SIMON SAYS

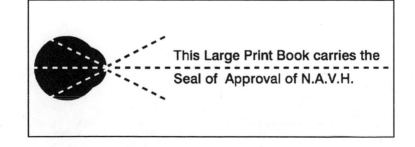

This Large Print Book carries the
Seal of Approval of N.A.V.H.

SIMON SAYS

LORI FOSTER

THORNDIKE PRESS

An imprint of Thomson Gale, a part of The Thomson Corporation

THOMSON

GALE

Detroit • New York • San Francisco • New Haven, Conn. • Waterville, Maine • London

THOMSON
GALE

LIBRARY OF CONGRESS CATALOGING-IN-PUBLICATION DATA

Foster, Lori, 1958–
   Simon says / by Lori Foster.
     p. cm.
   ISBN-13: 978-1-4104-0361-2 (hardcover : alk. paper)
   ISBN-10: 1-4104-0361-0 (hardcover : alk. paper)
    1. Boxers (Sports) — Fiction. 2. Family secrets — Fiction. 3. Large type
books. I. Title.
PS3556.O767S56 2007
813'.54—dc22   2007035722

Published in 2008 by arrangement with The Berkley, a member of Penguin Group (USA) Inc.

Printed in the United States of America on permanent paper
10 9 8 7 6 5 4 3 2 1

To Mike "Quick" Swick. A fantastic young man sure to be a future champion of the UFC. You're as dedicated to your fans as they are to you. You're not afraid to go new places, train hard, and most importantly help those in need.

Mike . . . a true UFC hero! Thanks for all the inspiration!

And to Shana Schwer, for all the wonderful friendship, support, and a shared love of the sport. You are truly one of the very best!

CHAPTER 1

"How come we're doing all the work, and you're just directing?"

Simon glanced at his friend Dean — better known as Havoc when he'd competed — and he grinned. "Both you dumb asses owe me, that's why." As one of the very best trainers in the SBC — Supreme Battle Championship — fighting biz, Simon had taken Dean to the top until Dean had retired to open his own gym. Before long, Simon would have Gregor leading the pack, too. Gregor had real talent, but he lacked finesse. They were working on it.

To Gregor, who held up the back end of the king-size mattress, Simon said, "Slow down. You're knocking Havoc over."

"Havoc is a pussy."

Quietly ornery, Dean planted his feet, throwing off Gregor's forward momentum and causing him to lose his balance, and the hold on the mattress. It dropped to the floor and Gregor nearly fell on his face.

Before things got out of hand, Simon unlocked the front door and stepped into the condo he shared with Bonnie. "Leave that in the hall until we get the old mattress out of here."

"A new mattress," Dean said around a chuckle. "Helluva way to celebrate five years with a woman."

"Yeah, Sublime," Gregor said, using Simon's fighting name, though Simon had given up fighting a few years back to manage fighters instead. "If you've worn out the mattress, don't you think you ought to go ahead and make it all legal?"

Acknowledging the sexual reference with a smile, Simon said, "We're waiting for the right time," as he led the way to the bedroom. He didn't add that the "right time" had come and gone more than once. For whatever reason, Simon always balked at the idea of tying himself down legally, emotionally, and officially. Not that he wanted anyone other than Bonnie; he was a one-woman man, through and through. Bonnie met all his needs, especially in the bedroom. And they got along well.

But still . . .

As usual, Bonnie had everything neat and tidy, with the bed made, the room well dusted, and all clutter put away. He really enjoyed her tendency toward neatness, given he was a bit of a neat freak himself.

Simon scooped the designer comforter and matching pillows off the bed and put them on a nearby chair. "Grab that side, Havoc, and we can move the mattress into the hallway."

Gregor took the opportunity to look around the large room with curiosity. "Jacki ain't much for housekeeping," he mentioned. "But then, I'm not either." He leveled a look on Dean. "And making the bed is pointless, since —"

"Shut up, Gregor."

Simon grinned. Ever since Gregor had married Dean's sister, he'd had a great time ribbing Dean. And Dean, who used to claim he wasn't a protective brother at all, always took the bait.

Ignoring his friends' knowing grins, Dean hefted up his end. "Eve is orderly, but not in an obsessive way."

"You've both found your perfect counterparts." The best part, from Simon's perspective, was that the women didn't fuss when Dean and Gregor had to spend months away, Gregor to fight and Dean to play corner man. Now that Dean had his own gym, they could do most of their training in town, but there were still extended trips out of the country to occasionally train with other camps. Variety added a lot to a fighter's repertoire. And then there was the endless promotion, finagling sponsors, and autographing events.

As icing on the cake, the wives enjoyed the sport, even if they didn't understand it. Not only did they not get in the way, they offered positive encouragement.

As they eased the old lumpy mattress to the side of the bed, several photos fell out to the floor. Dean froze, leaving Simon to balance the heavy mattress.

Gregor bent to pick up the shots. "What's this? You stashing porno, Sublime? Bonnie will have your head if she finds out you —"

The words dropped away.

Expression arrested, Gregor looked up from the photos. Anger tinged his obvious shock.

Simon frowned at him. "I'm too old to hide porno under the mattress, you ass." He set his side of the mattress onto the floor, leaving the bed only partially askew.

"Yeah, uh . . ." Tight-faced, Gregor pulled at his ear in uncertainty.

Finding his reaction more than curious, Simon stared at him. "What is it, Gregor?"

"Well . . ." Gregor looked at Dean as if

seeking assistance.

"You look ill, damn it." With an awful foreboding, Simon strode toward him. "Hand them here."

Gregor took a quick step back.

Dean said softly, "Wait, Simon."

"Wait for what?" He reached for the photos again, and Gregor dared to hold them above his head.

"Simon," Gregor murmured in miserable warning, "maybe you should —"

"Knock the shit out of you for playing games?" Sick dread crept through Simon. "Damn right. Now hand. Them. Over."

Because Gregor was such an enormous freak of nature, standing six and a half feet tall and weighing in at over two hundred and fifty pounds — all of it rock-solid, rippling muscle — few men ever confronted him. The twining of wicked tattoos around colossal biceps also offered discouragement to most.

But if Simon had to take the photos from Gregor, they both knew he could.

Rather than oblige Simon, Gregor looked to Dean for guidance.

Dean said, "Go ahead and give them to him."

It didn't bode well that Gregor turned away before complying with that instruction. The second Simon had the photos in his hand, Gregor split. He didn't just take a few steps away.

No, he left the bedroom.

And Dean followed him out, giving Simon privacy for God knew what.

But damn it, even before looking, Simon knew what he'd find. Only one thing would make his friends look and act the way they had. He ran a hand over his shaved head, hesitated, but he had to see for himself.

Simon turned over the first photo and without even seeing her face, he recognized Bonnie.

The woman he'd planned to marry one day.

The woman he'd just bought a new and expensive mattress for.

She was naked, her face turned away from the camera, sitting astride an equally naked man. In a detached way, Simon noted her long legs, her heart-shaped ass, her cascading dark hair.

He'd been intimate with that body for five years. In the photos, she was intimate with someone else, some nameless male face on a muscular body. The photos showed the man only from the shoulders down.

Bonnie looked to be enjoying herself.

It was the oddest thing, but the overriding

emotion that pervaded Simon was curiosity. Somewhere there was hurt, and definitely humiliation. But foremost was a weird loss of all sensation, and a resounding question: Why?

He locked his jaw.

Bonnie wasn't stupid, and in fact, her intelligence was one of the things that had initially drawn him. Why did she feel the need to wander? And why the hell had she hidden the photos beneath the mattress, where he might find them?

Simon no sooner asked himself that last question than his memory jogged and he recalled Bonnie's surprise when he'd come home early last night. She'd been sitting on the bed in a skimpy nightgown gazing at something, but he hadn't paid that much attention.

Before proceeding to his closet to change, he'd given her the same perfunctory kiss of greeting that he'd been giving her for years.

She'd kissed him back the same way.

Searching his memory further, Simon remembered her jittery responses to his questions, and her attempts to distract him.

When she asked if he was going to shower, he told her he had at the gym.

She jumped up to get him dinner, and he told her he wasn't hungry.

She wanted to check the front door locks, and he assured her he'd taken care of it.

He'd even left the bathroom door open as he brushed his teeth. But Bonnie had turned out the lights as if she planned to go to sleep.

That's probably when she stashed the photos under the mattress, because he hadn't given her an opportunity to hide them anywhere else. He hadn't given her the chance to hide them some place better. Of course, she had no way of knowing he planned to replace the mattress today.

Once he'd joined her in the bed, he found her stiff and aloof. But he'd softened her. Simon laughed at himself. Hell, he'd made love to her with determined patience, and unless her acting skills were well honed, she'd come with enthusiasm.

That reminder fisted Simon's hand around the photos, crinkling them. Had Bonnie already been with another man that day? His stomach lurched at the thought of playing second in line.

He thought about that, then he recalled that the bed in the photo wasn't his, thank God. But he'd thought the woman was.

Humiliation overtook the numbness; he felt like a blind ass.

Dean stuck his head into the room and

without a lot of emotion or sympathy, or anything else mushy that might have made the situation worse, he asked, "You okay?"

A pretty outrageous question for a man of his capabilities, his fighting record, his size and weight and strength.

So . . . was he okay? Simon queried himself, his mind and his heart, and actually . . . yeah, he was A-OK.

Embarrassed, sure. He had the same ego as any other man in the SBC. Pissed, you betcha. But he didn't have the need to find the unnamed man and pound on him. Far as he was concerned, the guy could have Bonnie.

He also felt determined to get through this new wrinkle without dramatizing things further.

But he didn't feel heartsick. Maybe that's why Bonnie had wandered, because he didn't love her madly and she knew it. It wasn't a good excuse, but it'd do for now.

Simon looked up at Dean. "You have anywhere you have to be?"

"No."

Havoc was often a man of few words, and he was always a man straight to the point. As his former trainer, manager, and agent, Simon appreciated that.

15

"Wanna help me move my shit out of here?"

One big shoulder rolled. "Sure. If that's what you want."

Simon nodded. "It is." He tossed the photos onto the nightstand. Bonnie would find them, and that'd be explanation enough for his departure from her life.

"Hey, Gregor?"

Gregor appeared in the doorway. He looked embarrassed for Simon.

"Knock it off, will you?"

Gregor glanced at Dean and then at Simon again. The sympathetic expression intensified. "Sure thing, Sublime."

Simon rolled his eyes. Gregor might look like a muscled behemoth, but he had a heart as big as the rest of his physique. The doofus. "You have time to hang around and help me move out of here?"

"Absolutely." Then with caution, "Where are you moving to?"

"Doesn't matter." Simon surveyed the now disheveled bedroom, wondering where to start. "Good thing I never got around to marrying her."

"Yeah. Good thing." Hands on his hips, Gregor looked around the room. "You've got a lot of stuff."

"I'm taking all of it." The finality in that

statement made Simon feel better. "Today will be a clean break. Once I walk out the door I don't plan to make any trips back."

"Right." Gregor rubbed at an ear thickened by too many precise punches. "How about I run up to the grocery and see if they have any empty boxes?"

"That'd be great. Thanks."

Gregor escaped with a stomping stride, but Simon noticed that he already had his cell phone in his hand. Great. He'd tell his new wife, Jacki, and she'd tell her sister Cam, and Cam would tell Dean's wife, Eve, if Dean hadn't already.

"Stay with Eve and me." Dean crossed his arms and stared at Simon. "You know Eve would welcome you."

Eve was a beautiful person, inside and out. Simon was pleased for Havoc to have found her. "Thanks, but no. I think I'll go home for a while."

"Home?"

"To Ohio. To see my parents."

That decision came out of nowhere, but it worked to stiffen Simon's backbone. Being around family was always a good thing.

Going to his closet and unloading the clothes, Simon added, "Mom and Dad will love it."

Suddenly a new voice intruded. "Simon?

What's going on? What are you doing?"

Havoc stiffened, but Simon smiled in evil delight. Talk about a clean break — this little confrontation ought to do it.

Without turning to face her, he said, "Hello, Bonnie."

Dean cleared his throat. "Hey, Bonnie."

"Dean," she said dismissively while moving further into the bedroom.

"Yeah." Dean coughed. "I think I'll go wait in the kitchen." And with that, he left them.

Bonnie's hand lightly touched his shoulder. "Simon?"

He shrugged her off. She had to have noticed the mattress in the hallway, the disarray of the bed, the crumpled photos on the nightstand. "I'll be out of here within the hour."

Typical of Bonnie, she refused to look anywhere but at him. She crossed her arms beneath her generous breasts. With a toss of her head, she sent her silky dark hair tumbling over her shoulders. "And just where do you think you're going?"

"That doesn't concern you anymore, does it?" Moving around her, Simon went to his dresser and removed a drawer, then upended it over the growing pile of clothes.

"Of course it concerns me." Bonnie fol-

18

lowed on his heels. "Today is our anniversary."

"Nope. Today is the day it all ends. Nothing more."

Her voice rose the tiniest bit. "Why?"

"Come on, Bonnie. You're smart. You already know why."

"Oh, just great. Because of one little indiscretion, you're going to throw away a five-year relationship?"

He couldn't help it; her dense perception of her perfidy struck Simon as funny. "Was it only one?"

"Yes!"

He still didn't look at her. "Was it little?"

Frustration and annoyance sharpened her tone. "I meant insignificant."

"I see. Well, that's too bad for you."

Bonnie sank well-manicured nails into his biceps. "Damn it, Simon, he was available when you weren't. I only took the photos to . . . to keep me company when you're not here."

What a joke. "I hope he's available nonstop now." Simon pried her hand loose, then immediately dropped it. "Because I'll never be available to you again."

"Bullshit."

The coarse word shocked him. "Such language for a lady." Bonnie prided herself

19

on her respectability.

"You're leaving me," she rasped. "The situation calls for harsh language."

"Suit yourself." His many sport T-shirts joined the stack on the sloping mattress.

Since her first tactic failed, Bonnie tried a new gimmick. "You're kidding yourself and you know it."

"Is that right?"

"You love me."

He shook his head on a laugh. "No."

"We have something special."

"I was dumb enough to think so." Simon nodded toward the photos. "Thanks for pointing out my error."

"Simon, *please!*"

Never had he heard Bonnie beg. He sure as hell didn't want to hear it now. "Save it."

She took a combative stance in front of him. "You're a family man, Simon. You like the security and familiarity of the same woman, the same place. You cherish stability."

"I like honesty and loyalty, too. What I don't like is being played for a fool."

"You could never be that."

He laughed again.

"Simon, listen to me. From the time we decided to move in together, you've been saying that love and commitment was give-

and-take, and —"

"Yeah, I know what I said, Bonnie. But you gave a little too much to the wrong man." Simon physically set her away from him.

"I won't just let you go," she stated. "I won't just stand by while you throw away five good years." When Simon said nothing, she screamed, "I uprooted and moved to Harmony for you!"

Once again, she shocked him. It was unlike Bonnie to cause a scene. "Save the hysterics, babe. You wanted the move, the fresh start, as much as I did. Don't use it as an excuse now."

"I'll win you back." Bonnie lifted her chin with that atrocious statement. "Onc way or another, you will come back to me."

Simon tossed his shaving kit toward the rest of his belongings. "Here's the thing, Bonnie. I'm not all that broke up about you cheating."

Her glossy red lips parted.

"Yeah, that surprises me, too, but I guess you weren't the big draw." Simon smiled. "Like you said, it was the comfort of familiarity."

"Simon . . ."

"Now that you shot that to hell, there's nothing here for me. Nothing."

"You can't mean that."

"Every word. So do us both a favor and don't waste your time pestering me."

Gregor chose that moment to reenter with more than enough boxes. God bless him and his perfect timing. Simon could hear Dean explaining the situation as he and Gregor came into the bedroom.

SBC fighters were nothing if not loyal to each other.

As if Bonnie weren't standing there, five feet nine inches of stacked female smelling of perfume and looking like a fashion icon, the three of them went about their business. Simon didn't look at her, but he was aware of her all the same. How could he not be? She stayed silent, but she continued to plead with her eyes.

And even distressed, she was one of the sexiest women he'd ever seen.

But the second he'd seen those photos, his interest had vanished as if it had never existed. He had no room in his life for rank disloyalty.

Within an hour, Simon had removed every trace of himself from the apartment. It took another hour at the manager's office, a lot of paperwork, and a chunk of his savings, but he got his name off the lease. While Dean drove and Gregor stewed, Simon used his cell phone and credit card to pay off all the utilities, and then have his name removed. He wasn't really worried about Bonnie running up deliberate bills. She didn't operate that way. But neither was he a man to leave things to chance.

When he finished, Bonnie was out of his life. Simon felt . . . renewed. Ready to start over. Challenged by upcoming changes. Yes, it'd be good to spend an extended time with his family.

And then . . . Looking at Gregor and Dean, he said, "You know what I want to do?"

Dean glanced at him before returning his attention to the road. "Yeah, I do."

Gregor frowned. "You do?"

Dean shrugged. "He's going to fight again."

Simon's brows shot up. Damned perceptive bastard. But then he and Dean had been a team for a long time, and they knew each other well. Dean would understand his sudden need for physical competition.

Gregor snorted. "No way. Simon's a trainer." No one said anything to that, which made Gregor reevaluate. "A damn fine trainer, for sure. But he's been out of the circuit too long to —"

"Whip your sorry butt?" Simon asked.

Though Gregor towered over both men, he merely grinned at the subtle threat. "Now, Sublime, I didn't say that."

Simon laughed. It wasn't that Gregor feared him. Hell, Simon doubted that Gregor feared any man. In almost any physical situation, he'd come out a winner.

Just not against Havoc or Simon. Not yet.

Still, it was respect and friendship that made Gregor turn away from a direct challenge.

"Don't sweat it, Gregor. You're good and getting better every day."

A look of conceit spread over Gregor's face. "Good enough to go up against Havoc now?"

Both Dean and Simon said, "No."

Gregor's expression pinched. "You might've retired, Havoc, but damn it, I haven't given up on the idea."

Dean said nothing, but Simon relented. "Dean's retired and he's not coming back just to accommodate you. When the time is right, we'll find the perfect contender for you. But for now, I'll need your help. You're right that I've been out of it for too long."

"You've probably forgotten more about submission fighting than most of the fighters will ever know," Dean told him. "And you're in great shape."

"For the average guy, maybe. But not for the SBC. I'm rusty and I know it."

Gregor rubbed his hands together. "Dean goes from fighting to owning a gym and training, and you go from training to fighting. The world has flip-flopped." Raw anticipation brightened his gaze. "So when do we get started?"

"Let me talk to the Powers That Be." Simon considered all the ramifications to reentering the circuit. "I'll see how they feel about me making a comeback."

Dean scoffed. "Are you kidding? You're a legend in your own time. Everyone will love it. You'll be the biggest draw the SBC has had in years. I don't have a single doubt that the organization will play up your first fight in a big way."

"Then I better be ready to win, huh?"

Gregor put his arm around him. "Don't worry, little buddy. We'll get you in top fighting form."

Because Simon stood six-two and weighed over two hundred pounds, only Gregor would refer to him as little.

His mind made up and his immediate future settled, Simon said, "I'm starving. Let's hit a drive-through for some loaded burgers."

"Hell, yeah," Gregor agreed. As the only

one of the three currently still competing, fast food, and especially anything as delicious as a hamburger, had been cut out of his diet for a while.

Happy to oblige, Dean pulled into the drive-through line for the next burger joint they saw.

Simon knew that once he hit home, his mom would have a healthy, home-cooked meal for him morning, noon, and night. And once he started training, his diet would be a big part of the program. He wanted to enjoy fast food while he still could.

It was the best way to celebrate his new freedom.

As if going to her mother's home — the home she'd grown up in — wasn't bad enough, it was barely nine in the morning, and Dakota Dream was a night person. Her eyes felt gritty, her brain foggy, and she needed caffeine in a bad way.

Not a good start.

Dakota stared at the man who had served as her stepfather from her sixteenth year until her mother's death.

Now he served as nothing in her life.

Nothing at all.

Yet . . . here she was, in a place she didn't want to be, at an hour she hated, and without the kick of coffee to keep her alert.

Wearing a deliberate look of disinterest, Dakota sauntered further into the familiar living room and took a seat where her mother's favorite chair used to be. Now, thanks to her stepfather, a very expensive leather lounger replaced it. "You're joking, right?"

Resting back with his shoeless feet on a new coffee table and a toothpick in his perfect teeth, Barnaby Jailer smiled that same smile that had always made Dakota's skin crawl. "Of course I'm not, honey. You owe me and you know it."

Hoping to brazen her way out of that claim, Dakota snorted. "Right. In what universe?"

A grating sound that Barnaby tried to pawn off as a laugh made Dakota's stomach lurch. Why couldn't he be a coffee drinker with a fresh pot waiting in the small kitchen?

From the moment her mother had brought Barnaby home, Dakota had hated him. Her reasons were sketchy at best. He was an average-height man with an average, rangy build and a pleasant enough face.

But at sixteen, she'd been very afraid of him.

Now, at twenty-three, he merely repulsed her. But it was years too late for second-guessing her first impressions.

Eyes closing on a familiar rush of pain, Dakota struggled to gather herself. She had few weaknesses left. As a survivor, she'd overcome obstacles and conquered nearly all of her fears.

With very few exceptions, she could face anyone and anything without flinching.

But those damn past regrets that encompassed her mother's death and her own grief always hit her like a concrete sucker punch. Time hadn't softened them.

Nothing ever would.

The hush of clothing against couch cushions and the squeak of a floorboard announced Barnaby's approach. Dakota didn't have to look at him to know he smiled, that his dark eyes glittered with satisfaction.

He was right, she did owe him.

"If it wasn't for me," Barnaby whispered from her right side, "you wouldn't have known your mother was dying."

"Shut up."

"If it wasn't for me," he continued, "you wouldn't have had anywhere to live."

"It was my home."

"Not after you left. Not after staying gone, without a word, for so long. She'd written you off, little girl."

Dakota smirked. "Little girl?" She slanted

her gaze up at him. "I'm only a few inches shorter than you are, Barnaby."

"And yet," he said, his voice frighteningly gentle as he moved to the back of her chair, "you're still so much smaller."

With every fiber of her being, Dakota felt Barnaby standing there behind her. Her skin prickled and the hair on her nape lifted as if touched by static.

"To Joan's mind," Barnaby continued, "she no longer had a daughter. Had she not been so ill, she would have refused to let you enter. Yet despite her wishes, I contacted you myself. I gave you a place to live and food to eat and most importantly, I allowed you back into your mother's life. I gave you a chance to say good-bye to her. Again."

"For good."

"Don't blame me for that. As soon as I knew your mother wouldn't pull through, I looked for you. But you weren't the easiest girl to find."

No, she hadn't been. When she'd run off with her boyfriend, she'd covered her tracks. Not once had she considered that her mother might be right in her arguments. No, Dakota had fostered her hurt, telling herself that her mother's reactions were because she loved Barnaby more than she loved her own daughter.

Like a spoiled child, she'd wallowed in her sense of betrayal while doing exactly as she pleased despite her mother's wishes. Thinking to herself, "She'll be sorry," she'd wanted her mother to regret her actions.

Oh, God. Her mother had been sorry all right. Sorry that she'd ever had a daughter.

Shoving to her feet, Dakota turned to face Barnaby. Despite the prickling of unease she got whenever in his presence, she wouldn't cower from him. But she wasn't dumb enough to let him linger at her back, either.

"So you think I owe you, and for that, you want me to find your son?"

"He'll be easy to find," Barnaby corrected. "What I need you to do is bring him to me."

"Why?" Suspicions began niggling around her brain. "If you want to establish some rapport with your son, why don't you just contact him yourself? Why send me?"

"I haven't seen him in a lot of years. It would be awkward." Hands stuffed into his pockets, Barnaby began circling her.

Dakota felt certain that restlessness didn't drive him. No, he wanted to unsettle her, to rattle her. For that reason more than any other, she kept her pose lazy and relaxed. "I didn't even know you had a son."

He shrugged at that. "No reason you

should."

"How old is he?"

"Thirty, maybe thirty-one."

"You don't know?"

He scowled, and ignored the question. "He might not want to see me after all this time. But you . . . you could get in on his good side, convince him to have a meeting with me."

Dakota watched him closely. He was up to something, but as usual with Barnaby, she didn't know what. "How am I supposed to do that?"

His dark-eyed gaze took her measure, crawling over her from head to toe in a way meant to disgust her. "You're a woman now, Dakota."

At twenty-three, she agreed, but that wasn't his point at all. "Yeah, so?"

"All women know how to sway men. I imagine you know better than most how to —"

Cutting off that tired insult, Dakota asked, "Why do you want to see him anyway?"

"It's a personal matter, honey."

Oh, that soft tone didn't hide a thing. It had fooled her mother, but it wouldn't fool her.

She shrugged. "Fine. Keep your secrets. It's no skin off my nose."

"Exactly."

"But here's a condition."

Barnaby's eyes narrowed. "You're giving *me* conditions?"

"Yes, and it's nonnegotiable." Dakota held his gaze. "Quit calling me 'honey.' "

The corners of his mouth lifted in a dawning smile of satisfaction. "It bothers you? I can't imagine why."

"You're sick."

That made him laugh. "Such squeamishness from a girl who dances onstage?"

"I sing more than I dance." And she was good, not that Barnaby would ever admit it.

"Rowdy songs meant to excite men. I know." He looked at her legs. "Your mother hated that about you."

Not again. How many times did she have to hear about her mother's disapproval and disappointment? Dakota drew a steadying breath. "Listen, Barnaby —"

"You know, she blamed herself."

Dakota braced her heart. Once on a roll, there'd be no stopping Barnaby until he had his say.

"Joan thought it was your name that caused you to turn so brazen. She said she'd wanted you to have a bright, cheerful name, different from other girls. Of course, when she named you, she didn't know that your married name would . . . enhance things."

Every muscle in Dakota's body tightened, but outwardly, she looked bored. "I've heard this tune too many times, Barnaby. Spare me, okay?"

"She said that had she known the choices you'd make, she would have named you something different. Because now your name makes you sound like a porn star."

Dakota faked a yawn. It was her name, her mistake, damn it, and she would keep it as a reminder — her version of donning a horsehair shirt.

"Dakota Dream," Barnaby intoned with slow and dramatic emphasis. "I think Joan was right. Definitely the name of a professional whore."

Her façade cracked. "Go screw yourself." Jaw tight and throat burning, Dakota pushed past him.

"Do this one thing," he reminded her, "and we're even."

Bastard! She paused near the door. It took two deep breaths before she could make herself turn and face him. "Give me his name and last known residence."

Victory did ugly things to Barnaby's disposition; it exposed his malicious nature.

Smug smile in place, he withdrew one hand from his pocket and held out a slip of paper. "This is all I have. He travels a lot, so you might have to use a few of your sneakier skills to locate him."

Careful not to touch Barnaby, Dakota closed her hand around the paper. She didn't look at it. Her sneaky skills included working part-time, mostly on a volunteer basis, to help locate missing people. Reuniting loved ones served as her lame way of making amends to a past she couldn't change.

At every opportunity, Barnaby threw it in her face.

"You'll have to cover my expenses."

"Of course." His lips stretched into a smile. "Keep a detailed tally and give me the total after you bring him to me."

She shook her head. "I see the lie in your eyes, Barnaby. We both know you won't give me a dime once you have what you want."

The smile pinched into a sneer, and even his perfect teeth couldn't make him appealing. "Before the accident stole Joan's ability to speak, she begged me not to contact you."

Dakota's heart thumped hard. "So you've said, many times." She knew it was true. If Barnaby hadn't found a soft spot in his cold heart, he wouldn't have gone against her mother's wishes and let Dakota move back in. She would have been hurt and home-

34

less, and all alone.

Worse, her mother would have died before she could touch her one more time, before she could hold her hand and beg forgiveness. Her mother never regained consciousness, but at least Barnaby had given her a chance.

And for that, she did owe him.

"Joan told me that you'd disappointed her and shamed her so much that she could never forgive you —"

"Yeah, I know." Already leaving the room, anxious to be away before Barnaby saw how he'd hurt her, Dakota said, "This is the last time, Barnaby. I'll drag your damned son to you if I have to, and then we're even."

"Of course." Voice moderate again, he added, "Don't slam the door, Dakota. You know how your mother despised your temper tantrums."

Breathing harder than she should have been, Dakota paused outside the house with her fist on the doorknob. It took an effort, but she loosened her muscles, relaxed them, and eased the door shut with a quick, quiet click.

The yard she'd played in as a child now looked like a showplace. There were no dandelions on the lawn, no bare patches from repeated games of tag.

While her mother lived, Barnaby hadn't spent a dime except on his own pleasures. But her mother hadn't been dead a week before he'd started throwing money around.

New shrubbery, enhanced with outdoor lights and framed with colorful fall flowers, circled the house. A large decorative fountain had replaced the cheap birdbath she'd given her mother on Mother's Day. Rather than repair the old broken sidewalk, Barnaby had paid to have it torn out so a new cobblestone walkway led to the front door.

New siding, windows, and doors. New carpet and furniture. New cabinets. The house was better. Improved. And it was no longer her childhood home. Maybe, Dakota thought, she should count her blessings.

"This is it," she said to herself. "The last time I'll ever come here. The last time Barnaby will ever hold me with guilt." She looked up into the sunny sky and breathed the brisk fall air. "The very last time."

Once in her car, to distract herself and gain some control so she wouldn't present a danger on the roadway, Dakota looked at the slip of paper.

Simon Evans.

Her eyes widened. Sickness gave way to fascination. Surely not *the* Simon Evans, renowned trainer of SBC fighters, once an amazing, unstoppable champion himself? Sublime, they called him, because of his incredible good looks, his way with the ladies, and his charming manner.

Her heart beat a little faster as she pictured him in her mind. Six-two. Ripped. Dark. He shaved his head, which only made the astounding intensity of his brown eyes that much more compelling.

What a hoot.

Barnaby was sending her to one of her favorite sporting events to fetch a superior icon in the industry. Hell, had she known, she'd have volunteered for the job.

Dakota recognized the address on the slip of paper as his hometown, confirming he was the fighter. But Simon wouldn't be there now. A few months ago, he'd announced his intent to compete again, and that meant he was at a camp somewhere, getting in shape. Or, she should say, getting in better shape. The man always looked delicious, no matter what position he chose in the SBC — trainer, fighter, or sex symbol.

She'd find him. She'd visit him.

And one way or another, she'd bring him to Barnaby.

If along the way she got to indulge her fandom, no one would hold that against her.

Her day was looking better. All she needed now was some coffee.

CHAPTER 2

Sweat poured over his shoulders and trickled down his spine to soak the waistband of his shorts. Training other athletes and training himself were two very different things. He'd never pushed anyone as hard as he pushed now. The passion was both exhilarating and exhausting.

Padded in protective gear, Gregor squared off with him again. Simon prepared himself — and a flash of blond hair distracted him just long enough for Gregor to knock him on his ass. His head rang, darkness crowded in, and then he had no more time to mollycoddle himself because Gregor attacked.

Six and a half feet of muscled fighter landed on him.

Shaking off the cobwebs, Simon went on automatic pilot, defending himself by rote, countering all of Gregor's attempts at submission holds and blocking most of his punches. With a few well-timed moves, Simon managed to reverse their positions and in seconds, he had Gregor in a rear-naked choke.

"Ho, hold up, Simon. He's tapping."

Dean's voice cut through the fog, and Simon immediately loosened his hold. Gregor rolled over to his knees, cursing himself.

Exhaustion pulled Simon flat to the mat. Eyes closed, he sucked air into his straining lungs while Dean took the time to tell Gregor what he'd done wrong, and what he'd done right.

Then he started on Simon.

"What the hell were you thinking? You dropped your hands and you looked away from him. That's your number one rule — to always keep your eyes on your opponent."

Simon didn't open his eyes yet. Gregor's slug had nearly knocked him out. Little stars danced behind his closed eyelids. "I know."

"Couldn't prove it by me," Dean said. "If you'd been looking at Gregor, you'd have seen a wild haymaker like that coming a mile away."

Damn harpie. "I know."

"Maybe Gregor is too damn big for you —"

"No."

"Then you're not putting enough into it.

You know if you can't handle him here, you sure as hell won't be able to handle someone in a competition."

"Stop bitching." Simon opened his eyes to see the bright lights on the ceiling of Dean's gym. What had distracted him?

Oh, yeah.

He sat up and twisted around in one motion to see a Barbie clone standing inside the gym doorway.

Yep. She was the distraction all right.

Dean followed Simon's line of vision and grunted. "You've got to be kidding me."

With a shoulder propped on the wall, her arms crossed, Blondie stared at Simon.

Dean asked, "Who is that?"

"Hell if I know." Without looking away from her, Simon pushed to his feet. "But spread the word before any of these bozos get lewd ideas — I've got dibs."

Because Dean had been after him to start dating again — without success — that statement earned him a double take. *"Now?"*

Simon shrugged.

"You're training for a fight, or have you forgotten?"

"Bad timing." Simon studied her negligent pose. "What can I say?"

"You can say that you're joking."

Simon flashed Dean a quick glance. "I'm

not." Then he shook his head. "But don't worry. I'll take my time, and I won't let her interfere."

"You don't even know if she's free."

That made Simon frown. For a woman to show up in Dean's gym, she'd probably come to meet someone. Was she involved with one of the other fighters? Married to one of them?

Dean made a sound of impatience. "Before you burn holes through her with that dark scowl, want me to find out what she wants?"

Just as Dean spoke, Blondie pushed away from the wall and sauntered toward them.

Simon shook his head. "Don't bother. I think we're about to find out."

Dressed in tattered jeans, black lace-up work boots, and a thick coat, Simon couldn't really see her body other than to note her height. But she had a loose-limbed gait, long legs, longer blond hair, and an eagerness in her eyes that consumed him.

Hell, yeah.

When the time was right, he'd have her. And then some.

Simon walked over to the ropes and propped his arms on them. Keeping his gaze glued to hers, he waited.

She stopped at the bottom of the ring and

looked up. "That was sloppy."

Inside, Simon grinned. Outwardly, he just looked at her.

"If you're going to compete in the next event, you need to do better than that."

Up close, Simon saw that the cold had turned her nose red. Not a dainty little nose, but not an unappealing nose, either. In fact, nothing about her features was dainty. She had a full mouth, thick lashes, strong cheekbones, and a stubborn chin.

Deliberately provoking, Simon studied her body from head to toes and back again. The heavy black work boots amused him. When his gaze returned to hers, he asked, "You're an expert?"

"More like a fan."

"Of the sport?" *Or of me?*

She nodded. "I've been watching it since the early days, back when it was no-holds-barred, no weight classes, and a lot more brutal."

Odd, to be having this conversation with her when he didn't even know her name. Yet. "So which do you prefer? The current rules or the older unrestricted freestyle?"

"I have favorite fighters from both. But I'd say it's more exciting now. More refined. By necessity, the fighters are well rounded in a variety of techniques."

43

"They have to be."

"Absolutely." She tilted her head to scrutinize him. "Your strength is your natural athleticism. You pick up quickly on nuances that others miss. You're strong and quick, but then so are a lot of the fighters." Without looking away from him, she nodded toward Gregor. "He's as strong as they get, but he lacks confidence. When or if he ever gets it, look out."

Because Simon thought the same, her insight surprised him. He glanced at her hands, but she had them tucked into her coat pockets. Curiosity ate at him, so Simon turned to Dean. "I'm taking a break."

Dean just rolled his eyes. Gregor sat on a stool getting further instructions. He looked royally pissed off.

Lifting the ropes, Simon jumped down from the ring. Now that they were on even footing, he guessed her height at only around five and a half feet. But she carried herself like someone taller.

Interesting.

The mandatory four-ounce gloves left his fingertips and palms free. Simon swiped the sweat from his face. "I'm roasting, but here you are all buttoned up in that thick coat."

As if just realizing what she wore, she glanced down at herself. Her hands came out of her pockets and she began unbuttoning the tan corduroy coat.

No rings.

No nail polish, either. Her fingers were long, her nails short and blunt.

"It's freezing outside, and I hate the cold."

Simon was so involved in visually exploring her that he barely paid any attention to her husky voice. Not since he'd walked out on Bonnie months ago had he been this interested in a woman.

Or more to the point, this interested in having a woman. Under him. In bed.

Or wherever she liked it. Hell, after months of celibacy, he wasn't picky.

As long as she wasn't the difficult type, too clingy or a psycho groupie, or . . . whatever. Easy, that's what he wanted.

Easy, ready, and willing.

"But you're right," she continued, unaware of his meandering and vivid sexual thoughts. "It's toasty in here."

Getting toastier by the second.

Simon waited as the buttons came undone and the thick material parted to reveal the shape of her body. She went one further in accommodating his imagination by shrugging out of the coat completely.

A loose, oversized V-necked gray sweater layered over a black T-shirt didn't disguise

45

her slim figure. The jeans were low-riders, and Simon got a glimpse of taut, pale flesh above the waistband until she tugged the sweater down.

As if she owned the place, she tossed her coat and a large, satchel-type purse toward a metal folding chair, and then stuck out her hand.

"I'm Dakota Dream."

Simon stared; she had to be kidding.

All types of quips came to mind. Like, *Weren't you in the last porno I saw?* Or, *Didn't you use to dance at a strip club?*

But one look at her face and Simon knew she expected it. Sarcasm, sexual harassment, assumptions — she'd pegged him to have them all. So the name was for real, not a gimmick, and though she might not admit it, it bothered her.

Despite the gloves, he took her hand in both of his. "Hello, Dakota."

Brief surprise flickered in her blue eyes before she smiled. "Hello."

Damn, that smile packed a wallop. "I take it you already know me?"

Slender shoulders rose in a shrug. "Of you." She propped her hands on equally slender hips. "Simon Alexander Evans. Sublime. You hung up your gloves a few years back after winning the championship

46

belt in the light heavyweight class. You only had two losses in your record, and one of those was a bad judges' decision."

Either she'd done her homework or she followed the sport as she'd said. "I agree. I got screwed on that decision."

"Everyone with any sense thinks so." She flashed him a cheeky grin. "Most of your wins were notable knockouts with a few incredible submissions thrown in. Since retiring your gloves, you've gotten the reputation for being the best trainer around. Anyplace you organize a camp, fighters show up in droves."

To test her, Simon asked, "You have a theory on why that is?"

"Sure. Too many guys train with repetitive conditioning, eight hours a day, seven days a week." She shook her head sadly. "It's a waste of time and energy. Your motto is that they need to train for intense five-minute bouts, because that's what they'll be doing."

"Right."

Mimicking him, she said, " 'Who cares if he can ride a damn bike uphill for hours on end? When I hit him in the jaw, his bike-riding skills won't help him at all.' "

Simon laughed. "Yeah, I remember saying something like that." Bonnie had soured him on involvement, but that didn't mean he wanted to be a notch on some loony broad's bedpost. If she was a regular groupie . . . well, he wasn't quite sure how he'd handle that. "Did you drop in for an autograph?"

Her smile slipped. "Actually . . ."

Simon watched as her chest expanded on a nervous breath.

"I came for you."

Such a sweetheart. Forcing his attention from her breasts back up to her face, Simon held her gaze and said softly, "Not yet, Dakota."

Confusion darkened the blue of her eyes. She tipped her head. "What?"

"You haven't come for me . . . yet." He still had a lot of work to do, so he headed back to the mat. Over his shoulder, he said, "But stick around, and I can guarantee you will."

Wow. Dakota watched as Simon ducked under the ropes and reentered the ring. He wore only black nylon kickboxing trunks and four-ounce gloves designed to protect his hands. He didn't shave his body, thank God, but he did shave his head. It proved one hell of a contrast to his dark chest hair and sexy eyebrows.

Without a doubt, Simon was the most

devastating man she'd ever seen.

And that sexual vibe . . . Dakota made a sound of regret. She wouldn't mind seeing if he had reason for such bragging, but she didn't dare get that involved with him. She had to remember that he was Barnaby's son. Once she delivered him to his father, she didn't plan to get within ten miles of Barnaby ever again.

Not even for a superhunk like Simon Evans.

After his outrageous prediction, he'd strolled off without giving her the chance to proposition him, so he still didn't know that his father wanted to reunite with him.

Not a problem, far as Dakota was concerned. Waiting around afforded her the opportunity to watch him work. She'd have paid good money for this, so to get to do it for free was a treat.

Fetching the chair that held her coat and satchel, Dakota seated herself ringside. All three fighters glanced her way, as if awaiting an explanation for her bold intrusion.

Dakota sat back, crossed her legs, and got comfortable. "Go on," she encouraged. "You won't even know I'm here."

The retired champion-turned-trainer, Dean "Havoc" Conor, looked to Simon for instruction. Instead of verbalizing his preferences one way or the other, Simon turned to Gregor Marsh, better known as "the Maniac," and said, "Let's go."

Gregor shrugged his enormous tattooed shoulders and grinned. "Sure thing, Sublime."

For the next five minutes, they sparred as if they were in a real competition. Dakota scrutinized every move, every countermove, and when they stopped for a break, she again approached the ropes.

"Hey, Gregor?"

The giant looked up from his conversation with Dean. His brows lifted in comical surprise.

"Come here."

Dean turned to glare at her, letting her know without words that her intrusion was unwanted.

Simon didn't say anything either. He just tipped up a water bottle and took a long swig.

Reluctantly, Gregor walked over. "What?"

She indicated he should lean down so she could talk to him without anyone else hearing. With even more reluctance, he bent down.

"Simon's killing you with those kicks."

"No shit, Sherlock." He grunted at the obvious. "At least he's not hittin' my liver."

"A deliberate choice on his part, because he wants to keep practicing." A liver kick would leave Gregor done for at least an hour.

"What's your point, dollface?"

Gregor looked annoyed enough to send most people scampering away. But Dakota wasn't the least bit intimidated. "I don't think you've noticed, but he's telegraphing those kicks. You can block them if you know what to watch for."

Bemused with the conversation, Gregor looked back at Simon — who stared at them both with piercing intensity. Proving that he enjoyed provoking his friend, Gregor faced her again. "You don't say?"

She nodded. "Right before he kicks, he tightens his jaw."

"So?"

"It's an indication of what's to come. I've seen him do it every single time." Dakota stepped back and put her hand on her right thigh. "You're leading with your right leg, which is why he keeps going after it with that low roundhouse kick. When he tightens his jaw, get ready to lift your leg, like this." She demonstrated what he should do. "That'll block it, and confuse him at the same time."

"I know how to block a kick."

"When you see the kick coming. So far, you haven't seen it, so Simon isn't expecting you to block it. When you do, that'll be your opening."

Intrigued, Gregor studied her with new awareness. "My openin' for what, exactly?"

She looked around Gregor, saw Simon's scrutiny, and hurried through the rest of her instruction. "You need to get Simon's attention upstairs, instead of downstairs with your legs. Do this." She demonstrated a fast combination of hits.

"That's a basic combo," Gregor argued.

"Yeah, but you're not using it! And its effectiveness is why it's so basic. So you throw the jab-cross, and then a rear roundhouse. You'll be kicking his leg instead of him kicking yours."

Gregor rose back to his full arresting height. "You know a lot about this stuff."

"I follow the sport. And I've trained a little." What an understatement. "I love it."

"I figured you were here for Simon, what with the way you two chatted each other up so cozy and all."

"I am here for him."

"But you want to help me to kick his ass?"

She snorted. "Ain't gonna happen, Gregor, at least not today, so forget it. The only way you'll take Sublime is by a freak accident. But the best way for him to improve is to have a fighter challenging him. Right now, you're not doing that."

Gregor pulled in his chin and glared at her. "You're a strange broad, you know that?"

Dakota grinned. "Yeah, I know. Now go get him!"

Shaking his head, Gregor went back to the center of the mat. Simon immediately joined him.

"What the hell was that all about?" Dakota heard Simon ask.

"She gave me a few tips for kicking your ass."

Simon looked deliberately blank over that. "You're joking."

"Nope." Gregor took a stance. "Let's see if your little lady friend knows shit from shinola."

Simon glanced at her, Dakota saluted him, and without changing expressions, he faced off with Gregor.

Less than a minute into the practice, Simon kicked out but Gregor blocked him, and then quickly threw his punches. Simon managed to dodge the blows, but not Gregor's reciprocal kick. Simon winced at the impact to the outside of his thigh on his left leg.

It happened again.

And again.

So Simon changed tactics. When Gregor went to kick, Simon shot in on him. With incredible speed, he switched to a double leg and the big man went down with the resounding thunder of muscles landing hard on the mat. Gregor made the huge mistake of leaving one of his thick arms vulnerable, and within seconds, Simon forced him to tap out from an excruciating arm bar.

Huh. While digging in her satchel for a stash of peanut M&Ms, Dakota shook her head in disgust. Gregor needed a lot more finesse to take someone like Simon. His strength and size might carry him through the ranks of men with less technical ability, and as she'd told him, he might occasionally get lucky with a shot. But he needed fine-tuning, and then some.

After popping a handful of M&Ms into her mouth, Dakota looked up at the mat. Simon stood leaning on the ropes, watching her.

He looked sinful and sexy, and as macho as one man could look.

"Sorry, but I can't offer you any candy. I'm sure it's a no-no while you're training."

Simon continued with his burning stare. "What did you tell Gregor?"

With an insulting lack of haste, Dakota left her chair and approached the ring. "You want the truth?"

"Is that a rhetorical question?"

"Yeah." She swallowed down more of her candy. "I don't suppose you have a cola machine around here anywhere."

"No."

"I didn't think so." She eyed his water bottle, but plain old water wouldn't do much to revive her. She needed the kick of caffeine. "Coffee?"

"At a diner two doors down, across the street."

Uh-oh. Simon wasn't exactly in a talkative mood now. "Right. Thanks." Admiring his tight abs and bulging biceps, she gave him the once-over before meeting his dark-eyed and somehow challenging gaze. "The thing is, you announce your kicks."

"The hell I do."

She shrugged. He could believe her or not. Didn't really matter to her. "I told Gregor what to watch for, and how to counter it. It helped him, just not enough, obviously."

His voice going a little grittier, Simon said, "I don't announce shit."

"I'll show you. But just real fast, because I do need that caffeine. I can feel myself fading, and a little chocolate isn't going to cut it." After tossing back the last of her M&Ms, Dakota grabbed the ropes, put one foot up on the mat, and hoisted herself onto the perimeter of the ring. She lifted a rope and ducked under.

Bending to unlace her boots, she said, "It's not a supernoticeable thing, but I've watched all your fights at least a half dozen times, so I saw it right off. Havoc would have seen it, too, but he had his attention on Gregor instead of on you."

She straightened, dropped her clunky lace-up boots into the corner, and meandered to the middle of the mat. When she turned back, Simon still stood there near the ropes.

"Well, c'mon. We gonna do this or not?"

He tried to look impassive, Dakota would give him that. But sheer disbelief showed in his eyes. He didn't move.

Dakota rolled her eyes. "Don't worry. You won't hurt me." And then, just to be devilish, she added, "And I won't hurt you. I promise."

That unglued his feet, but the second he moved, both Gregor and Dean started roaring with hilarity and anticipation. Their laughter abruptly died when Simon reached her, bent one knee, tossed her over his shoulder, and carried her back to the ropes.

Dakota did nothing. What would be the point? With the others watching, she didn't feel threatened. And his hold wasn't so much restrictive as functional.

But the feel of his big hands on her, one on her calves and one seriously close to her behind, set her heart to thumping. She breathed in his raw, hot scent. Where she braced her hands on the middle of his back, he was sweaty and so solid that his flesh didn't give way at all.

The man had serious sex appeal.

"Down you go," Simon said, and he slid her off his shoulder, over the side of the ring, and all the way down to the floor.

Dakota stared up at him. It took her a second to find her voice, and then all she said was, "Chicken."

"Yeah, you scare me all right. And that's a real shame." He smiled and turned away, already busy talking to Gregor and Dean.

Dakota chewed over what he said, but only because he sounded so serious, as if his words had double meaning. Did she alarm him? Did he maybe have deranged groupies who threw themselves at him? Stalker women who wouldn't let him be? Or did he just consider her nuts, and therefore dangerous?

And why was it a shame? Had he thought

to ask her out? Maybe ask her over? For sex?

The jerk.

Determined to prove him misguided on all counts, Dakota bolted right back into the ring. When Dean looked her way in amazement, Simon jerked around to face her, too.

"Un-fucking-believable."

She held up her hands. "Don't jump the gun."

Dean laughed. "Is she for real, Simon?"

"Hell if I know."

Dakota suffered through their arrogance with impatience. "Look, I don't want to spar with you. I just want to show you what I'm talking about."

Dean propped his hands on his hips. "Lady, not to be rude, but anything Simon needs to know, he can hear from me."

Gregor rubbed at his ear, saying nothing.

"Well, you haven't told him, now, have you? You're too busy watching Gregor so you can teach him, but Simon plans to reenter the ring, and *mister,* not to be rude to you, but you're not giving him the feedback he needs."

All three males blinked over her audacity at chastising the well-known and sometimes revered Havoc.

Oh, for the love of . . . "If you guys could just tuck away the testosterone for a minute, you might find that I actually know what I'm talking about. I trained in Muay Thai for three years, and I've studied grappling and kickboxing. I'm not saying I'm a competitor, because I know what it takes to compete."

Dryly, Simon said to Dean, "She's not a competitor."

"Thank God for small favors."

Obnoxious asses. Dakota glared at them. "What I'm saying is that I know enough to recognize the difference between a little knowledge and enough experience and talent to get in the ring. You have to admit that's more than some of the guys who try to compete."

There'd been several instances where a hard-ass bozo stupidly wanted to compete in the ring, but a barroom brawler never stood a chance.

"And that's exactly why Simon should hear me out, because I don't have any delusions, just good practical advice."

Again, Simon strode toward her. "Tell you what? Why don't you hightail it out of here now and let us get back to work, and we'll just forget all about this."

"I had no idea that SBC fighters had such

pigheaded arrogance."

Simon reached for her arm — and Dakota reacted on instinct. Well . . . instinct and short temper; after all, he had insulted her with his macho baloney.

Moving fast, she knocked his arm aside and in Muay Thai fashion, kicked out — stopping just sort of hitting Simon in the temple.

Simon stiffened in shock.

Dean and Gregor gaped at her.

Standing there like that, balanced on one leg with the other extended straight in the air, her foot inches from Simon's head, Dakota said, "Be glad I can control myself. Otherwise, that kick would have knocked you out."

His eyes narrowed.

Smiling, Dakota tapped her toes against his temple so he'd know the exact spot she'd pinpointed, and then she dropped her leg and turned her back on him in one smooth motion.

Unwilling to press her luck, Dakota snatched her shoes from the corner and left the ring in a barely veiled hurry. Once on the ground again, she turned back to Simon. "Same bat time, same bat station?"

Frustration, confusion, and antagonism all flashed in his gaze. *What?*

Dakota fought back her grin. "I take it you're not a Batman fan?"

The antagonism took over. "No."

"Figures." She sat to pull on her boots. "I was asking if you'd be here tomorrow at the same time."

"Why?"

Simon's responses had fallen into one-word clipped replies. Dakota wondered if that had any significance for anything. She didn't know him well enough to decide.

Lacing up her boots took a minute and gave her a good excuse not to look at him. "I still need to talk to you, that's why."

"You want to talk, then talk. I'm listening."

"No way. This isn't a good time."

"Why not?"

Did he hope to convince her to finish her business now because he didn't want her coming back tomorrow? Oh, no, she wouldn't let him off that easy. "You're too busy beating your chest and playing Tarzan, which makes me want to clock you for being a jackass, and I need a liquid pick-me-up in a bad way before I put up with any more of your macho bullshit."

Dakota spared a quick glance his way, but couldn't tell what he thought of her deliberately abrasive statement. She finished her boots and stood again. "So, is tomorrow good for you?"

For about fifteen seconds, Simon stood undecided, and she held her breath. Then he crossed his arms on the ropes and nodded. "I'll be here."

"Great." Relief revived her as she pulled on her coat. "I'll bring a thermos of java. We can share."

"I have my own drinks."

"Protein junk, I bet." After wrinkling her nose, she buttoned up her coat to ward off the fall breeze. "To each his own." Anxious to leave while she was still ahead, Dakota gave a negligent wave and headed for the door. She could feel Simon's gaze boring into her back, but rather than uncomfortable, it felt . . . exciting.

Once outside, cold air stung her face and cut through her layers, making her shiver. Steaming, fragrant coffee sounded better and better by the second.

Halfway down the block, Dakota still felt the tingle of interested attention. She couldn't resist looking over her shoulder.

All three big men stood in front of the gym, watching her departure. When she grinned at them, Gregor waved — until Dean slugged him.

Now that she'd seen them, they all went

back inside. Huh. Maybe she hadn't been such a pain in the butt, after all. Maybe she'd been a novelty instead.

And maybe Simon was as anxious to see her again as she was to see him. Dakota didn't know if that'd be good — or very, very bad.

Simon didn't know he was grinning until Dean shook his head at him.

"What?"

"You look moonstruck."

Simon shrugged that off. "She intrigues me, that's all."

Gregor threw an arm over Simon's shoulders, almost knocking him to the floor. "Sorry, bud, but you're trainin' and that means no nooky for you. You gotta save that juice for fightin'."

Simon laughed and shoved him away. "So Jacki's out of luck tonight, is that what you're telling me?"

A slow smile spread over Gregor's face. "Jacki never takes no for an answer."

"And that's more than enough on that subject," Dean insisted, since Jacki was his little sister. "But he is right, Simon. A brief fling is one thing, but you can't afford to get played by some skirt right now."

"Dakota wasn't wearing a skirt."

"Dakota?"

"Dakota Dream."

Gregor and Dean shared amused looks. Dean said, "With a name like that, she sounds like a —"

"Yeah, I know," Simon cut in. "But she's touchy about it, so don't tease her."

Dean's amusement turned to a scowl. "How the hell do you know she's touchy?"

"I could tell."

"I have a solution for you: No one can tease her if she doesn't hang around."

"She's coming back tomorrow." And Simon added, "Same bat time, same bat station."

Dean ignored all that. "If she shows up, you need to send her packing."

"It's a free world, Dean. Women can go wherever they want these days." He smiled at his friend. "Even to your gym."

Gregor said, "But she'll have to pay to stick around tomorrow."

Simon nodded. "I know."

"And there'll be a lot more guys here then, too. It's always the busiest day. Crowded as hell. I thought we'd skip it."

"I thought so, too," Dean added.

Simon frowned. Fridays were always busy because a handful of veteran fighters made the trip to Dean's gym, which meant that all the newer men also showed up to observe, listen, and learn.

It worked out well for all involved. The established fighters got to spar with fresh blood and bone up on new and varied techniques, and novices got the opportunity to get in some authentic practice.

"I've decided to be here."

Gregor and Dean studied him.

Simon didn't care what they thought, but still he said, "I figure I should get in as many days as I can before competing again."

They studied him some more.

"Hey," Simon snapped, fed up with their awkward looks and insulting conjecture — even if they were right. "You two don't have to hang around if you've got something better to do. I only plan to work out, not spar."

To Simon's chagrin, they both jumped on his excuse.

"Eve would enjoy having me home for a full day for a change." Dean barely smiled while saying that. "And Haggerty will be here to run the place. It's not like I'm needed."

"Jacki will be thrilled to have me all to herself," Gregor added.

"Selfish bastards," Simon said without venom. Ready to call it a day, he headed for the corner where the clean towels were kept.

A hot shower sounded heavenly. "You know, since you mentioned skirts . . . I wonder what Dakota would look like in something less rugged."

"Don't," Dean told him.

"Don't what?"

"Wonder about her." Dean tapped himself on the forehead. "Let the bigger head do all the thinking, and think only about the competition."

"I had no idea you were such a mother hen."

"She's trouble, Simon. We both know it."

Given her behavior and outrageous way of talking, Simon had to admit the possibility. But for whatever reason, that only intrigued him more. "Maybe." Then to reassure both his friends, he said, "I have my priorities straight, and I've been in the business too long to get sidetracked by a piece of tail."

But even as he said that, Simon regretted the coarse reference to Dakota. She was different. A little odd, but in a cute way. Ballsy beyond belief. He liked that.

And he had a feeling that beneath the street-thug clothes, she had a killer body, lean and limber, just as he preferred.

"God help us," Dean muttered. "I see it on your face. If you want her that bad, just go after her. She'll still be at the diner. Hook up, get it out of your system, and then tomorrow we can all three take a break."

Hell of an idea — except that Simon would never allow Dean or even Gregor to think him so weak that he'd allow a woman to influence him. Never again. "I'll pass on that, but thanks for the offer." He slung the towel around his neck. "Dean?"

"Yeah?"

"I hate to admit it, but Dakota might've been right about a few things."

Gregor nodded. "The little darlin' did clue me in on how to spot your kicks before they happened."

"How's that?"

"You tightened your jaw. Like this." Gregor clenched his teeth. "See?"

"She spotted *that?*" Dean asked.

"Said she did. And she was right. That's the only reason I was able to block those last few."

"I'll be damned," Dean muttered.

Simon nearly laughed. Something so simple, and Dakota had noticed. Usually, if a fighter telegraphed his intent, it was by planting his legs, bracing his shoulders . . . something more obvious than a mere expression.

"So I tighten my jaw." Bemused, Simon shook his head and made a quick decision.

"Monday morning I want Dean in the ring with me."

When Dean said without argument, "You've got it," Simon knew that he'd already come to the same conclusion.

"What the hell?" Gregor joked. "I'm being replaced?"

"We'll alternate," Simon suggested. "And whoever isn't sparring with me should damn well watch for more tells."

Less than an hour later, they all left the gym to go their separate ways. Simon did slow his car near the diner, and sure enough, Dakota still sat inside. At a booth. With two young men chatting her up. With each word she spoke, Dakota gestured with her hands. She wore a steady smile.

She looked really, really cute.

Simon almost weakened. He almost parked and went inside.

Instead, he stepped on the gas and drove away. Dakota Dream would not lure him off course. No woman could. He planned to win his return fight in a big way.

The spectators would get their money's worth, and then some.

But afterward, when the belt was his and the Internet sites heralded him as still the victor . . . then he'd find Ms. Dream. Until

then, it wouldn't hurt to have a little fun
with her.

CHAPTER 3

Dakota drew up short just inside the gym door.

Like yesterday, warm, humid air and the drone of noise greeted her. But unlike yesterday, today the place was packed.

Men were everywhere, many of them in various stages of undress. Most wore kickboxing shorts and nothing else. All of them were big, hard, dangerous-looking men.

A good dozen of them eyeballed her entrance into their semiprivate sanctum.

Well, this was uncomfortable.

Not that she'd let a little discomfort slow her down.

Before Dakota could take more than a few steps forward, a welterweight too old to still compete stopped her. "The gym's closed today."

Dakota's brow went up as she peered at the wiry little man. He sat at a barely noticeable corner desk, a newspaper opened over his lap, his feet propped up. He wore a white T-shirt, baggy athletic pants, and wrestling shoes. Other than some artistic tattoos on his forearms, the most noticeable thing about him was a very close-cropped Mohawk and a little goat beard.

The very sight of him made Dakota smile.

"That's odd," she said, and still gained no attention from the man. "There are so many people here, it looks open to me."

"There are men here, not just people. They're members." He turned a page of the paper. "We're closed to the public. You're the public. So we're closed."

Suspicions bloomed. "Did Sublime put you up to this?"

"Closed is closed. Dean's rules. Sublime ain't got nothing to do with it." But he glanced at her over the edge of the newspaper. His gaze dipped to her feet, crawled up to her face, then went back to his paper. "But I reckon Sublime wouldn't want to send ya off no ways."

"Really?"

"Known as a ladies' man, that Sublime." His gaze peeked over the paper again. "You're a lady, ain't ya?"

"Last time I checked."

"There ya go." And he went back to reading.

One thing he'd said caught her attention. "Dean Conor owns this gym?"

"Yup."

She knew the gym was ultra popular with fighters, and that Dean was always on hand. But as an owner rather than a spokesman? Surprise, surprise.

"I didn't realize."

"No reason you should, you being the public and all."

Well, shoot. None of that was very productive. "So let me see if I understand this. You're telling me that I need a membership to get in today?"

"Everyone needs a membership to get in today. Not just you." He rattled the paper. "Don't be conceited."

"Conceited?"

He huffed. "Thinking it's all about you. Doesn't matter to me who you are or who you're here to see. You need a membership, just like everyone else."

"Right. Got it." And people called her strange! "How do I get a membership?"

In a well-rehearsed spiel, he said, "You pay eighty bucks. That'll cover the month. Come as often as you like. Any equipment you see, you can use. First come, first serve. You need your own gear. We ain't got no ladies' shower room, though. Not that the men'll kick ya out, but you might not like it in there." He turned another page. "It smells."

Dakota stiffened her spine. "I have no intention of using the men's shower."

"That's a good thing, I reckon."

"I'm Dakota, by the way."

"Name's Haggerty. I play referee when needed, bust heads when it's called for." He lowered the paper and even went so far as to drop his feet to the floor. "And I collect memberships."

"Lovely." Well, he'd certainly brought that one full circle! Dakota loosened her satchel from her shoulder. "Do you take checks?"

"Nope. But I'll take a credit card. That'll get you a temporary ID and use of the place."

"Thank you, Haggerty. You're being most helpful."

He grinned, stunning Dakota by the beauty of that smile. How such a gnarled little man kept such wonderful teeth, she couldn't guess.

As he ran her credit card, she asked, "I hope Sublime is here today."

"I seen him earlier."

"You seen . . . er, saw him where?" In that crowd, she'd never find Simon without a little help.

"Weight room. Toward the back." Haggerty tipped his head in the general direction then returned her card to her, along with a temporary ID. "Just so you know — it's smelly back there, too. Not every day, but today's not every day. Today is busier."

"I appreciate the warning." Dakota stared across the floor toward the door Haggerty had indicated. A dozen scarred, curious, muscle-bound hulks kept her in their sights as they continued with their routines.

It'd be like walking the gauntlet.

She might as well get it over with. Looping her satchel strap over her neck for safekeeping, Dakota lifted her chin and began her trek. It wasn't easy. Sweaty bodies ebbed and flowed around the room. She got bumped four times, three of those times on purpose, she was sure.

A hand grazed her behind. She ignored the insult of it. For now. But she did turn to lock eyes with the offender.

She wanted him to know that she was on to him.

A little more handsome than some of the others, he grinned at her. "Looking for someone, honey?"

"A man."

He held out his arms. "Mallet Manchester, at your service."

"Oh," she said, "I think you misheard me. I'm looking for a *man*."

Everyone around them roared with hilarity.

Except Mallet.

Dakota could tell that he took himself far too seriously.

Separating herself from him, she stepped around one bruised fellow with the worst cauliflower ears she'd ever seen, and sauntered past another who smelled like a sewer; Haggerty hadn't lied about that.

After much maneuvering through human traffic, she finally reached the door — and it opened on its own.

Simon stepped out and almost ran into her. He drew up in what she chose to interpret as pleasurable surprise. "Dakota."

"Simon." Man-oh-man, he looked good, sweaty and hot and, again, wearing only kickboxing shorts, these a royal blue. Not a single foul odor arose from him. If anything, he smelled good. Earthy. Manly. Strong. Sexy.

Dakota shook her head of those fanciful notions. "You bum," she teased. "You know, you could have warned me."

His firm mouth didn't smile, but his dark eyes did. "About what?"

"The eighty dollars, naturally." Never in a

million years would Dakota admit that the crowded gym discomforted her. "I had to use my credit card just to get in."

His fingers touched her chin in a brief apology. "I'll try and make it worth the cost."

That single nonsexual caress immobilized her. Hell, she couldn't even breathe. She stared at Simon, waiting for . . . she didn't know what.

Three swearing, disgruntled men pushed toward them, and Simon took her arm, tugging her out of the way. But rather than stop once he'd cleared their path, he released Dakota and kept going — toward another group of men.

Dakota hurried after him. "You're still working out?"

"I'm done, but I want to watch some of the others for a while."

"How long is a while?"

If he found her question pushy, he didn't say so. "Half an hour or so."

Not too bad. Dakota looked around at the other men, and although she almost suffocated on the thick testosterone in the air, she decided it might be fun to talk to them. Some of them she recognized from fights; others looked new to her. "Okay, so then . . . maybe we could do lunch after that?"

"Doubtful." Simon stopped in front of two men practicing strikes. He took a moment to instruct one man on the positioning of his legs before giving a portion of his attention to Dakota. "While I'm training, I'm on a specialized diet. No fast food for me."

Dakota patted her fattened satchel. "I figured as much. I packed our lunch in a thermal bag."

Simon's dark brows rose a good inch. "You assumed I'd agree?"

"I was hopeful, yeah."

He crossed his arms over his chest. "Let me know what you're offering first."

That sensual smile of his wasn't restricted to her offer of food. But Dakota wouldn't let him bait her. Playing dumb to his innuendo, she said, "For me, a cold cut trio, coffee and chocolate cake for dessert. For you, lean turkey with dark greens and tomato on a whole wheat pita and a power drink."

He looked at her mouth. "Do I get dessert?"

Such a loaded question! Dakota almost asked, *What do you want?* but she caught herself in time. "Of course. One cup of cottage cheese with fresh pineapple slices."

He reached out and tucked a wayward strand of her long blond hair behind her ear. "I'm impressed."

Today he'd taken to touching her, and the intimacy of that left her flustered. Dakota hoped she hid her reaction to his familiarity. "That I know my business?"

"That you went to so much trouble."

Trouble would be going back to Barnaby empty-handed. And that, she wouldn't do. She wanted Barnaby, and the reminders of her awful mistakes, wiped from her life once and for all.

Pasting on a grin, Dakota assured him, "If I get what I want, it'll be worth it."

If she gets what she wants.

If her thoughts had traveled in the same direction as his, Simon could almost guarantee her satisfaction on that score. If her thoughts varied from his, well, then, he'd just have to convince her.

One way or another, he had to get a handle on his reaction to her.

Maybe he'd been celibate too long, and maybe, without even knowing it, he was still stinging over Bonnie's deceit. Whatever the reason, Dakota got to him in a big way.

She removed her coat to reveal a bulky, unattractive navy blue sweatshirt with white lettering that read, BARBERS KNOW WHERE TO PART IT.

Simon scowled. Was she dating a damned barber?

Too many washings had left the sweatshirt misshapen, giving an ill fit over tattered jeans and those same manly black boots. And still she looked so damn sexy to him that his heart beat faster.

Standing outside a circle of men practicing submission moves, Simon pretended not to watch her.

Ha. What a joke.

Even though he'd already told them all that she was off-limits, every guy in the place watched her. A few were ignorant enough to ignore his warning and approach her.

Like Mallet Manchester.

Simon didn't like Mallet much, but he had to give him some leeway for stupidity. Dumber than a heavy tool, that was Mallet. Simon thought his real name might be Michael, but no one ever called him that, on or off the mat.

Mallet was the type of moron who never took good warnings to heart. He thought he could bully men and harass women, and sometimes, he was right.

Within the SBC family, he was dead wrong.

Every organization had its bad apples, but

for the most part the SBC fostered honor, good sportsmanship, hard work ethics, and camaraderie. Those traits were necessary to succeed in the rigorous competitions. Fighters worked together to learn. They congratulated each other and competed with goodwill.

Mallet, Simon predicted, would never succeed beyond the occasional win. He wasn't championship material. He didn't have the heart.

Chatting with people, examining machines, and assessing biceps, Dakota flitted around the room. She admired a few tattoos, and two fighters even went to the back to retrieve photos of their wives and kids to show her. Like the belle of the ball, she charmed them all.

Except Mallet.

When Dakota didn't give the young fool enough attention, he tried to steal the show by brazenly copping a feel of her ass. She was facing Simon at the time, so he witnessed the shifting expressions of shock, fury, and finally malice that overtook her smile.

Simon saw red.

Then he saw Dakota backhand the guy right in the balls.

She didn't turn to face Mallet for the attack. Nope, she took him off guard by striking without looking at him. And she hit the nail on the . . . head.

Mallet's face froze for a horrified instant before twisting into awful pain. He cupped his jewels and dropped hard to his knees.

The gym room went silent, partly in shock, partly in amusement, and partly in anticipation of what would happen next.

As Dakota turned to Mallet, everyone watched. She put her hands on her hips. She even looked a little sorry for him.

Bending down, she made sure to have Mallet's attention. "Oh, quit the bellyaching. That wasn't much more than a tap. But let me warn you, if you paw me again, next time it'll be a punch." She straightened, dusted off her hands, and went back to chatting as if it hadn't happened.

Simon didn't realize that he'd headed toward her until he reached her. Once there, he wasn't quite sure what to do. Mallet remained on his knees, still wincing in pain, so it'd be pointless to deck him — as he wanted to.

And Dakota didn't seem the least bit upset by the incident, so he couldn't comfort her or defend her, or anything lame like that.

He didn't know what the hell to do.

Dakota saved him by asking, "All done?"

Unable to lighten his mood or his expression, Simon nodded. "Yeah. I just need to shower."

"Great. Are you a ten-minute kind of guy, or one who lingers?"

Everything she said had sexual connotations to Simon's lust-inspired brain. "That depends on what I'm doing, Dakota."

"Oh?"

Damn, but he couldn't keep from looking at her mouth. She didn't wear lipstick, and her mouth looked soft and full, always ready to smile. His voice dropped. "Sometimes lingering is just the right move."

Those sweet lips parted, then closed tight. "Well, now isn't a good time to linger. I'm starving. And if you don't mind, do you think you could take that one with you?" She nodded toward Mallet. "I think I swatted him a little harder than I meant to."

The hell he would! "He can damn well crawl in on his own."

Dakota frowned. "He's carrying on so, I'm starting to feel a little guilty, even though he had it coming."

"Yeah, he did." But on second thought, Simon didn't want to leave Mallet alone with Dakota while he showered. He caught Mallet's upper arm and hauled him to his feet. Training mode kicked in, and Simon said, "Let's go, son. I think you could use a cold shower. And no, don't complain to me. You're lucky she got to you before I did, because I'd have broken your hand."

To his credit, Mallet kept his mouth shut, but his expression was enough to make most women shudder in fear.

Not Dakota.

She laughed.

Beyond the obvious ideas of bedding her a half dozen times until he got her out of his system, Simon wondered what he was supposed to do with a woman like her. She'd made herself at home in the gym, when few women would even venture inside, much less linger.

Simon cleared the floor with Mallet in tow, and then used a forearm to pin the much younger man to the wall. "I warned you, Mallet."

"She was flirting with everyone!" he strangled out.

"No, she was visiting while waiting for *me*. If you're too stupid to know the difference, that's your problem. But this is the last time I'm going to tell you: hands off."

Mallet tried to pry Simon's forearm away from his throat, but he couldn't. "You don't own her, Sublime."

Simon gave him an evil smile. "Far as you're concerned, I do. And if I catch you so much as looking at her the wrong way again, my fists are going to have a discussion with your face. You got that?"

Trying for a smidge of bluster, Mallet said, "Maybe I'm not afraid of you."

"Then you really are dumber than I thought." Simon released him so that he could show him the error of his ways — and Haggerty materialized out of nowhere.

"If you're going to draw blood, do it outside the gym. You know Dean's rules."

Simon looked at Haggerty, and guessed aloud, "Dakota sent you in, didn't she?"

"Said she was afraid you'd kill the young'un." He shrugged, then latched onto Mallet's arm. "I thought she might be right, so here I am when God knows I have better things to do than babysit idiot fighters." He led Mallet away, all the while chewing the young man's ear on rules and propriety and good common sense.

With no release for his anger, Simon fumed. Damn meddling woman, he thought.

Meddling, but also smart. After all, she'd known what he would do. Apparently, Dakota had a big heart, too, if Mallet's well-being mattered to her after he'd dared to grope her.

Now Simon was the one who needed a cool shower, to bring both his anger and his ardor under control. He wasn't used to excesses of temper. He fought with brains, not emotion, and he dealt with others the same way.

All his life he'd seen things as black and white. A man needed to work hard, treat others honorably, accept his responsibilities, and along the way have some fun.

Dakota would definitely be fun.

But in his gut, he knew she'd also be dangerous. And he couldn't ignore the fact that she'd shown up at the worst possible time. He had to prioritize, and that meant training first, fighting second, promoting third . . . and having fun with a sexy, mouthy, surprising broad fell somewhere way down on the long list.

He'd be smart to get the hell away from her.

That is, if she'd let him. As he'd pointed out to Dean, it was a free world and if Dakota chose to hang out at the gym, he couldn't stop her. Right?

While he showered, Simon made up his mind. He'd find out what Dakota wanted, then he'd send her on her way.

He wouldn't touch her, damn it.

85

He wouldn't seduce her.

He wouldn't do all the things to her that he really wanted to do.

That decision put him in a bad enough mood. But after he redressed and went out to the main floor to find Dakota, his mood took a dangerous turn for the worse.

Dakota had removed her ridiculous black work boots. One of the heavyweights sat on the floor holding those and her satchel in his lap. He was joined by other fighters, some standing, some sitting.

None working.

They were all too busy watching Dakota, encouraging her, ogling her as she halfheartedly sparred with Mitch McGee.

Damn it, did no one take him seriously anymore?

McGee spotted Simon before Dakota did. He froze, which was unfortunate because Dakota expected him to block a kick. He didn't. She spun around, and her foot connected with Mitch's chin. Eyes crossing, mouth going slack, Mitch staggered backward and bounced against the ropes.

"Oh, my God!" Dakota ran to him. "Mitch! I'm so sorry. Are you okay?"

With growing irritation, Simon watched her fawn over McGee. What he felt was not jealousy. No. It wasn't.

Hell, no.

But McGee should have known better than to play with her, damn it. "Let's go, Dakota," Simon ordered.

"Yeah, just a sec," she said back.

McGee, showing some intelligence, slumped against the ropes, shook his head to clear it, and said, "I'm fine. Don't keep Sublime waiting."

"Why? Waiting won't kill him. I've been waiting on him for an hour now."

"Yeah, but . . ." McGee glanced at Simon with apology. "He's ready now."

She snorted. "He's not a raw turkey. He'll keep without souring too much."

McGee's brow puckered in confusion. "What?"

That was Simon's reaction, too. Dakota did say the oddest things that, from what he could tell, had no meaning to anyone but her.

Rather than look like an ass, Simon said, "Suit yourself, Dakota. I'm outta here." And he forced himself to turn and walk away from her.

"Oh, for the love of . . ." Her voice dropped to a growl. "All *right* already. Keep your pants on."

Simon stopped. He took one deep breath, then another before he turned to see Dakota scrambling under the ropes. "I think I'd rather not."

She flashed him a look of incomprehension. "You'd rather not what?" Dropping to sit on her butt by the heavyweight, she tugged on her boots and sped through tying her laces.

"Get it in gear, Dakota, and I'll explain it all to you once we're alone."

Most of the men understood that Simon would prefer to have his pants *off* with Dakota, and they snickered and hooted — until Dakota silenced them all with a frown.

"Don't encourage him," she said. "He's bad enough as it is."

So she intended to give them all orders. Ballsy beyond belief, that's what she was.

But the men went quiet.

Done with her boots, Dakota jumped up and pulled on her coat, thanked the heavyweight for his assistance, and grabbed her satchel. She raced to Simon, hooked her arm through his, and smiled brightly. "All ready. Let's go."

Simon glanced around to see all the men smiling like adoring saps. How the hell did she do that so easily? Few women could infiltrate an all-male domain and be treated as both a pal and a lady.

Especially if she looked like Dakota Dream.

It wasn't just her name that made Simon think of porn stars. She had a natural comfort with her body and presence, and a load of confidence that rivaled a championship fighter.

Dakota was dangerous to one and all. But still, Simon's look issued another warning, and one by one, the men all went back to their drills.

Okay, so maybe he wouldn't be able to escape her without at least a small taste. And touch. And maybe even . . . full satisfaction.

But just once.

Then he'd send her packing and get back to the business of reclaiming a title championship.

Chapter 4

She drove a truck. Why didn't that surprise him?

Simon glanced around at the interior of the aged Ford F-150 and decided that it suited her. Rugged, but well equipped. Economical, but still attractive. A string of Mardi Gras beads hung from the rearview mirror and a newspaper, with cheap hotel ads circled, lay on the dash. On the floor of the passenger's side was a large thermos, no doubt filled with coffee.

If someone had asked Simon last week — or even two days ago — if he ever thought to eat lunch in a truck in the rain, he'd have assured the person it wasn't possible.

Yet here he was.

A slow steady rain added to the chill in the air and limited the visibility through the windows.

It was cozy. And intimate.

Simon took another bite of his pita sandwich and wished like hell he had the same loaded cold cut triple-decker that Dakota devoured.

She'd driven them just a few blocks from the gym to a deserted park. She kept the engine running with the heat on low and a CD playing. He wore only a long-sleeved tee and jeans; she'd taken off her coat.

Around a mouthful of food, she asked, "Is my hair curling?"

Simon settled against the passenger door and surveyed her. "Do you realize that your conversational topics are usually pretty hard to follow?"

"Yeah, I know." She shrugged. "Sorry. But see, it's raining and I didn't expect that. The humidity makes my hair curl. And frizz. I'd have pulled it into a ponytail if the weatherman hadn't outright lied to me, claiming it'd be a nice day."

Her hair was frizzing a little, but it looked cute. "You're fine." Simon eyed the sweat-shirt again. "I take it you're into barbers?"

She glanced down at her chest and smiled. "A friend gives me this stuff on holidays. I have a whole line of barber-joke apparel."

"He's not a boyfriend?"

She shook her head and said emphatically, "No."

The way she stressed the negative made

Simon wonder, so he kept quiet and waited for her to elaborate. She did.

"I'm too busy for any steady dating or anything. And besides, I'm picky."

"Picky how?"

"No smokers, no druggies, no heavy drinkers."

He avoided the same people. "You call that picky?"

"In today's world, yeah."

"What else?"

"Hmmm." She considered her preferences while wolfing down another big bite. "Well, I'm not keen on stuffed suits, or guys that are into total grunge. And definitely no wimps or whiners."

"I don't like whiners, either. Anything else?"

"No young'uns. A man has to be at least my age or older."

A perfect lead-in. "And you are . . . ?"

"Twenty-three."

Simon snorted. He'd thought her a little older, maybe closer to his thirty-one years. "Any younger than you and he'd be in high school."

She ignored that. "And because I have to travel a lot, no one who's too clingy. I hate all that mushy heartbreaking drama, ya know?"

She really did have a long list, Simon realized. But fortunately, he didn't fall into any of her taboo categories. He respected his health too much to do drugs, smoke, or overdrink. And he'd never been clingy or whiny a day in his life. "So do you ever date?"

"Not very often." She averted her gaze — and that got Simon to speculating.

"When was your last date?"

For the longest time, she didn't answer, choosing instead to stare out the window. The CD played, vying with the howling wind.

Simon was about to change the subject when she said, "It's been so long now, I can't remember exactly." Suddenly she turned to him. "What about you?"

"A few months." But he didn't want to talk about Bonnie. "So tell me, Dakota, what do you do when you're not hanging out at gyms waiting for men you don't know? You mentioned that you have to travel a lot?"

A big smile brightened her expression. "Most of the time, I perform."

"Dare I ask?"

She laughed. "I'm a singer. Sometimes I go solo, sometimes I hook up with a band. Depends on the job, and they vary a lot.

I've done weddings and parties for a one-shot deal. And I've done bars and clubs where I stayed on for a few months at a time."

Yeah, Simon could see her front and center, entertaining men. She'd be a hit. Her voice was mellow and rich, and easy on the ears. "So you do have a real job, just not an ordinary one."

"Listen to who's talking!" She reached over to slug him on the shoulder. "Like being a professional fighter for the SBC is in any way ordinary."

"You've got me there." Simon pried the lid off his cottage cheese and pineapple. It looked good. "You want to sing me something while I eat this?"

She laughed again. "No way."

"Shy?"

"Nope, not even a little. But this is hardly the time or place."

"Why not?" Simon glanced around at the interior of the truck, then the empty grounds of the park. "Eating in a truck in the rain in the cold is a first for me. We might as well top it off with live entertainment."

Dakota shoved her empty food containers back into a bag. "I had thought we'd sit outside to eat. I was going to brave the cold

94

for you, Simon. I'm sorry it didn't work out."

"Why?" He ate the rest of his meal in a few big bites. "Why go to all this trouble? You still haven't told me what it is you want."

"I know." She put her hands together. "I needed to talk to you, but not in a busy diner, and not at the gym. What I have to say . . . well, it's better done in private."

Simon eyed her. "If we'd ever had sex, I'd think you were pregnant or something." Her eyes widened. "But that sure as hell can't be it since I haven't touched you."

"No."

He watched her, and added, "Yet."

Her mouth opened, but nothing came out.

"So what is it, Dakota?"

"Well," she hedged. "You know, it's ironic that you'd mention fatherhood."

Enough was enough. Simon cleared away the empty containers with an edgy type of impatience. "Stop dancing around about it and just tell me."

She sucked in a deep breath and, watching for his reaction, said, "Your dad wanted me to fetch you home."

Alarm slammed into Simon. "My dad?"

"Yes. He wants . . . needs to see you."

But he'd just seen both his mother and

his father not that long ago. Still, fear took over. Simon dug out his cell phone from his pocket and punched in the familiar number.

Alarm brought Dakota upright. "What are you doing?"

"Calling my dad." She started to say something, and he held up a finger to silence her. "Dad? Hey, what's going on?"

His usual jovial self, Reid Evans laughed. "Not much, son. What's up with you?"

As briefly as possible, Simon explained Dakota. As he spoke, she shook her head at him and kept trying to interrupt, but Simon didn't give her a chance. Finally, she threw up her hands and slumped back in her seat with a mulish expression.

Reid Evans had never met anyone named Dakota Dream. He knew nothing about her. He had no idea who she might be or what she might want.

He exposed her for a fraud.

"Thanks, Dad. That's what I figured."

Reid didn't let it go at that. "You know, she could just be trying to wheedle a date from you."

"Maybe." But Simon didn't think so.

"Is she a looker?"

"Hard to tell," Simon lied. "She's not the best dresser I've ever seen." Simon stared at her. Dakota frowned back in irritation.

"Sweet disposition?" Reid asked.

Simon chuckled. "Somehow, I have my doubts on that one."

"You should bring her home, let your mother meet her. She's a good judge of character."

"Don't count on it." Before Reid started insisting, Simon said, "I gotta run, Dad. Take care, okay?"

"You, too, son. Keep in touch."

"Will do." Simon disconnected the phone. He worked his jaw while studying Dakota. Obviously, she'd lied. But why? "You care to explain?"

"If you care to listen," she snapped back.

Simon chastised her with a shake of his head. "First you lie to me, and now you act surly."

"I didn't lie."

"That was my dad I spoke to, Dakota."

"Really? Your biological father or a step-father?" Without giving him a chance to react to that, she said, "I'm guessing step-father, since your filial father is the one who hired me."

Ice ran in Simon's veins. He didn't re-member his father at all. According to his mother, the man had left when Simon was little more than a year old. Not once in the thirty years that had followed had he ever contacted Simon.

Why would he contact him now? "You say he hired you?"

Dakota gave a dismissive wave of her hand. "When I'm not singing, I work on a volunteer basis to help find missing people. Usually runaway teens, but I guess Barnaby thought that qualified me to find you."

Growing colder by the second, void of emotion, Simon said, "I'm not a teen, I haven't run away, and I don't know anyone named Barnaby."

She flattened her mouth. "I'm sorry, but you didn't give me much chance to explain."

"And now there's no reason to." Simon put on his seat belt. "You can take me back to the gym."

"But . . . I have to talk to you about this."

"The answer is no."

"I haven't asked a question yet!"

"Doesn't matter." He wanted away from her. He wanted away from the idea of his real father seeking a meeting with him. "We're done here."

"Simon, come on, don't be stubborn. At least hear me out."

A strange hollowness bloomed inside him. "I can walk if you don't want to drive me back."

Her jaw locked. Simon thought he might

have heard her teeth grinding. Then she cursed softly and snapped her own seat belt into place. She put the truck in gear. "Fine. I'll take you back."

No way would Simon thank her.

Dakota stayed silent until they got into traffic. Then, knowing he couldn't very well get out of the truck unless she stopped, she launched into explanations. "His name is Barnaby Jailer, and he just wants to meet you."

Disgusted, Simon closed his eyes and ignored her.

"I don't know why, but he said it's important, and he said he never contacted you before now because he couldn't."

"Save it, please."

"I can't just go back empty-handed."

"I don't think you have a choice, honey."

"I'm not your damn honey, and we all have choices. You could choose to see him so that —"

"So that you get paid?" A fresh rush of anger burned away the apathy. "Is that it? You low on cash?"

"Great." Dakota's hands flexed on the steering wheel. "Now you're going to be a jerk again?"

"Again?"

"I haven't forgotten that you refused to

even listen to my suggestions about your fighting style."

Simon's anger prickled and sharpened beyond all measure. No woman had ever affected him this way. No woman had ever been outrageous enough to talk to him like this.

Insane, he thought, but disappointment drove him as much as anything else did. Despite her being a royal pain in the ass, he'd wanted her.

Bad.

And now he knew he wouldn't have her.

He felt the loss like a solid punch to the liver. "You want to know something, Dakota? I put up with you so far because, for whatever odd reason, I thought you were a little sexy."

"Sexy?"

It seemed she found that idea as ludicrous as he did. "I figured I'd play along with your whacky nonsense, get laid, and then bid you farewell. But now I have to wonder."

Her eyes narrowed. "Wonder about what?"

Simon leaned close and put his hand on her thigh.

She stiffened straight as a flagpole.

Voice low and mean, Simon said, "If I go between your legs right now, am I going to find warm woman, or a set of brass balls?"

Taking a sudden sharp turn, Dakota slammed on her brakes, throwing Simon to the side of the truck. She snarled, *"Get out."*

Simon already had his seat belt opened and was reaching for the door. "Gladly."

Her hands had a death grip on the steering wheel. From her neck to her knees, she looked rigid enough to crack.

She didn't look at him.

She didn't blink.

Simon had the awful suspicion that she wasn't just pissed, she was hurt.

And damn it, he regretted that.

He stepped out of the truck and started to say something — he didn't know what — but she sped away, tires squealing, rain puddle splashing to drench his legs. The door swung shut on its own.

Standing there in the pouring rain, Simon watched her truck disappear from sight. Well, shit. None of that had gone at all as he'd hoped. He hadn't even gotten a small taste of her, much less the full-blown release he'd hoped for.

Rain soaked him to the skin. His brain churned. His guts burned. Never in his life had he found himself in such a position. He always knew just what to do, when to do it, and how to do it. Hadn't he walked out on Bonnie without a single regret?

But now . . . it felt like he had many loose ends, most of them surrounding an uncontrollable need to have Dakota Dream in his bed.

With nothing else to do, Simon started walking toward the gym, which was still a block away. He paid no attention to the rain.

His real father's name was Barnaby.

What could the man possibly want after all this time?

Stretched out on her hotel bed, a gigantic bowl of popcorn balanced on her abdomen, an ice-cold Coke leaving another ring on the already ruined nightstand, Dakota wallowed in her defeat. Light from the television flickered around the darkened room, but she had no idea what was playing. She'd yet to taste either the popcorn or the cola.

Damn, damn, damn.

It had been three days since she'd forced Simon from her truck and into the rain. Three days of rethinking and wishing and . . . regrets. She *hated* regrets. God knew she'd lived with enough of them plaguing her for most of her life.

Why did she let Simon get to her? And with his refusal so final, why was she still sitting in a hotel room in Harmony, Kentucky? By now, she should have packed up her meager belongings and moved on to something less annoying. Singing jobs awaited her. Work would help distract her. She had a life elsewhere. Sort of. If you could call her day-to-day existence "life."

She liked Simon, she realized. She respected him. Worse, she was very attracted to him when no man had drawn her in years.

But he'd thought her no more than a quick lay.

Bastard.

Closing her eyes, Dakota imagined how she could have done things differently. But she'd been over that scenario a hundred times. She'd chewed it every way imaginable, and always come to the same conclusion: Simon deserved better than Barnaby.

So maybe she hadn't really put her heart into convincing him. Maybe she'd even done the right thing by not getting his agreement, and now she should let him —

Her cell phone buzzed, vibrating over the nightstand until it bumped into the Coke. Great. A diversion.

Not bothering to check the number, she snatched it up, hoping to hear the voice of a friend, or even a salesman. "Yeah?"

"How are things progressing, Dakota?"

Barnaby. A familiar lead weight settled around her. Slowly, she set the popcorn aside and sat up. "They aren't. Progressing, that is."

"Explain that please."

Oh, she'd explain all right. "Funny thing, Barnaby, but Simon wants nothing to do with you."

Two heartbeats of silence passed before Barnaby gave an audible sigh. "You need to convince him, honey."

"I'm no one's honey." The words were harsher than she'd intended, but not since her ill-fated marriage and demolishing divorce had she willingly been "honey" to anyone.

"Convince him, Dakota."

"Impossible." She took a measure of glee in telling Barnaby the truth. "Things were going fine, he seemed nice enough, then I mentioned you and he became a real dick. Seems he doesn't like you much. Odd, since he hasn't even met you, huh? Then again, maybe his mother told him all about —"

"I doubt his mother ever mentioned me, one way or the other. But if she did, she would have kept it brief."

"Really?" That sounded odd. "How come?"

"Shall we discuss mothers, honey? There are plenty of things I haven't told you yet."

God, Dakota hated herself for asking, but

she couldn't stop herself. "Yeah? Like what?"

"Like the fact that your mother wrote some letters before her death."

Her heartbeat thundered as an invisible fist clenched around her throat, making speech difficult. "Letters? To who?"

"Some to me."

"Why would she write you letters when you were always with her?"

Rather than answer that, he said, "And some to God."

Dakota frowned. Had her mother written them out of suffering? Out of grief? Breathing seemed impossible. "I want to see them."

"I destroyed them," he said. And then, calculating, "But a few were to you. And I still have them."

Her body and mind went blank. "No."

"Yes. You see, it seems Joan was struggling with a lot of decisions, especially those decisions that concerned you."

Tears rushed to Dakota's eyes, but her voice sounded steady enough when she asked, "You read them?"

"Of course. As her husband, I had every right to know her secrets, and her state of mind."

Dakota's eyes closed, forcing the tears to

trickle down her cheeks. She dashed them away. Barnaby took great pleasure in tormenting her. She wouldn't give him the satisfaction of knowing how he succeeded. "You're just dying to tell me what they said, so go ahead."

"You couldn't be more wrong. I have no intention of telling you anything."

Her eyes snapped open again. If Barnaby didn't want to tell her the contents of the letters, that could only mean one thing — they hadn't all been hateful. If they were, he'd have already told her. He'd have relished telling her.

Unless he'd just found them.

Dakota calmed herself, thinking through her next few questions. "Funny that you've never mentioned any letters before. Why is that?"

"I saw no point in mentioning them . . . until now."

"Or maybe you just decided to make this up, and that's why you haven't mentioned them."

"It matters little to me what you believe, Dakota."

Damn it. "How long have you supposedly known about them?"

"I found them right after Joan's death. The silly woman had them hidden."

Now Dakota knew he lied, and told him so. "Get real, Barnaby. Mom was in a coma. She couldn't speak, couldn't move. How would she have hidden anything?"

"Obviously, she wrote them before she got so badly hurt."

But why? Why would her mother do such a thing? "I don't believe you. You're making it up."

"She hid them in the oddest place," he said, ignoring her accusation. "All the photos of you had been stored in a drawer, if you'll recall. Joan didn't want daily reminders of the daughter who had disappointed her so badly. But after her death, I gathered the photos to send to you." He paused for effect. "That's when I found the letters hidden behind one of your framed photographs. It was a high school picture, I believe."

Disbelief, excitement, and hope brought Dakota to her feet. A memory danced through her mind — her mother hugging her, her mother smiling.

Her mother trying to protect her from things Dakota had never even imagined.

She again heard her mother's words as they sat together on the sofa. "Dakota, listen to me. There are too many times when you're home alone while I'm at work. We never know what might happen, so I've put some emergency money behind your photo." Her mother showed her five one-hundred-dollar bills neatly stashed within the frame, behind the photo.

She'd been so young and innocent then, she'd laughed at her mother. "What would I need with that much money?"

Another smile, this one tinged with sadness. "I don't ever want you to feel helpless. We don't have any family to turn to, and sometimes things happen. If I was in a wreck, or I got hurt some other way —"

"Mom, don't talk like that." Dakota could still feel the security of her mother's arms when she'd hugged her close. "You should take that money and buy those new shoes you liked. Or get us a new TV or —"

"Shhh. Dakota, listen to me. Things happen. I know, because I wasn't ready for your father to die so young. We hadn't planned at all, and . . . I want you to be better prepared. Five hundred isn't much, but it'll help you for a few days if . . . if you ever need it." Her mother stroked her hair, kissed her forehead, then held her away so she could smile at her again. "It's not for pizza or a new CD, but you and I are the only ones to know about it. Do you understand, Dakota?"

That was so long ago, before things had deteriorated with her mother — before Barnaby. Far as Dakota knew, the emergency money had remained there . . . and now Barnaby claimed her mother had also stashed letters in the same place.

"You never sent me any letters, Barnaby."

"No."

"But if they were meant for me —"

He laughed. "I decided I'd hold on to them. I thought they might come in handy someday, and I was right."

Loathing him more by the moment, Dakota asked, "Handy in what way?"

"If you want to read the letters, bring my son to me." His voice gentled. "I'll gladly hand them over to you then."

Of course. Barnaby hoped to use the letters — if in fact they existed — as a bargaining tool. "You weren't listening, were you? Simon said no. He wants nothing to do with you."

In a softer tone, Barnaby crooned, "You're a woman, Dakota. You have the means to convince him."

He had to be kidding. "You're disgusting."

"You have ten days — and then I'm burning one of the letters."

And he would, too. Panic clawed at Dakota, but reasoning with him would never work. "You're —"

"Smart? Calculating? Devious? I know. You only have three letters, honey, so stop wasting my time. Bring Simon to me. Soon."

He hung up on her, and Dakota had to struggle to keep from throwing the cell phone across the room.

So many thoughts zigzagged through her mind. Why would her mother have written letters? Was there any chance at all that she'd forgiven Dakota? Had she softened toward her only child? Had she . . . still loved her after all?

She had to know.

New conviction chased away Dakota's doubts and worries. Damn it, one way or another she would get Simon to Barnaby. She had to.

Those letters could be her salvation.

Going back wasn't easy, but Dakota hid her apprehension with a wide smile and a lot of inane chatter toward any fighter who got close enough to hear her.

She hadn't seen Simon yet, but she knew by the uneasy way the others watched her that he had to be around somewhere. Sooner or later, he'd show himself, and then he'd notice her.

With any luck at all, he'd give her a chance

to convince him to see Barnaby.

After two hours, Dakota was about to give up when Simon came onto the floor, freshly showered, in conversation with Dean and Gregor. Despite the cold weather, he wore a T-shirt with his jeans. Beneath the concealing material, fluid muscles drew her attention. He wasn't smiling, but he didn't look unhappy, just deeply involved in their topic.

When Dean pointed toward a fighter making use of the ring, Simon looked up — and spotted her. He stopped dead in his tracks. Even across the distance separating them, Dakota felt the burn of his scrutiny. She wanted to look away from him, but couldn't manage it.

Frowning toward her, Dean said something to Simon, they briefly debated, and Dean threw up his hands. He and Gregor headed in a different direction.

Simon approached her alone. When he reached her, he just stood there, looking her over, his expression inscrutable.

"Hi." Dakota felt like an idiot, but she couldn't take the silence any longer. "How've you been?"

"I thought we'd seen the last of you."

"Afraid not." Her smile hurt. Except for a cut on his cheekbone, Simon looked outright gorgeous. "I see you got caught. Did

Dean do that, or Gregor?"

"Neither."

So he was going to be difficult. She'd deal with it. "A wild bull, then? A bus? What? Come on, Simon, give me details."

He looked her over again, and she knew now that it was with disapproval. He'd made it clear that she didn't appeal to him, that he considered her too pushy and too mannish. But so what? Approval from him wasn't what she needed the most.

While looking at the front of her shirt, he said, "Actually, it was Mallet."

"Ouch." She winced, feeling a moment of pity for the young fighter. "Is he dead, then?"

A small smile touched Simon's mouth, but only for an instant. "No. I took it easy on him. I got the cut from his elbow."

"Instructing him, then, and not fighting."

"What makes you think so?"

She shrugged. "That's easy enough. No way Mallet would be able to hurt you like that unless you let him."

"Your faith is humbling," he said with dry sarcasm. "Dean asked me to give him some pointers, but Mallet jumped the gun a little on a move I showed him. He's young and impetuous, and at times too eager. I wouldn't kill him over that, you're right.

But he's catching hell from everyone else."

Pleased that he'd strung together so many pleasant words, Dakota nodded. "No one wants to spar with a dirty fighter."

"Something like that."

She grinned. "At least now you know he has good elbows, right?"

"There is that." Distracted, Simon nodded at her chest and read aloud, " 'Barbers have all the right tools.' " His gaze clashed with hers. "You sure this guy isn't more than a friend?"

"Like you'd care." Those words had no sooner left her mouth than she wanted to take them back. Her eyes widened and she bit her bottom lip. "Forget I said that."

Simon didn't change expression, he just waited.

Sighing, Dakota rubbed at her forehead. She didn't understand him at all. "It really isn't any of your business, but since you asked — again — he's just a friend."

"All right." Simon crossed his arms over his chest. "Why are you still here?"

Hoping he wouldn't send her packing again, Dakota measured her words. "Maybe we could talk about that over lunch?"

"I have other plans."

Yeah, right. "Tomorrow, then?"

"No." Resolute, he kept her gaze snared

in his. "Not today and not tomorrow."

Somehow, without her realizing it, he'd moved closer. Suddenly Dakota could smell the mingling scents of fresh soap and heated male.

She looked at his sternum. "But —"

"You're wasting your time."

If she believed that, her despair would be great. She shook her head. "I don't think so."

"Suit yourself. But the answer will stay no."

Before Simon could walk away, Dakota caught his arm above his elbow. At the feel of his rock-solid biceps and taut skin, a secret thrill coursed through her.

She licked lips that went dry and pleaded with him. "Could you at least tell me why?" And then maybe she could talk him around his reasons.

He looked first at her hand, then at her mouth. "I have a father, Dakota. I don't need Barnaby . . . whatever his last name is."

"I thought I told you. It's Jailer."

"Perfect." He gave a short laugh lacking humor. "Barnaby Jailer. Now I'm doubly glad he decided to cut me out of his life, because Dad filled in and he's the best. I wouldn't insult him by associating with

Barnaby, and even if he wouldn't be insulted, I don't have room in my life for another paternal figure."

"Maybe —"

"No. Do us both a favor — go back to Barnaby, tell him thanks but no thanks, and move on to something more lucrative." He pinched her chin. "Maybe you can sing a song somewhere or something."

Dakota jerked her head away. "You don't have to be so hateful."

"And you didn't have to be so conniving about what you wanted."

She gasped at that accusation. "Conniving?"

"Damn right." Simon towered over her, and she cringed back. He frowned over her reaction, and allowed her the small distance without comment. "You led me to believe you were here out of personal interest."

"No." Annoyed that she'd let her fear take hold for even a heartbeat, Dakota squared off with him. "That was your colossal ego that led you to that assumption. As I recall, you didn't even give me a chance to tell you what I wanted."

"And you didn't bother to correct me." Suddenly he cupped the back of her head, drew her up to her tiptoes, and put his mouth over hers.

Dakota went limp, hot, and alive, all at the same time.

His mouth opened, urging her mouth to do the same. Without reserve, his tongue explored over her lips, the edge of her teeth, then past her teeth to twine hotly with her tongue. Bold and curious, Simon adjusted for a better, deeper fit.

Holy cow.

Needing to ground herself, Dakota clutched the soft cotton of his T-shirt. She leaned into him, overwhelmed, excited, ready . . . and the murmuring of the men around her sank past her numbed psyche.

Good God. She opened her eyes and saw that Dean and Gregor, along with a half dozen other men, stood there watching in various expressions of amusement, speculation, and disapproval — the latter coming from Dean.

Horrified, Dakota jerked away. But Simon's hold on her nape didn't let her get far, which was a good thing given the shaky support of her legs. She did not want to end up on her ass.

Through eyes that burned with emotion, Simon stared at her. "Damn, I needed that." His thumb moved over her sensitive skin, reviving her and lulling her. Then he said, "Good-bye, Dakota."

Good-bye? No way. He had to be kidding, she thought. But he released her, stepped around her, and walked out of the gym.

Leaving *her* standing there with the audience.

And they all waited to see what she'd do.

Well, hell. Praying her face wasn't as hot as she suspected it might be, she took a bow and said, "Glad you enjoyed the show."

Trying to look nonchalant when she could barely walk, Dakota collected her coat and satchel and left the gym, too.

For once, the cold air felt good. She glanced around for Simon, but she didn't see him anywhere so she made a beeline for her truck. She got in, slumped behind the wheel, and wondered what the hell she should do next.

But no matter how she tried to formulate a plan, her thoughts kept coming back to that kiss.

She hated to admit it, but more than anything, she wanted Simon to kiss her again.

CHAPTER 5

Simon couldn't believe it when for the fifth day in a row, Dakota waltzed in. They made eye contact, she smiled and waved, and he wanted to punch holes in the nearest hard surface.

Why did she have to plague him? After that one hot kiss — which he'd *had* to take and now wanted to repeat — he couldn't get her out of his thoughts. He'd tried, he really had, but with her constant annoying presence, his efforts were futile.

Ignoring her hadn't done him any good. She just pretended that it was otherwise by showing up in those snug jeans and goofy shirts, looking soft and cocky, and all too fuckable.

She smiled at him a lot.

And she watched him. His every move.

Every so often, she even took notes, and it made Simon crazy wanting to know what she wrote. Pointers on his style? Or something else?

Today she only slumped down to sit on the floor, her back propped against the wall. She looked at Simon for a few moments, then closed her eyes.

She looked beat. Defeated. Not at all like her usual perky, determined self.

For some reason, that bothered Simon even more than her galling upbeat enthusiasm.

For the next ten minutes, he divided his attention between his sparring partner and watching Dakota. She swilled down a whole thermos of coffee in no time flat. She rubbed at her eyes, chewed on a fingernail, then stretched and sighed — and Simon took a heel to the center of his torso.

It hurt like hell.

"Nice shot," he gasped, and he felt himself going down. He landed on his knees and struggled to get oxygen into his lungs.

Dean tried to call a halt, but Simon waved him off. "No," he wheezed. "I'm okay."

Billy, his sparring partner, bounced back and forth on the balls of his feet, anxious to keep going after a taste of success. In a real fight, he'd have finished Simon. Luckily, this wasn't a real fight — but Billy should have treated it as one just the same.

The trainer in Simon briefly took over.

Once he got upright again, he said, "You should have followed through with some ground work, not stood back and waited for me to recover. Until Dean says otherwise, you go one hundred percent, got it?"

Being young and stupid, Billy laughed. "Whatever you say."

So Simon put it to him.

The laughter died as the other man back-pedaled, but not fast enough. Simon threw one punch after another, forcing Billy into a corner and giving him no defense except to cower and give up.

"And that," Dean told the other man, "is why you don't laugh. If Simon Evans gives you advice, you soak it in. You're getting something most fighters would love to have, but couldn't afford, and here at my gym, you're getting it for free."

Between desperate gasps for air, Billy panted out, "Free, hell." He lifted the towel from his bloody mouth, shook his head, and stretched his swollen lips into a grin. "But, yeah, I've got it. Thanks."

Simon knelt in front of him. "You okay?"

"Yeah." He laughed again. "You're fast."

"So are you. That kick might've done me in if you'd followed through." Simon looked at Dean. "How's he at grappling?"

"Better than he is with his stand-up game."

"Really?" Simon's brows lifted with respect. "Then I'd say you've got real talent." He clapped Billy on the shoulder and stood.

Dean followed him to his corner. "You're letting her get in your way."

"I know."

"That's stupid."

"I know that, too." Simon sucked air into his lungs, chewed over his thoughts, and looked at Dakota. Again. She'd sat so long on the floor waiting for him that she'd fallen asleep. Her head had slumped to the side, and her limbs were boneless.

To keep his next suggestion private, Dean leaned in close. "Do something about it, Simon, before she screws up your comeback."

Simon chugged down a gulp of water without taking his gaze off her. After he wiped his mouth, he asked, "What do you suggest I do?"

"Whatever it takes."

Simon glanced at Dean, his brow raised.

"But do it," Dean insisted. "Preferably today." And with that, he walked back to Billy to give him a few more pointers.

Simon dropped the water bottle back into the corner and gave all his attention to Dakota.

Right off, he'd noticed the signs of exhaustion on her usually animated face. Now he also saw the dark circles under her eyes, the paler complexion, and the slump of her proud shoulders.

He didn't like it, damn it, any more than he liked her dogging his heels like some determined puppy.

He laughed. Puppy, hell. More like a pit bull.

Dripping sweat, soaked through to his jock, red faced and fed up, Simon stormed over to Dakota. He could hear her deep, even breathing.

Why come here to sleep?

Why was she so damned tired that she couldn't stay awake?

Simon nudged her foot with his and she stirred. "How much is he paying you?"

At his raised voice, she jerked awake with a start. Her long legs shot out, almost kicking him. She gasped, looked around in alarm, and finally focused on Simon's knees. Her chin tucked in and she did a slow visual trip up his body, pausing over his groin, then his navel. She visually tracked the line of dark body hair up his abdomen to where it spread out over his chest and finally, she met his gaze.

Her eyes looked dazed. "Hey, Simon."

Having just awakened, her husky voice sounded even more mesmerizing. "How much is Barnaby paying you?"

"Barnaby?"

Impatiently, Simon swiped his wrist over his temple to remove a trickling bead of sweat. "You don't remember Barnaby? He's the reason you're here, right? Or was that a lie, too?"

"I remember Barnaby."

"So tell me, how much will you earn for this job?"

Taking a moment to get her bearings, Dakota straightened, stretched, rubbed at her eyes. Then she looked up at him. "He's not paying me anything."

"Bullshit."

She laughed, apparently too tired to be insulted. "Believe whatever you want, but Barnaby probably won't even cover my expenses — and they're adding up pretty quick."

Simon tamped down on the surge of anger. "Then *why?*"

Resting her head back against the wall, Dakota stared up at him. Simon knew the moment she decided to give him a small truth.

"We're on the barter system." She turned her face away from him and shrugged. "I give him you, and he gives me something I want in return."

Simon dropped to a crouch and caught her chin. "What is it you want?"

"That's for me to know."

"Then maybe I'll have Dean refund you and ban you from the gym."

"He'd do that?"

"In a heartbeat."

Scowling, she scooted away from him and pushed to her feet. "Look, I'm sorry, really I am, but it's none of your damn business."

Simon stood, too. "And that's supposed to stop me from asking, when what I want doesn't matter to you at all?"

She made no apologies. "Since you won't go, it's a moot point anyway, isn't it? Without you, he won't give me what I want."

"Sounds like a hell of a guy."

Her face came up and she snapped, "He's a prick, if you want the truth."

Her vehemence surprised him. "Is that so?"

Dakota blanched, and took a quick step back. "Damn, I'm sorry. I know he's your father, but —"

Cutting a hand through the air, Simon said, "Forget it. Insult him all you want. He means nothing to me."

But then he thought about what she'd

said. What could Barnaby have that she wanted? And if she truly disliked him, why work for him at all?

"You're making me crazy, damn it."

"Sucks for you, huh?" Shoving long tresses of thick blond hair away from her face, Dakota said, "Gawd, I'm tired. I'm heading out for some coffee."

Simon looked down at the gigantic — and empty — thermos sitting beside her satchel. "You drink too much of that."

"Yeah, thanks. I'll make a note of your concern." Her smile mocked him. "See ya tomorrow, Simon."

No way in hell. He'd had enough of her lunatic behavior. Before she could saunter away, he caught her arm and brought her back around. "Give me his number. I'll call him."

So much hope shone in her pretty blue eyes that Simon wished he'd made the offer sooner.

"Really? That is, I don't know if that'll do it, but it's worth a try if you really —"

"Just leave the number with Haggerty and I'll call him tonight." Still holding on to her arm, and feeling like a cunning high school boy about to cop a feel, Simon added, "Leave your number, too, and I'll let you know what he has to say."

A wide smile put dimples in her cheeks and drove away some of her tiredness. "If you weren't so gross with sweat right now, I'd hug you."

A man could only take so much. Simon trailed his hand up her arm to her shoulder and urged her in closer.

As he bent to her mouth, he said, "I'll take a rain check, then." And he kissed her. Not as long this time, not as deep or hot. But it fed something in his soul, and made him want more.

A whole lot more.

Even after he ended the kiss, Dakota stayed poised, eyes closed, lips slightly parted — tempting him. He touched her soft mouth with a fingertip. "No more displays, woman. We've caused enough gossip."

She swallowed, nodded. Finally, she sighed. "You are one hell of a kisser, Sublime. Maybe even the best." As if in regret, she shook her head at him and turned to walk away.

Simon watched her go to Haggerty. She had to find the number in her cell, and he watched her every move, knowing he should get away from her, but hating the thought of seeing her so exhausted.

As Dean said, he had to handle the situation somehow, the sooner the better.

Calling Barnaby was a compromise, nothing more. He'd talk with the man, tell him himself that he wasn't interested, and then maybe he'd regain some peace in his life.

Because then, Barnaby wouldn't be between him and Dakota.

And that meant she'd be available. He could hardly wait.

Barnaby paced the small living room that he'd once shared with Joan. He liked this house, the coziness of it and the quiet middle-class ambiance. Thanks to the insurance money and his renovations, he could be comfortable here for the rest of his life. He could relax.

He'd earned that right, damn it.

But unless Dakota succeeded, he'd lose it and everything else that he'd become accustomed to.

Poor sweet Joan would have died for nothing.

Barnaby looked at the young man sprawled in his favorite chair. He despised him. He always had. "I already told you, Marvin. I haven't gotten the money yet, but I will. Soon."

"You better start pushing the right buttons, old man, before I get tired of waiting and push them myself."

Barnaby's eyes narrowed. "Are you threatening me?"

All congeniality disappeared. Marvin shoved out of his seat and, giving way to a ferocious temper, overturned the coffee table. Drinks and magazines dumped across the pristine carpet.

"Threaten you?" he screamed. He threw a lamp against a wall, breaking it into chunks, then stomped on the linen shade with his dirty boots. "I don't fucking threaten."

Praying there wouldn't be any more damage, Barnaby stood still and waited for the anger to subside.

"I'm *telling* you, God damn it. If you want to keep what you have, I better get paid."

"All right, all right." Shaken and furious and, though he hated to admit it, afraid, Barnaby tried to placate him with fast promises. "I'll take care of it."

Jutting his face toward Barnaby, Marvin asked, "How?"

He gulped. He wasn't fond of Dakota, but he didn't particularly want her harmed, either. Still . . . better her than him. "I sent Dakota on an errand."

Eyes brightening, Marvin eased into a more relaxed stance. "Dakota?" His mouth curled. "Tell me everything, Barnaby. Now."

Seeing no hope for it, Barnaby detailed his plan for getting the money Marvin extorted. When he finished, he added, "If you'll just give me a little more time, I'm sure Dakota will succeed."

"She better." He gave one hard shove to Barnaby's shoulder and, laughing, he stormed out.

After locking the door, Barnaby looked around at the mess. His beautiful home. His beautiful lamp and table. Now ruined.

The thought of murder teased his senses. He'd done many reprehensible things in his time, but he'd never killed anyone. Right now, he thought he could do it.

After years of wheeling and dealing and always coming out on the short end, he'd finally played a winning hand. He *owned* his life. He had a nice, quiet existence. He was able to watch game shows in the morning and in the afternoon he relaxed in the shaded yard. Sometimes he took pleasure in trimming the lawn, sometimes he paid others to do it.

He didn't want to risk it all for a punk-ass thug. Not when there were easier ways. . . .

The jarring sound of the phone brought Barnaby jerking around, ready to defend an attack. He laughed at himself when he realized the intrusion was a call.

Stepping over the destruction on the floor, he lifted the receiver. "Hello?"

"Barnaby Jailer?"

Quiet satisfaction lifted his tension. Instinctively knowing who called, he affected the proper tone and attitude. "Yes. May I help you?"

"This is Simon Evans. Dakota Dream asked me to call you."

Call him? That little bitch. She knew that wasn't what he wanted. He couldn't get anything accomplished unless he met with Simon face-to-face.

Barnaby's hand tightened on the receiver. "Simon. Oh my. Yes, thank you. Thank you." He conveyed just the right amount of uncertainty and gratitude. "This is wonderful. But . . . I was so hopeful that we could meet. In person, that is. You see —"

"No." Firm, with no room for indecision, Simon cut him off. "I'm only calling to tell you that I'm not interested in meeting you. Dakota has been damned insistent, but I won't change my mind. I hope you'll tell her that you accept my decision."

"But I don't." Barnaby moderated his tone. "I can't. You see, it's imperative that I meet with you."

"I said no."

Desperation unfurled in his guts. "Just let

130

me explain."

"There's no point, because it won't matter what you have to say. I'm not interested."

Barnaby stepped on broken glass without realizing it. "I understand that you must be hurt, or perhaps angry at my long absence. There are no good excuses, of course. But maybe if you'd hear what I have to say, you'd change your mind."

"No." Lacking any inflection at all, Simon said, "I'm not hurt or angry. I just don't care. Period. That won't change."

His hand nearly crushed the receiver. "At least give me a number where I can call you back. Or perhaps your current address." He wouldn't go to him, but he could write to him, endearing letters that might soften his stance.

"No."

"Then maybe —"

"Good-bye, Barnaby. I'd prefer that you not bother me again."

The line went dead. Barnaby's arm dropped to his side and he looked around at the destruction in his home. All because of *her.*

"You'll care," he predicted in a whisper. "Trust me, Simon, before it's all said and done, you most definitely will care."

Knowing what would likely happen next,

Barnaby went into the kitchen to get a broom and dustpan. He needed to restore order to his new, tidy life. He wanted to keep everything perfect . . . for as long as he could.

Even the bright sun couldn't remove the chill from the morning air. Dakota shivered inside her layers of clothing and coat, and still, the last thing she wanted to do was go into the gym. She hovered at the entrance, trying to give herself a pep talk, trying to work up some courage.

But really, what choice did she have?

None.

She straightened her shoulders and had started to push the entry door open when an odd sensation skated up her spine. Someone was watching her.

As she glanced over her shoulder, she didn't give it much thought — until she saw the black SUV just cruising by.

Slowly.

An eerie sense of déjà vu made her skin prickle. The darkened windows of the vehicle kept Dakota from seeing anyone inside.

But she knew without a doubt that someone saw her.

And she knew that someone was smiling

at her obvious alarm.

She stiffened and stared harder, determined not to turn tail and run. The car stopped. The tension built. Unsure what she'd do, but knowing she had to do something, Dakota took a step toward the vehicle.

And finally, it rolled away.

Heart pounding hard, Dakota shoved the gym door open, stormed angrily inside, and ran headlong into Mallet Manchester. It was like barreling into a brick wall.

"Oompff." He caught her to him as they both stumbled back.

"Mallet!" Together, they barely regained their balance. "Sorry about that."

His big hands opened over her back and he smiled with awareness. "No harm, honey. I don't mind at all."

Oh, good grief. Dakota gave him a droll look. "You just refuse to learn, don't you?"

He laughed — but released her and held up both hands. "Ah, come on now. You're not still holding a grudge, are you? Especially after you laid me low?" His smile widened. "It wasn't my fault really. It's just that you're irresistible."

"Uh-huh. And you want to sell me a bridge, right?"

That made him laugh again. "This time I'm innocent. You ran into me, not the other way around." He tipped his head. "Any reason you came charging in here?"

Recalling the car she'd seen, Dakota frowned. "Yeah, I was distracted."

"With what?"

She shook her head and said without thinking, "I thought someone was following me."

"Following you?" Mallet's attention went to the glass doors and he looked toward the street. "Who?"

"Well, not really following me, I guess. Just . . ." How could she explain the inexplicable alarm she'd felt? "Look, it's nothing. Just a car that went by and it seemed like someone was looking at me —"

"I'm sure lots of men look at you." Going all serious on her, Mallet said, "You're hot."

"Uh . . . thanks. I think." Dakota gave a quick glance at the doors, but saw only the regular ebb and flow of traffic. "It was probably my imagination."

"Well, just in case . . ." He eased closer. "Why don't you let me know when you're ready to leave today, and I'll walk you out."

Such a nice offer — a much-appreciated one, too. She could face the threats on her own, but maybe showing off Mallet would be a good deterrent. "Thanks. I just might take you up on that."

"Good."

Suddenly Dakota felt another stare, this one not the least threatening. She looked beyond Mallet and found Simon standing there, full of intimidation and strength and sex appeal. He wore no expression at all, and still he managed to look irked.

Mallet must have felt his presence, too, because he stiffened. "Okay, then." Pretending not to know that Simon stood right behind him, he said, "I'll see you around."

He turned, hesitated only a split second in front of Simon, and strode around him as if he had someplace important to be.

Simon let him pass without a word so that he could address Dakota. "You'll take him up on what?"

"Nothing important." Simon's nearness and the impact of his presence set Dakota's heart to pounding. To cover that reaction, she went on the verbal attack. "I thought you were going to call me after you spoke with Barnaby. I waited up half the night for you."

The corners of Simon's mouth lifted. "Most women wouldn't admit to waiting for a man's call."

Most women didn't have Barnaby Jailer breathing down their necks. "Yeah, well, I'm unique."

"I noticed." Gesturing at the door, Simon said, "Why don't we step outside to talk in private?"

She balked — and he wondered at it.

"Dakota?" He scrutinized her, and given his new mood, he must have come to some conclusions. "You want to tell me what's going on?"

"Not really." She wasn't about to share her deepest darkest secrets. "Let's talk in here instead."

"All right." Simon took her arm and urged her toward the wall. There were others around them, but no one close enough to overhear. "We'll talk — as soon as you tell me what Mallet offered to do for you, and why you don't want to go outside."

"You are so pushy."

He laughed. "That's the pot calling the kettle black, isn't it?"

Dakota had to admit that he had a point. "Look, I already told you, it's nothing." She tipped her face up to him and smiled. "Let's talk instead about your conversation with Barnaby."

"Sure. After you answer my question."

Given everything she'd been through, and everything she had to lose, his stubbornness annoyed her. "What do you care, anyway?"

Simon crossed his arms over his chest in a

pose she now recognized. Instead of "Sublime," he should have been nicknamed "Ass" for sheer stubbornness.

"This is ridiculous, Simon. It was nothing."

"Probably," he agreed. "So why not tell me?"

"Unbelievable." Dakota crossed her arms, too. "All right, fine. I thought someone was watching me."

"Who?"

"I don't know who," she lied. "When I looked, all I saw was a car with darkened windows, and no, it wasn't a car I recognized."

"But you suspected someone, someone you don't like or someone you fear, otherwise it wouldn't have worried you."

A likely conclusion, she supposed. "You could be right. But some things are none of your business, and this is one of those things."

"So you were afraid?"

Dakota threw up her hands. "Did I say that?"

Very gently, Simon touched her cheek. "You didn't have to. It's odd, but I can already read your expressions."

Not good. The last thing she needed was Simon poking around in her psyche. She scowled at him. "Okay, smart-ass, so what am I thinking now?"

Simon laughed. "That you're done with this topic. I'll let it go — for now." He held out a hand to her. "Let's sit in your truck to talk, and then you can head on home."

She hadn't planned to turn around and leave so soon, but he didn't give her much choice as he led her outside. Dakota noticed that he scanned the area, and that he kept her tucked in close to his side.

She felt safe.

She felt . . . protected.

Dangerous. She absolutely would not let herself start relying on others. She most especially would not rely on Barnaby's son. "Did it occur to you that I might not want to go home yet?"

Simon spotted her truck in the side lot and led her toward it. "Where is home, by the way? You're staying in a motel?"

"Yeah. A cheesy little place not too far from here."

"A friend owns the Cross Streets Motel. Dean stayed there when he first came back to Harmony. You should check it out."

Dakota's heart tripped at that suggestion. She barely noticed when Simon opened her driver's door and waited for her to get inside. As soon as he settled in on the passenger's side, she asked, "Are you suggesting I stay in Harmony for a while?"

Staring into her eyes, Simon hesitated only a moment before he leaned forward to kiss her.

Dakota didn't move out of reach, but she did groan. Against his mouth, she asked, "Why do you keep doing this to me?"

"Hell if I know." His breath warmed her; he caught her bottom lip in his teeth for a gentle nip. "I can't seem to help myself." His hand settled in her hair, his long fingers cupping her skull and tipping her head so that he could seal the kiss, take it deeper, make it hotter.

Even knowing she had a hundred things to discuss with him, Dakota gave in and relished the taste of him, the heated scent that clung to him, the confident way he touched and kissed her.

When Simon finally ended the kiss, they were both breathing harder. He put his forehead to hers. "I didn't call last night because I wanted to talk to you in person."

"All right." She took a few more seconds to calm herself. "Let's hear it."

"I spoke with Barnaby."

Still tasting him on her lips, Dakota said, "I know."

He leaned away to frown at her. "You do?"

"Yeah. He called me."

Simon's expression darkened. "What did he say?"

He'd said a lot, all of it ugly and mean and, in some ways, desperately threatening. Not that Barnaby scared her. He was a worm and she despised him, but he'd never really gained that power over her.

Dakota saw no point in sharing all that with Simon. If he found out that Barnaby was her stepfather, one thing would lead to another and eventually she'd reveal her past — a past that shamed her, a past she'd worked hard to overcome.

Dakota shrugged. "He said that I failed. That you refused to see him. That I can kiss my —" She caught herself. "The thing he has that I told you I wanted? He said he's destroying it because I didn't get you to agree to see him."

"Shit." Simon settled fully into his seat and put his head back. "I tried, Dakota. But I don't want anything to do with him."

"Yeah. I gather you made that much pretty clear." Not that she blamed him. She didn't want anything to do with Barnaby, either.

Unfortunately, she didn't have the same choices that Simon had. One of the letters would already be gone, if they'd ever existed in the first place. That made it more impera-

tive than ever that she get his cooperation
— and soon.

As if he'd read her thoughts, Simon
turned toward her. "I'm asking you to give
up, Dakota."

If only she could. "I'd rather you give in."

"No."

Guilt kept her from looking at him when
she asked, "What would it hurt, really?"

Suddenly, Simon tried a new tactic. "I
don't like your boots. They look clunky and
mannish. Not at all attractive."

Now Dakota looked — stared, in fact — at
him. What in the world did her boots have
to do with anything? "You're kidding,
right?"

"No. They're ugly."

She affected her best snarky smile. "Good
thing you don't have to wear them, huh?"
Personally, she found the boots comfortable
and they kept her feet warm.

If her reply insulted Simon, he hid it well
as he stretched out his long, muscled arm
and fingered a wind-tossed lock of hair that
hung over her shoulder. "I don't like scruffy
women, either." His gaze locked on hers.
"Are you ever put together?"

"Put together?"

"Polished. Groomed. Less . . . disheveled?"

Dakota felt like slugging him. "It's cold, Simon. If by scruffy and disheveled you mean dressed in warm layers, then tough titty, because I'm not going to be cold for anyone."

He laughed, and when she wrenched away, freeing her hair from his teasing fingers, he laughed some more. "God, you amuse me."

"Great. At least I'm good for something, huh?"

The laughter faded to a warm smile. "I suspect you're good for many things." His voice went low and deep. "That's part of my problem."

Dakota watched him warily. Did she have what it took to use an attraction to her advantage? Never in her life had she tried to use seduction to get her way. If it meant kissing, touching, being closer to Simon, then it wouldn't be a hardship.

Anything beyond that . . . she just didn't know.

"But," Simon added, "as much as I want you, I refuse to upset my parents by associating with a man who has never contributed to our lives in any way."

Still considering any unknown wiles that she might possess, Dakota asked, "Have you told your parents about Barnaby?"

"No, and I don't plan to."

"Maybe it wouldn't be such a big deal to them."

"I have enough respect for them both that I consider it a big deal." His gaze pinned her in place. "I won't change my mind, Dakota, you should know that. You should also know that if you insist on hanging around, I'm not going to be able to keep my hands off you."

Her temperature rose a few degrees. "And I don't have anything to say about it?"

"Of course you do." Once again, he cupped her head and brought her forward for a firm, quick kiss. "But so far you've been saying yes, and we both know it."

"Yeah," she sighed. "I know." If Simon meant to scare her off with his warning, it had the opposite effect. She wanted him, too, and that was about as unexpected as it could get.

His next kiss was soft, gentle, and consuming. Dakota relished every second of it.

For more than the obvious reasons, it'd be dangerous to court his attentions. If he decided to push the boundaries, she truthfully didn't know if she could follow through.

Until meeting Simon, all she'd thought about sex was how to avoid it.

But now . . . Dakota opened her eyes as Simon slowly released her. Feeling warm and almost liquid, she smiled and started to ask him just how far he wanted to take things.

Then she saw the black SUV pulled up along the passenger side of her truck, idling there, *watching them.*

Instinctively, Dakota lurched forward, trying to see into that other vehicle. She cursed as she half crawled over Simon, reaching for the door handle to open the door. Her heart pounded in dread, but she refused to sit inactive like a coward.

Taken off guard, Simon stared at her in concern.

Then the SUV gave one small blast of the horn and drove away. With another curse, Dakota retreated back into her seat.

Simon swiveled around to see the car driving away. He looked back at Dakota, and though she tried to wipe all expression off her face, she knew too many emotions were there for him to see.

"All right, Dakota. Who was that?"

Furious with herself, she shook her head. "How the hell should I know?"

"Who do you *think* it might have been?"

"A Peeping Tom?" She forced a scratchy laugh. "You do seem to have a propensity for public displays."

Simon exploded. "*Damn it,* can't you ever give me a straight answer?"

She pulled back in surprise and affront. "Don't yell at me."

He got himself under control with an effort. Jaw tight and eyes narrowed, he said, "Then try giving me a straight answer for a change."

Insulted, troubled, and unsure what to do, Dakota tried to come up with a suitable story, but her mind felt too numbed with apprehension to think clearly. "I hope it was just someone Barnaby hired to see if I'm being successful with you or not."

Doubtful, Simon asked, "He'd actually do that?"

"Probably." She shrugged. "Who knows? He does seem to have plenty of money to play with these days."

"He's well-to-do?"

"I wouldn't go that far. It's just that he's bought stuff lately, things for . . . his home and yard. He lives comfortably."

Simon absorbed that. "Since he saw me kissing you, will he assume you're successful?"

She snorted. "I have no idea how Barnaby's mind works."

Bracing one hand on the steering wheel

and his other on the back of her seat, Simon caged her in. "And if it wasn't someone sent by Barnaby, then who else might it have been?"

Dakota sized him up, decided what the hell, and shrugged again. "You'll think I'm nuts, but I have an odd suspicion that it might have been my husband."

CHAPTER 6

Simon went so stiff that he could have broken with just a touch. Beyond a red-hot rage, he wasn't sure what he felt, but he felt it a lot. "You're *married?*"

She flapped a hand toward him. "Divorced." She added, "And you're yelling again. I don't like it."

His anger deflated. So she was free for the taking. Not that it should matter, since Dakota could be no more than a fling, and as such, having her or not shouldn't have such an impact on him.

But it did matter, he realized, and that made his tone harsher than he intended. "That'd make him your *ex-husband,* woman. Get it straight."

Anger replaced the apprehension he'd seen in her gaze, relieving Simon. "I have it straight, damn it," Dakota snapped right back. "*He's* the one who conveniently forgets."

Simon wanted her, and issues of Barnaby aside, he now planned to have her. Marriage would have changed everything, because honorable men did not poach.

But a disgruntled, bothersome ex he could handle. Gladly.

"Why? Is he still in love with you?"

And just that easily, Dakota's anger vanished, too. She covered her face and laughed. "God, no. Definitely not love."

"Dakota?" Her humor seemed very out of place, alarming Simon.

She shook her head, then on a groan, dropped her hands and, for only a moment, let down her guard. "He never loved me. But he wanted to keep me."

"What happened?"

Her smile flickered. "I didn't want to stay."

"Why not?"

She straightened in her seat so that she faced the windshield. Bracing her arms on the steering wheel, she said, "It's getting late, Simon, and I've got a dozen things to do. If you aren't going to agree to see Barnaby, then I should get going."

He wasn't about to go anywhere. Not yet. "You don't want to tell me about your ex?"

She slanted him a look through burning blue eyes. "Get real, Simon. No one wants to hear about someone's ex. It's boring, and it's old news."

"Apparently it's not old enough if he's following you and it scares you."

"I wasn't scared!"

Simon knew fear when he saw it, but he wouldn't push it. "Concerned, then."

"Look, it doesn't matter. It probably wasn't him." She glanced at the watch on her wrist. "It was a big mistake on my part, all of it."

"How so?"

She flexed her hands on the wheel, struggled with her thoughts, and finally snapped, "I'm just a little jumpy where he's concerned, okay?"

"Why?"

Her jaw worked as she calculated her next move. She turned her head toward Simon. "Are you going to go see Barnaby?"

He hated to disappoint her, but . . . "No. I already told you that I wasn't."

Her temper flared, and her voice rose. "Then get your nose out of my business, and your butt out of my truck."

Instead, Simon crossed his arms. "We're dealing now, is that it? What's at stake here, Dakota? Let's get it all clear right now."

She didn't back down. "All right, fine. If you want to know my private business, though I have no idea why you would, then you have to do me a damn favor and go see Barnaby."

"What if I want to sleep with you?"

That took her by surprise and her face went blank.

Simon wondered at it. Surely Dakota knew her own appeal, and he sure as hell hadn't been subtle about his interest. "I do, you know."

Recovering, Dakota said, "Forget it. Ain't happening."

"Wanna bet?"

Her eyes widened. "You can't be serious!"

"Why? You want me, too. We already established that." Curious at just how desperate she might be, Simon pushed her a little more. "If I go see Barnaby, will that guarantee you in my bed?"

All the small muscles in her face pinched taut. Simon half expected her to slug him, and he braced for it.

What he got instead was her embarrassment, and an admission.

"I'd probably sleep with you either way. But no, it wouldn't have anything to do with you seeing Barnaby."

He badly wanted to believe her. A hundred questions went through his mind, but all he said was, "Probably?"

"Yeah. I can't guarantee anything because

I just don't know." She turned the key in the engine. "Now, unless you plan to go driving around with me today, you'd better get out."

"Could I have a kiss good-bye?"

"No." She stared out the front windshield.

Grinning, Simon slowly leaned in close to her. She looked worried, but she didn't retreat. He put his mouth on her cheek for a soft, nuzzling kiss.

Her breath came a little fast.

He kissed a slow path to her neck, licked one sensitive spot, sucked gently.

She moaned.

He kissed his way up to her ear, nibbled on her earlobe — and she turned toward him in a rush, kissing him hard and fast.

Silly woman.

It wasn't a question of "probably" as much as "when." He'd prefer sooner to later, but she did seem concerned about it, so he'd take it slow.

Withdrawing by stages, Simon kissed the corner of her mouth, her jaw, her cheekbone. "I won't be at the gym tomorrow."

Eyes still closed, Dakota gulped and nodded. "Thanks for letting me know."

"You're welcome." He didn't want her to hang out all day waiting for him, when he wouldn't be there for her to needle. Other men would be there, and though he'd never been the possessive type, he didn't like that setup at all.

Mallet had already proven that Simon wasn't the only man interested.

Slowly, Dakota's lashes lifted to show him dazed eyes filled with confusion. "What is it about you?"

"What do you mean?"

She sighed. "Never mind. You're cocky enough as it is." Settling back against her door, she asked, "Where will you be tomorrow?"

"Just taking a day off."

"Really? You do that?"

Simon shrugged. He trained hard, but he didn't believe in working at it 24/7. "There's a party tonight, and I'll be out late."

She thought that over. "So you're not just avoiding me?"

"There are a lot of things I want to do with you, Dakota, but avoiding you isn't one of them. Not anymore."

"Good." She looked more than a little confused. "Well then, I'll see you the day after."

"I'll be there." On impulse, Simon said, "Let me see your cell phone."

Even as she pulled the phone from her pocket, she asked, "Why?"

"I want you to have my number." He took the phone from her and programmed in his number. "If you see your ex, or even if you think you've seen him, give me a call."

"Why should I?"

"Just do it."

"Because Simon says? I don't think so."

Simon finished with the phone and handed it back to her. "Yes."

"Your concern is so sweet, but I can take care of myself."

She made *sweet* sound like a foul insult. "I'm sure you can, but —"

Her finger smashed against his mouth. "You want to do something for me, Simon? Go see Barnaby. Otherwise, I don't need your help."

"Is your middle name Stubborn?"

"Go see Barnaby, and I'll tell you."

Simon grabbed her for another smooch, this one teasing, and Dakota laughed against his mouth.

He opened the truck door and got out. "Behave yourself, woman, and *if* you decide you could use some help, you have my number."

"Yeah, yeah. Got it."

Knowing she wouldn't call, Simon shut the door. He'd been prepared for her to ask him more about the party, to maybe wheedle an invite so she could work on him some more. But she hadn't.

He'd miss her tomorrow.

Hell, who was he kidding? He'd only taken a few steps from her truck and he already missed her. She took up far too much of his attention; he needed to get his head into the competition, and the party tonight would help.

Not inviting her had been a deliberate decision on his part.

Roger, the owner of Roger's Rodeo Bar, was throwing the shindig as a tribute to Dean, and to the other fighters who had flocked to Harmony to train with Dean and Simon. Roger had become a big fan and contributed financially to the gym and the SBC.

Tonight, the organization would announce the fight card via a special hookup to the Internet. Roger had it set up for a big screen. There'd be a live band, lots of laughs, talk on techniques, and good-natured ribbing.

There'd also be plenty of single women, but that didn't interest Simon at all.

Tonight was to promote Dean's gym and show appreciation to Roger, period. It was all part of the business.

And once the business was finished, he'd

find Dakota, and take care of the pleasure.

Dakota waited until Simon reentered the gym, then she turned off her truck and called Barnaby at home.

He answered on the third ring. "Hello?"

"Did you send someone to watch me?"

"Dakota, honey? Is that you?"

Knowing he called her "honey" just to irk her didn't make it any less annoying. "Stick it, Barnaby. I asked you a question."

He tsked at her bad manners. "Why would I waste good money having you tailed when I know you'll be doing your absolute best?"

She believed him. But if it wasn't Barnaby, then it had to be Marvin. Or was she just being paranoid? "I am doing my best, but Simon's still saying no."

"You need Simon to say yes."

"It's not going to happen, I tell you."

"Then I have no choice but to burn a letter. Perhaps the first one she wrote. It's the longest."

Bastard. "Not so fast." *What to do, what to do?* Squeezing her eyes shut, Dakota said, "I'll think of something."

"Think of seducing him. That would work."

God, she hated the smarminess of his voice. Ignoring his suggestion, she said,

"Give me a few more days to work on him."

"Go to him tonight. Do what you have to do and then —"

"No." Sick bastard. "He'll be at a party tonight, so I can't. I have to time things right." Time things? Good grief. What kind of stupid lie was that? "He's in the middle of a lot of stuff."

"What stuff?"

If Barnaby hadn't already made Simon's connection to the SBC fighting organization (which she doubted was the case), then she didn't want to be the one to tell him. Whatever his reasons for wanting to meet Simon now, they'd double once he knew his son was famous in certain circles.

"His job keeps him busy."

Rather than ask what his job might be, Barnaby said, "How many days would you need?"

"Another week."

"Seven days?" He chuckled with spiteful humor. "You only have to screw him once, Dakota, not become his live-in lover."

Rage took hold of her and she forgot about the letters. "Take it or leave it, Barnaby, because this conversation is over."

He took it. "One more week, Dakota. Don't disappoint me by disappointing him." And he hung up on her.

Slowly, Dakota lowered her hand and let her cell phone drop to the seat. She felt guilty, as if she'd betrayed Simon in some way. She was so lost in her own thoughts that when someone tapped on her window, she almost screamed.

Mallet Manchester stood there, his hair damp from a recent shower, an apologetic smile aimed her way.

Dakota rolled down her window. "You startled half my life away."

"No kidding. You jumped a foot." He leaned down with his forearms braced on the window frame. "Sorry about that."

He was so close that Dakota could see the individual eyelashes of his blue eyes. She scooted back a little. "What's up?"

"I was going to ask you that. I saw Simon inside, asked him where you were, and he said you'd just left." His gaze dipped over her. "Yet here you are, sitting all alone and staring into space."

"You asked Simon about me?" She couldn't believe his nerve.

"Yeah, well, I was just going to ask him if you were going to the party."

The same party Simon had mentioned? Why hadn't she thought of that? It'd be the perfect opportunity to let Simon see her without her boots or frumpy extra layers.

She didn't like dressing up and seldom saw the point of it, but she could clean up as well as the next gal.

Though Dakota hated to admit it, she wanted Simon to see her at her best, to know that she could look feminine and pretty.

She wanted his admiration, damn it. And it didn't have a single thing to do with Barnaby's assignment.

"I don't know yet." Hoping she didn't look as devious as she felt, Dakota dug for more information. "Where is it again?"

Mallet wasn't fooled for a second. "Sublime didn't invite you, did he?"

Well, hell, wouldn't be much point in lying about it now. "Nope, but he did mention that he was going."

"I don't get it. What's going on with you two?"

Unfortunately, not a whole lot of anything. Yet. "What do you mean?"

"The very first day you came in, Sublime warned everyone to stay away from you."

Her back stiffened. "He did what?"

Uncomfortable, Mallet cleared his throat. "Maybe I shouldn't have said anything."

"Too late now." Dakota tapped her fingers on the top of the door frame. Why would Simon do such a thing? "Do I look like a

158

threat somehow? Did he think I'd disrupt the practice or throw off the routine?"

Amused at her assumption, Mallet grinned. "You misunderstand. Simon gave the warning so he could keep you to himself."

Dakota just blinked at him. Keep her to himself? For what?

Seeing her confusion, Mallet clarified, "He laid claim."

"Laid claim?" she repeated. "On me?"

"Yeah. But I'll be damned if I can figure out why, when he doesn't seem to be pursuing you all that hard. At first, everyone figured he was ready to get back in the game. You know, after breaking things off with Bonnie."

Who the hell was Bonnie? "Yeah, uh, I'm not up on Simon's personal relationships."

"He and Bonnie had a thing going on. They'd been together something like five years, or so I've been told. That was before I got to know Sublime better here at Havoc's gym."

Dakota wondered what Bonnie might have done to cause Simon to end their relationship. Not for a second did she think to blame Simon. He wasn't the type to cut bait and run unless he had good reason.

"Anyway," Mallet continued, "far as I've

heard, Bonnie's been chasing him hard and fast, trying to get him back, but Simon's steered clear of women since. It's been a while, too."

"No dating, huh?"

"He's been in training," Mallet said with a shrug, as if that explained it all. "But then you showed up and he spread the word that you were off-limits before you'd even been here five minutes."

Of all the nerve. Caveman tactics had never impressed Dakota. But now, well, it was kind of sweet to think of Simon wanting her all to himself. And romantic, too.

Had her lack of fashion sense appealed to him after all?

But then maybe after getting to know her better, he'd rethought his claim. As Mallet pointed out, he hadn't exactly been in hot pursuit. Sure, he'd kissed her a few times, but other than when she shanghaied him, he barely paid her any notice at all.

She'd have to see what she could do to get Simon a little more motivated.

Repositioning herself in her seat, Dakota leaned in closer to Mallet. "So. Are you going to the party?"

"Hell, yeah. It's an SBC party. They're going to announce the fight cards. I can't wait to hear the matchups. All the guys from the gym will be there."

Hoping she didn't look as frumpy as Simon had indicated, Dakota smiled at Mallet. "Do you have a date yet?"

His blue eyes warmed . . . with laughter. "No, but I don't have a death wish, either, so if you're looking for a ride, forget it. Sublime would have my head."

His humor rubbed Dakota the wrong way. "He doesn't own me."

"Tell him that."

"I plan to." She'd tell him that and more.

"Really?" Now Mallet looked alarmed. "Well, for God's sake, don't tell him I'm the one who squealed to you."

"Now, Mallet, you know that Simon wouldn't actually hurt you."

Affronted, he drew himself up, showing off his extraordinary height. "I'm not afraid of any man in a fight. But Sublime has clout and I don't want to get on his bad side."

"You think he'd blackball you?"

"No." Mallet complained to himself, and then admitted, "He's a good guy, the best in the business."

Dakota touched his arm. "And you want his respect?"

He scoffed at that, but said, "I deserve his respect."

He probably did, Dakota thought. Mallet

wasn't a bad man at all. A little too much of a flirt, and far too bold at times, but he wasn't irredeemable. "All right, Mallet. Take me to the party, and your secret will stay safe with me."

He stepped back from the window. "You're blackmailing me?"

"Just get me in." Dakota stuck her head out the window to appeal to him. "I'll tell Sublime . . . I mean Simon, that I twisted your arm. I'll tell him I was going to go anyway, and you didn't want me to have to walk in alone. He won't blame you, I promise."

Mallet weighed her offer while looking her over again. "You gonna dress up?"

Did he also think she looked scruffy? Men. "You betcha," she assured him. "Dress, high heels, the whole nine yards. Hell, I'll even throw on some makeup." She'd do whatever she could to blow Simon's mind.

"No kidding?"

While Mallet thought about her request, Dakota thought about Simon's audacity.

How dare he lay claim to her, but then not invite her to an important party? Did he plan to flirt with other women? Did he have a date with someone else?

Had Bonnie won her way back into his heart?

The very thought made Dakota's stomach tighten and soured her mood. "Make up your mind, Mallet. I don't have all day."

At her grouchy impatience, a wide smile lifted Mallet's ears. "Why not? If nothing else, watching Sublime watch you ought to be enough fun to make up for any trouble this causes."

"Great!"

Before Dakota could do too much celebrating, he held up a hand. "But there's a condition."

"There always is. Let's hear it."

"Call me Michael. Mallet is fine when I'm in the ring, but it doesn't sound right coming from such a pretty woman."

Pretty. How sweet. "Thank you, Michael." Dakota wrote down the name of her motel and her cell phone number, in case of any problems. "What time will you pick me up?"

"Eight o'clock."

"I'll meet you in the lobby." She briefly gripped his wrist, and was stunned at the thickness and vibrant strength. No, Mallet had no reason to fear any man. "Thank you, Michael. I owe you big time."

He said nothing to that, and so Dakota drove off. But she saw him in her rearview mirror, standing there watching after her truck, until she turned the corner and couldn't see him anymore.

Simon was bored and trying to hide it.

Twice now, throngs of women had ambushed him. They waited for him everywhere — near the bar, in the billiards room, even by the men's john. He'd had more offers tonight than most men got in a year.

There used to be a time when all the female attention amused him.

Tonight wasn't it.

Everywhere Simon looked, people laughed and joked. Men razzed each other, women flirted. The four-man band was great, and though he'd kept to his strict diet, the food and drinks looked good. Dean and his wife, Eve, danced. Gregor and his wife, Jacki, huddled in a corner, smooching. The entire lower level of the bar, including several private rooms, was at the disposal of SBC fans and fighters.

Not even the mechanical bull could hold Simon's attention. He'd moseyed in there once, only to dodge back out before the female crowd could reach him. There didn't seem to be enough men to occupy all the women.

Knowing Dakota wouldn't call him, Simon still checked his cell phone. Again.

Nothing.

He tucked it back in his slacks pocket and leaned on the wall. He should have found a good excuse to skip this. He could have gone to Dakota's motel, locked them both in a room, and rid himself of pent-up sexual frustration.

That thought came with a visual, and his body stirred. Damn. Not good.

Would the night never end?

A group of five fighters came over to him, followed by twice that many females. They insisted he share a few of the more gruesome stories of broken bones and popped ribs. Using the interruption as a diversion from his thoughts, Simon obliged, laughing with them, telling the tales without embellishment. By the end, he had a woman squeezed up on each side of him.

The conversation turned to tattoos. Some fighters sported so much ink, they looked like comic papers. Most displayed tats with meaning, while still others tried to add menace with a well-placed, frightful design. It amused Simon how someone would always try to outdo someone else with the most outrageous artwork.

"You got any tats, Sublime?" one young man asked.

"On the top of my feet," Simon told him around a swallow of cranberry juice over ice. During training, he didn't allow himself any alcohol at all. "When I was twenty-two, I got drunk enough and cocky enough to think it'd be cool to have matching bullet hole designs there."

"Bullet holes?" one petite brunette asked. "I don't understand."

Remembering his reasoning at the time, Simon grinned at himself. "I had just gotten really good with a high kick, and when I hit someone just right, it sounded like a gunshot."

"Awesome," one young man said with near reverence.

Right. Awesome. Simon grinned and shook his head. He got a real kick out of the new recruits to the SBC, their enthusiasm and naiveté, along with their determination. Training them was very rewarding.

"I think it sounds sexy." A chesty blonde smiled at him. "Will you show us?"

"Not tonight." Simon was about to comment further on tattoos when the band called a halt and the lead man jumped down from the stage.

It wasn't until then that Simon noticed his shirt. It read, BARBERS HAVE BIG POLES. Alongside the text was a thick red-

166

and-blue striped barber pole.

Barber. That was too much of a coincidence for Simon to let it pass. He excused himself from the group and started toward the bar where the singer had just ordered a drink. On his way, Simon studied him. He was tall, maybe as tall as Simon himself. Unlike most skinny musicians, he had a thick, muscular frame. As he lifted his drink and tossed it back, the flex of his arm showed a bulging bicep.

Not the typical musician at all.

Before Simon could reach him, Bonnie waltzed in, redirecting Simon's attention. As usual, she looked gorgeous, decked out from head to toe in designer duds. With her hair twisted up in some deliberately loose, sexy style, she caught the attention of every male she passed.

Keeping Simon in her sights, she ignored all others and made a beeline for him.

Simon sighed. Bonnie hadn't given up on him. Since the fateful day he'd left her, she'd done everything imaginable to get him back. Usually he could refuse her calls, dodge her come-ons, and ignore her apologies. Inside the crowded bar, it wouldn't be so easy.

Could the night get any worse?

Simon no sooner had that thought than

167

he heard a familiar voice screech, *"Barber!"* and everything masculine in him went on high alert.

Bonnie reached him, started to say something, but Simon caught her shoulders and moved her to the side in time to see Dakota — at least, he thought that was Dakota — dashing across the floor toward the bar.

The singer had already left his seat with his thick arms spread wide to greet her.

Jealousy burned red hot.

"Simon?" Bonnie complained. "Whatever are you looking at?"

"I'm busy, Bonnie." He tried to step around her, but she jumped in front of him and put her arms around his waist. Dakota slipped out of his line of vision, and he couldn't free himself from Bonnie to get her back in his sights. "Let go."

"Simon, don't be like this." Bonnie tightened her arms and put her head to his chest. "I've missed you so much. I came all this way in the hopes we could talk."

"We don't have anything to talk about. I've made that as clear as I can." Simon saw the flash of Dakota's legs — gorgeous legs, damn it — when the singer lifted her off her feet and swung her around in a circle.

"But there's something important that I have to tell you."

"Forget it."

With her hands clenched into the fabric of his shirt, trapping him, Bonnie pushed back enough to see Simon's face. "You will listen to me, Simon. I insist."

God, he'd forgotten how pushy Bonnie could be. He caught her wrists and pried her arms away from him. "Insist all you want, but I'm not interested."

She blurted, "The man I slept with is the man you'll be fighting."

"Harley Handleman?" Simon barely paid any attention. "So?"

The crowd shifted and he could see Dakota again. A rush of heat left him breathing faster. Damn, she looked better than he'd even imagined.

"Yes, Harley. Simon, he planned all this."

"What?"

"Sleeping with me to get to you."

Now she was really reaching. "They just announced the fight cards tonight, Bonnie. Harley couldn't plan shit."

Dakota's casual clothes had hidden a sleek, sexy, athletic body. She wasn't a small woman by any stretch, but she wasn't overweight, either. An off-the-shoulders black dress hugged her all the way down to her knees, tight enough to show off straight, proud shoulders, a narrow waist and concave belly, generous hips, and toned thighs.

In three-inch heels, her legs looked impossibly long and strong. And without a baggy shirt to conceal her curves, he could see that her breasts were round and firm. His gaze tracked her body back up to her face.

Dakota met his gaze.

For one second, her blue eyes shone with awareness. Then she took in Bonnie plastered to his side, and her smile turned mean.

Damn, she looked incredible. Long blond hair curled over her back and shoulders. She'd done something with her eyes, making them smoky and sensual. Her lips were shiny, her skin flushed.

Again, Simon pried Bonnie away. "Later." He started toward Dakota.

Bonnie latched on to his arm. "Did you hear me? You'll be fighting my lover, Simon."

"And you think I care?" He wanted to get to Dakota, but he didn't want to maim the singer.

And that's what he felt like doing, because Dakota kept hugging herself up to him, and he kept hugging her back.

They were both smiling like saps.

Barber his ass. The man did not work in a salon, but he wasn't a typical musician, either. Sure, he had the overgrown hair and pierced ears. But he probably spent as much time in a gym as he did on a stage. Earlier, when he'd sung a slower love song to a heady beat, Simon heard a few women calling him sexy.

His teeth locked. Did Dakota find him sexy, too? Given how she smiled up at him, probably.

"Simon, I'm sorry," Bonnie said. "I didn't know that Harley was using me to find out about you until just recently. As soon as I realized it, I knew I had to come to you, to tell you."

"Thanks." He watched as Dakota took the singer's hand and started him in Simon's direction. Everything about her fascinated Simon, how her hair moved, the slight bounce of her breasts, her comfortable stride in the high heels.

Obviously, despite her preference for mannish boots, Dakota wasn't unfamiliar with heels. She had the same confident gait, only now, instead of just self-assured, she looked killer ambling toward him.

And she held another man's hand.

An edgy sort of anger burned in Simon's gut, urged on by sharpening lust.

"Simon," Bonnie said a little louder, "I *love* you. I'll always love you."

Dakota reached them just in time to hear

Bonnie's announcement. She stopped abruptly, then straightened herself and sent a sardonic glance at first Bonnie and then Simon. Her eyes burned with fire. "Wow. Pretty sucky timing on my part, huh?"

CHAPTER 7

Simon couldn't get over Dakota's new appearance. Not because this sexier façade made him want her any more than he already did; that'd be impossible.

But because now he knew every other man would want her, too. He didn't like that idea at all. "Your timing is just fine."

Like an angry wet cat, Bonnie turned on Dakota. "No, it's not. Surely you can tell that you're interrupting a very private conversation."

"My bad." Dakota started to go.

Simon wrapped his fingers around her wrist and encountered warm, silky skin and deceptively delicate bones. When she turned her head toward him, her long hair cascaded over her shoulder.

Dakota smelled like misted perfume and looked like scalding temptation. His heart beat faster. "What are you doing here, Dakota?"

A seductive smile curved her mouth. "Just hoping to have some fun." She freed her wrist, and tipped her chin up to him. "Is that a problem?"

"Depends on who you plan to have fun with." He directed his attention to the singer — and found him giving Bonnie an interested once-over. Great. If he kept his focus on Bonnie and off Dakota, they just might get along.

"All things considered," Dakota said with her gaze lingering on Bonnie, "I can't see how that's any of your concern."

"Don't believe everything you see."

When the singer felt Simon's stare, he gave up his scrutiny of Bonnie and held out his hand. "Hey, brother, how's it going? I'm Barber, a friend of Dakota's."

Simon took his hand and held on. "Define 'friend.' "

A smile flashed. "You know Dakota. She's a heartbreaker. I've tried, but she won't let me past the front gate."

"Stop trying."

Finally catching on to Simon's hostility, Barber didn't retreat. His hand tightened on Simon's and he closed the space between them.

Eye to eye with Simon, and every bit as determined, Barber said, "Out of respect for Dakota's wishes, I've done just that. What about you?" He turned his head to size up Simon. "You been all that's proper and respectful?"

"Enough already." Dakota wrapped both arms around one of Barber's. "If we could bypass the pissing contest, I'd like to get out of here so Simon and his lady friend can get back to their *personal* discussion."

"We're done," Simon said.

"No, we are *not*," Bonnie asserted.

Barber looked between them all, and settled on Simon. His congenial smile returned. "Got a little situation on your hands, don't you, brother?" He winked. "Too bad for you."

Before Simon could explain that Bonnie wasn't an issue, Barber slung an arm over Dakota's shoulders.

"Hey, babe, I have an idea. Come onstage and do a song with me."

As if they'd both just dismissed Simon, Dakota laughed. "No way. I'm not horning in, Barber, so forget it."

But Barber refused to take no for an answer. He headed for the stage, dragging a playfully resistant Dakota with him. When the other men in the band spotted her, they greeted her with familiarity, issuing catcalls and wolf whistles. Dakota just laughed at them.

Simon seethed.

He realized Bonnie was still talking to him when she caught his chin. "Simon! Are you listening to me?"

Fed up, he glared down at her. "No, I'm not listening. If you can't tell, I'm a little preoccupied here."

Barber jumped up on the stage and grabbed a mike. "I need y'all to give me a hand in getting my favorite lady, Dakota Dream, up here. Now c'mon, Dakota, honey. Come sing us a song."

With the band's encouragement, applause broke out. A group of fighters from the gym looked at Dakota with awe. They knew her, but Simon doubted they knew she performed. Odds were even better that they'd never heard her last name.

They got into the game quickly, making the most racket, pumping their fists in the air and shouting Dakota's name.

Dakota laughed aloud, shook her finger at Barber, and finally relented. She took off those sexy shoes and handed them to . . . Mallet?

Simon did a double take. So that's how she'd gotten to the party? With Mallet as an escort?

That dumb-ass stood there grinning like the village idiot, doing his fair share to convince her to sing.

Bending down, Barber held out a hand to Dakota. She hiked up her snug skirt to display her legs all the way to the top of her thighs. More wolf whistles pierced the air as she planted one foot onto the edge of the raised platform stage and took Barber's hand. He hauled her up.

Dakota positively beamed, Simon realized, as if she belonged onstage.

And maybe she did.

The band fell into a thrumming tune. Still smiling, Dakota shook back her hair, lifted a mike, and the second she began to sing, everyone went silent.

Damn, she was good.

It amazed him that such a deep, rich voice could come from such a delicate woman. But then, Dakota was full of surprises. Like her knowledge of mixed martial arts and training within the SBC.

And his filial father.

Simon stood there, as mesmerized as everyone else. The rock-and-roll tune bounced off the walls of the bar. When Dakota brought her hands together in an accompanying clap, the audience joined in.

Out of the corner of his eye, Simon noticed the owner, Roger Sims, strolling up to the stage to listen.

Beside Dakota, Barber played the guitar, but midway through the song, they switched. Dakota lifted the strap of the guitar over her head and picked up the beat where Barber had left off, segueing right into a solo.

She looked hot enough to catch the stage on fire. When the solo ended, Barber turned to sing the song with her, and together, they made one hell of a show.

When they finished, the room erupted into applause. Simon grinned, unaccountably proud for some reason, and all the more determined to have her.

To quiet the crowd, they started another song. But this time the drummer called Dakota over and, to everyone's surprise, she played the drums as well as she sang and played guitar.

"Damn, she's talented," Simon said to no one in particular.

Bonnie sniffed her disdain. "She looks cheap with her skirt hiked up like that and her hair going everywhere."

Simon stepped away from her.

Bonnie followed in disbelief. "Oh, please, Simon," she sneered. "Don't tell me that *she's* the reason you won't forgive me?"

"She's got nothing to do with you cheating, Bonnie."

She sucked in a gasping breath, but wasn't deterred. "At least stop ogling her long enough to let me explain how that fighter deliberately duped me." She waited for his reaction, but got none. "Harley's main goal all along was to get you in the ring, Simon. He wanted you to come out of retirement and —"

"Enough." Simon leaned close so no one else would hear. He didn't raise his voice, didn't show any anger. But he tried to be as clear as possible. "I don't give a damn who you fucked, Bonnie, or why. You can fuck him again tonight if you want."

"Simon!"

"His reasons don't matter to me any more than yours do. We're through, and nothing is going to change that."

"But . . . you'll be fighting Harley for your comeback. I wanted you to be prepared."

"You think the fact that you slept with him will somehow impact the outcome? You think I'll be emotionally involved?" Simon shook his head. "It means no more to me than what he had for breakfast."

Her face colored. "You can't mean that. You aren't that cold."

Simon laughed. "No." He glanced at

Dakota, and his voice dropped. "Far from cold."

Lacking his discretion, Bonnie yelled, "Meaning you're hot for her?" And she pointed her arm toward the stage, singling out Dakota for all who were close enough to witness her lack of tact.

Simon felt a moment's pity for her. She was not a happy woman. "Think whatever you want, Bonnie, but think it away from me."

He strode toward the stage to join Dean and Eve.

"I didn't know she performed," Dean said. "She's good."

"Yes, she is."

Eve elbowed Simon. "Has she fallen under your spell yet?"

"Hard to tell."

"You're kidding." Eve laughed, but when he didn't change expressions, she said, "You're *not* kidding?"

"No."

"Wow." She looked at Dakota again. "I like her already."

"I knew you would." Simon admired the way Dakota moved in time with Barber, doing a brief dance step that flowed with the beat of the music.

Dean spoke to his wife loud enough for

Simon to hear. "Simon's not used to women giving him grief or making demands, and it's interfering with his training."

"I'm sure with a little effort he could win her over," Eve said just as loudly. "After all, this is Sublime we're talking about. He carries that name for a reason, right?"

Dean stopped being subtle to say directly to Simon, "Whatever he decides, he'd better get a handle on things soon so he can get his focus back on training."

"I've been training."

"And you've been preoccupied. The two don't mix."

"I'll take care of it," Simon said. But how, he didn't know.

Dean shook his head. He and Eve headed toward Roger and took up a new conversation.

Gregor showed up next, with Jacki in tow. "This is a hell of a show, Sublime."

"Yeah, she's good."

"Didn't mean her performance, exactly." Gregor grinned. "I meant the way you're leering at her, along with every other guy here."

Simon glanced around and saw that every unattached man, and some that weren't single, watched Dakota with spellbound intensity.

"Not *every* guy," Jacki said to Gregor.

"No way, darlin'," he told his wife. "I've got my hands full with you."

"Damn right," Jacki said happily.

"Can't you two take that nauseating marital bliss elsewhere?" Simon asked them.

Jacki slugged him in the shoulder. "Come on, Simon. You know it's funny."

It was a novel thing, the way Dean's sisters treated him like a brother. But Simon liked it. With most women, friendship was out of the question because they wanted intimacy more than anything else.

But with Dean's sisters and his wife, Eve, he could enjoy the female perspective with no strings attached. "I have no idea what you're talking about."

"Yeah, right." Jacki hung on Gregor's enormous shoulder while poking more fun at Simon. "Look around you, *Sublime*. All the guys might be watching her, but all the women are watching *you*, hoping to get your attention. And here you are, spellbound like the average Joe with the one woman who's giving you grief."

Simon scowled at that. "Who says she's giving me grief?"

Gregor cleared his throat. "C'mon, darlin'. Let's go find Eve and Dean. They make better company."

Simon smiled as he watched them go. For a former wild child, Jacki had really taken to the settled life of a married woman. She and Gregor made a good pair — which was apparently something Gregor had realized right off, given his hot and heavy pursuit of her from jump.

Simon looked at Dakota again. She really was something, but marriage material? He snorted. Not likely. It wasn't that Bonnie had soured him on marriage; he wasn't shallow enough or dumb enough to cast every woman in Bonnie's mold.

But every time he turned around, Dakota had another surprise for him. First her attempts at schooling him, the master, on martial arts. Then that bombshell about his father. And now this incredible onstage persona.

Was she an athlete or a femme fatale? A PI or a performer? Did she really want him, or just his cooperation with Barnaby?

Would the real Dakota please stand up?

Or better still, lie down.

In his bed.

Maybe when he had her soft and sated from an extended sexual marathon, all her defenses would be down and he'd be able to uncover her secrets. That idea appealed to Simon. A lot.

For three more songs, Dakota stayed on-stage, dancing, singing, playing different instruments. When she took her last bow, Simon saw that her hair clung to her forehead and throat, and that her cheeks were dewy from her exertions and the bright lights.

He was so turned on that he hurt with it.

She exited off the back of the stage, and Simon circled around to meet her. Mallet had the same idea.

They almost ran into each other.

Mallet halted first. "Hey. What's up, Sublime?"

Simon cut through his small talk. "You brought Dakota here?"

"She insisted."

"Twisted your arm, did she?"

Suddenly Mallet's reserve left him and he planted his big feet in a defiant stance. "Actually, she promised to wear a dress, and I couldn't resist. Now that I've seen her, I have to say I'm glad I agreed."

Simon was glad, too, but that wasn't the point. "I told you to stay away from her."

Mallet shrugged. "Yeah, you did. But then you didn't exactly follow up with her, so I figured you'd lost interest."

"I haven't."

"Can't prove it by me."

Shit. Would every fighter at the gym now want to challenge him for Dakota's attention? If so, Simon supposed he'd have to cement things with her, and fast, in order to deter the others. "Stay tuned, then. But do it from a distance. Do I make myself clear?"

"I hear ya. But I'll have to ask Dakota about it."

Dakota came around the corner just then. With one hand she held a fistful of her hair off her neck, and with the other she straightened the hem of her dress. "Ask me about what?"

Mallet smiled while handing her shoes to her. "Whether or not you want me to keep my distance."

She released her hair and bent to step into her shoes, but her gaze darted between both men. "We're friends. No one tells me who I can or can't be friends with."

Simon crossed his arms over his chest. "You seem to have a lot of male friends."

She shrugged. "I haven't counted, but maybe. Men are easier to get along with than women." With her heels back on, she sauntered over to him. "Case in point is your little lady friend who kept staring daggers at me. She doesn't even know me, but she made it clear that she doesn't like me."

"Don't worry about Bonnie."

"Oh, I wasn't worried. But if you care about her, keep her away from me. I'm not big on putting up with snippy bitches."

Simon grinned. Acrimony? Jealousy? He hoped so. "She's probably already left."

"And you aren't going with her? That's not very gallant of you."

Mallet rolled his eyes. "If you two are all made up now, I think I'll go scope out the single women."

Dakota spared him a glance. "Just hang by Simon's side and women will find you." Her smile taunted. "Seems like that's where they all want to be."

So she'd seen that, too. "Maybe if you keep me company, the rest of them will leave me alone."

"And that'll leave more for me," Mallet added with good humor. "I'll see what I can do about keeping them happy."

Dakota nodded to him. "Have fun, Michael. I'm sure we'll find each other later when it's time to head home."

"Why would you?" Simon asked.

She put her shoulders back. "I rode here with Michael."

Simon towered over her. "But you'll be leaving with me."

Dakota patted his chest. "Not unless you plan to give Barnaby a visit." And with that, she turned on her heel and sashayed away. "I need to visit the ladies' room to freshen up."

Mallet stood beside Simon and watched her go. "Hell of a woman."

What an understatement.

Simon looked down the long hall where Dakota had disappeared. "You've been here more than me. Is there any other way out from the ladies' room?"

"Nope. She'll have to come back past you to leave."

"Perfect." Simon parked himself against the wall to wait for her. "So, *Michael,* do we understand each other now?"

He laughed. "She's all yours, Sublime." Then the humor disappeared. "But only because it's obvious that's the way she wants it."

Was it obvious? "Noted."

Rather than leave, Mallet took a position on the wall beside Simon. "Can I ask you something?"

"Depends on what it is."

"Who's Barnaby?"

Seeing no reason not to tell him, Simon said, "Apparently he's the man who hired Dakota to find me."

"Why?"

"She says he's my father."

Mallet went still. "You don't know?"

"Never met the man. I was raised by my stepfather — and he's Dad. I don't give a shit about meeting this Barnaby character."

"But Dakota does?"

It was odd to have Mallet as a confidant, but at least he wasn't harping on the SBC and fights and training. "From what she's said, Barnaby has something she wants. The only way she can get it is to trade me to him." He slanted his gaze at Mallet. "So you see, it's not my charm that has her here."

Mallet stared at him. "You think she's just working a business deal?"

Simon thought Dakota was more involved than that, but he couldn't be sure. "You heard her. Everything hinges on me meeting her terms."

Mallet pushed away from the wall, paced a few feet, and came back. "I don't know her well —"

"Let's keep it that way."

"— but I can't see Dakota being so mercenary."

Simon couldn't either, not really. "She told me about Barnaby herself."

"Don't you think there has to be more to it than that?"

"I've been considering the possibility," Simon admitted.

A small group of women came around the corner, led by Dean's wife, Eve. They spotted Mallet and Simon, and surged forward with new purpose. Eve laughed. Simon groaned.

Mallet leaned closer to whisper, "You better consider it quick, Sublime. I wasn't the only one with thoughts about Dakota tonight, and I doubt you'll be able to warn everyone off forever."

"What the hell does that mean?"

"I'll give you a few days."

Simon stiffened.

The women reached them, and Mallet finished, saying, "After that, I'm going to offer to get her whatever it is she needs from this Barnaby dude. And I don't give a damn whose dad he is." Mallet saluted Simon seconds before he allowed himself to be drawn into conversation with one of the women.

Eve went on past with a wave.

That left three other females to circle Simon.

He called out to Eve, "Tell Dakota to get a move on, will you?"

Eve laughed again, and disappeared into the ladies' room.

■ ■ ■ ■

Dakota dampened a few paper towels and patted her face and neck. Wow, it felt good to work. She loved it.

Simon hadn't mentioned her performance, but everyone else had shown appreciation, so she wouldn't let that bother her. Especially when she knew that he'd taken notice of her clothes and makeup.

Her hair looked a little worse for the fun she'd had. "I should have bought a purse," she said to her reflection.

"Maybe I can be of assistance." Eve held out a hand. "Hi. I'm Dean's wife, Eve. I loved your performance."

Surprised, Dakota accepted her hand. Eve was just about her height, but with dark hair and beautiful blue eyes. "Thank you. It was nice of Barber to include me."

"He's a good-looking man."

"Barber? I suppose so."

Eve smiled and handed her a comb. "Will this help?"

"Thanks." As she turned to straighten her hair, Dakota explained. "I'm from out of town, and when I came here, I packed pretty light. I had to run out earlier today for the dress, hose, and shoes. But I didn't even think about a purse and what I usually carry is big enough to be luggage."

"Do you plan to be in town much longer?"

"I guess that depends."

"On Simon?"

Her hair as tidy as she could make it, Dakota turned back to Eve to return her comb. "He told you?"

Eve dug in her own small, stylish purse until she found a pen and a small slip of paper. "Dean told me that you two have been cozy. That's all I know. Here." She handed Dakota the paper. "That's my number. If you need to borrow anything while you're here — like a purse — just give me a call." She smiled. "I'd be happy to help out."

"Hey, thanks." Dakota took a quick, surreptitious glance at Eve. She was a very fashionable woman, very attractive. "So you're married to Havoc, huh?"

"Yes." She gave an exaggerated sigh of pleasure. "He's incredible. Oh, and you know that he and Simon are best friends?"

"I know that Simon trained him."

"And was his agent and his manager and . . . his everything else, I guess. Dean told me that most of the more successful fighters had a whole team working for them, but all he needed was Simon."

"And now Simon's going to fight again." Dakota shook her head. "If I was a betting woman, I'd put all my cash on him."

"Me, too. But Dean's a little worried." Eve touched up her lipstick.

Guilt hit Dakota like a sledgehammer. "Because of me, you mean."

Eve looked at her in surprise. "No one would blame you. Dean expects Simon to do what he needs to do. Period. I guess this Harley Handleman is a real tough guy. Hungry, Dean says. Simon shouldn't underestimate him."

"The fight is still a while off."

"Plenty of time for us to get better acquainted." Smiling again, Eve said, "Maybe you and Simon could join us for dinner one night."

Dakota ducked her head. "I don't know. I think maybe it's time for me to move on." She glanced at Eve, saw her very honest interest, and decided that it couldn't hurt to trust her. "I saw Simon with someone named Bonnie."

Eve wrinkled her nose. "She used to be his fiancée. But that's over."

"I don't know." She recalled the way the other woman had clung to Simon. "Bonnie didn't seem to think it was over."

"She cheated on Simon. Trust me, he's

not going back to her."

A dash of icy water couldn't have shocked Dakota more. "She cheated? But . . . *why?*"

"Exactly." Eve shook her head. "It's incredible enough with Simon being so sinfully attractive. But he's also nice, dependable, hardworking, and very honorable. Add to that the fact that he's a fighter with a fighter's ego, and any woman dumb enough to cheat deserves to be dumped."

Dakota ran all that through her head. "So what was Bonnie doing here then?"

"Just hoping to manipulate him, I think. See, after months of trying to get Simon back, Bonnie is telling anyone who'll listen that the man she cheated with is Harley Handleman."

Dakota's jaw dropped. "Hard-to-Handle? The guy Simon will be fighting in his comeback?"

"Yes, but that doesn't matter. Bonnie thought it'd make it more personal for Simon, but he's not that way. He doesn't fight with emotion. He fights with ability and training."

Training that she'd interrupted. Dakota closed her eyes. And worse, she'd tried to manipulate him the same way Bonnie had. God, what must he think of her? On every level, she was batting a big fat zero.

It was time to face reality. "I should head home."

Eve asked, "Where are you staying?"

"At a motel, but I meant home, back to Ohio. I should never have come here." Her mind made up, she nodded. "In fact, that's exactly what I'm going to do."

Eve looked alarmed. "What?"

"I'm going to leave. First thing tomorrow."

"No. You can't." Eve trotted after her as Dakota left the restroom. "I mean, you should talk to Simon about this first."

"Why?" Resolute, Dakota kept going. "Simon doesn't want me here."

"Now, I know you're wrong about that."

She shook her head. "I meant that he doesn't want me here for the reason I came." And he only planned to use her for sex if she stuck around. Dakota wasn't sure that was possible, even with her agreement. "And no, I can't explain my reasons for coming because it's not my story to tell. Ask Simon."

"I intend to!" Eve barely kept pace with her. "But I think —"

They rounded the corner and saw Simon waiting.

With other women.

They were all animated and laughing, and

194

one woman was toying with the buttons on the front of his shirt.

Dakota's temper came to a slow boil. "You see? Simon won't miss me at all."

Eve rolled her eyes. "Can't you tell that he's trapped? This kind of thing happens to him all the time. He can't help it that he's gorgeous and women want him."

As Eve said that, Simon caught the woman's hand and moved it away from his chest.

Laughing, she brought it right back.

He sidled out of reach — and bumped into another woman behind him.

"There, you see?" Eve shook her head. "I feel so sorry for him."

"Yeah," Dakota said with saccharine sweetness, "he's suffering badly from all the attention."

Simon looked up and spotted them. His brows snapped down. "Finally." Lacking subtlety, he freed himself from the women. The one who'd been clinging to him stumbled as he stepped away.

Dakota started forward, saying, "Don't break up the private party on my account."

His long legs carried him quickly to meet her halfway in the hall. "There wouldn't have been a damned private party if you hadn't taken a vacation in the john." He scowled at Eve, who had just caught up.

"What the hell did you two do in there? Knit a blanket?"

"Talked about you, mostly," Eve explained.

His dark gaze locked with Dakota's. "Is that so?"

Her face went hot. "We talked about how I'm leaving."

"Not with Mallet, damn it."

Why Simon persisted in thinking he could give her orders, Dakota couldn't imagine. "His name is Michael and I'll leave with anyone I want to leave with."

Roger stepped into the fray. "I hope you have time to talk with me first."

Everyone went blank.

"You, too, Roger?" Simon asked. "But you're married, damn it."

Eve barked a very unladylike laugh. Dakota frowned, having no idea what Simon meant.

Roger fried him with a look. "Happily married, yes." He dismissed Simon. "Ms. Dream, I'm Roger Sims, the owner here. Your performance was incredible."

"Thank you."

"The guests loved you, and a few have already asked me when you'd be back. I spoke with Barber, and he claims that you might be available for employment. I'd like to discuss that with you, if I could."

"Oh." Employment? In Harmony? And she hadn't even been looking. "Thank you, Mr. Sims —"

"Roger, please."

"All right, Roger."

Simon growled.

Dakota glanced at him. "I appreciate the offer, but I'm not going to be here much longer."

"We're open any night that you are, and I'd be happy to have you here for as long as you are in town."

"I'm flattered, really I am. But actually, I was planning on leaving tomorrow."

Simon stiffened. "When the hell did you decide that?"

"While we were in the bathroom," Eve told him. "Talking about you."

"Great." Simon frowned at her. "Thanks for nothing, Eve."

She shrugged.

"There's no point in me staying," Dakota explained. "That's real clear to me now."

"I think her decision has something to do with Harley," Eve added helpfully.

"Harley?" Simon drew back in disgust. "What the hell does he have to do with this?"

Things were quickly spiraling out of

control, Dakota decided. She put her hands to her head. "Get real. It doesn't have to do with any one person. I just need to think about a few things."

"And you can't think in Harmony?" Simon demanded.

Roger took her arm. "I understand. Rather than make any decisions tonight, why don't you let me buy you a drink, make you an offer, and then you can have the night to consider it?"

"Well . . ." Dakota just didn't know. She looked at Simon. The longer she stayed near him, the more she wanted him, and the more impossible she knew that to be. Whether he acknowledged Barnaby or not, he was still his son. If that wasn't awkward enough, she'd be utterly humiliated when Simon found out about her past. And if she stayed, he'd definitely find out. "No, I don't think —"

Simon started to say something, and Eve latched on to him. "Really, Dakota, what will it hurt to hear the offer? I'm sure Roger won't keep you long."

"Not long at all."

With Eve clutching him in a determined way, Simon glanced at her in confusion. "What are you . . . ?"

"Roger is family," Eve interrupted. "Did

you know that, Dakota? He's married to Dean's oldest sister, Cam. She's Jacki's sister, too."

"Ah . . . okay." Dakota had no idea what Dean's family tree had to do with anything.

"You two go ahead. I need to talk to Simon anyway." Eve shooed her away. "You have my number, Dakota. Give me a call sometime tomorrow, okay?"

"Maybe. If I can." *If I'm still here.* Then Eve was dragging Simon away, and Roger tried to urge her along, too. Dakota gave up. "Where are we going?"

"To my office upstairs. It's quieter there."

Quiet sounded good. "Is there a back way out from there?"

"A back way? Of course, but why?"

Feeling like a coward, Dakota lied, "I'm getting a headache and I'd just as soon not struggle through the crowd again if I don't have to."

"I understand. It won't be a problem at all. Let's talk business, and then I'll show you out myself."

"All right. But I need to do something first. Tell me how to get to your office, and I'll meet you there in five minutes."

Roger smiled. "That'd be wonderful. Thank you. I promise you won't regret it."

CHAPTER 8

"What the hell are you doing, Eve?"

She sighed, and finally stopped hauling him along. "I'm butting in."

He liked Eve a lot. She was perfect for Dean. "Is that right?"

"You're interested in her, Simon. And she cares for you."

What had they talked about in the restroom? Had Dakota admitted to caring for him? Simon wasn't sure. "You're basing that on what?"

"On the fact that she doesn't want to interfere with your fight." She held up a hand to stall any comments from him. "I've seen it plenty of times now, Simon. The women who really care don't get in the way. The ones who whine and want all the attention are only in it for that — the added attention that comes with dating a well-known SBC fighter."

"Why would Dakota think she's interfering?"

"I'm afraid that was my fault. I told her Dean was worried. I wasn't insinuating that he was worried about her, and when she made that jump, I corrected her." She touched Simon's arm. "But he is worried, and you understand why. Harley isn't an untried rookie."

"I wouldn't make a comeback against a rookie."

"Stow the ego, okay? You know exactly what I'm saying. Harley is making his way to the top by demolishing experienced fighters. You can take him, we all know that. But you have to be ready for him."

"And I will be." Harley was the least of Simon's concerns right now. But then, maybe that's what worried Dean.

"You were a trainer for a long time. I'm sure you know what you're doing. But if you were training you —"

He smiled. "That'd be a little hard to do, Eve." Just then, Simon spotted Dakota making her way across the floor.

She was heading straight for Barber, damn it.

Exasperated, Eve said, "You know what I'm asking."

"Yeah." Simon ran a hand over his head.

"I'd be kicking my ass and telling me to focus." But how could he, with Dakota filling his head?

"And you know why you're not focusing?" Eve lifted her arms to make her point. *"Dakota."*

Though he'd just pegged her as the source of his distraction, Simon chided Eve. "Don't blame her."

"As I told her, no one blames her." Eve pointed her finger at him. "Everyone blames you. But Dakota put it together. She's not a dummy."

"No. She understands more about the sport than any woman I've met." As Simon watched Dakota finally reach Barber, he thought about Dean's wife and sisters. They liked the sport, and they tried to learn more about it, but they weren't into it the way Dakota was. She genuinely liked it, had followed it from the beginning, and she knew as much about him and his experience in the SBC as Simon knew himself.

"Dakota told me that she shouldn't have come here. That she should have left long ago. Then out of the blue, I could see that she'd made up her mind. She will leave, Simon."

Still staring at her with Barber, he said, "I have to talk to her." No way in hell was he ready to let her go.

"Let Roger convince her to take a job here first. That'll be a good bargaining chip."

"Maybe." A job she loved would be a good incentive for staying. But she wasn't talking to Roger. She was talking to that damned Barber.

"If he doesn't convince her, you can encourage her in that regard. First, though, you have to show her that you have your priorities straight."

With obvious annoyance, Barber caught Dakota's arm and led her to a more private corner of the floor. "My number one priority being . . . ?"

"The upcoming fight. As long as Dakota thinks she's keeping you from doing your best, she won't stick around."

Hoping to appease Eve so he could go to Dakota, Simon said, "Right. Got it."

"But she can also be a priority, just in a different way."

"Okay." Had Dakota already finished with Roger?

"Simon, listen to me. You have to resolve whatever conflict you two have going on. If Dakota knows that you're committed to her, then seeing you with other women won't affect her the same way."

"Committed to her?" That got his attention off Dakota and her friend. He snorted. "I've only known her a week, Eve."

"So?"

So Dakota had only come to Harmony because Barnaby hired her, which was something she hadn't bothered to admit up front. Not a good basis for trust or commitment. But Simon didn't want to go into that right now. "You haven't heard the whole story, Eve."

"I don't need to hear it. Dakota wears her heart on her sleeve, and anyone who knows you can see that you're more than casually interested. Let Dakota know it, too."

"I have."

"Then let her know that she's special." Eve propped her hands on her hips and looked him over. "Let's face it, Simon, you're gorgeous."

She said it like an accusation. "Thank you."

"And sexy."

He looked around for Dean, but didn't see him. "Okay."

"And like my Dean, you have a divine body."

"You hitting on me, sugar?"

Eve waved away that teasing comment. "There's no avoiding those damn annoying female fans, so Dakota *will* see you with other women."

Simon tweaked her chin. "That sounds like experience talking."

She shrugged. "I see women coming on to Dean all the time. But I know his different looks, and I can see that he's not interested, that he's only being polite and removing himself from the situation as quickly and nicely as possible."

True. Dean had eyes only for Eve. And speaking of Dean . . . Simon looked beyond Eve and saw his friend approaching. He said loud enough for Dean to hear, "Havoc's whipped."

"He's *happy,*" Eve corrected. "There's a difference."

"Exactly." Dean's arms slid around Eve and he hugged her from behind. "The party's still going full speed, but Gregor and Jacki just left."

Eve used that opening with the finesse of a master. "Dakota is thinking of leaving, too. I mean, not just tonight, but for good."

Dean glanced up at Simon. "Since when?"

"She's not going anywhere," Simon assured him.

Resigned, Dean released his wife to talk business. "Simon —"

"Yeah, I know. I need to get my head out of my ass." He gave a crooked grin. "Your wife has explained it all to me in detail."

Dean looked down at Eve with surprise. "She has?"

"Starting Monday, you'll have my undivided attention. But tonight, I'm going to take care of some unfinished business with Dakota."

As Simon walked away, he heard Dean ask Eve, "What was that all about?"

"Just sharing a little female wisdom with him, that's all."

Simon grinned. Yep, he was definitely benefiting from Dean's family connections.

Barber tucked Dakota safely into a more private corner of the crowded floor, then shielded her with his body before demanding, "What do you mean, you thought someone was watching you?"

Dakota shook her head and leaned around him to look around the room once more. Her sharpened gaze went right past Simon and Bonnie, though they both were giving her more than a little attention. "I don't know. It just felt . . ." She frowned and gave up. "Not right."

Barber didn't like it. Dakota wasn't a woman given to hysterics or dramatics, but her life had been such that, no matter how much time passed, he would never discount a possible threat toward her.

"Let me take you home."

That made her smirk. "To Ohio? Tonight?"

"No." Unamused, Barber made note of the fatigue on her face. He didn't like that, either. "Where are you staying?"

She named the motel, and then turned him down. "There's no reason for you to drive me there, Barber. I already have a ride." Before he could voice his opinion on that, she added, "And even if I didn't, I know how to call a cab."

"But why should you when I'm right here, ready and willing to be at your service?" He held out his arms like a sacrifice, trying to tease her into agreeing.

"Thanks, but no thanks." Distracted, her gaze continually scanned the room.

She must've really been spooked to be so vigilant.

"Dakota . . ." But Barber didn't know what to say. He hated to mention the past. She'd had so much fun tonight that he didn't want to ruin it for her with ugly memories. And after her rousing performance, odds were that any number of horny men were eyeballing her with hungry thoughts.

"It could have been my imagination."

Neither of them believed that. But in the

crowded club, Barber doubted any real trouble could find her.

And if a guy tried to press his luck, Dakota had the training to make mincemeat of him.

She smiled up at him. "Roger's waiting for me, so I better get going. I just wanted to say good-bye first."

"I'll see you when you finish with him."

"Sorry." She shook her head. "Soon as he and I are done talking, I'm outta here."

Barber glanced at his watch. He had hours to go before he finished for the night. "If you'd hang around till our break, I could —"

Dakota gave him a level look. "No."

Her insistence wore on Barber, and he knew why. "What's the matter? You worried lover-boy will have a hissy?" Simon had clearly challenged him, and Barber had been tempted to accept. "I can handle myself and you know it."

Dakota let out an exasperated breath. "I've never doubted that. You're the one who's not interested in competing."

"I've got nothing to prove." But Dakota did. From the day he'd met her, she'd been trying to prove to herself that she was worthy of forgiveness. And that was why he'd ignored Simon's provocation and instead had talked her into doing what she loved best: performing. "What does Romeo mean to you, anyway?"

Barber watched her face and saw the second she put up her defenses.

"Nothing." She didn't quite meet his gaze when she muttered, "And his name is Simon, not Romeo."

"I know his damned name." Barber crossed his arms over his chest. "If he means nothing, then how come you were drooling when you looked at him?"

"Drooling." Dakota slugged him in the arm. "I did no such thing, and you know it."

"A slight exaggeration." At least he had her attention again. He hated it when she shut him out. "So if you're bailing on me tonight, what do you say about hooking up tomorrow? We could grab a nightcap somewhere, gab all night, and watch the sun come up."

"Just like old times, huh?" A faint smile curved Dakota's mouth, easing the signs of tension. "We haven't closed out the bars in years."

The mention of old times reminded Barber just how far she'd come. In a blink of time, she'd grown from a scared little girl still in her teens, allowed in the bars only because the owners liked him, to a mostly confident, take-charge woman who captivated an audience of men when she sang onstage.

In many ways, he saw Dakota as a little sister, best friend, and fun companion.

In other ways, she tempted him to push for more than platonic sharing. But Barber knew it'd never happen, and he cared too much for her to drive her away by acting like a randy goat.

"I'm still a good listener, Dakota."

"I know that." She leaned into him for a big hug. "But let's plan on catching up somewhere in Ohio, after I've gone home. Tonight I just want to hear Roger's offer, then hit my lumpy motel bed to sleep for a good eight hours."

Knowing she wouldn't relent, Barber nodded. "You got it, babe." While rubbing her back, he looked beyond her — and saw Bonnie. A real hellcat, that one. "I'll call you when I get back to Ohio next month."

She looked up at him. "That'd be great."

Barber cupped her face. "So before you split, tell me what you know about your beau's ex."

"Simon is not my beau," she said, before she realized exactly what he'd asked. Then she stiff-armed away from him. "Oh, please. You've got to be kidding."

"Nope."

"She's a bitch."

"Yeah." Barber watched Bonnie search the room. Hunting for Simon? Probably. She wasn't a woman who'd like rejection. "But a sexy bitch."

"If you like claws and a forked tongue."

Barber laughed. "I'm male, Dakota. I like any kind of female tongue." Even the acerbic ones could be sweet when coerced into the right use.

Disdain curled her lip. "Whatever. It's your life. Have at it and good luck."

Barber saw Bonnie visually lock on to someone to her left. Given the change in her posture, from determined to seductive, he'd bet his last pair of underwear he knew who she saw.

When Simon came into view, heading straight for them, Barber had his assumption confirmed.

On impulse, knowing Simon would see, he kissed Dakota's forehead. "He's heading this way, love."

Dakota went on the alert. "Who? Simon?"

"Yep. And I think I'd like to snag Ms. Bonnie before she snags him, so now's your chance to make your getaway if you still want to make an early night of it."

"I do." She gave him one last hug and headed off in a rush. Barber watched her disappear through a darkened doorway.

Just as Simon reached him, Barber stepped into his way. "Hey, bud."

Simon almost plowed over him. "Excuse me."

"Sorry." Still blocking his way, Barber said, "No can do."

Disbelief brought the fighter to a standstill. Deadly serious, he said, "Trust me, you don't want to do this."

"But you do?"

"Not really." Though his gaze remained direct, Simon relaxed his stance. "But I can. And I will."

A laugh took Simon by surprise. Barber clapped Simon on the shoulder. "Put away the brass knuckles, my man. I just want to ask you something."

"I'm busy."

"Chasing Dakota, I know." Simon's expression made Barber laugh again. "She'll be busy for a few minutes, and I won't keep you any longer than that."

Impatience showed through Simon's attempt at civility. "What is it?"

"It's about your woman."

"Dakota?"

Leaning back on the wall, Barber asked, "How the hell did I miss your sense of humor?"

Unamused, Simon started away, and Barber said, "Actually, I meant Bonnie."

Simon paused again. "Bonnie's not mine." He searched the area, trying to find Dakota. "If you're interested in her, feel free."

"No warnings about her?"

Dark eyes took Barber's measure. "You're a big boy. You can make your own assessments on Bonnie."

"Right." Shaking his head, Barber mused aloud, "Wonder why Dakota never believes that."

"Who can understand women?"

Okay, so maybe Simon wasn't quite as unlikable as he'd first figured. Though there was obviously bad blood between them, Simon hadn't bad-mouthed Bonnie. And he hadn't felt compelled to push the confrontation to a physical level.

Not for a single second did Barber think Simon avoided a fight out of fear of losing. No. Simon carried himself like a man who knew he could dominate any situation.

But maybe, like Barber, he had nothing to prove.

Barber respected that.

"Dakota went up the back way to see the manager. You can wait here for her if you want." He pushed away from the wall. "I think I'll do us both a favor and head off your little hedgehog for some one-on-one."

Simon turned, saw Bonnie bearing down on them, and gave Barber a nod. "Thanks." And with that, he sidled out of Bonnie's path.

Just as he'd done to Simon, Barber put himself in Bonnie's way. "Hey, beautiful."

She started to push past him, but after the compliment, she preened. "Hello." Her gaze skipped beyond him. "Did Simon say where he was going?"

"Off with Dakota somewhere."

Her huff nearly parted his hair. "I thought he had better taste than that."

Barber chuckled and took her hand. "You insulting yourself, darlin'?" When her dark eyes narrowed, he explained, "Because the way I heard it, he was with you not so long ago."

She tugged at her hand, and when he didn't free her, she lifted her chin. "He'll be with me again, eventually."

"That so? Huh. It looks different from where I'm standing, but I'll take your word on that." He lifted her fingers to his mouth and pressed a warm, damp kiss on her knuckles. "So in the meantime, what do you plan to do?"

"Do?"

"With your sexy self. Surely chasing after

a reluctant swain isn't your thing. If I could make a suggestion . . . ?"

Her breathing deepened. She hesitated, and then nodded. "Go ahead."

"I'll be in town for a week, performing here." Barber closed the space between them until he could touch his nose to her hair and breathe in her warmed scent. "I'd be real grateful for the company, and I can promise not to bore you."

She studied him through calculating eyes.

With his mouth only an inch from hers, he said, "If anything's going to get another man's attention, that ought to do it."

"Yes." She licked her lips. "That would do it."

"I get done here at one thirty. That's a while off yet, so in the meantime, why don't you think of something interesting for us to do?"

"Interesting?"

"Yeah." Gently, he kissed the corner of her mouth, just teasing her. "Something that involves us both being naked. Maybe in a bed." He dropped his hand and stepped away from her. "Or not."

Every line of her body showed her interest. "You're presuming a lot."

"Ah, darlin', I'm just real hopeful, that's all. Been that way since the moment I first saw you."

The compliments worked, putting a sly smile on Bonnie's lush mouth. "All right. One thirty." As she went past him, she said, "Between now and then, I'm sure I'll be able to think of all kinds of fun activities."

For her benefit, Barber clutched his heart in theater-worthy drama. Bonnie laughed — and she hadn't even noticed his boner. It looked like his visit to Harmony would be eventful after all.

That is, if he could stop worrying about Dakota.

Dakota badly wanted to accept Roger's generous offer. He had a nice place, sort of a low-key honky-tonk with dancing, drinking, easy food, and private rooms galore. The upper floor, where he kept his office, circled the other floors with a cool steel railing, giving guests a nice view of the activities below. Both floors served drinks, but most of the fun happened downstairs with the live band, mechanical bull riding, billiards, and more.

Roger had offered good pay, and staying in Harmony held a lot of appeal.

But for every good reason to stay, there were twice as many reasons to go.

She wasn't a person who liked to meddle

in the lives of others. She wasn't a manipulative person who used others for her own ends. She wasn't a woman who had casual affairs.

Who was she kidding? Since her divorce, she wasn't a woman who had sex, period.

Yet, in Simon's case, she'd meddled unforgivably, put her own needs above his, and for the first time in years, the thought of sex appealed to her.

None of that really mattered, though, because Simon didn't want to meet Barnaby. End of story. Time to leave the man alone and accept defeat.

That decision depressed the hell out of Dakota, even if she knew it was the right thing to do. At least she was alone in her unhappiness instead of caught in the middle of the laughing guests. From his office, Roger had kindly escorted her to the back of the building. A private stairwell led to empty storage rooms on the first floor. There she'd find a door to the street.

Roger would have walked her out, but his cell phone rang and Dakota, who wanted nothing more than to return to her motel room to accept defeat in private, assured him she could see herself out. For days now, she hadn't gotten enough sleep. Her feet hurt. And she still had to go to the front of the building to get her coat. She didn't want to wait for him to complete his call, and she didn't want to inconvenience anyone any more than she already had.

Reluctantly, Roger agreed.

After leaving a message for Mallet, Dakota called a cab. She appreciated the chance to sneak out — if only she hadn't had that awful sense of being watched. Not Simon, and not Bonnie.

But someone.

Worry edged at the back of her mind as she opened the stairwell door and, shivering at the rush of cold air, stepped inside. The heavy door slowly closed with a loud creak and a final thunk, leaving her in heavy shadows and subdued silence.

Since she wasn't likely to see anyone on the stairs, Dakota bent to remove her shoes. Her toes thanked her as she wiggled life back into them. She took two steps, listening to the sounds of the party behind her.

Then she heard something else.

Going still, Dakota listened. Her heart skipped a beat and her breath strangled in her lungs. Sure that someone was behind her, and equally sure that she was mistaken, she started to turn — and something hit her hard in the middle of her shoulder blades.

She screamed as she went tumbling head-first down the long flight of stairs, and didn't stop screaming until she slammed up against the door at the landing.

CHAPTER 9

Simon found Mallet on the dance floor, having himself a good time to a fast tune. Raising his voice so Mallet could hear him over Barber's band, he asked, "Have you seen Dakota?"

Mallet paused, letting his dance partner fall into step with others. "She's not with you?"

"Would I ask if she was?"

Moving off the busy and noisy dance floor, Mallet shook his head. "I suppose not." When they reached the outer perimeter of the room, he pulled out his cell phone, saw he had a message, and checked it. "Hey, she said she's taking a cab home."

"When was that?"

He glanced at the phone again, then at his watch. "Maybe ten minutes ago."

Hands on his hips, Simon stewed. "Damn it." Why had she come to the party, only to sneak off without telling him?

Mallet started to commiserate with Simon when Dean showed up. He didn't look happy. "Haggerty just called me. Dakota's hurt."

Both Mallet and Simon froze at that news. Simon recovered first. "How bad?"

"I don't know yet. I came for you before asking other questions." Dean started away and both men followed.

Pushing the pace, Simon asked, "What happened?"

"All I know is that she fell down some stairs."

Dean wound back through the crowd with Simon and Mallet right behind him. They went downstairs, and then into a storage room.

Dakota sat in a chair, shoeless, her dress and hose torn, her face turned away. Beside her, Haggerty fretted with a large cup of ice and some hand towels clutched in his hands.

"I found her," Haggerty blurted, and for the first time since Simon had known him, he sounded frazzled as he rattled off explanations. "She was all crumpled up against the door at the bottom of the stairs. She screamed, that's how I found her." His Adam's apple bobbed as he swallowed hard. "Thought she was dead at first. I really did."

Because Simon was watching her so

closely, he saw Dakota stiffen.

"I was outside there, takin' a smoke," Haggerty continued. "Then she screamed. Real loud. I heard her even through the storage room and the outside door and I came running in, and I found her there. Lookin' dead."

"Thanks, Haggerty." Simon went to his knees in front of Dakota. "What happened?"

Dakota shrugged. When she spoke, she didn't sound shaken or scared, or upset.

She sounded pissed.

"You heard Haggerty. He certainly tells it with flair."

Gently, Simon touched her jaw to bring her face around so he could see her. He knew it wouldn't be good, and still his stomach cramped. "Ah, shit."

A large bruise colored her forehead. A cut on her cheekbone oozed blood. The corner of her mouth was swollen and she had the beginnings of a shiner. "Dakota, honey, are you all right?"

"I'd be better if I hadn't landed on my face." Her attempt at a sarcastic smile only made her look more injured.

Simon looked up at Haggerty. "Did you call an ambulance?"

"You try," Haggerty charged him. "She threatened my manhood if I did it."

"I don't need an ambulance." Gingerly, Dakota prodded her lip, then licked it. "Other than suffering from embarrassment, I'm fine."

"Embarrassment?"

"The girly scream?" She looked up at Haggerty. "I asked you not to repeat that part, remember?"

Simon couldn't believe she was worried about that.

Haggerty looked ready to jump out of his skin. "I had to tell them what happened!"

"Well, then, thanks for nothing."

Mallet and Dean stood in appalled silence. All of them had seen men battered and bruised. Broken wrists, dislocated elbows, torn ligaments. Knockouts and choke-outs and blood galore. They'd seen it all — on fighters.

Not on women.

"Are you hurt anywhere else?" Simon lifted her arm, but she pulled away.

"I said I'm fine."

So defensive. Dakota didn't like it that she was hurt, and she absolutely hated showing any signs of weakness. Funny that although he hadn't known her for long, Simon knew that much without a single doubt.

"How about letting me check for myself?"

Her gaze fried him. "How about you don't treat me like a damn baby?"

"Dakota . . ."

Disgusted, she said, "Look, my knees are a little sore, and I banged up my thigh. That's it. No biggie."

"Let me see," he insisted.

She laughed and gave in. "Sure, doc, whatever you say." Lifting her dress a little higher, she showed an awful swelling bruise on her outer thigh, visible through her shredded nylons. "Not too bad, considering I went down all but the top two steps."

Simon settled his hand warmly over her thigh, covering the obscene bruise. "Did you trip on something?"

She laughed again. "No."

The way she said that gave Simon pause. "Then how . . . ?"

For only a moment, she closed her eyes, looking vulnerable and scared. But when she opened them again, she scowled at the other men. "I don't like having an audience."

Dean stared at her. "Since when? You're a performer, remember?"

Simon scowled at him. "Knock it off, Dean."

Dean worked his jaw. "I didn't mean —"

"No, he's right." She pressed her fingertips

to her temples. "But let me restate that. I don't like a bunch of guys looking at me like I'm a sad little girl. Don't you all have something better you could be doing?"

Mallet said, "I don't."

Dean drew in a slow breath. "I suppose I should let Roger know, since you fell in his place."

"I didn't fall."

Haggerty shoved an ice-filled towel into Simon's hands. "Make her use that before she gets any more colorful."

"I didn't fall."

Simon had a bad feeling about this. "Tell me what happened."

Again, she looked at everyone, seemed to give a mental shrug, and said, "All right, boss. If you want the truth, I was shoved."

"Shoved?" Mallet demanded. "By who?"

"That's the funny part. See, I was too busy crashing down the stairs to notice."

They all looked at each other.

"Well, now." Haggerty's voice became all rough and edgy. "Ain't no shame in falling, honey. I've fallen. Hell, we've all fallen."

Dakota slumped back in the chair. "Yeah, well, shame or no, if I had fallen, I'd say so. I'm not a liar." Her gaze bounced off Simon's, and she added, "Not usually. Not this time. I was pushed."

"Then we'll call the police," Dean announced, and he already had his phone in his hand.

"Butt out, Dean."

They each looked at her, and she rubbed a shaking hand under one eye to remove some smeared makeup. "Look, guys, I don't mean to be rude, I really don't. But it's my business, not yours. I don't need some big macho fighters to take care of me. If I wanted to call the cops, I could damn well do it myself."

"Then why don't you?" Mallet asked.

"Right." She turned dry and sarcastic. "None of you really believe me, so why would the cops?"

Dean, Mallet, and Haggerty all wore identical looks of guilt.

"You see? It's not like I can prove that someone shoved me, and without proof, what'd be the point? The cops can't do anything."

"They could look around," Dean pointed out.

"Wouldn't do any good. Whoever pushed me was long gone even before Haggerty came charging in like a white knight."

"She did look around when I was there." Haggerty rubbed at his chin. "I thought she was looking for you, Sublime."

Dakota rolled her eyes. "I wanted to make sure that he wasn't there to hurt you, Haggerty."

He? Simon thought. Dean glanced at him, and they shared a look of comprehension. So Dakota had an idea who had done this, but she didn't want to say.

He'd get it out of her, Simon decided. Soon. After they were alone.

Haggerty drew up in affront. "You wanted to protect *me?*"

With a crooked smile, Dakota said, "No offense."

"I'd have kicked his ass."

"Sure you would have." She looked away from him. "Guess I wasn't thinking straight."

Before Haggerty could get more insulted, Simon said, "First things first." He was so furious he shook, so that instruction was as much to himself as to Dakota. "You need to go get checked over."

"Nope." As if she weren't black and blue all over, Dakota pushed to her bare feet, and though discomfort showed on her face, she stood straight with her shoulders back. She held out her arms, putting herself on display. The arm seam of one sleeve had given way. Her nylons were shredded. "See? No breaks, no sprains." Her eyes narrowed.

"No reason to pamper me."

Mallet gave a lurid curse.

"Your every sentence starts with a no," Dean pointed out.

"That's right, and here's a few more for you." She crossed her arms under her breasts. "No police and no hospital."

Dean leveled a look on her. "If you were a fighter, I know what I'd tell you." He crossed his arms, too. "But you're not."

"Right." She smirked. "I'm a weak little female."

"True enough."

"So let me guess," she said, ignoring Dean's agreement with her. "If I wasn't female, you'd tell me that this little cut on my face doesn't need stitches."

"No, it doesn't."

"And I should ice the bruises for now, then hit the hot tub tomorrow to ease the stiffness."

"Probably."

"Sounds like the perfect plan." Snatching the ice away from Simon, Dakota pressed it against her forehead. "There, you see, it's all under control."

They stared at her.

She turned to Haggerty. "Thanks for the ice."

"Welcome."

Simon couldn't take it. "I'll drive you home."

"I called a cab."

"I'll cancel it." Done with letting her call the shots, Simon turned to Haggerty and Mallet. "Since she insists, we'll skip the police, but I'd like for you two to go back upstairs and ask around. Someone pushed her. I want to know who."

Dakota looked momentarily surprised that he believed her. He could see her relief, and something more.

Mallet nodded. "Someone might have seen another person up near the office."

"It's possible. Or maybe they saw someone coming back downstairs. Can't hurt to check."

Dakota said nothing.

Simon chose to see her silence as trust. "Dean, if you'll get rid of the cab and then let Roger know what happened, I'd appreciate it."

"I don't hold Roger responsible," Dakota insisted.

"He'll still want to know. And since you were with him right before this happened, he might have noticed someone else around the area."

"Sure thing." Dean gave Simon a level look. "You'll call me in the morning to let me know how it's going?"

Simon nodded.

"And if you need anything . . . ," Mallet added.

"Got it."

One by one, the men touched Dakota — her hair, her arm, her jaw. It was their way of offering sympathy and support as they left her in Simon's care.

Suffering their concern, Dakota thanked them and tried to hurry them on their way. To Simon, she looked like a stoic trooper ready to collapse.

As soon as the others had gone, Simon made another ice pack so that she had one for her bruised face and one for her injured thigh. "Come home with me."

She looked mildly surprised, then very defensive. "Why would I want to do that?"

Why indeed? "I want to take care of you."

Her face scrunched up in indignation. "What am I, an infant? You guys all get beat up worse even when you win a fight, and you don't sit around bellyaching, waiting for someone to —"

Simon kissed the bridge of her nose, effectively cutting off her tirade. "I want to talk to you, too, Dakota. And get to know you better."

"Get to know me better?"

"That's right." Simon didn't mention any form of intimacy. She wasn't up to it, and right then, what he wanted most was for her to be safe, comfortable, and cared for. Sex would wait.

He kissed the corner of her injured mouth, curved his hand around her nape, and gave her a direct look. "And Dakota, I want you to tell me who did this to you."

Now that they were alone, her bottom lip trembled. She immediately firmed it. "I already told you. I didn't see anyone."

Her shaky voice tore at his heart. "I know you didn't."

Her makeup was ruined, her hair tangled, and she looked as if she'd gone the distance with a heavyweight and lost. But still, she cleared her throat and made her voice strong. "Right. So how do you expect me to —"

Simon brushed her hair away from her face. "You still have a good idea who it is, don't you, honey?"

She didn't deny it.

"Dakota?"

As if her bold façade had worn thin, she rested her forehead on his shoulder. "You know, I pretty much hate it when people call me honey, but all of you do it."

"All of us?"

"You and Haggerty and Mallet."

"I'll tell Mallet to knock it off." Her husky and warm laugh teased Simon's senses. He breathed in her scent, felt her heart beating against his chest, and said again, "Come home with me. Please."

"Yeah, all right." She lifted her face and sighed. "But just for tonight, and only because I want to get to know you better, too."

Not understanding himself or what he wanted, Simon accepted her stipulation of one night only. But tomorrow he'd reevaluate the situation. "Let's go."

Wrapped in Simon's jacket, riding on heated seats in his SUV, Dakota finally felt warm. Even the ice bag on her thigh didn't cause her a chill. There was no one staring at her with doubt and pity. The evening was quiet, the streets mostly deserted. She no longer shook.

She almost felt safe.

But then, out of nowhere, her muscles would clench again at the awful sensation of being jabbed in her back. She'd see those hard steps coming up at her face, feel the helplessness of falling and falling, and fear burned in her veins.

She couldn't stop thinking of it. As she'd

tumbled, there'd been no recognition of pain. Numbness had taken over. When she crashed at the bottom of the stairway, she didn't know if she was hurt bad or not. The echo of her scream assaulted her eardrums, making it impossible for her to hear anything else.

One thought had gripped her: Was her assailant still behind her?

Would she feel the blade of a knife? Would her clothes be torn away?

Or would this time be *worse?*

For long seconds after the assault, she couldn't open her eyes, didn't dare look for fear of what — or who — she'd see standing there. Then Haggerty had charged in and shouted her name and —

"Dakota." Simon reached across the seat, taking her hand and pulling her from her black thoughts. "Try to put it out of your mind for now."

"Easier said than done." Dakota gladly laced her fingers through his. He was so warm and alive, strong and gentle. His touch helped to calm her racing heart.

Nothing and no one would ever scare Simon. He was a rock.

And she wasn't. "I hate being such a coward."

Simon glanced at her. "You're not."

It hurt her throat to laugh. "Nah, of course not." She held out her free hand, showing Simon the slight tremors that still haunted her. "I feel sick."

"Do you need to throw up?"

His look of alarm would have amused her under different circumstances. "Not that type of sick." Sick at heart. Sick down to her soul.

When she'd first felt someone watching her, she should have taken it as a warning, instead of writing it off as nothing. She knew better, damn it.

She eased her hand away from him. "I shouldn't be imposing on you."

"I feel better having you with me."

Because he was such a good man. Dakota stared out the darkened window, disliking herself immensely. "I've done too much of that already."

His voice edged with anger, Simon asked, "What exactly does that mean?"

Self-pity made her maudlin. It was unforgivable. She'd changed. She wasn't a selfish person, not anymore. It was past time she remembered that. "I've hounded you to do things you don't want to do. I've tried to use you to get what I want. I apologize for that."

He steered his car into the motel where

she stayed. "We have a lot of talking to do. Let's just wait until you're comfortable, okay?"

Dakota looked around the lot in confusion. "Changed your mind about spending the night with me, huh?"

"No. And without debating it, we both know it'll probably be for more than one night. So why keep paying for this room when you won't be using it?"

More than one night? He must be a glutton for punishment. "I think we need to debate it."

He sighed.

"Come on, Simon, I can't just throw myself on your doorstep because of a few bruises."

"You met Roger. Well, the bar isn't the only place in Harmony that he owns. He has a nicer motel. It wasn't always, but after Dean had some problems there, Roger put in better lighting and better security. If you decide to go back to a motel, go to his."

That sounded reasonable enough to agree. "Not a bad idea."

"This place isn't the best. You know that."

"It's a dive — but it's cheap."

"Is money an issue for you?"

She grinned. "Not yet." But it would be soon.

"All right, then. Cheap or not, after what happened tonight, don't you think it'd be a good idea to move out of here?"

If the push down the stairs hadn't rattled her so badly, she'd have thought of it herself. "Yeah, I do." She started to open her door, but Simon told her to wait.

Like a true gentleman, he came around and opened the door for her, then stayed close, holding her hand while they went inside to gather her few belongings.

When Dakota flipped on the light, Simon looked at her room with curiosity. Her satchel, overflowing with snacks, rested on the dresser. The empty shopping bag, evidence of her impromptu trip to the mall for a party dress and shoes, lay crumpled on the bed next to her open suitcase. Her thermos stood on the nightstand, her boots on the floor.

"You didn't bring much with you, did you?"

"I didn't expect to be here long."

Hands on his hips, Simon stared at her. "I disappointed you by not agreeing right away to see Barnaby."

She'd disappointed herself more by asking. "Forget it. Far as I'm concerned, Barnaby is one topic we should kill, bury, and never mention again."

Her vehemence had Simon frowning, but after a few moments, he nodded his agreement. "Do you need to check your phone for messages before we get out of here?"

"No." She was a cautious sort by nature, but especially when dealing with Barnaby. "I didn't tell anyone where I'd be staying. Anyone who might need to reach me has my cell number."

He picked up her thermos, which was empty, and replaced the lid. "Do you want to change before we leave?"

She hadn't thought about it, but one look at her ruined dress and hose, and it seemed like one hell of an idea. "Yeah. Thanks." Going to her suitcase, Dakota withdrew a worn pair of jeans, a sweatshirt, and warm socks.

As she ducked into the bathroom, Simon busied himself by strolling restlessly around the small room.

The mirror provided something of a shock for Dakota — she looked hideous. Worse than hideous. No wonder Simon hadn't mentioned sex. Why would he want to?

After changing, Dakota made a face at herself and took a few more minutes to remove her destroyed makeup and the traces of blood from her cut, which, once cleaned, looked to be no more than a deep scratch with discoloration around it.

Every movement caused an ache. Her muscles were stiff, her flesh black and blue. Her stomach still roiled and her head pounded. Before gathering up her few toiletries, she brushed her hair and pulled it into a loose ponytail at the nape of her neck.

Stepping out of the bathroom, she said to Simon, "I hope you have a coffeemaker."

"I do." He scowled at her sweatshirt, which was another gift from Barber. "But you drink too much of that stuff."

"Right." She offered up a sneer. "I'll start a twelve-step program soon, I swear. But not tonight."

Simon drew her to him and examined her injured cheek. "Not too bad, but you might end up with a small scar."

That struck Dakota as so ironic that she said without thinking, "Won't be the first." The words had no sooner left her mouth than she caught her breath. *Idiot!*

She tried to ease away from Simon, but he didn't let her go, and she didn't want to make an issue of it.

"You have other scars?"

"Doesn't everyone?"

"How?"

"Come on, Simon. Not another inquisition. Let's get out of here, okay? I'm beat."

Simon's dark gaze scrutinized her. She

could tell he didn't want to, but he let it drop. "Are you sore?"

"Yeah, all over. But Dean's right." She held up the now soggy ice bag. "I'll refill this at the ice machine on the way out. Tomorrow, a good soak in a hot tub will do wonders. Is there one at the gym?"

He touched the corner of her mouth. "Yes. There's also one at the house I'm renting."

"You're renting a house?"

"I've been in Harmony for a while now. I plan to stay on until the competition. Rather than share the hot tub with a bunch of fighters, you can use the one at the house."

"Cool." She freed herself from him to sit on the edge of the bed and pull on her boots. "Only problem, I don't have a suit."

"You won't need one." He zipped up her suitcase.

Dakota stared at him until he held out his free hand to her. Was he hinting about sex? Or did he mean he'd give her privacy?

She had no idea. She wasn't even sure which option she preferred.

After she took his hand, Simon led her out the door, saying, "Don't worry about anything, Dakota, okay? I'm not going to rush you."

"I wouldn't let you rush me."

He smiled. "But I will join you in the hot

tub. And while we're soaking, we'll talk about things. Like what Barber means to you, whether you want your own room or you'd rather share the bed with me, who pushed you, and what other scars you have."

With dread, Dakota realized that he wanted to know everything.

The desk clerk smiled at them, forcing Dakota to blink away her wariness. She had to check out. She had to think. She had to get control of her fear.

This whole night was one huge mistake.

But she'd rather go with Simon and answer impossible questions than spend the night alone.

Chapter 10

"It's small, but since I don't officially live in Harmony, I didn't see any reason to rent anything extravagant."

Arms wrapped around herself in a pose that looked far too contained and alone, Dakota nodded. The drooping ice bag hung from one hand, sending a trickle of icy water to darken the side of her sweatshirt and the top of her jeans.

By the minute, her skin turned more colorful, the reds and blues deepening to purple and green.

Yet she kept quiet, not issuing a single complaint.

Simon fought back his frustration. He knew Dakota's physical pain hadn't caused her remote attitude. It was his need to know more about her, and her uncertainty at exposing herself.

But he wouldn't relent, damn it. Dakota fascinated him more than any woman he'd ever known had. It'd be nice if she felt the same.

Before he could know her true feelings, he had to know her. All of her.

Whether she liked sharing herself or not.

"You have some messages." She indicated the blinking red light on his phone, sitting on the end table.

Simon walked over to the phone and pressed a button. "Normally I'd wait to check them, but it could be Dean or Mallet. I assume they'd call my cell, but just in case . . ."

Simon shrugged, then listened to the messages. Dakota looked stunned to hear him offered a commercial for a health drink, two sponsorships for clothing, and a reminder that his article would be due soon.

She stared at him. "You're writing an article?"

"Yeah. One of the sports magazines offered me a good deal to do a piece for them."

"What's your topic?"

"Ego." Still holding her suitcase, he said, "It has no place in training."

"I'd like to read it."

"All right."

"Is it always like this?" She nodded at the answering machine. "So many offers and so

242

much attention?"

"Pretty much." Simon stepped closer to her. "Now it's my turn for a question."

Her blue eyes narrowed as she turned her gaze on him.

"Do you want to sleep with me or alone? Before you answer, understand that I mean *sleep.* You're in no shape for sex, and I know it."

Her jaw tightened. "I can sleep alone."

"Of course you can. But do you really want to?"

She opened her mouth to reply, but said nothing. Her arms tightened around herself and she looked away. "I don't know."

So honest — or at least it seemed that way. But she'd duped him several times already and Simon didn't want to be taken in again. "I'd prefer you sleep with me, if that helps you decide."

"All right." She swallowed, and her gaze wavered. "If you prefer, then sure. Why not?"

"Good. This way." Simon led her down the short hall to his bedroom. "It's a big bed. We'll each have plenty of room. But I don't mind cuddling, if you're so inclined."

He set her suitcase down and turned to her. "The bathroom is right through there. If you want more privacy, there's another one in the hall."

"Thanks." She stared at the bed.

It all felt very awkward, given that Dakota looked wary and, despite his need to protect and pamper her, he was so horny he could barely breathe. "Next question. How about some aspirin?"

"How about half a dozen? And coffee?"

"Two aspirin and a cup of coffee if you insist." He took the ice bag from her and led her back the way they'd come, into the kitchen.

"This is a nice place."

"It came furnished, so I can't take credit for more than paying the rent."

While Simon dumped the makeshift ice pack and retrieved a real one from the freezer, he asked, "Something to eat?"

Favoring her injured leg, Dakota slumped into a chair. "I'm always up for food."

That made Simon smile. True, she did have a fast metabolism that she constantly fed.

First, he gave her the aspirins with a glass of water, then handed her the ice pack. She automatically put it against her thigh, which seemed to be her worst injury. Simon looked at the large bruise on her forehead, her black eye, and the other marks on her face.

Fury and empathy warred inside him.

"What are you in the mood for? Sandwich, soup, cereal, eggs?"

"Cheese sandwich?"

"Got it." When Simon opened the fridge, she set the ice pack on the table and came forward.

"This is ridiculous. I don't need you to wait on me."

"I don't mind."

"But I do. It's not what I'm used to and it makes me feel like a slug. Let me get the sandwich and you can do the coffee."

Simon studied her. She'd regained some warmth in her cheeks, and she wasn't trembling as much. Dakota Dream was not a woman to be coddled.

"Your leg is feeling better?"

"Let's put it this way. Making a sandwich isn't going to hurt it any more, but sitting and stewing is for the birds."

"All right." He pointed out the location of plates, glasses, bread, and chips. "Make me one, too."

She glanced at him over her shoulder. "You're allowed, with your training?"

"I'm strict, but not that strict. One sandwich won't hurt anything."

"Long as you're sure."

After they sat at his small table with the

food in front of them, coffee for Dakota, water for Simon, she went back to icing her various pains. She took turns, first holding the ice against her face, then her leg. She timed it perfectly, like a pro, making Simon wonder how much experience she had with injuries — and why.

Simon said, "Next question."

"Gee, I'm starting to feel like a world spy being interrogated."

Teasing? By the moment, she returned to her old self. "How do you know Barber? You realize that I assumed it was his vocation, not his name."

"I know." She grinned at him, but it was a crooked grin, given the battery on her face. "He thinks the different slogans are funny."

The sweatshirt she wore now said, BLOW JOB? and had a picture of a blow dryer in the background.

Brows raised and temperature elevated, Simon said, "That one's suggestive."

"Yeah, Barber claims he had this one made specifically for me. It's huge, so I usually wear it to sleep in, not in public. But I didn't even think about it when I pulled it out of my suitcase."

"You and Barber seem really close."

"We are." With most of her sandwich gone, Dakota downed half her coffee and said nothing more.

She didn't plan to elaborate? Simon snorted. He wouldn't let her off that easy. "How did the two of you meet?"

She set down her coffee and began pulling at the crust on her bread. Not to discard it, but to eat it. "It's a long story."

"I'm not going anywhere."

She sighed, gave him a grievous look, and wolfed down more food. Around a mouthful, she said, "I'm wrong. Actually, it's a short story." She chewed, swallowed. "In addition to the band, Barber teaches self-defense. I met him at some classes."

"What kind of classes?"

"Muay Thai. Remember I told you that I'd been studying off and on for three years now? Barber's been instructing me. I've also taken some grappling and kickboxing classes."

"With Barber?"

"No. He only teaches Muay Thai." She tilted her head. "He's really good, Simon. With some additional training, he could probably compete in the SBC. But he's totally into his music and only teaches now to stay in shape."

"How good are you?"

"Good enough to defend myself, but without enough guts." Propping her elbow on the table and her forehead on her hand, she slumped. "Like on the stairs tonight. Defending myself never entered my mind. I panicked, and forgot everything I know. Like I said, I have some courage issues."

"Anyone can be caught off guard, especially when an attack comes from behind."

She sat back in her seat and stared at him. "It wouldn't happen to you."

Simon didn't deny that, but he did qualify it. "I've been studying mixed martial arts most of my life, and competing for over a decade. You can hardly compare yourself to me."

"Because it's instinctive for you." She nodded. "I know. I wish I could learn to react like that. I need to somehow trigger an automatic response." She sat forward again, and her voice rose in frustration. "What good is it to learn technique if I don't apply it? I might as well be an ignorant, helpless girl."

"I can't see you ever being ignorant or helpless."

She sent him a look of disgust. "Then you don't have much imagination or insight."

What the hell did that mean? "Dakota . . ."

In a massive mood switch, she shoved back her chair. "Sorry, Simon, but I've changed my mind. I'd rather sleep alone."

"Why?"

She headed to the sink with her plate. "I'm getting whiny, and I despise whiny women. It disgusts me. It's stupid."

Simon tried to keep her talking, to give him a chance to figure her out. "You're not whiny, Dakota, but under the circumstances, you'd be allowed."

Her laugh had the effect of nails on a chalkboard. "No thanks. Hopefully I just need some sleep." She put her dishes in the dishwasher, returned the ice bag to the freezer, and without looking at him, turned to leave the room. "Thanks for the food and meds and . . . attention. Right now I —"

Simon grasped her wrist.

And to his surprise, she turned on him. He ducked one fist, then another.

Shooting to his feet, Simon said, "Dakota, calm down."

Silently, not even breathing loud, she struggled until Simon let her go and held up his hands.

She stumbled back from him so quickly that she bumped into the sink.

From across the kitchen, they stared at each other.

Still keeping his hands out in a supplicating position, Simon said, "I'm sorry. I didn't mean to . . ." *What?* Dakota stood in front of him as if held at gunpoint. "I'm sorry," he said again, his voice firm.

"No." Dakota didn't look away from him. "It's not you, it's me." But she didn't move. Her gaze still locked on his, she curled her hands into fists and clenched her jaw. "God, I feel like an idiot."

So did he. "What happened?"

She shook her head. "I don't know. You grabbed me, and I . . ." Her muscles tightened more. "I don't like to be grabbed."

"I wasn't grabbing you, honey. I mean, not with any evil intent. I just wanted to talk."

"Yeah, I know." Her shoulders were so taut, she looked ready to snap.

Simon struggled to find the right words. "I only wanted to ask you why you had the change of heart."

Expression pained, she nodded. "Yeah. I know."

With her so spooked, there didn't seem to be any reason to beat around the bush. He might not have known Dakota that long, but he knew genuine fear when he saw it.

Simon put his hands on his hips. "Your husband abused you, didn't he?"

Her eyes narrowed and her mouth firmed in mulish denial.

Too many things were coming together

for Simon to relent. "He hurt you, and that's why you took self-defense." He eased one small step closer to her. "What happened tonight, the push down the stairs and being here alone with me, brought it all back."

"So you're not only a fighter, you're a shrink, too?"

The bitter wisecrack didn't faze Simon; he recognized it as a defensive tactic.

But the idea that someone had hurt Dakota damn near killed him. "You think he's the one who shoved you tonight?"

He expected her to dodge the question, to maybe tell him to butt out of her life or to flat-out refuse to answer.

Instead, she lifted her chin. "I'd bet my favorite boots on it."

Even now, she had her wit, and Simon knew he was a goner. "He's the one you thought was watching you yesterday."

"Someone definitely was. I felt it. But Barnaby denied keeping tabs on me. So who else would it be?"

That she'd trust him made Simon that much more determined to protect her. "If you're so sure, then why not tell the police?"

"What would be the point? He's not stupid, so he probably has an alibi lined up if anyone asks." Her mouth twisted. "He always has an alibi. He always covers his tracks."

He always has an alibi. Those words reverberated in Simon's head. Had the bastard attacked her before this? How many times?

Either Dakota didn't notice his rage or she ignored it. "Besides, where he's concerned, I'll admit I'm paranoid. What if it wasn't him?" She shook her head. "I won't do anything without proof. I tried that once and it didn't do me a damn bit of good."

In that moment, Dakota looked very alone and resigned to staying that way. Simon couldn't take it. "I won't let him hurt you."

At his announcement — which surprised him as much as it did Dakota — she seemed to wilt. Just as quickly, she straightened with new resolve. She looked at his face, his throat, down to his chest and arms. Lower.

She breathed faster, harder. "I've changed my mind again."

Simon didn't understand her at all. "Okay." He tried to read her expression, but couldn't. "What do you . . . ?"

In three long strides, Dakota reached him. Going on tiptoe, she grabbed his head and yanked his mouth down to hers. She was so frantic that her first attempt missed his mouth and landed on his chin. "Damn." She tried again, this time hitting the mark.

She kissed him. Hard.

Simon was stunned. In a very short time, Dakota had gone from defensive to shaken to sexually dominant. He tried to take her shoulders, to hold her back.

She wouldn't let him.

"Sit down, Simon."

Without giving him a chance to comply, she pushed him backward toward his seat. Simon let her have her way. She was rough, determined, and he fell into the chair off balance. Before he could figure out how to handle this new mood of hers, she straddled his lap.

What the hell was this?

His cock didn't care — whatever it was, he liked it.

Her long legs opened around him, her lush bottom snuggled atop his crotch. He was sinking fast, and he knew it.

Dodging her kiss, trying to be noble, Simon said, "Dakota, wait."

"Be quiet." With ruthless pursuit, her mouth found his again and she kissed him with blind hunger, grinding her mouth against his, nipping him with her teeth. Simon was both concerned and wildly aroused.

Concern won out.

Doing his best not to hurt her, he turned

his head away and held her shoulders. "Hold up, honey."

"For what?" She licked his jaw, gave a love bite to his neck, his shoulder. "You said you wanted me."

"Ow, damn it, Dakota —"

Her hot little tongue soothed over his skin, ending with a soft, luscious suck. "You taste so good, Simon." Rubbing her nose against him, she added, "And you smell even better."

She sounded turned on, but damn it, he didn't trust this swift about-face. That didn't stop him from getting a boner, but he wasn't a man who lacked control. Just the opposite. And he *did* care for her, so before things got too far out of hand, Simon caught her wrists and pinned her arms behind her back.

Her wild gaze shot up to his, and her voice went high and shrill. "What are you doing?"

"Shhh." Gently, Simon kissed her. "Slow down and talk to me, sweetheart."

"Talk?" She struggled to free her arms, realized she couldn't, and thrust herself away from him so hard and fast that she toppled them both from the chair.

Simon felt them falling. With one arm, he kept Dakota close to protect her while bracing for the impact with his other arm. They hit the floor with a thud, Dakota pinned under him.

She went perfectly still for two heartbeats. Then exploded. "Get *off.*"

Knowing he couldn't let this continue, Simon again caught her wrists and pinned them above her head. Her knee struck him hard in the back. "Damn it." He scooted down until he sat on her thighs.

He had her totally immobilized.

And she hated it.

"Dakota, listen to me."

Her body bowed, lifting him from the floor. Her eyes squeezed shut, her teeth clenched.

Jesus, he hated this. But what to do? Let her molest him? Let her use him for . . . what? He had no real idea.

What if she despised him for it later? And how the hell would that work anyway, when she seemed on the verge of panicking with every other breath?

Transferring both her wrists into one of his hands, Simon touched her cheek. "Dakota, stop fighting me and listen to me."

"Go to hell."

"You attacked me, honey, not the other way around. I don't want to hurt you. I would *never* hurt you. You know that."

She turned her face as far away from him

as she could manage. "Let me go, Simon."

"I will. I promise. But will you please talk to me first?"

"Fine." She swallowed. Took two breaths. Finally, she looked at him. "We'll talk."

Having no idea what to say, Simon waited. Seconds ticked by like gunshots. Their combined heartbeats rocked together.

Dakota squeezed her eyes shut, then slowly opened them. "Simon?"

"Yeah, honey."

"I have a little problem."

He'd figured out that much. "I know." He offered up a small smile of encouragement. "Wanna tell me what it is?"

She no longer struggled, but she was still so frozen. "I'm not sure it's worth the trouble."

"I'm more than sure that it is." Carefully, Simon lowered himself over her, but only for an instant, only long enough to hold her close and then roll to his back so that she rested atop him. "Better?"

She sighed loudly, hid her face against his chest, and truly relaxed. "I'm an idiot, but yeah."

Simon smoothed her wild hair down her back. "Will you tell me about it?"

"I guess I've got nothing better to do, do I?"

Patience, Simon decided, and just kept stroking her hair, her back. Despite the awful situation and possible reasons for it, he enjoyed the special moment of closeness with her.

Finally, he felt like he might get some real insight into the elusive Dakota Dream.

"When I was seventeen, I ran away from home." Her fingers curled into his shirt. "Talk about stupid. I don't know what I was thinking."

"You were seventeen, just a kid. And kids do things they later regret."

"I was a thoughtless, spoiled brat."

He stroked down her back to her hip, and back up again. "I find that hard to believe." She said nothing. "Was there a reason you ran away?"

"Yeah." She squirmed around and got comfortable on him. "To marry Marvin Dream and live a fairy-tale life."

Marvin Dream. "So that's how you got the name?"

"The name and a whole lot more." She rubbed her cheek against him. "My mom didn't like Marvin at all. When she found out that we'd been hanging around together, she refused to let me see him. He was so much older than me, or at least, at the time, it seemed that way."

Simon stared up at his kitchen ceiling. When he'd set out to have Dakota, he hadn't imagined anything like this. His ballsy, outspoken Dakota giving confessions on the kitchen floor. It boggled his mind. "How much older?"

"Five years."

So when she was seventeen, he was twenty-two. "A big gap at that age. He was a man, and as you said, you were a kid."

Dakota shifted, moving to sit up beside him. She kept one hand on his abdomen, and with the other she tucked her hair behind her ear. "I can do this better if I'm looking at you."

She could look all she wanted, as long as she kept talking. "Do you want to stay here, or go to the living room?"

Looking around at his floor, the toppled chair, her mouth slipped into a sheepish smile. "I guess a couch would be more conventional, huh?"

Stretched out on the tile, at his leisure, Simon reached out to touch a long lock of her hair. "Doesn't matter to me, honey. Wherever you're most comfortable."

"You are the oddest man." She pushed to her feet and offered him a hand up.

She was less than half his size. She'd been through an attack. She was now black and blue, and swollen. She had something horrible in her past.

And she wanted to help him off the floor.

One novelty after another, Simon thought, and took her hand.

Dakota had strength, both physical and emotional. Keeping hold of his hand, limping only a little, she led him back to his living room and then plopped down on the couch. She'd left the ice pack in the kitchen, so she rubbed absently on her thigh.

Simon eased down close beside her.

"Barber says I should get counseling, but I don't have time for that mumbo jumbo."

So Barber already knew all about it. Simon stewed over that.

"There's no point anyway." She met his probing gaze. "Since I don't date, it usually isn't an issue."

"Is this a date?"

She grinned. "More like me chasing you down at a party I wasn't invited to."

"I'm glad you showed up." Simon meant it. "I'm damn sorry you got hurt, but seeing you in that dress and heels was . . . interesting."

"Interesting, huh?"

And enlightening and provoking, but he saw no reason to share all that. "I also enjoyed hearing you sing. You're good."

Accepting the compliment without modesty, she said, "Thanks."

Simon teasingly lowered his brows. "Now, about this date."

"Should I have said I don't have sex?" All innocent, she touched his chest, stroked, then flattened her hand there and looked up at him with big, serious eyes. "I don't, you know. Not since my divorce." Moving carefully with her injuries, she turned on the couch to face him, and started stroking him again. "But now . . ."

Simon kept his smile contained. "Eventually, we will be intimate."

Her hand stilled. "Yeah."

"No objections?"

Her shoulders lifted. "I kind of figured that we'd end up there. That is, if I stay in town."

"Stay."

She nodded. "I think I will. Maybe. I *want* to. We'll have to talk about it."

She sounded very undecided. Simon caught her hand and tugged her toward him. As gentle as he could manage, he kissed her and whispered again, *"Stay."*

Her gaze darted away from his. "Before we get to that, remember my little freak-out in the kitchen? Well, you might've figured out already that I can't bear to be held down, or out of control."

"Held down, as in beneath me when we make love?"

His plain speaking brought her wide eyes back to his. "Being" — she cleared her throat — "*beneath* you would count as not in control. It's not that I want to freak out. I don't. I hate it. But sometimes it just happens."

"Sometimes, meaning you've tried with other men?"

She snorted. "No. Meaning that in my Muay Thai practices, I could only go so far without panicking."

A deep breath didn't alleviate the tightness in Simon's chest. "You practiced with Barber?"

"Yeah."

"And he had you under him?"

"Well, duh." She rolled her eyes over his venomous expression. "You know how training goes. Grappling isn't really part of Muay Thai, but you practice moves, and then sometimes it's actual sparring. Someone is in the guard, someone is mounted."

Jealousy was a new emotion for Simon and he had a hard time getting it under wraps. "I could practice with you."

"Wake up, Simon. You already saw in the kitchen how successful that'd be." Shaking

261

her head, she said, "No, I'm admitting defeat on that one. I don't like it, and I don't think I ever will."

Simon thought about it, then shrugged. "I liked having you in my lap." Hell, he could think of a dozen ways to have her where she'd think she was in control. "If we'd both been naked, that would have worked just fine for me."

Color bloomed in Dakota's face.

It was interest, not embarrassment.

Trailing his fingers down her cheek to her jaw, her throat to her shoulder, Simon caressed her. "Whatever it takes, Dakota."

Agitated breaths drew his attention to her breasts. "Then why did you stop me?"

"You're hurt." Moving his hand lower, Simon skimmed down the outside of her left breast. "You had a bad scare today and you aren't thinking clearly. I don't want to take advantage of you. And there's a lot more we have to talk about yet."

At the mention of talking, she yawned. "The gabfest will have to wait. I really am getting tired." She started to rise.

Simon gently held her in place. Reminding her of where they'd left off, he said, "You could change the last name, you know."

Before he'd finished, she was shaking her

head. "No. I took the name and I'll damn well keep it."

"Sort of like, you made your bed and now you intend to lie in it?"

Her chin lifted. "Something like that."

"When you remarry —"

She laughed. "Yeah, right. Me, marry again? No, thanks."

For now, Simon let that pass. Talking about marriage made him uneasy. Already he didn't want Dakota with anyone else, yet it was way too soon to think about her with him on a permanent basis. "Let's backtrack a minute. You said your mother didn't want you to see Marvin Dream, so you ran away."

"I was such a fool."

"Did Marvin know how your mother felt?"

"Oh, yeah. Mom told him to his face. At the time, I was so embarrassed that she'd treated me like a kid. Now . . ."

"Now you understand how she felt."

Her knee touched his thigh. Her hand clenched on his shirt. "Took me long enough. Too long, in fact."

"You eloped?"

"Just like a fairy tale, huh? Marvin was older and handsome, and strong, and he told me we didn't need anything from my mother as long as we had each other. I left behind most of my clothes and books and . . . everything. Marvin said he'd buy me whatever I needed." She shook her head and gave a hoarse laugh. "These days, anything I need I prefer to get for myself."

Except that Barnaby had something she wanted, and she couldn't get it for herself. Simon frowned, pushing that thought and the guilt it caused to the back burner; he had other, more pressing issues to resolve right now. "What did Marvin do to you?"

"He was a creep, that's all."

"I'm sure. But he was more than that, wasn't he?"

"Maybe." Dakota looked at his restraining hand still on her wrist.

Simon let her go, only to lace his fingers with hers instead. It wouldn't be easy to remember her fear, when he thought of her as so indomitable and outspoken, confident in every situation. "Tell me."

She gave up. "How about I give you the short story? Tomorrow, if you want more of the details, I can elaborate then."

Simon easily read her. She thought that tomorrow, he wouldn't want to know. She honestly believed he'd give up on her. "All right."

After a deep breath, she gave him the explanations he wanted. "Our marriage was a farce from the start. Marvin was abusive.

By the time I realized it, I was stuck. And then it didn't even matter because I returned home too late to ever see my mother again."

"When you said short story, you meant it."

"The details are . . . embarrassing."

Simon lifted her hand and kissed her knuckles. "Of all the things I want, what I want most is for you to be comfortable with me."

She laughed. "Really? Now why do I find that so hard to believe?"

"Because you were married to an asshole, and you haven't dated much since."

Expression bemused, she said, "It was a rhetorical question, Simon."

"I know." He lifted her hand again, and this time he kissed her wrist. "You assume I want sex first and foremost, right?"

"You did tell me that you thought I was sexy and that you hoped to get laid."

Remembering that less than auspicious moment, his mouth quirked. "You're very sexy, and I definitely want you. I know it'll happen eventually, so I can be patient. But trust, that's something else entirely."

"You want me to trust you?"

"Yes."

"Do you trust me?"

"I'm starting to."

"*Starting* to?" She yanked her hand away, but she was smiling, too.

Simon leaned forward and kissed her. "One step at a time, Dakota." And while they were both stepping . . . Simon's arm went around her. "About your marriage — I take it the honeymoon didn't last long?"

"A few weeks, maybe a month." As if they'd known each other longer, Dakota settled in beside him, putting her head into the crook of his shoulder. "We were poor, but at seventeen, who cares about money or material possessions?"

Most everyone he knew, regardless of age, but Simon didn't say so.

"I had Marvin and for a while that seemed like enough. Then I realized what he expected from me, when I'd never had that many responsibilities. He insisted that I work, which was okay except that it wasn't easy to get a decent job at seventeen. He helped me to fudge my age and get hired on at some seedy places. He also wanted me to keep our run-down apartment looking good, buy the groceries, do the laundry, have dinner ready for him every night, and . . ." She quieted, the words falling off into nothingness.

Without her saying it, Simon knew what

Marvin had wanted: He'd expected her to keep him satisfied in bed.

He was glad that Dakota couldn't see him or the anger in his expression.

"None of that was *horrible,*" she explained. "But he didn't want me to visit my mother either because he knew she didn't like him. I felt guilty about the last fight we'd had. I wanted to talk to her, to show her that I was doing all right for myself so she wouldn't worry. And I wanted to see if she'd softened toward me at all."

"Marvin refused to let you see her?"

She nodded. "We argued about it." Agitated, Dakota shifted, looked up at him, then away. "I told him I was going to see her no matter what he said, and he slapped me. Not a punch or anything, but it blacked my eye. I didn't want my mother to see that, so I didn't go."

Simon had expected physical abuse, but having it confirmed made his gut clench. He didn't know what to say, so he said nothing at all. He knew the story was going to get worse, and he braced himself.

"After that first time, he lost his temper a lot, sometimes for no reason at all. Every time he got mad, the situation got worse. I realized that I'd made a colossal mistake. But after a few months, when I'd had enough and knew I had to leave, he . . ." Dakota faltered, drew another breath. She tilted her head back and locked her gaze with Simon's. "He raped me."

CHAPTER 11

Simon went cold inside.

Rushing into defensive speech, Dakota said, "I know, everyone thinks a husband can't rape a wife, but —"

"I'm not everyone."

She paused, and her small nod thanked him. "It wasn't like being attacked by a stranger. I know there's a difference, a huge difference. I really do. But Marvin made sure that I'd hate what he did to me. He deliberately made it an ugly punishment."

Plain and simple, Simon wanted to kill the bastard. If Marvin Dream were to materialize right now, Simon would demolish him with pleasure.

"Afterward," Dakota whispered, "when he finished with me and started to stand up, I was so furious, so sickened and so afraid and fed up, that I kicked him in the face."

"Good for you."

"I was still wearing my shoes."

"I hope you broke his goddamned nose."

"No. But I did bloody it. And seeing his own blood did something to Marvin. He went crazy. Crazier than I'd ever seen him." Dakota sat up, moving away from Simon. "He stabbed me."

A rush of heat chased away the chill of Simon's anger. *"What?"*

"He had a switchblade that he always carried. Not a teeny tiny one, but not exactly a giant blade either. I'd seen it plenty of times because he'd get it out and show it off to people, or he'd just sit and polish it, sometimes for an hour or more." Dakota twisted a little, lifted the hem of her sweatshirt, and showed a narrow scar on her left side below her ribs.

Staring at that thin cut, Simon's vision blurred. "Jesus."

So unemotional that it spooked Simon, she said, "That's the worst one, and none of them are really bad." Then she raised the sleeve on her right arm and showed another silvery scar on her forearm. "He got me here, too, and once on my thigh. After that, he just looked at me, like maybe he was shocked, too. He punched a hole in the wall and stormed out of the apartment."

"The police —"

"I didn't tell them right away. I wanted to

leave, but I didn't have my own car, and wasn't sure when Marvin might come back. I didn't really have any friends or anyplace to go. I'd alienated my mother, and put myself in that situation, and I was so . . . embarrassed and ashamed of myself."

Simon wanted to crush her close, but given their topic and the guarded look in her eyes, he didn't dare.

"After I stopped feeling sorry for myself, I cleaned up the cuts and realized they weren't life threatening or anything. They stopped bleeding and didn't even hurt that much."

More appalled than he could ever remember being, Simon stared at her.

"Marvin stayed gone all night, and that next morning a PI found me. He told me that my mother had been hurt in a bad accident. She was in a coma and not expected to live." Dakota covered her mouth with a shaking hand. "I forgot about me and went home to see my mom."

Simon swallowed down his rage. It was so much for a young woman to have to deal with. Though he somehow already knew the answer, he said, "She didn't recover, did she?"

"No." A new sadness seemed to weigh Dakota down. "The last time I'd talked to

Mom was in that big argument before I ran away with Marvin. We both said awful things, but hers were warranted." She shook her head. "Mine weren't."

Simon wanted to pull her into his lap. He wanted to comfort her somehow. But he knew Dakota wouldn't appreciate that. She'd see it as a weakness on her part.

"I stayed with her until she passed away, but she never regained consciousness so she never heard how sorry I was."

"Did you ever see Marvin again?"

"Yeah, I saw him." That fatalistic sadness evaporated. Determination took its place. "Even before Mom passed away, he came to the house and wanted to see me. He tried being apologetic, but I was so numb I didn't care about him or what he said or thought. Then he got threatening. For a month, he hounded me. He kept coming to the house and calling me."

"He scared you."

"Yeah, he did. After Mom's funeral, I talked to the police. I told them about Marvin's attack, but I hadn't yet filed for divorce and so much time had passed, they didn't think much would come of it. They said everyone would want to know why I was still married to him if he was so bad and why I hadn't come to the police right away if he'd really attacked me."

"They didn't do their job."

"They were honest with me, that's all. They said they'd try, but truthfully, I didn't have it in me to push the issue."

"What about your father?"

She dismissed that with a shake of her head. "Dad died when I was eight. He was out of town on business, had a car wreck, and . . ." She shrugged. "I remember that my mom cried for weeks."

"So after your divorce and your mother's death, you were all alone?"

Her shoulders lifted in a shrug.

She hadn't had anyone to help her deal with Marvin, to share her grief or her pain. "That must have been difficult at your age."

"In some ways. I hadn't yet gotten my GED so finding work was almost impossible. But things really improved when I met Barber and he let me perform with him a few times."

Grateful that she'd had someone, Simon tamped down on the surge of renewed jealousy. "Perform?"

"He'd run an ad for a singer to round out the band. I'd never really thought about singing professionally before, but I'd enjoyed it in school and I needed money so I figured, why not? The moment I met Barber, it seemed like he knew me and my situation. He went out of his way to make things easier for me." She smiled. "I guess he's the closest thing I have to a big brother."

If Barber had his way, Simon thought, he'd be more than that; he'd made that clear. "I'm glad he was there for you."

"Singing got me through the rougher times. I love it. And when I can, I volunteer to help find missing teens. I've recovered a few." Her smile flickered. "It's great, really great, to see a family reunited."

And now she wanted to reunite him with his father? Somehow, Simon didn't think so. So what motivated her the most? He'd have to figure that one out another time.

Simon trailed his fingers through her hair, lifting it away from her face and examining her black eye. "You haven't had sex since your husband?"

The question took her by surprise. "God, no. I haven't had any interest, either." Trying to act cavalier, she patted his cheek. "Till you, that is."

Odd, Simon thought, that he'd be the one. Not that he was overly modest; he knew women found him attractive. It was a running joke in the SBC that women threw themselves at him. It was because of the female fans that he'd been dubbed "Sub-

274

lime" instead of a more appropriate kick-ass name.

Before Dakota, he'd never really cared or paid that much attention to it. "I'm flattered."

"But not surprised, so don't pretend that you are."

"All right." He cupped his fingers around her skull and brushed the delicate, bruised skin beneath her eye with his thumb. "Thank you for sharing."

"Pretty pathetic, huh?"

"Sad. But no, not pathetic."

"If you say so." With an exaggerated yawn, she stretched and rose to stand in front of Simon. "Since you've so generously offered me a night here, I think I'll turn in."

Simon didn't move. "I want you to sleep with me."

Hands on her hips, she stared down at him. "I thought you said I was too banged up."

"Sleep, Dakota."

"Oh, yeah. You did clarify that once already, huh?"

Her cheeky grin didn't fool Simon. "Will you sleep with me?"

"I don't think it's a good idea."

"You can trust me."

"Yeah, I know. I do." She crossed her

arms. "But I'm not sure I trust myself. I've got a lot of aches and pains, and today's been an overload of crazy crap. You've already been so nice about everything. . . ."

Simon stood. "That's because I'm a nice guy. Always remember that." He took her hand and led her down the hall to his room.

"I need to shower."

Her blurted statement showed her nervousness. "Okay. Get your stuff together and I'll get you some towels."

Watching Dakota dig out panties and a long-sleeved T-shirt from her bag, Simon felt a little edgy himself. Despite the mix of sympathy, rage, and concern over her past, he was at half-mast. He wanted her, and there wasn't a damn thing he could do about it.

In the five years he'd spent with Bonnie, of course there'd been nights when they'd slept without having sex. But he'd never strayed. In five long years, Bonnie was the only woman he'd been with sexually.

Since leaving her, sex hadn't even been a consideration. He had too much to do to prepare for his fight.

But now . . . sharing a chaste bed with Dakota would be torturous. Sleeping without her, however, would be worse.

He went into the bathroom and found her

standing there fully dressed. Her demeanor was one of defiance and dogged determination.

"Here you go." He laid the towels on the toilet seat and went to the tub. "I'll adjust this for you, and then wait in the bedroom."

"Appreciate it."

When Simon had the water just right, he turned to her, slid his fingers over her jaw, and bent to kiss her with ultimate care.

She kissed him back, but didn't object when he pulled away.

"I'll be right outside if you need anything. Just give a yell."

She nodded, and the second he left the room, he heard the door lock.

Twenty minutes later, the water still ran and Dakota hadn't yet come out. With the covers turned back and the television on, Simon had propped himself up in the bed. Normally he slept naked, but in consideration of Dakota, he'd chosen to wear flannel lounge pants.

He didn't watch the TV.

He didn't relax.

He was too busy listening for Dakota.

When the water finally shut off, Simon stared at the door. She'd be stepping out of the tub right now. Wet. Naked.

As he listened to the subtle sounds of her

dressing and watched the shift of light from beneath the bathroom door, he breathed slow and deep. He was taut and anxious and rigidly in control of himself.

The bathroom door opened.

Dakota looked toward the bed where Simon reclined, at his leisure. He appeared totally relaxed, as if having a woman join him in bed for sleeping purposes was nothing out of the ordinary. And of course, after his longtime relationship with Bonnie, it wouldn't be.

For her, it was about as routine as a trip to the moon.

Dressed only in an oversized T-shirt and panties, her hair now loose, she shivered and gooseflesh rose on her skin. "I'm done."

Simon stared at her legs. "Feel better?"

"Yeah." On top of looking relaxed, Simon also looked wonderful, almost too wonderful to be true. The idea of curling up beside him thrilled her.

As long as she could keep her ridiculous fear under wraps.

Faking a yawn, she said, "I think I'm ready to sleep."

Pulling his gaze off her body and onto her face, Simon said, "Come on." He patted the empty side of the bed. "Climb in or you'll get chilled."

Without giving herself more time to think on it, Dakota rushed over and crawled under the covers.

Simon turned his head to look at her. "Wanna watch a movie?"

Oh. She focused on the television. Maybe she didn't need to fake-sleep yet. "What's playing?"

"I can skip around the channels and see."

As keyed up as she felt, a movie would be a great way to unwind a little. "As long as you don't pick a sappy love story, I'm in."

They had just settled on an ancient horror flick when Simon's phone rang. Without a word, he handed the TV remote to Dakota and reached over to the bedside table to grab up the cordless.

Forgetting the movie, Dakota listened in as Simon apparently talked with someone important. After cordial greetings, he threw back the covers and sat up on the side of the bed. A few minutes later, he pushed to his feet to pace the room.

A soft, loose pair of cotton flannel pants rode low on his trim hips. He wore nothing else. He had a gorgeous body. She visually measured the breadth of his wide shoulders, the solid strength of his biceps and forearms. As he turned, she looked at his back and imagined rubbing her hands over him. His skin looked sleek and dark, and she already knew he'd be warm to the touch.

Dakota was so enthralled in studying Simon's body that she missed most of the conversation — until he looked at her.

After snaring her in his gaze, he said, "I can make it tomorrow, but I'd rather wait if —" He frowned, nodded and said, "All right. No, no, it's not a problem at all. I appreciate the opportunity. Of course. Yeah, thanks. You too." He disconnected the call, but remained standing, watching her.

Dakota had a feeling he was about to share bad news. "What's up?"

"I need to go out of town tomorrow."

Not so bad. "Where to?"

"Vegas. There's a promotional gig. . . ." The words trailed off as he looked at the shape of her body beneath the covers. In obvious frustration, he rubbed a hand over his head. "You've heard of *The Sports Connection?*"

"A talk show, right? Athletes get on there and clown around and stuff."

"Yeah. Someone canceled on them, so now they have an opening."

Dakota sat up in excitement. "And they want *you?*"

He smirked at her surprise. "Incredible, huh?"

Flushing, she rushed to say, "I didn't mean it *that* way."

"I know. Actually, I travel my ass off doing promotion." He didn't look happy about it. "I just got back from Palm Springs, and I was in New York before that."

"What kind of stuff do you do?"

Simon shrugged. "There was a lengthy documentary on Dean with me as his trainer. There are always ads — you know, dressed in athletic shorts, or wearing certain running shoes. Power drinks, customized mouthpieces." He ran a hand over his smooth head. "I've even done ads for razors."

Dakota couldn't believe how casual he was about it. "You're a celebrity."

"In small, exclusive circles, with a contained audience."

"No way. The whole world is talking about the SBC. It's overtaken boxing."

"Maybe." He paced in front of her. "The talk show is nothing new, and I'd pass on it in a heartbeat, but that was Drew Black on the phone."

"The owner of the SBC?" Dakota had followed Drew's story and knew how instrumental he'd been in making the SBC a highly recognized association. "Do you know him well?"

"Yeah, sure. He's a good guy. When I told him I was returning to fight, he jumped all over it. They've been giving it top billing, so it'd be lousy of me to turn down any additional promotion for the organization."

"Of course you wouldn't turn them down! It's an awesome offer."

Very softly, Simon said, "I don't want to go."

She could see that. "Well, for heaven's sake, why not?"

He gave her a look that spoke volumes.

"Oh, come on." Dakota crawled over to sit on the edge of the mattress, facing him. "You can't go changing your itinerary on account of me."

"Why not?"

He had to be kidding. "I'll be here when you get back."

The intensity of his stare unnerved her. "Will you?"

Oops. Until she said it, she hadn't really made the decision to stay. Simon knew it, too. Hoping to retrench, Dakota said, "Maybe."

He took a step closer to her. "Too late, honey. You said it, now promise me that you meant it, and I'll go to Vegas with fewer misgivings."

When she hesitated, he said, "Or I could still call Drew back and cancel —"

"That's blackmail."

He shrugged.

Dakota doubted he really meant it. Hadn't he just said he felt obligated to go? But she didn't want him conflicted over such a fun opportunity, so she rolled her eyes and said, "All right, all right. I'll be here."

Smiling, Simon set the phone back on the nightstand and said, "Scoot over, woman."

Putting an end to the discussion, he had them both settled back in bed in no time. With an arm around her shoulders, Simon tugged her in close. Dakota rested her cheek on his naked chest, her hand on his bare abdomen.

In that position, she didn't feel the least bit threatened. But she did feel warm and secure and . . . excited.

By silent agreement, they watched the movie.

Or at least, Dakota tried to watch it. But on every level, she was aware of the crisp chest hair tickling her cheek, the solid muscles and warm skin under her palm.

With every breath, she inhaled Simon's stirring scent.

With every heartbeat, her blood rushed a

little faster through her veins.

An hour later, she started to tremble with the need for more. It was unexpected, but then, she'd never gotten this close to a man except to grapple, and it wasn't the same. Not at all.

What she'd felt with Marvin couldn't compare to this. She'd been too young and inexperienced to understand her own needs. With him, her pleasure had come from the excitement of doing the taboo, of knowing an older guy wanted her, exploring the unknown.

Losing her virginity.

She'd been so immature, and wasted so much on him. But now, with Simon, every feeling was deeper, hotter, so sharp that it stole her breath away.

Ready to take a chance, Dakota smiled, looked up at him — and realized that Simon must have been exhausted.

He was sound asleep.

Amazed, Dakota turned her head further and stared at him in disbelief.

She knew he gave his all during every workout and practice session. His day started early and today it had run late. But still, how could he *sleep?*

Carefully, unwilling to wake him, she eased into a sitting position. Various aches and pains in her body vied for attention, but with Simon there beside her, offering her an opportunity to study him without reservation, she paid them no mind. Light from the television screen gave plenty of illumination to the room.

Even before meeting Simon in person, she'd admired him on television in pay-per-view events and in her DVD collection. She'd always thought him a devastatingly handsome man. Now, up close, she knew she'd missed so many nuances and details.

Everything about Simon Evans was gorgeous.

Dakota took her time scrutinizing his face. Even relaxed in sleep, there was an undeniable capability to the set of his features — the strong jaw, high cheekbones, firm lips. . . . She wanted to lean down and kiss him, but he obviously needed his sleep.

She loved his brows. They were thick, dark, and level, a perfect match to his incredible eyes. Never before had she thought of eyebrows in such a way, but on Simon, sexy described them best.

Years of competition hadn't left any disfiguring marks. There was no sign of a broken nose, and he didn't have cauliflower ears. He did have a few small scars, but they only added to his machismo.

He had a naturally dark complexion, but the sun had enriched his skin tone. Given the bronze of his shoulders and chest, Dakota believed that he did his morning jogs without a shirt.

Imagining the reaction of any woman who'd seen Simon run past, Dakota smiled. He probably left tongue-tied broads everywhere he went.

He certainly left her that way.

Growing more curious by the moment, she looked at his lap. The blankets concealed him, so she eased them away. Through the soft pants, she could make out the outline of his heavy sex.

Her temperature raised another few notches.

Earlier, he'd been bigger, thicker, maybe from a semi-erection. Because of her? Thinking that sent a thrill of delight up Dakota's spine.

Now, sound asleep, he looked full but softer, and she badly wanted to touch him, to weigh him in her hands and feel the heat of him.

Dangerous thoughts, given how they affected her.

Simon shifted then, raising one arm to put above his head. She held her breath until he stilled again and settled back into even breathing.

The underside of his arm was lighter, but just as muscled. The dark hair under his arm seemed very intimate, and very masculine.

With a sigh, Dakota settled back against the headboard, got comfortable, and continued to study him. Sometime later, she, too, fell asleep.

In the wee hours of the morning, the party finally broke up and Roger Sims came around to pay the band. He also invited them to prolong their contract, and without any other dates pressing, they agreed. Extending their stay in Harmony wouldn't be a hardship for any of them.

At the end of the gig, most of the band had alternate plans, so Barber knew they wouldn't be holding up the van for him. He didn't have to announce his plans with Bonnie.

Stretching to ease his tired muscles, he looked around the floor until he spotted her. Seeing her again gave him the same kick of hot desire. She lounged in a chair, eating him up with her gaze. Several empty glasses crowded her small table, proving she'd been sitting there a while.

Anticipation hummed in his veins.

Jumping down off the stage, Barber made his way over to her. Other than tilting back her head to maintain eye contact, she didn't move.

Sexual tension hummed between them.

Barber ran his finger along her sleek jawline. "Well, now," he said softly, "don't you look enticing, waiting here for me?"

Her smile came slow and easy, a little crooked — and Barber took a closer look at her eyes. He softly cursed.

She looked more than a little high.

Knowing his plans were shot to hell, he asked anyway. "How much you had to drink, darlin'?"

"Jus' enough to help pass the hours and hours and hours. . . ."

Shit. The slurred words said it all. Resigned to disappointment, Barber said, "Come on, then," and he took her upper arm to help her from her seat. "I'll see you home safe and sound."

Once upright, Bonnie collapsed against him and giggled like a maniacal schoolgirl. "I've been thinking and thinking about wha' we'll do, Barber."

Yeah, he had, too. But now he knew she'd pass out before reaching her bed, and he'd be going back to his hotel room alone.

When he had sex, he wanted the woman

288

wide-awake, willing, and very involved.

Not numb from alcohol.

"Let me have your keys, sugar."

She handed them over without argument. "I'm goin' to make you *crazy,*" she whispered suggestively.

"Shouldn't be too hard, considering you already got me halfway there." Getting her out the door and to her sporty little Mazda in the deserted parking lot took some finessing.

She kept trying to cop a feel of his crotch.

"And here I thought you were a lady," Barber chided, when he eased her grip away for the fifth time.

"Are you insinuatin' tha' I'm not respectable?" she asked with a little too much spit.

"Wouldn't dream of it." Just as Barber got the passenger-side door open for her, he heard the rush of footsteps behind him.

He jerked around in time to successfully dodge the chunk of pipe aimed at his head. Instead of caving in his skull, it caught him in the shoulder, slamming him sideways. Bonnie screamed at the top of her lungs.

She had very healthy lungs.

Going with the momentum, Barber hit the ground and rolled, surging back to his feet in one movement.

His shoulder thumped in pain, but not

enough to keep him from facing the attackers.

He encountered three men, one standing back as if in charge, another with a pipe, a third grabbing for Bonnie as she struggled.

Like hell.

They all wore ski masks, disguising their faces, but Barber didn't need to see a face to hit it.

He shot in low and took down the pipe wielder in a full body slam. Aware of the other two behind him, he landed one solid punch to the chin, hard enough to break the man's jaw. The idiot didn't even see it coming, and went limp from the blow.

Bonnie let loose with another scream, this one muffled from a hand over her mouth. Barber turned and saw her clamped up tight between the other two men.

Neither of them rushed him as he got to his feet. They were too busy looking at their fallen friend.

Taunting them, Barber said, "You're both too fucking stupid to know you're already dead." He grinned to add menace to the threat — and attacked.

Bonnie got tossed to the side.

The battle lasted no more than two minutes, but in that time, Barber took and gave his fair share of blows, and still came out ahead. The difference was his training. He knew how to strike with more power, to cripple with a blow, to fend off two against one.

In the end, the three men scrambled off together, disappearing into the darkness.

Barber watched them go, knowing it was the sound of sirens that had chased them away.

He turned to Bonnie. She huddled on the ground near the front tire of her car, covering her head with her arms and sobbing uncontrollably. Damn.

Dropping to his knees, Barber asked softly, "Are you hurt, little honey?"

She launched herself against him, nearly knocking him over again. He winced at the added discomfort to his battered body, and held her close.

Two police officers showed up.

Standing with Bonnie held to his chest, Barber explained what had happened. The officers called it in, took a report, promised to look around, and said they'd let Barber know if they found anyone.

He knew they wouldn't.

Tipping up Bonnie's chin, he said, "Shhh. You okay now?"

"Nooooo."

No? Huh. He wasn't quite expecting that

now that the excitement had ended. He didn't see any marks on her, and other than her hair falling loose, she looked okay.

"Yeah, well . . ." Feeling a bitch of a headache coming on, Barber rubbed the back of his neck. "So, what's hurt, exactly?"

She slugged him, stumbled away, then shot right back into his arms. Barber could feel her shaking all over, and accepted that attacks in darkened parking lots weren't exactly Bonnie's speed.

"It's okay now, sugar. Just take a few deep breaths."

"Get me oudda here." She hiccuped on a sob. "Please."

Sounded like a hell of plan. "Sure thing." Barber levered her away to see her pale face. "You need to visit a doc for anything?"

She shook her head and crowded back in close to press her face to his shoulder. Given the sound of her sniffling, Barber was afraid that she might be using his shoulder for a hanky.

Not an appealing thought.

Easing her away again, he got her in the car and in her seat with her seat belt latched. As he rounded the hood to the driver's door, he glanced at his shirt. Phew. Only damp from tears.

He seated himself, started the car, and

pulled out of the lot. "Where to, baby?"

She gave him mushy directions while she continued to shake and lament the fates.

Barber glanced at her. Not exactly the charitable sort, he couldn't wait to unload her. Even for a one-night stand, he wasn't used to weak women.

Hell, he was used to Dakota.

In all the years that he'd known her, with everything she'd been through, he'd never once seen Dakota drunk or heard her wail. For certain she didn't sit around sniffling and looking pathetic.

Following Bonnie's directions, Barber drove about twenty minutes while she kept her nose pressed to the window as if unsure of their exact destination. Finally, in inebriated excitement, she said, "Tha's it! Right there. Pull in to tha' driveway."

Barber parked in front of the darkened house, turned off the motor, and came around to open Bonnie's car door. "Once I've got you settled, I'll need to use your phone to call a cab."

Given her earlier display of lust, he expected an argument, but she only clamped on to him to steady herself and nodded agreement.

When they reached the shadowy porch, Barber let her lean on him so he could hunt on her key ring for her door key. Before he could find it, she lurched away, fell against the door, and banged both of her fists repeatedly against it.

Drunks, Barber thought. They did the oddest things.

Now where the hell was the key?

CHAPTER 12

A noise startled Simon awake. He jerked upright.

Dakota sat up, too. *"What?"*

The television sent flickering light around the room. They looked at each other, and Simon started to smile, but ended up wincing instead. "Oh, honey. Your poor face."

Confused, Dakota blinked at him. "Why, you flatterer you." She rubbed at one eye. "Did you really wake me up just to tell me how bad I look?"

"No." He didn't smile. "But damn. The puffiness is worse and the color's deepened." Simon grazed her cheek with his fingertips. "You're beautiful, but sort of in a pea green mixed with purple way now."

She made a face. "Perfect. I guess I should be glad you didn't scream."

He snorted. "I don't scream, Dakota."

She grinned as she looked around the room, then glanced at his lap. "I must have fallen asleep after you did."

Feeling like an ass, Simon ran a hand over his head. He remembered wanting her, but also enjoying her company, the closeness and familiarity. He'd listened to her breathing, felt the gentle thumping of her heartbeat . . . "Sorry about that. I guess I'm not used to the late nights right now."

"I didn't mind." Bobbing her eyebrows suggestively, she said, "It gave me a chance to check you out real close."

"You don't say?"

Still with her gaze on his lap, she said, "The last thing I remember was thinking how different you looked after you fell asleep."

"Different?"

"There." She nodded at his lap. "But you don't really look different anymore."

Knowing exactly what she meant, Simon grinned. "Morning wood. It's not you. Or rather, not you just yet. But give me a minute. . . ."

Another loud banging sounded, making Dakota jump and Simon scowl. Someone was at his door making a terrible racket.

"Ah, well. Male anatomy 101 will have to wait." Throwing back the covers, he said, "Stay here," and left the bed.

At the sound of yet more banging, he bel-

lowed, "Keep your pants on! I'm coming."
He couldn't imagine who'd be visiting him
at . . . he glanced at a clock on the wall and
cursed. It wasn't even close to morning yet.

He looked out the peephole — and stiffened in incredulity. "No fucking way." After
jerking the door open, he demanded, "What
the hell is this?"

Barber leaned against the porch wall, his
hands folded behind his back, his eyes
closed. He looked disgusted, half-
embarrassed, and resigned to the inevitable.

The second the door opened, Bonnie
threw herself against Simon and started
babbling. Fury and confusion warred together. Simon turned to Barber for an
explanation. "I'm listening."

Barber shrugged. "Sorry, bud." He
stepped in around Simon. "I thought she
was taking me to her place, but apparently
not."

"You got her drunk?" Simon pried Bonnie
loose and held her away from him.

"No, I didn't get her drunk. She got
herself drunk while waiting for the band to
finish."

Simon's eyebrows climbed high. He didn't
know Barber well, but given that he was
Dakota's friend, he'd had certain expectations about his character. Now Simon

wasn't so sure. He had no respect for men who took advantage of women. "And you were going home with her?"

"That's right." His expression turned stony. "In case you failed to notice, she's wasted. I wasn't about to let her drive. But then we got jumped in the parking lot, and Ms. Had-Too-Much-to-Drink gave me directions here. I didn't know it was your place. But all the same, I'd like to call a cab."

"Hell, no." Simon dodged Bonnie as she tried to kiss him. "You're not leaving her here with me, so forget it."

"What am I supposed to do with her?"

"Take her home."

Bonnie said, *"Noooo . . . ,"* and Simon found himself back in her embrace.

Barber shrugged. "You see my predicament. I can't exactly force her."

It needed only this, Simon thought. "Start at the beginning. What do you mean that you got jumped?"

"Just that. I was unlocking her car when three guys showed up." He rubbed his shoulder. "One was swinging a pipe."

Holding Bonnie at bay, Simon tried to maneuver her toward Barber. She wasn't having it. Somehow she plastered herself to him and put her face in his neck. He felt her mouth sucking at his throat, felt her nails digging into his flesh.

In disgust, Simon turned toward the couch — and found Dakota standing there. She looked both stunned and annoyed. Though she'd pulled on her jeans, she also had a blanket wrapped around herself. Her long hair hid the bruising on her face.

Perfect, Simon thought. Just freaking perfect. "I thought you were going to stay in bed."

Barber's head jerked up. At the sight of Dakota, his eyes widened and he looked genuinely shocked, then derisive. He tsked. "Well, well. Now I'm doubly sorry we intruded."

"What's going on?"

Barber snorted. "I don't need to ask you the same thing, do I?"

Simon growled. The sound startled him as much as it did Bonnie, who levered away in surprise.

Barber just laughed — the annoying ass. "Well, Dakota darlin', for the most part, mine is a tale of drunken revelry."

Stepping further into the room, Dakota said, "Funny. You don't sound drunk." Clutching the blanket with one hand, she used the other to tuck her long hair behind her ears.

As she did so, Barber took a second look. His slouched posture was exchanged with rigid outrage. "What the hell happened to you?"

Almost as quickly, he turned on Simon with accusation.

"Don't." With Bonnie squeezing the breath out of him, Simon said, "Not for a second."

Barber continued to glare, but not long. "Right." He headed toward Dakota. "You wouldn't be here with him if he'd done this."

"Don't be an idiot. Simon wouldn't hurt me any more than you would."

Simon watched as Barber gently held Dakota's face, examined each hurtful mark, then bent and kissed her brow.

And Dakota let him.

"Tell me what happened," Barber whispered.

"You first," Dakota insisted.

"No way, doll."

Rolling her eyes, Dakota said, "I fell down some stairs, that's all."

So she didn't plan to tell Barber her suspicions? For whatever reason, that made Simon feel better.

"Uh-huh." Barber continued to hold her in a far too familiar way. "Try again."

Seeking his help, Dakota looked at Simon in exasperation.

He peeled Bonnie's arms away and urged her into a chair. She fell back, sunk into the cushions, and looked ready to pass out.

"Now." He faced Barber. "You said you were jumped?"

"Yep. Three guys."

"Are you hurt?" Dakota asked.

"A little banged up." He smoothed her hair. "But not nearly as much as you."

Fed up with all the cooing, Simon put his arm around Dakota and hauled her in to his side — away from Barber. "You chased them off?"

"Wish I could tell it that way," Barber said. He made a point of noting Simon's possessive hold, then moved to the chair where Bonnie sat. He put a hand on her shoulder, maybe to help keep her there, or maybe to reassure her. Simon wasn't sure. "I was holding my own, probably broke the jaw on one of them, but then the cops showed up and they hightailed it out of there."

Dakota looked from Simon to Barber. "Did you recognize . . . that is, do you know who it was?"

"Sorry." He absently patted Bonnie as she

301

mumbled about something. "They wore ski masks."

Simon looked down at Dakota. "I don't believe in coincidences."

"Right." She let out a breath. "Me, either."

Barber eyed them both. "I already know that Dakota tangled with more than the stairs, so how about some details?"

Putting on a bright smile, Dakota said, "I do believe this is the perfect opening to coffee."

Simon shook his head. "You would think so." But he had to agree. "Let's all go into the kitchen. I'll make the coffee and we can compare stories. Maybe it'll help the police. Maybe not."

Bonnie fought her way off the chair, stumbled, and fell into Barber. "Doesn't anyone care what happened to me?"

"Course we do, darlin'." Holding her upright, Barber looked at Simon in accusation. "Jesus, man, you could have warned me."

Before Simon could reply, Dakota said, "I *did*." And then, to Simon's surprise, she joined Barber in helping Bonnie to the kitchen. "The coffee will help to sober her up."

One strange predicament after another, Simon thought. Maybe life with Dakota

would always be this way.

Life? He shook his head at himself and trailed behind the others. "Dakota thinks coffee is the cure-all for everything."

"That she does," Barber agreed.

"I can promise you one thing." Dakota looked over her shoulder at Simon and winked. "It can't hurt."

In that moment, Simon knew he was in trouble. Even in such a ridiculous situation, Dakota impressed him with her poise, amazed him with her control, and made him proud of her for her kindness.

Mallet wanted her. Barber did, too. For all he knew, there was a man around every damn corner just waiting for a chance with her.

Yet she'd chosen him.

She was an incredible woman. Maybe too incredible to ever let go.

"You didn't tell me he was a fighter."

Marvin Dream glanced at his moronic friend sitting in the front seat, and his temper got the better of him. He punched him in the back of the head, and when that didn't take the edge off his anger, he did it again and again.

Unfortunately for Marvin, violence only spurred him toward more violence. He liked it. He fed off it.

Cowering, the other man cried out. "What'd I do? What? Stop it." He ducked, trying to avoid Marvin's rage. Blood trickled from his already-injured ear.

But Marvin couldn't stop.

The driver swerved, cursed.

And Marvin realized that the cops might notice them if they drove crazy. That helped him regain his control, and he retreated to his seat in the back of the SUV.

"I'm bleedin' again," the other man accused in a whine as he rubbed his sleeve over his ear. He snuffled and hunched his shoulders, and cast a wary eye into the backseat at Marvin.

Jesus, Marvin thought. He hated gutless sheep who couldn't take a hit. No one ever stood up to him. No one ever dared.

Except Dakota.

She'd not only stood up to him, she'd kicked him in the face, left him, divorced him. . . .

His rage burned bright again, and he burst out, "Fucking idiot, I didn't know he was a fighter, now did I? He's a long-haired freak in a band. He plays a goddamned guitar."

"I'm sorry. I didn't mean nothin' by it, Marv."

"Shut up." Marvin shoved himself into the

corner of the vehicle, staring blindly out the window, stewing over his anger, and remembering.

He knew he'd grown obsessed over Dakota, but she was the most elusive woman he'd ever known. The longer he went without her, the more he wanted her. Over and over in his mind, he remembered his last night with her.

How she'd fought him.

How he'd taken her anyway.

His breath hitched in stirring excitement. He wanted to taste her again. He *needed* to feel her under him, struggling, cursing. . . .

But she'd moved on to other men. Too many other men. Tonight, while he'd lurked in the shadows, anonymous and unnoticed, Dakota had joined the band onstage. As if she no longer feared anyone or anything, she'd strutted her stuff in one hell of a show.

He'd seen every little detail. The flex of her strong thigh muscles accentuated by the clinging dress. The bead of sweat that ran down her chest and between her tits. How her long hair danced around those too-proud shoulders.

She'd deliberately made him wild to have her back.

With a sound of disgust, the driver interrupted Marvin's thoughts, saying, "I should have gigged that fucking musician for busting my jaw."

Marvin barely managed to keep the reins on his temper. "I don't want him dead, you asshole." His hands tightened into fists and he continued to stare out the window. "The cops will blow off a mugging, especially outside a bar. But a murder's altogether different. They won't let that go without a lot of digging. And I don't need that kind of hassle right now."

No, all he needed was Dakota back where she belonged. With him, tied to him, where he could control her. Thanks to Barnaby's cowardice, he'd found her again. He wouldn't let her get away this time.

That fantasy redirected his anger and gave him time to think.

To lessen their odds of being caught, they'd driven to Harmony separately, then hooked up to ride together to the bar. They hadn't used his car — he wasn't stupid. If anyone caught the license plates, they wouldn't lead to him and neither of his cronies had the cojones to point the finger at him.

They knew he'd kill without remorse.

The driver pulled over to the crowded convenience store so Marvin could reclaim his sports car. He got out, but instead of walking away, he tapped on the passenger-side window of the SUV.

Still holding his bleeding ear and looking pathetic, his friend rolled down the window.

Marvin gave him a friendly slap on the face. "Go home. No bars, no women. I mean it. I don't want either of you to fuck around or get into any trouble."

"All right."

Nodding, Marvin said, "You did good. Thanks."

Both men grinned at him, grabbing at the small token of appreciation like starving dogs.

His smile frozen, Marvin walked away before he got sick. Or enraged.

Once in his own car, he dialed his cell phone. Barnaby answered on the second ring.

"Hello?"

"Thanks to me, you should be hearing from your darling stepdaughter soon."

"Marvin?" The voice went gruff with suspicion and alarm. "What the hell did you do now?"

Stupid Barnaby. He thought himself so ruthless with his gambling habit and occasional fits of temper, but he didn't have the guts it took to play real hardball. In fact, if he hadn't taken matters into his own hands, Barnaby would still be married to that prissy, complaining bitch and living in middle-class squalor.

"I just offered the gal a little inspiration, that's all."

Marvin heard a gulp. "Did you . . . ?"

"Kill her?" He laughed at the thought. "There are a lot of things I want to do to Dakota, but offing her isn't one of them. Not yet anyway. Not till I get my fill."

"Haven't you done enough?" Barnaby snarled, and that made Marvin laugh.

"You have balls, Barnaby. I'm impressed." His voice hardened. "But don't shove aside the blame. You owe me big-time. We both know this is the only way you'll be able to pay, so don't blow it or the next time I visit, it won't just be your furniture I break."

"I accept my part in this mess."

"Lighten up, man. You should be hearing from Dakota soon." His ex-wife was nothing if not protective of others. Look at how she'd gone running back to that bitch mother of hers. Marvin shook his head. "When you hear from her, take the credit and she'll hand the fighter over to you."

Barnaby didn't ask for what he should take credit. He said only, "You sound sure of yourself."

"I always am." Marvin closed his phone

and tossed it on the leather seat beside him. Dakota might think herself tough, but when it came right down to it, he knew she was still just a sad, lonely, and scared little girl.

She couldn't bear to see anyone hurt, especially not one of her few friends. She'd deliver Simon, all right. Then Barnaby would get the money he owed. He'd get his debt cleared.

And Marvin would get so much more.

Two hours of talking and comparing hadn't lent them any more clarity to the situation. Barber only knew that there'd been three men of medium height, one of them muscular, the other two soft from overindulgence. He didn't know what they wanted, only that they'd intended no good.

He and Simon both thought the incidents were related.

Dakota knew they were.

They both assumed it was Marvin behind the attacks.

Dakota didn't have a single doubt.

While the two of them chewed over possibilities, she acted blasé, but she knew what she had to do. And soon. She wouldn't let Barber be hurt. She wouldn't let anyone be hurt because of her.

In the two hours that they talked, Bonnie

started to sober enough to become a bigger pain in the butt. She alternately wanted to cry on Simon, make out with him, or accuse him.

And when she wasn't doing that, she stayed busy glaring at Dakota and calling her names that were too incomprehensible to make out.

It amazed Dakota that even after tying one on and surviving an assault, Bonnie still looked polished in a way Dakota could never be.

Her nylons weren't torn. Not a speck of dirt marred her pale skin. Her dress fit impeccably. Other than missing her lipstick and her hair now hanging loose, Bonnie looked the same as she did when she'd started the night. If she'd keep her mouth shut and sit still, it'd be hard to know she was drunk.

That Simon wore only his flannel pants hadn't gone unnoticed by Bonnie. She'd spent more time gazing longingly at him than drinking the coffee that Barber kept putting in front of her.

Dakota tried to ignore Bonnie's fascination with Simon, but it wasn't easy. Knowing that she'd come running to Simon, and knowing that Simon had once cared enough to spend five years of his life with the woman, worked on Dakota's temper.

Just as the earliest rays of sunrise crawled through the window, Bonnie seemed to fall asleep. She even started to snore.

Barber half smiled at her, then glanced at Simon. "Think she'll remember any of this?"

"I don't know. I've never seen her drunk before."

"I don't think anyone was trying to hurt her. She was just with me."

"And you're Dakota's friend."

Barber nodded. "Marvin's a real pain in the ass. He's continued to harass her since the divorce. Slashed car tires, rocks through a window, a lot of chicken-shit stuff like that."

"No way to prove it's him?"

"Not so far. The thing is, he doesn't much like for Dakota to have friends, but he knows we're close. He's seen her onstage with me." Barber rubbed at his now bristly chin. "A while back, he was hanging out at this bar where we had a week run. He'd sit in the audience and wait for her."

Dakota could feel Simon watching her, but she gave her attention to her coffee mug. She didn't want him to know how Marvin affected her.

"What came of it?" Simon asked.

"He hassled me a few times," Dakota admitted. "He likes to intimidate people."

"Especially you?"

She shrugged. "Maybe. He'd wait until I was alone in the hall, or he'd slip into the back room with me. Then he'd try to crowd me. He'd say a few veiled threats, make a few threatening promises. That sort of thing."

Simon looked at Barber, who said, "I didn't realize what was going on at first."

Just remembering it made Dakota's stomach turn. "He could never follow through because it was a public place. Marvin can punk out some people, but not a packed bar where half the men there would take pleasure in a brawl."

"So he finally went away?" Simon asked.

Barber nodded. "After I had a talk with him."

That was news to Dakota. She looked up to find Barber watching her, too. "What did you do?" she asked.

"I told him if he touched you, I'd take him apart."

She sucked in a breath, then shoved back her chair. "You never told me."

"No, I didn't."

Flattening her hands on the table, Dakota leaned toward him. "You had no business doing that."

"Bullshit." Barber looked more tired than riled. "No man would sit by while that jerk bullied you."

Dakota laughed, because one man had: Barnaby. "You should have stayed out of it."

Simon asked, "Should I stay out of it, too?"

"Yes." Appalled at her raised voice, Dakota reined herself in. "For God's sake, I don't mean to yell, but this is ridiculous. We don't even know for sure if it was Marvin. But if it was, I'll take care of it."

Simon tipped his head at her. "How?"

She flattened her mouth. "I don't know yet. But I think maybe talking to the police is a good idea after all." And talking to Barnaby was an even better idea. It seemed too much of a coincidence that both Barnaby and Marvin would reappear in her life at the same time. She had no idea what the connection might be, but once Barnaby knew she wouldn't play, no matter what, he'd have no choice but to withdraw.

With both men staring at her, Dakota re-seated herself. "Look, I'll be extra cautious. I won't take any chances. But there's no point in either of you getting caught in the middle of the mess."

Simon said, "I hope you're joking."

"She's not," Barber told him. "She's worrying because someone tried to hurt me. She wants to *protect* me."

"Huh." Simon frowned. "That's kind of insulting, isn't it?"

"Yeah. Like she thinks she can take better care of this stuff than I can."

Dakota wanted to kick them both. "It's not about who's more macho, damn it. This is my problem, that's all I'm saying."

"No," Simon said. "You're not responsible for what your ex might do."

"Then I'll just go home." Dakota reached for the coffeepot, found it empty, and slumped in disappointment. She needed more caffeine. "If I'm not here, the problems won't be here. End of story."

Ignoring most of what she'd said, Simon pointed out, "That was the second pot."

"You're keeping count?"

"Dakota does like her java." Barber saluted Simon with his mug. "We have that in common."

Simon nodded at the jelly jar on the table. "You both like your sugar, too."

Because Simon's kitchen didn't boast any cookies or other sweet treats, she and Barber had chowed down several pieces of toast and jelly with their coffee.

Simon drank water.

His eating and drinking habits might be the biggest obstacle to her comfort when visiting him.

Dakota no sooner had that thought than Bonnie roused herself. She looked around the table at everyone. Except for her blood-shot eyes, she looked beautiful. She finger-combed her long, dark hair away from her face and over her shoulders. With determination bright in her expression, she stumbled over to stand by Simon's chair.

Simon glanced up at her.

Barber looked over his coffee mug at her.

Dakota considered throwing the empty carafe at her.

Now that Bonnie had everyone's attention, she pointed a finger at Dakota. "You're des-pic-able."

She barely got the word out, and Dakota yawned.

"Bonnie," Simon warned. "Don't start."

Bonnie put a hand on his bare shoulder, either to caress him or to help balance herself. "Iz all right, Simon. She haz to know that you're in trainin' for a very important fight."

Simon looked at Dakota, but said nothing.

Bonnie curled her lip in Dakota's direction. "Gettin' involved with someone like *her* jeopardizes everythin' you've worked for."

"Don't worry about it, Bonnie."

That's it? Dakota thought. That was Simon's idea of defending her? Not that she needed him to defend her, but he could have done a better job of it.

Dakota straightened in her chair.

Smoothing her hand over Simon's shoulder to his neck, Bonnie began massaging him. "You need someone who understands wha' you do."

"Dakota understands." He smiled at her. "Don't you, honey?"

Dakota's eyes narrowed. She'd about had enough of Bonnie.

"If she understood," Bonnie insisted, "she wouldn't be here."

"I invited her."

Dakota could feel Barber's amusement, the jerk.

"You're a man," Bonnie declared, excusing Simon of any responsibility. "But you barely know her. It iz incredible that she woul' spen' the night with you already."

Barber choked on his coffee, wheezed for breath, and coughed out a loud, obviously forced, laugh.

With the precision of a laser beam, Bonnie's gaze drilled into him. "And just *what* iz so funny?"

"Oh, come on, darlin'. You don't see the irony of you playing judge and jury?"

Bonnie drew herself up to her full height. "I see nothin' humorous in thiz situation at all."

As if he mourned the loss of a fine attribute, Barber muttered, "And to think I used to be such a gentleman." He met Bonnie's gaze. "All right, doll, let me point out the obvious."

"I don' see —"

"You and I just met today, but you were headed home with me. And it sure as hell wasn't to play checkers."

Watching Simon, Dakota saw his expression of boredom.

Through gritted teeth, Bonnie said, "Everyone here knows tha' I'm *drunk.*"

"But you weren't when you agreed to my offer." Barber eyed her head to toe. "It was your impatience in waiting for the monumental moment that drove ya to imbibe, my sweet."

Bonnie gasped.

Lounging back in his seat, Barber stretched out his long legs and laced his fingers over his abdomen. "Not that I blame you, me being such a treat and all."

Bonnie snatched up Simon's water glass. She would have thrown it if Simon hadn't caught her in time.

Dakota snickered.

And Bonnie swung around on her so quickly that she lost her balance and Simon had to catch her. She ended up in Simon's lap — and made herself at home very quickly.

With her arms tight around Simon's neck, Bonnie said, "You bitch, how dare you?"

Name calling? And still in Simon's lap? Slowly, while staring at Bonnie, Dakota smiled — and stood.

Simon stood, too, setting Bonnie on her feet at his other side, safely away from Dakota. "That's enough." Then to Barber, "It's time for you two to go."

"I'll call a cab."

"Not until you've gotten Bonnie home."

Barber looked up at the ceiling. "Will the trials of this day never end?"

"Forgit it," Bonnie insisted. "I'm sober 'nuff to drive myself."

Neither man agreed.

While Simon and Barber convinced Bonnie, Dakota went back to the bedroom to wash up and finish dressing properly. She needed to go see Barnaby. She needed to settle things with him before someone got hurt.

She needed to protect her friends, and herself, from Marvin.

By the time Simon got rid of his guests, Dakota was ready to go. He closed the front door, turned, and almost ran into her.

One look at her and he asked, "Where do you think you're going?"

"It's almost morning." She didn't feel like smiling, but did so anyway. "With everything we know now, I have a lot of decisions to make."

To her surprise, he bent and kissed her.

Dakota yanked back. "And I'm not tired anymore."

He kissed her again, his mouth open, hot.

Her knees went weak. "Simon? What are you doing?"

"Convincing you to stay." He caught the shoulders of her coat and eased it off her.

She started to tell him what he could do with that idea, but he kissed her again, and her thoughts scattered.

It took her a little longer to remember she was mad about Bonnie, and that she needed to talk to Barnaby, and . . .

When her coat hit the floor, Dakota recalled herself and pushed Simon back, not hard, but not really easy either. "I don't see why I should —"

"Come with me." He caught a fistful of her sweatshirt and tugged her toward the bathroom.

"Wait a damn minute!"

"Why?" In the bathroom, Simon released her and picked up his toothbrush. "I need to freshen up so I can kiss you properly."

Dakota stared at him.

He brushed with enthusiasm, and glanced at her askance. "What?" he asked around a mouthful of toothpaste.

"I don't understand you."

"Which part, honey?"

She shook her head.

"The kissing part?" He spit in the sink and rinsed his mouth.

Dakota had never watched a man brush his teeth. Not even Marvin or her father, definitely not Barnaby. It felt oddly intimate.

Simon grabbed up the hand towel, dried his mouth, and grinned at her. "By properly, I mean really deep and wet and . . ."

Turning in a rush, Dakota grabbed for the doorknob. The door had barely opened when Simon's hand landed flat against it and slammed it shut.

Her heart shot into her throat and her brain scrambled to find the right words. Simon crowded in close to her back.

When he said near her ear, "You okay?" she could smell the toothpaste on his breath.

Still grappling with the meaning behind his actions, she asked, "What do you mean?"

Gentle, light, and in no way threatening, his free hand slipped around and opened over her belly. "I'm not scaring you?"

He had a little at first, but his concern took care of that. To brazen through the moment, she said, "No," and sent her elbow back hard, gouging his abdomen.

It felt like she'd run her arm into a wall. Simon barely grunted.

"Good. I don't ever want you to be afraid. Not of me, not of anyone."

His voice was so warm and compelling that Dakota had to force herself to remember that she was annoyed with him. "Let me out of here, Simon."

"Soon as I apologize." His palm pressed more firmly against her. "And then maybe you'll let me kiss you the way I want to."

Her attention wavered between the warmth of his touch and the promise in his words. "Apologize? For what?"

"For making you jealous."

"I wasn't!" She tried to turn, but Simon held her in place.

He nuzzled the sensitive skin behind her ear. "If you can't admit it —"

"Can't?" Again, she struggled against him.

"Can't, won't." He nibbled on her earlobe. "You see, if you don't go first, then how am I supposed to admit how much it bugged me to see you and Barber acting so damned cozy?"

She went still.

Simon smiled as he explained, "Bonnie kept looking at me as if I were her last meal, and you didn't even care. You were too busy sharing coffee and food with Barber."

Dakota could feel Simon all along her back. Hot. Powerful.

Wonderful.

All this teasing mixed with seduction put her way out of her element. "It sounds to me like you were the jealous one."

"Yeah." His fingers contracted on her belly, gently caressing. He pressed a damp kiss to her nape. "Barber's okay. I like how he defends you, and I'm glad he was there for you when you needed him. But it pisses me off that he wants you."

How asinine. "He doesn't."

"Yeah." Simon turned her to face him, and he looked very serious. "He does."

"No —"

He took her mouth again, deeper this time, just as he'd said he would. But he didn't lean into her, didn't smother her with his closeness.

He scooped his hand down to cuddle her bottom. It was the oddest feeling to Dakota, to have a man kneading her derrière and groaning softly about it. It was Simon's reaction to touching her more than the touch itself that excited her.

"Damn, Dakota." He put his forehead to hers. "Mallet wants you, too, you know."

She started to roll her eyes — and his hand came around to wedge between her thighs. Her breath hitched, her heart skipped a beat, and a wave of heat rushed through her.

Simon looked at her, gauging her reaction, and Dakota tried to be blank, to show no emotion so that he wouldn't stop.

He searched her face, then smiled, and Dakota knew that he was schooled enough to see the difference between fear and arousal.

She was flushed, breathing hard and fast. But she couldn't help it.

"You are so damned sexy," he murmured.

Vanity niggled at her comfort zone. "I'm all banged up."

"I know." Simon kissed her bruised forehead, the bridge of her nose, the deep scratch on her cheek. "Whoever did this to you, Marvin or someone else, I'd like to find him and stomp his sorry ass into the ground."

The meaning of the words, and the gentle way Simon said them, left Dakota floundering. He sounded seductive, caring, and furious, all at the same time.

Her eyes were about to close when Simon said, "Let's get in the hot tub to . . . ease your sore muscles."

With his hand still between her thighs, just pressed against her, not really moving, Dakota assumed he had a lot more in mind than merely easing her muscles.

She swallowed, nodded. "Yeah. Sure. Okay."

Grinning, happy and teasing her, Simon kissed her again. "Bonnie means nothing to me."

Dakota did not want to talk about Bonnie. "If you say so."

"I do. And you can always trust me." He moved his fingers, and it was like a jolt of sensation that ebbed out to every inch of her body. He stilled again. "Dakota? I want to do more than soak in the hot tub."

God, he made her crazy. "Yeah, Simon, I figured as much."

His cheek brushed hers as he kissed the side of her throat, her shoulder, under her chin. "You're okay?"

Dakota couldn't help it; she laughed. "I would be a lot better if you'd shut up and get on with it."

He leaned back to see her, and Dakota said, "I'm not a shy woman, Simon. I won't suffer in silence. If you do anything I don't like, trust me, you'll hear about it."

"And if I do things you like?"

She sighed. "I imagine you'll hear about those, too."

"Perfect." He took her hand. "Let's go."

CHAPTER 13

A high wooden privacy fence with the gate locked kept the hot tub hidden from the yard. The house gave the only access, and the doors were all secured. They were alone, and Simon had hours before he had to pack for his trip to Vegas.

There were so many things he wanted to do with Dakota, but the number-one thing on his list was to give her pleasure. He wanted her to know that sex with him would never be anything but good. Men were easy — just seeing a desirable woman could put most near the edge. He was there now, aware of Dakota standing beside him, her arms around herself to ward off the early morning chill as he uncovered the hot tub and turned it on. From the second she'd agreed, he had a boner.

But Simon wasn't a boy. He was thirty-one years old, and he knew women, knew how complicated and elusive an orgasm could be for a woman.

For someone who'd been sexually abused, it'd be an especially tricky business because there was much to overcome, and old expectations didn't die easily.

For someone like Dakota, with her strong personality and strength of will, the past would play an even bigger role. More than anyone else ever could, she condemned herself for past mistakes. It'd take finesse, experience, and a little faith to ease her past her false impressions and apprehension.

When Simon first realized that she'd kept her last name as a sort of punishment, a constant reminder that she had erred in judgment, he knew he'd have his work cut out for him. Dakota caught a lot of flack on the name. And granted, Dakota Dream did ring of a suggestive stage handle.

But she could change it easily enough, if she only would.

He'd work on that, along with giving her pleasure.

Though Simon wore only boxers, he barely noticed the weather. Dakota was still fully dressed and shivering as the hot tub churned and steam rose into the air.

Heart thumping and muscles tight, Simon turned to her. "You need to skin out of some of those clothes."

"Yeah, I know." But she stood there, watching him.

Pretending that it meant nothing, Simon stepped up to her and caught the waistband of her jeans. While he unsnapped and unzipped, he talked to distract her.

"At the gym, I've seen you taking notes."

Dakota blinked at him, trying to hide her nervousness. "Notes?"

"Yeah. When you're watching me." He eased his hands into the pants and, fingers spread, cupped her hips. God almighty, she was soft and well rounded. Simon swallowed down the surge of lust. "What the hell do you write?"

She looked at him, then at the hot tub and down at herself. "Uh . . ."

"Training tips on things you think I'm doing wrong?" As he said it, he shoved the jeans down to her knees.

"No," she said on a high note. And then: "Don't be stupid."

"Sorry." He grinned at her reaction to having her pants down. "So what is it, then?"

She licked her lips as if trying to gather her thoughts. "I write down stuff I see that I think maybe I can learn. Stuff that'd be good to know."

Simon absorbed that, and nodded. Going

to one knee, he held the jeans and said, "Step out."

Dakota braced a hand on his shoulder and did as he asked.

She wore thick white socks, and again, he noted her legs, lightly muscled, shapely and smooth.

A T-shirt, panties, and crew socks. Not exactly an outfit meant to seduce, except that this was Dakota, and he was on fire for her.

He lifted her left foot. "I could spar with you, you know."

"Forget it." Her fingers tightened on his shoulder and her voice rose an octave. "You're in training. You need to train."

"All right, then." It choked him to say it, but he offered, "Dean, then."

"Ha! Hell, no."

What did she have against Dean? Or was it just that he was male, and therefore getting physical with him didn't appeal to her?

Given that he didn't really want her to be physical with any man except him, Simon couldn't fault her for that.

Lifting her other foot to remove that sock, too, Simon said, "I want you to be confident in your skills, honey."

"I am. That is, I'm learning."

"You're smart, Dakota." He stood, and

now she wore only a T-shirt and panties. It made him nuts. "You know more about the sport than any other woman I've met."

"I love it."

She no longer looked so cold. Her shivering had subsided and she had a warm flush to her skin just barely visible in the shadows of the privacy fence.

But her nipples were hard, and Simon couldn't seem to get his gaze off her chest.

"I've learned a lot just by watching."

Unable to help himself, Simon brushed the backs of his fingers over her left breast, teasing that taut nipple. "And you know the best way to learn is to do. Real confidence comes with experience." His gaze locked with hers. "And that means not just practice, but out-and-out, full-blown contact."

Her breathing accelerated. "I've done that with Barber."

Simon clenched his jaw. "Fine." *Son of a bitch.* He did *not* want to say it, but her safety was a priority. "Have Barber come to the gym to work with you." And he'd watch over them both.

Dakota drew in a shuddering breath. "Why are you so worried about me improving my skills?"

"You know why." Her beautiful legs and trim waist weren't a surprise for Simon, not after seeing her in that dress. But a woman's breasts could easily be enhanced with the right bra.

He didn't think Dakota bothered with enhancements.

And when he opened his hand over her breast and held her, he discovered that she was heavy and firm, more than perfect. He could feel her puckered nipple against his palm.

"Damn," he said, surprised at how hoarse he sounded. "You really are stacked, but somehow you've managed to hide it."

"I see no reason to show it."

No, why would she when she didn't want male attention? Except for his, Simon reminded himself.

Before he got any further off track, Simon took her hand and led her to the hot tub. He stepped in first, then helped her in.

"There's a ledge for sitting."

She started to move to it but, still holding her hand, Simon sat down and pulled her to him until she straddled his lap.

It was wonderful.

And torturous.

And the pleasure of having her lush behind cuddling his cock damn near took his voice.

Dakota stationed both hands on his shoulders and just looked at him. Her eyes were dark and heavy, her lips parted to accommodate her fast breaths.

The water level reached just to her nipples, and the shirt quickly became transparent. With her panties and his boxers soaked, they barely existed. Her belly rested against his abdomen. His hands naturally went to her backside.

"Comfortable?"

She nodded — and stared at his mouth.

Ruthlessly controlling himself, Simon asked, "No bad feelings?"

She shook her head, and leaned forward to kiss him. He let her do that without taking over; he just accepted her kiss, opening his mouth when she nudged at his lips, touching his tongue to hers as it licked into his mouth.

"Simon?"

"What do you want, Dakota?"

Her nose bumped his. Her breath fanned his mouth. "I'm not sure."

He should be sainted. "Will you trust me?"

"To do what?"

She didn't sound wary so much as keenly excited. "Turn around."

That confused her.

She lifted her head and stared at him, and Simon explained. "I'm not about to come in my hot tub, babe. It's not cool."

"Then . . ."

"I want to play with you a little. That'd make me a really happy man."

"Play with me?" Her slim brows pinched over her nose. "That sounds sort of frustrating."

"For me, yeah." But he hoped not for her. "I'd like to get more familiar with your body, and let you get familiar with me touching you."

She squirmed, and suggested, "We could just go back to your bed —"

"Shhh. No, not yet."

"Why?"

How did he tell her that he didn't want to be a quick conquest? He didn't want to have sex with her once, just to prove to them both that he could. What he did want, Simon couldn't say. Not in the long run.

But for right now, here, this moment, he wanted to hear her groaning with a climax. He wanted to feel her shivering with release, wanted to hold her as she went soft and limp and spent.

So he lied. "I'm in training, remember?"

Suspicion firmed her mouth. "Yeah, so?"

"Sex is a no-no."

She straight-armed away from him and glared. "You're a tease, aren't you? If you had no intention of —"

"Dakota." He brought her to him for a quick, hard kiss. "I asked you to trust me. Do you think you can do that?" Playing dirty, knowing she hated to admit to any weakness, Simon added, "Or will your fear get in the way?"

Through her teeth, she asked, "Tell me what you want me to do."

So much pride. Simon kept his grin contained and helped her to stand. "Just turn around, and then sit back down."

Water splashed as Dakota gave him her back, then dropped onto his knees. Silly woman. She was so adorable to him. Hands at her waist, Simon said, "Ease back. Careful, because I've got a boner that I'd just as soon leave in one piece."

That stiffened her spine, but she eased back against him until she felt his erection, then she stilled.

"Keep coming." Simon helped her until her back rested against his chest. "Now try to relax."

She made a small sound and remained stiff, put off, and antagonistic. Her hands were on his upper thighs, her fingers digging hard into his muscles. He rather liked that.

Deliberately, Simon rested one hand low on her belly. "If you open your legs, I can touch you."

Not a sound.

Not a single movement.

"Maybe I'm rushing you —"

Her legs parted over his, not far, but enough that Simon could ease them wider himself. It was a favorite foreplay position of his, but this wasn't foreplay, and never before had the woman on his lap been so rigid and wary.

Rather than rest her head back on his shoulder, Dakota kept her neck stiff so she could lock her gaze on his hands and watch his every move.

It was awkward, but not enough to deter him.

"That's perfect," Simon lied. Lightly, he trailed his fingers up and down her inner thighs, and added, "For now."

Then he just kissed her, her nape, her shoulders, wherever he could reach. He knew Dakota expected a quick attack, but he'd disappoint her on that. He wanted to take his time with her, to build anticipation for them both.

One by one, he lifted her hands and nibbled on her knuckles, licked her wrists, and sucked on her fingertips. Dakota breathed so hard, he could hear her over the bubbling water.

"Are you warm enough?"

She nodded and said, "Oh, yeah," in a rough, breathless rush.

"Would you mind if I brought your shirt up above your breasts?"

She finally dropped her head back and said on a near wail, *"No."*

"No, you don't mind, or no, you don't want me to?"

She yanked the T-shirt up herself, then held it there, trembling, panting, anxious.

Looking over her shoulder, Simon admired her breasts. "Beautiful." Not only her breasts, but . . . "I can see through your panties now, too. Not clearly with the water and bubbles, but . . ."

Dakota turned her face into his throat and held herself very still. Her hands remained fisted in the wet T-shirt below her chin.

Simon hefted one breast in each hand, gently cuddled her, squeezed, and then caught each nipple. He tugged, and Dakota nearly arched off his lap.

Pausing, he whispered, "Settle back, honey. Try to relax and let me enjoy you." He still had each nipple clamped firmly.

"This is crazy."

"I know," he said, soothing her. "Sit back now."

She did, but she'd started to squirm again,

and Simon realized just how sensitive her breasts were. He'd barely touched her, had mostly teased a little, and she couldn't sit still.

Loving Dakota would be a lot of fun.

For now, it'd be his torture.

He pulled gently at her nipples as he spoke to her. "You're twenty-three, Dakota. I assume you've had a climax before?"

"No. Yeah." She shook her head in frustration and said low, *"I don't know."*

Interesting. "Let me rephrase that, then. Have you had a climax with a man?"

"No."

No hesitation there at all. "All right. But by yourself —"

"Do you want me to drown you, Simon?"

Because she couldn't see him, he grinned. Her harsh voice sounded both excited and embarrassed. "I'd rather you didn't."

"Then stop trying to embarrass me."

"Okay." He flicked his thumbs over her. "Do you like this?"

She nodded.

"What about this?" Holding the weight of her breasts in his hands, he compressed her nipples with his thumbs.

"Yes."

"You have a pretty belly."

She cursed.

Simon said, "I'm going to put my hand inside your panties."

Her shoulders tensed. "You don't need permission, damn it."

"I wasn't asking, just letting you know." Because he could tell it heightened her arousal for him to talk to her, and because he didn't want to startle her, or rush her in any way. "Let me know if you don't like it."

"Yeah, sure."

Simon felt the muscles in her thighs contract. Slowly, so slowly that it made him a little wild, too, he slipped his fingers into her panties. This time he wasn't content just to touch her. He explored, parting her, sliding over her swollen lips, dipping his middle finger barely into her, then pressing in further.

"Oh, God."

Near her ear, Simon whispered, "You feel so good. Hot and slick." Making himself hot, he added in a growl, "I wish I could taste you."

Her trembling increased, making Simon wonder.

"Has any man ever —"

"No."

With his free arm, Simon hugged her. He could be first at something. *Would* be first. And it thrilled him. "We'll save that for another time, okay?"

She didn't bother to answer.

"Two hands, honey." He kept his finger pressed in her as far as he could go, and with his other hand, he found her little clitoris. She was swollen, distended, and he groaned low in his throat, ready to come regardless of what he'd told her.

With ultimate care and experience, he slipped his fingertips over her, again and again, his rhythm steady and easy and light. At the same time, he moved inside her, felt every tightening of her inner muscles, each new rush of warmth that bathed his hand.

Putting his mouth to the side of her throat, Simon sucked at her sensitive skin to give her a hickey. As the sensations built, Dakota moaned, went first boneless and then so taut that her back arched and her feet pressed hard against the floor of the hot tub.

He stayed with her, encouraging her with small sounds, murmuring to her — and finally he felt her coming.

His heart expanded as she locked her teeth and clenched her muscles. Her hips moved against him. She groaned, guttural, earthy, real sounds that echoed on the still air around them.

Simon held her close and relished the moment more than any other that he could recall. More than his first win or when he'd gotten a championship belt or . . . anything.

As Dakota finally eased, resting limply in his hold, he turned her, cradling her on his lap and kissing her. She held on to him, snuggled in close, and damn, but it felt like trust. Bone-deep trust.

And so very much more.

Ten minutes later, Dakota was so still and silent, Simon wondered if she'd fallen asleep. He gave her a squeeze. "Hey. You okay, honey?"

"Yeah." She slowly inhaled, stretched luxuriously. "I'm great."

He liked the sound of that. "You didn't hurt your thigh, did you?"

"Nope."

Simon tipped up her face and kissed her. She looked relaxed and as sated as he'd hoped. Smiling in satisfaction, he asked, "Do you want to go in for a nap?"

"I'm not sleepy. Just . . . sort of amazed and maybe a little self-conscious and kind of tingly all over."

"Perfect." He kissed her again. "You're totally, completely perfect."

That had her snorting. "Yeah, right. Lack of nookie must've made you delirious." She sat up and, to Simon's surprise, she straddled his lap again.

"What's this?"

Shrugging, she looked at his chin and said, "I'm wondering if there's something I can do for you."

Sexy, strong, and generous to boot. His smile widened. "There are all kinds of things you can do for me. Later. After I get back from Vegas."

"What about right now?"

"Right now, I'd like to talk."

"You're serious?" She scowled at him, took in his expression, and accused, "You *are*." She made a sound of disbelief. "Good grief, you are the most talkative man I've ever met."

"Most men enjoy a little conversation, Dakota. It's not unheard of."

"Really? Even when a near-naked woman is sitting on his lap?" She nodded. "I'm sure guys everywhere would agree with you. I mean, what else would a man have on his mind but some chitchat?"

She had a point. "This is a unique situation."

"For me anyway. I've never been in a hot tub with a man. Never sat on a man's lap. Never . . . well, you know. That other stuff."

"Come with a man?"

341

Tucking in her chin, she gave him a reproachful frown. "It didn't need clarification, Simon."

"I think it did." Locking his fingers behind the small of her back, Simon ensured she couldn't bolt away if she didn't like what he had to say. "There's something special going on here, and that gives me certain rights."

Her eyebrows lifted. "Is that so?"

"Yes."

"Spell it out for me."

Simon took heart in the fact that she didn't move away. She sounded more curious than offended. "We both know it was probably Marvin who pushed you and attacked Barber."

"I don't have any doubts."

"Neither do I. And that's why I want you ready and able to defend yourself if it becomes necessary." Simon knew he couldn't be with her 24/7. No man could. She was an independent woman who lived her life as she should — free and on her own terms.

He liked and admired that about her. But at the same time, he couldn't bear the thought of her being vulnerable to a man who'd already abused her.

She had skills, but she needed to improve

in order to fend off an attack by someone like Marvin Dream.

Dakota leaned forward and kissed his chin. "I don't take chances, Simon. There's no reason for you to worry about me."

"It's not about taking chances. If someone wants to get to you, he can. You can't live your life and always be protected. The very best defense is preparation. You need to be prepared."

When she leaned away, that only afforded Simon a better view of her breasts beneath the wet, clinging T-shirt. "I'm not sure what it is you want."

"You." He wanted no mistakes about that. "I want you, Dakota. A dozen different ways. I want to be inside you when we're sitting like this, and I want you over me, riding me."

"Simon." Once again, her breathing hitched.

"And I want you under me, unafraid, with your legs around my waist and your face tight with pleasure."

She bit her lip, and then nodded. "Sounds good to me."

Simon held her face in his hands. "I want to know that you trust me and that some prick from your past no longer has a hold on your life."

After letting out a shaky laugh, Dakota said, "Gee. That's the sweetest thing any man has ever said to me."

Simon smiled with her. "I think the best way for us to make that happen is to move slowly, at least where sex is concerned. And yes, before you ask, I'll be fine. Contrary to schoolboy claims, I won't explode from unrequited lust or suffer painful lasting effects or any of that."

"No blue balls?" she teased.

Simon shook his head. "I'll just want you more day to day, but I can handle it." Hell, he'd wanted her from the moment he laid eyes on her. What would a little more patience hurt?

"Didn't you just say that guys in training are supposed to skip sex anyway?"

He snorted. "Yeah, right." If she knew that Dean had told him to "have her and get it out of his system," she might not understand. "In theory, I guess that's true. But the only men I know who skip sex are the ones who don't have an option either way. And then they're probably unloading on their own, so it doesn't matter."

The most comical expression came over Dakota's face. She choked out, "Unloading?"

With a crooked grin, Simon said, "You

get my meaning."

"Yes, I do. And oh, the visuals it brings to mind . . ."

Laughing, Simon waggled his head and then drew her close for a teasing, smacking kiss. "Knock that off, woman. It's time to get serious." He eased her against him so that her head again rested on his shoulder. "How long have you been divorced now?"

She shrugged. "A couple of years. I'm not exactly keeping count or anything."

"And in that time, how often have you seen your ex?"

"Hmmm." While she thought about it, Dakota toyed with his chest hair. "Not that often, really. I'd say he shows up two or three times a year. Occasionally more often."

Just often enough that she couldn't relax and forget about him. "He's threatened you since the divorce?"

"Now that would depend on what you consider a threat. He says things, or looks at me a certain way, and I feel threatened, but you wouldn't."

No, he wouldn't, Simon silently agreed, but then, he hadn't been raped.

Thinking it enraged him all over again. As Simon gently moved long tendrils of wet hair away from her face, his hand shook. "I already told you that I know you're smart."

He hugged her tight. "If you feel threatened, then I'm sure there's a good reason." After pressing a kiss to her temple, he said, "Dakota . . ."

"I don't like that hesitation."

His arms tightened even more, and he stopped waffling. "Would you mind too much if I asked a few friends to keep an eye on you?"

Surprised, she lifted up to look at him.

"Understand, Dakota. I could have done that without you even knowing. But you're an independent sort and I don't want to insult you in any way."

She appeared thoughtful, but not offended, as she chewed that over. "If I'm staying in town —"

"You are."

His quick insistence made her smile. Softly, she agreed. "I am." In a stronger voice, she added, "Actually, now that you mention it, I'd appreciate some backup. Other than Barber, I'm not well acquainted with anyone in town, and I don't think I need to go running to the police. But it'd be reassuring to know someone had my back."

Her sensibility shouldn't have surprised Simon, but it did. And the fact that she didn't consider herself well acquainted with

Mallet reassured him, too. "You know, I think I expected you to curse me."

"Bastard," she whispered with a grin, so as not to disappoint him. Then she kissed him again.

Simon liked it a lot that she kept kissing him, touching him, and that she hadn't blown up at his suggestion that she could use some help. "I appreciate your co-operation."

"The appreciation is mine. Just tell me who and where, and I'll make sure I'm not alone until I know for sure if Marvin is behind any of this."

"You are the most amazing woman."

"Uh-huh." She rolled her eyes. "I am a rapidly fading woman. I need coffee and food, and I think you need to pack, so how about I get a cab to my truck and then I'll find that motel you suggested."

Simon wasn't ready to say good-bye to her just yet. "I have a better idea. Give me fifteen minutes to change and pack and I'll take you to your truck, then the motel, and *then* I'll head to the airport."

"You have time for all that?"

It'd be close, but Simon just nodded. "Yeah. I have time." To get them on their way, he caught Dakota under the arms and lifted her to her feet. Her transparent clothes nearly caused him to choke. The woman was a warm, walking temptation.

Simon leaned forward to put one fast kiss on her belly. "This'll be the longest, most agonizing trip I've ever taken — and that's saying something, because I've traveled a lot."

Dakota turned and stepped out of the hot tub, and that, too, was a unique experience guaranteed to haunt his dreams. "Fair warning, Simon." Shivering at the cold air, she reached for a towel. "When you get back, I plan to molest you."

Oh, God. The trip just got more excruciating. "You don't say." He cleared his throat. "I'll look forward to it."

CHAPTER 14

As soon as she was alone in her motel room, Dakota called Barnaby. He sounded half-asleep still, but at the sound of her voice, he quickly grew alert.

"I hope you have good news, honey."

"Not much has changed, Barnaby — except that I'm done." Not giving him a chance to argue, question, or complain, she rushed on. "If you have letters, then go ahead and burn them. I don't care."

"Liar. You can't mean that." When she said nothing, he raged on. "This is the last link you have to your mother!"

Dakota ignored that. Her stomach felt tight at the thought of losing the letters, but her spirit felt freed. "Simon wants nothing to do with you and that won't change. I want nothing to do with you, either. Don't ever call me again."

Sounding strained, he said, "You'll regret this."

"If you think to send someone after me again —"

"Again?"

"Don't act innocent, Barnaby. We both know you had something to do with me getting shoved down the stairs."

A long pause left Dakota uneasy. "I don't know what you're talking about." He sounded harsh and upset. "Were you hurt?"

Suddenly doubtful, Dakota tightened from her toes to her temples. "You sent Marvin here."

"I have as little to do with that miscreant as I can manage." Tension throbbed in his tone. "Years ago, I told you not to get involved with him. I warned you. But you were Ms. Know-It-All and did just as you pleased, so if he's in your life now, you have no one but yourself to blame!"

His words rang true. "You know, it's odd, Barnaby, but I almost believe you." And Dakota hated that. She'd been so sure that Barnaby was behind the trouble. But now . . .

"I thought you loved your mother. I thought you'd do anything for those stupid letters. Why would I waste my time with a common thug?"

What he said made sense. "So you haven't seen Marvin at all?"

Dakota could hear him breathing during another extended pause. Finally, he said, "You listen to me, girl. Sometimes in life, you don't have a choice. It's not about what you want or don't want. Get Simon to come to me. Or at least get him to call me again. It's important. You *will* regret it if this doesn't work out."

"That sounds an awful lot like a threat, Barnaby."

"No!" He seemed almost panicked. "Give me his number. I'll call him. Just let me grab a pen and paper —"

Squeezing her eyes shut, Dakota said, "If you bother Simon or me again, I'll contact the police. I'll tell them everything and let them decide if you're involved or not. I mean it, Barnaby. Don't test me." She closed the cell phone, disconnecting the call.

For a few minutes, Dakota sat on the edge of the bed and considered Barnaby's last warning. What did he need with Simon? Would she ever know?

She looked at the phone in her hand. The thought of calling Marvin made her pulse trip. He wouldn't tell her anything, but maybe he'd give himself away somehow. He liked to brag, almost as much as he liked to bully.

Carefully, Dakota set the phone on the

nightstand. She wouldn't call him.

Not yet.

When Simon returned, she'd tell him what Barnaby had said, and he could decide what he wanted to do. For now, Dakota only wanted to eat, and then sleep. Unfortunately, she didn't feel like going out for food, and sleep proved elusive. Visions of Barnaby and Marvin kept intruding. She managed to block them only by concentrating on Simon — and missing him.

He was right. This would be a very long trip.

Dakota found Barber at the bar of Roger's Rodeo. He sat facing the crowd with his long, jean-covered legs extended. He'd hooked his left elbow on the edge of the bar behind him, and in his right hand, he held a drink.

Dakota followed his line of vision and saw that he studied a group of women gathered together.

She approached without his notice, and poked him in the ribs.

He barely stirred. Only his gaze moved toward her, but then went back to the gaggle of flirting women. "Look at them, Dakota. You'd think there'd be one in the bunch, huh?"

Dakota had no idea what he meant. Seating herself on a stool beside him, she asked, "One what?" She glanced at the women again, but all she saw was that they were youngish, attractive, and outgoing.

"One worth bothering with. One that'd spark some interest. But nope. They're all out of the running."

"The running for . . . your attention?" she guessed, trying to gauge his odd mood.

"Yeah."

"So what puts them out of the running?" The bartender approached and she ordered a plain cola. "They all look nice enough to me."

"You aren't a guy, that's why." He tipped his head. "The sexy one with the long hair? She's a smoker. Do you know what it's like to kiss a smoker?"

"Um, no."

"Like sucking on an ashtray. It's gross."

Dakota smothered her grin. "I had no idea."

"And look at the fake fingernails on that blonde."

"High maintenance?" Dakota guessed.

"Scars on my back."

"Oh." Dakota took a sip of her drink, trying not to imagine that. "I can see where that'd be bad."

"The one with the short hair has fake boobs. I hate fake boobs. They feel like footballs."

Dakota choked. "They do not."

He turned to her. "Have you felt any?"

"Well . . . no. But I can't believe —"

"The pickin's are too slim here." He swiveled around to face the bar again, downed his drink, and signaled for the bartender to give him another. "I think it's time I got out of Harmony."

Dakota took the liberty of sending the bartender away before he could refill Barber's glass. "I think it's time you stopped drinking."

"Maybe." Scrubbing a hand through his hair, then over his face, he groaned. "So what's up with you, darlin'? Did you take Roger up on his offer to perform here?"

"I'm going to. At least for a few weeks." He looked so morose that Dakota shouldered him playfully. "Roger said you extended your contract, too. I was hoping we could make it an act."

"You don't need me."

The way he said that, as if his words had a hidden, deeper meaning, gave Dakota pause. "Of course I do. I always have."

"Nope. You're the most independent, capable, smart, considerate —"

Good grief. Half laughing, she said, "That's enough, Barber. Don't saint me, okay?"

"You're too sexy to be sainted."

Dakota drew herself up. "What in the world is wrong with you?"

"Nothing new." He grinned, and then leaned toward her.

Uncertain of his intent, especially given his odd mood, Dakota leaned out of reach.

But Barber kept coming, and if she leaned any farther away, she'd fall off her stool.

When he got close enough, he gave her a loud smooch on her surprised mouth, then touched her cheek. "You really are a doll."

"No, I'm not. And until today, you never thought so."

"Wrong." He stood and stretched. "I'm not drunk, you know."

"No?"

"You refused my second drink for me."

Only his second? "Hmm. Sorry about that. I just assumed —"

"It's okay. I sing better dead sober anyway." He sent her an intense, probing inspection and held out a hand. "Let's find someplace quieter to talk."

"About what?"

"Anything you want."

"All right." Worried about him, Dakota

355

took his hand and let him lead her to one of the smaller interior rooms of Roger's Rodeo. At the early evening hour, the mechanical bull sat still and silent, and no one else intruded.

"You hungry?" Barber asked.

Her appetite still hadn't returned, so she fibbed. "I ate before coming here."

He pulled out a chair and straddled it. "I'll be coming to the gym tomorrow."

"Dean's gym?"

"Yeah. Simon called me. He wants me to work with you some more." One side of his mouth kicked up. "He wanted me to wait until he got back from Vegas, but why make it easy on him?"

"Easy on him?" Dakota crossed her arms on the small round table. "Is that supposed to mean something?"

"Yeah." He winked. "But don't worry about it."

"I'll worry about it if I want to. Since I walked into here tonight, I've understood about a tenth of what you've said. What's going on with you?"

Rather than answer that, Barber narrowed his eyes. "You're in love with him, aren't you?"

She straightened so fast that she nearly knocked over the table. "What are you talking about now?" *Love?* He had to be kidding — only he didn't say it like a joke.

Barber's expression softened. "You shouldn't be so afraid of the idea, hon."

"I'm not." But her heart started punching and her lungs felt restricted. Dakota shook her head in denial. "I haven't known Simon — you are talking about Simon, right?"

A surprised laugh escaped him. "Yeah, I'm talking about Simon."

She shook her head hard. "I haven't known him that long."

"So? It is what it is."

"That's just it. What is it?"

"You really don't know?"

It was hard to explain, but this was Barber, her best friend. So she gave it a shot. "I've never really felt like this before, so I don't know what to call it." She lifted a hand, feeling helpless. "I'd rather not call it anything."

"You'd rather just enjoy it while it lasts?"

If it lasted. She and Simon hadn't met under ideal circumstances, and she was worried that once he knew all about her, his interest in her would disappear. "Something like that."

Barber took both her hands in his. "I know you well enough to see it, Dakota. Take my word for it, Simon is the one."

He sounded pretty sure of that. "What if

Simon doesn't feel the same? What if he's just looking to entertain himself for a little while?"

"I hate to break it to you, hon, but you aren't the entertaining sort. You make a man work for it."

Affronted, Dakota scowled at him. "What does that mean?" Okay, so she knew she wasn't the typical female, but Barber made her sound like a real pain in the tush.

"It means you're special." His gaze warmed as he looked at her. "Very special. Remember that more than anything, I want you to be happy."

Enough was enough. "You're talking all screwy, Barber. If you have something to say to me, just spit it out."

His thumbs rubbed the backs of her hands. "I'm saying that I care a lot about you. I think I know you better than anyone else does, including Simon. And you deserve to be happy."

"What brought this on?"

"Deep introspection and the realization that I dragged my feet too long."

Jerking her hands away from him, Dakota pushed away from the table. "All right." She crossed her arms. "Enough with the cryptic remarks."

He laughed. "Not cryptic at all." He

stood, too. "I'll meet you tomorrow at the gym bright and early. In fact, didn't Simon tell me that you're staying at Roger's motel now?"

"That's right. Usually I rent the cheapest room around, but after everything that happened, we both thought it'd be a good idea for me to stay at a better place. Not that Roger's motel is ritzy. Far from it. But it is in a better part of town."

"I know. I'm staying there, too."

"You are?" Cautiously, because his mood was so different, Dakota said, "Maybe we could just ride together to the gym tomorrow morning."

"With us both knowing what Marvin is capable of, I think that's a great idea."

"Safety in numbers?"

"There is that. And I'm half hoping the bastard does make a play while I'm with you. It'd give me the chance to demolish him." Having said that, Barber started away, but when Dakota didn't follow, he looked at her over his shoulder, one eyebrow raised.

"Like you said, you're my best friend, so I wanted to ask your advice on something."

He gave one sharp nod. "Shoot."

"Do you think I should call Marvin —"

"No."

"— and ask him if he was behind this —"

He turned to face her fully. "Absolutely not."

"— to find out what he might say, maybe see if he gives himself away somehow or —"

Barber thundered back over to her and grabbed her shoulders. "*No.* Damn it, Dakota, don't be a nitwit."

Never before had she seen Barber act so strange. He was always a goof, always irreverent, but now he seemed totally out of sorts.

"What is your problem?" she demanded.

"I want you to ignore the bastard. Pretend he doesn't exist. I want you to have zero contact with him."

She knocked his hands away. "You want a lot."

Raising his arms, Barber shouted, "You have no goddamned idea!"

Dakota buried her hurt behind indignation. "I don't know if I did something to piss you off or if you're just having your monthly, but I've had enough." Confused and fed up, Dakota started to shove past him.

Barber drew her back around, then quickly held up both hands when she squared off. "You want to know what's wrong with me? Fine. I'm horny."

Dakota did a double take. *"What?"*

He laughed at her. "Well, you wanted to know, doll. That's it."

"You've lost it, Barber."

He laughed again. "Lust does strange things to a man, and as you've already figured out, things went south with sweet Bonnie."

"Sweet? Now I know you're nuts."

"Sweet on the eyes, at least." He chucked her under the chin. "And now I'm finding that no other woman appeals to me. Not enough anyway."

"Please don't tell me you got hung up on Bonnie."

"Nope. Not even close. I just don't feel like wasting the time with any other woman when I know it won't satisfy the itch."

Barber had always been open with her, and she knew he leaned toward the uninhibited side. But this was outrageous, even for him. "Itch, huh? Poor baby. Want me to spring for some Calamine lotion?"

"I have a better idea. You're a natural night owl. I'll be up late performing. And Simon's out of town. Let's grab a bite to eat tonight. There's this little Greek place where a lot of the fighters hang out. They do a mean chicken plank. I know, you weren't expecting me to say fried chicken, but it's to die for. What do you say?"

He'd rattled all that off so fast, Dakota felt her head spinning. But since the idea of sitting alone in her motel room didn't appeal to her, she shrugged. "Sure. Why not?"

With Simon gone, she didn't have much else to do to occupy her time except stew on Marvin and Barnaby, and neither of those topics appealed.

She glanced at her watch. "I need to go talk to Roger. Then I was going to do a little shopping to get a few more clothes. I hadn't planned to stay here this long and I'm running out of stuff."

Barber rolled his eyes. "Uh-huh. And lover-boy likes you spiffed up some, right?"

She did want to clean up her act a little for Simon, maybe show him that her one display of feminine dress wasn't a complete aberration. "He doesn't like my boots."

"I think it's more a case of him liking you without your boots, but sure, shopping sounds like an easy way to occupy yourself. Who's going with you?"

"I'm a big girl, Barber. I know my wardrobe lacks inspiration, but I'm not hopeless. I can pick out clothes all on my own, *and* make them match."

"Sure you can. I happen to like your boots, and you clean up with the best of them." He tugged at one earring. "I just thought women liked to do that sort of thing in gaggles."

Dakota grinned. "I'm not like most women."

"Ain't that the truth?" He put his arm around her. "Come on, babe. We don't want to keep good old Rog waiting."

He walked her as far as the office, then turned her over to a smiling Roger. Dakota didn't know what had happened, but Barber was as different as he could be.

She briefly wondered if he'd actually been smitten with Bonnie, and was suffering disappointment. But she didn't think so. Bonnie wasn't his type. He tended to lean more toward earthy, easy women, not up-tight ladies with ulterior motives.

Tonight, over dinner, she'd grill him. She'd get to the bottom of his odd behavior. But for now, she wanted to work out terms with Roger. She wasn't an idle type of person and she needed something to occupy her time in Harmony.

She looked back just once to see Barber making a call on his cell, and once again, he didn't look happy.

Barber waited impatiently for Simon to pick up. When he finally did, Barber didn't bother to identify himself. "She wants to call Marvin."

Apparently, Simon didn't need any further explanation. "Like hell."

"Yeah, that's sort of what I told her." Barber rubbed the back of his neck beneath his ponytail. Simon didn't know it — or maybe he did — but he'd put Barber in something of an awkward predicament by asking him to stick close to Dakota. "But Dakota's an independent sort. She's used to doing everything on her own. Maybe I should give the chump a call before she does."

"I'd rather you let it go for now, at least until I'm back in town."

"And that'll be . . . ?"

"I only landed a few hours ago, but the driver had an itinerary for me."

Barber heard the rustling of paper as Simon checked his schedule.

"I do the show tomorrow morning. Meet with some folks for lunch after that. I don't know. With any luck, I can be back on a plane by the late afternoon. But I'm not sure yet. Sometimes things come up. It depends on what Drew might have planned. I'm having dinner with him, so I'll ask and get back with you tonight."

As Simon spoke, Barber kept walking. He needed to be onstage in ten minutes. "I'm hooking up with Dakota for dinner tonight."

Silence.

Barber smiled. "No need to worry about her, then. I'm not about to let anything happen to her. But before that, she plans to do some shopping. It's weird, because Dakota isn't one who likes that sort of thing. I think she's only going shopping now because some asshole made her feel bad about her boots, so —"

"I'll give Dean a call," Simon interrupted; he sounded more irate by the second. "He and Eve can shanghai her so she won't be alone."

Misery loves company, Barber thought, and added, "With us being at the same motel, we'll hook up in the morning for breakfast, then hit the gym. I'll work on some new moves with her."

A low growl sounded through the phone. "I thought you were going to wait a few days on that."

"No time like the present, right?"

There was a long pause, and then very softly, Simon asked, "Are you going to make me regret asking for your help?"

"Yeah." Barber laughed. "But Dakota's a one-man woman, so all you have to suffer is a few ribbings from me."

"Then if that's all —"

365

"Don't rush off till you've heard the real punch line." Barber had no doubts that Dakota was head over heels in love. Now he wanted to know for sure how Simon felt.

"Punch line?"

"Yeah." Anticipating Simon's reaction, Barber said, "See, I asked Dakota if she was in love with you."

More silence.

Barber grinned to himself. "Hey, you still there, Sublime?"

With dry impatience, Simon asked, "What did she say?"

"It was more how she reacted than what she said." Barber embellished things enough to try a saint. "I swear, man, she looked like someone goosed her with a cattle prod. Her eyes went huge and she gagged a little. Or maybe she was choking. Hard to tell."

"You don't value your teeth much, do you?"

Barber laughed. "It was an interesting reaction, if you want the truth. So now I'm wondering how you'd react if asked the same."

"It's none of your damned business."

"Is that a yes or no? Because if it's a no, then Dakota is fair game again and —"

"Don't even think it."

Well. That reaction spoke volumes. Barber

366

worked up a convincing chuckle. "All right, dude. Calm down before you hurt yourself. I was just making sure."

"Go fuck yourself."

"Yeah, right now, no one else is appealing much to me." Before Simon could out-and-out challenge him, Barber added, "Give her a call. Convince her that she shouldn't talk to Marvin. The guy's a nut-job. Any acknowledgment from her will just encourage him because he'll know he's getting to her."

"I'll call her as soon as we hang up. But I have another question for you first."

Barber reached the floor where he'd perform. The band was set up and ready to go, waiting on him. Already the bar began to fill, so he hung near the perimeter, out of the chaos. Soon, the noise level would make conversation impossible. "I'm all ears."

"Since you know Dakota so well, have you ever met Barnaby Jailer?"

Barber forgot about the band. "Why?" What could Dakota's stepfather have to do with anything?

"He's my father."

Falling back against the wall, Barber said, "No fucking way."

"So you do know him?" When Barber didn't immediately answer, Simon said, "He bailed on my mother when I was just a little kid. We haven't heard anything from him since. But now he's hired Dakota to find me and bring me to him for a meeting."

"Why?"

"I don't know and I don't care. I want nothing to do with him. But somehow, he's twisting Dakota to get her to cooperate and, more than any other reason, that makes me not trust him."

That rotten son of a bitch. Yeah, he knew Barnaby. Or knew of him. All of it straight from Dakota. All of it bad.

Barber had no idea what Dakota might have told Simon about her stepfather, and until he knew, he wouldn't say too much.

But one question clamored in his brain. "If that's true, then someone needs to visit him to find out what hold he has over her. And it's not going to be Dakota."

"After what's happened," Simon said, taking the edge off Barber's temper, "I agree. I don't want Dakota anywhere near him. I thought about seeing him myself, but she told me to forget about it. She went from wanting me to see him, to insisting that I not."

"That might just be because she cares about you now."

"Maybe. But the more I've thought on it, the more I wonder if Barnaby could be involved with her tumble down the stairs, or your incident in the parking lot."

"You're ruling out Marvin now?"

"No, but I don't want to dismiss Barnaby, either. Out of nowhere, after nearly thirty years, he's suddenly so insistent on seeing me that he pressured Dakota into helping him. I can't help wondering why. If Marvin and Barnaby know each other, they could both be involved somehow."

"I suppose it's possible." Barber worked his jaw. Marvin would be the obvious choice, but knowing now that Barnaby wanted to meet Simon . . . yeah, he could guilt Dakota into helping him. "Let me talk to Dakota, see what she has to say." He'd find out what she'd told Simon, and how Barnaby had finagled her into this mess.

"So you do know Barnaby?"

"I didn't say that. Look, I gotta run. The band's ready to start and you need to get hold of Dean if you don't want Dakota in and out of mall parking lots on her own."

"Right." Simon paused, then said, "Listen up, Barber. I don't think I need to tell you —"

"Yeah, yeah. She's off-limits. Touch her, and you'll kick out my kneecaps. Got it." He grinned again. No matter how hollow he felt about losing his opportunity with

Dakota, he couldn't pass up the chance to prick Simon's jealousy. "Just remember, if she ever tells me otherwise, it's every man for himself."

He hung up on Simon's heated curse.

Simon hadn't said if he loved Dakota, but he hadn't denied it either. It was going to be fun watching the two of them muddle through.

Fun, and torturous.

But what the hell. Sooner or later, another lady would appeal to him. Dakota was unique, but she couldn't be the only woman around with her distinctive qualities. While he waited for the right woman to show up, he'd work on his character flaws a little.

Or not.

Right now, he only had to concentrate on putting on a good show. Given how he loved his music, it'd be easy to shake off his melancholy. And tonight, he'd have Dakota all to himself.

He'd find out everything he needed to know — and then some.

Dakota picked up another pair of jeans, and at the same time, she looked at Dean out of the corner of her eye. He wore a frown, the same frown he'd had when he picked her up. Hands shoved in his jeans pockets, his attention constantly moved between his sister Jacki, his wife, Eve, and Dakota.

He looked watchful, miserable, and resigned.

Knowing that Simon had put him up to babysitting, she lost her patience. "Look, this is ridiculous."

Startled, Dean narrowed his gaze on her. "What's that?"

"You don't want to be here. Hell, I don't even want to be here." She pointed at the other side of the small boutique where Jacki and Eve gushed over a sequined top. "They're enjoying it, but you and I look like we're being tortured. I know why I'm here. But why the hell are you here?"

If anything, his eyes narrowed more. "I'm accompanying my wife."

"Bull. You're playing bodyguard. Simon called, nagging at me about what to do and what not to do, and I'm willing to bet he did the same to you."

"No one tells me what to do." Dean rethought that and said, "No one other than my wife, that is."

"Fine. He suggested, then. Strongly." She shook her head. "The thing is, I don't like shopping anyway, but I especially don't like it with you moping behind me!"

Without changing expression or position,

Dean managed to look more imposing. "I do not mope."

Unfazed, Dakota snorted. "No? Then what would you call it?"

"Suffering silently."

"Ah." She couldn't help it, she snickered. "Well, let me tell you, your silent suffering is annoying as hell. Why don't you go get something to eat and we'll call you when we're done?"

Dean loomed closer so he could speak to her without his wife or sister overhearing. "You have a whack-job ex-husband stalking your stubborn ass. My wife and sister are with you. I'm not budging."

That was pretty straightforward and to the point. Dakota could tell Dean expected more arguments from her, but in reality, his attitude made her want to sigh.

So much affection and devotion. She smiled. "You care for Eve a lot, huh?"

Dean didn't so much as flinch. "I love her."

"That's nice, ya know?" When he looked suspicious of her attitude, she tried to explain. "I mean, it's great that you two found each other."

A little confused, Dean glanced at his wife, then back to Dakota. "What are you up to?"

"Nothing." It annoyed her to be so mistrusted. "What am I, an ogre? I'm just saying, it's not every day that two people meet, fall in love, and choose to spend their lives together."

Dean studied her, then nodded. "It's better than nice." Relaxing a little, he took the jeans she had and tossed them aside. "Those are butt-ugly. They look like men's jeans. Try these."

Dakota stared at him, bemused. Then she looked at the jeans he'd just sort of snatched up off another table.

Huh. Not bad. "Those are nice."

"Yeah, I know. Get two pair, one in washed denim and one in black. Between the two pairs, you ought to be able to find enough tops to mix it up and get you by, and then we can all get the hell out of here."

Dakota grinned. "What about tops?"

He went stiff for only a second before indulging a quick cursory glance at her upper body. Dakota had the feeling he'd just taken her measurements in a heartbeat.

Stepping around her, Dean went from rack to rack and when he came back, he had five shirts in various materials, colors, and styles. They all looked warm and soft, and not at all revealing. Perfect for her.

Dean Conor was a rather amazing man.

"Here," he said. "Do you need to try them on?"

Dakota checked the sizes and smiled in relief. "No way. If you think they'll work, we're done here. All I need is a different pair of shoes and those are in another store."

"Come on." He took her arm and led her toward the other women. "You two about done? Dakota is ready to pay but she needs shoes still and wants to hit a few other stores."

The way Dean had worded his question made it sound like Dakota was the one anxious to go.

And she was.

Both women had an armload of items, and they each wanted to inspect Dakota's purchases before they'd go to the checkout with her. After enthusiastic approval, they finally paid and got their items bagged.

Once out of the boutique, Eve and Jacki just naturally drifted ahead again. They got along so well that Dakota envied their easy friendship. Nodding toward them, she said, "Eve is really, really nice."

Loaded down with shopping bags, Dean hung back by Dakota. "She's incredible."

Dakota hid her smile. "The thing is, I don't interact real well with ladies."

"You don't try."

"No, I do. That is, I think I do." How to explain it? Eve and Jacki had both been so nice, trying to draw her in, to include her. But she never knew quite what to say to them. "See how they're laughing and chatting? They've been doing that since I got in your car."

He shrugged. "Yeah, so?"

"Do you ever wonder what they're talking about?"

"Woman stuff."

"Well, sure. But whatever that entails, I already know I'd be out of my element. I guess I'd rather talk about guy things, like fighting and training, than fashion or makeup or that sort of junk."

Dean rolled a shoulder. "Me, too. So pick a subject."

"If you're serious . . ."

He let out an exasperated breath and looked down at her. "Something on your mind, Dakota?"

She had so much on her mind, all of it centered around Simon, that it felt like her head would explode. "Do you think I'm interfering too much in Simon's training?"

"No."

That quick answer didn't convince her "Because I don't want to."

"He wouldn't let you."

How could everything be so cut-and-dry for men? "He told me once to get lost."

Dean smiled. "I know."

"But I didn't."

"I know that, too."

Dakota was so set on finding out what she needed to know, that she barely registered Dean's words. "At the time, I didn't mind bugging him. But now . . . he's got a lot to do to finish getting ready for the fight, and I don't want to get in his way."

"Most of the guys have significant others. If they can't juggle a relationship, they won't be able to make it in this sport."

"I suppose." Gregor was in training, too, but Dakota doubted that Jacki ever felt like a nuisance. Of course, they were in love, like Dean and Eve. "But you know, Simon and I don't have a . . . normal relationship."

An arrested look came over Dean. "Now you're treading into territory that I don't want to hear about."

"But . . ."

"Sex talk is out."

She gasped. "I wasn't talking about sex!" Without thinking, Dakota punched his shoulder hard enough to make him nearly drop the packages.

Cursing low, Dean juggled things until he had them balanced again.

Eve looked back at them, and though her hand tingled in pain, Dakota pasted on a smile. Dean just kept plodding forward down the mall toward the shoe store.

Feeling like a blockhead for overreacting, she muttered, "Sorry."

"For?"

"Hitting you."

Dean glanced at her. "You hit me?"

Did all SBC fighters have a warped sense of humor? "Very funny." But she did want to set the record straight. "I was talking about how Simon and I met, not . . . anything else. And seriously, I am sorry for slugging you. I sometimes do that without thinking."

"It's a guy thing, being physical." Dean shrugged. "Simon told me you've had some training."

"Yeah, but I need more." What an understatement. "A lot more. Barber and I are coming by in the morning. I've worked with him before."

He nodded. "I'll be there anyway, so I'll watch and see if I can give you any pointers." He looked at her again, this time lingering on her many bruises. A touch of worry darkened his light brown eyes. "That is, if you're sure you're up for it."

"They're just bruises, Dean, not breaks.

No reason to sit on the sidelines."

His mouth lifted in amusement before a laugh escaped. Shaking his head, he said, "Definitely a guy thing."

She didn't understand him, but then, she didn't understand Simon either, and Barber had totally thrown her for a loop. "If you really don't mind, I'd appreciate the feedback. I know you're one of the best trainers out there."

"Simon is better."

"Simon is out of town, and when he gets back, he has to concentrate on his own training, not on fooling around with me."

Dean choked, looked down at her, and laughed aloud. "Don't sweat it, Dakota. Somehow I think Simon will manage just fine doing both."

She started to reply to that when Eve and Jacki disappeared into a shoe shop that looked very high end, making Dakota curl her lip. "They have to be kidding."

" 'Fraid not. Eve is a walking fashion statement."

"Great. So how much are shoes going to cost me here?"

"More than they should, if you ask me. And if you're asking me, it's a waste of time and effort, too, because Simon doesn't give a" — he glanced at her, and modified his speech — "flip what kind of shoes you wear."

"If that's so, then how come he told me he didn't like my boots?"

"You probably had him pissed about something."

"Yeah, that's happened a lot between us."

Smiling over that disclosure, Dean nudged her into the store. "Look. Eve has found the perfect pair for you already. If you bite the bullet and buy the things so we can call a halt to the shopping spree, I'll stop and get ice cream for everyone."

"Ice cream, huh?" Dakota looked at the boots Eve held up for her inspection. They were narrower than her clunky lace-up boots, with two-inch heels, side zippers, and buckles that offered edgy appeal.

Unwilling to trust her own sense of fashion, Dakota asked Dean, "Do you like them?"

"Yeah, sure, but then with what you're wearing, anything will be an improvement."

Grinning, Dakota said, "All right, then. If they have my size, I'll take them."

CHAPTER 15

Marvin stood just outside the glow of a light pole and watched Dakota across the parking lot of the mall. She'd been in there for a couple of hours, though he knew she wasn't much of a shopper. But now the big bruiser beside her was loaded down with packages. Ahead of them were two laughing women.

Her damned backup. What a joke.

Wind blew his hair across his face and cut through his jean jacket. When Dakota had shown up at the bar, as Marvin had known she would, he had his chance to follow her.

Only she didn't leave alone, and that added to his rage. Dakota could be so damned elusive, sneaking out of town, changing her phone number, switching hotels. He hated this damn town. He wanted to head back to Ohio.

But not before squaring things with Dakota.

His cell phone buzzed again, and for the

fourth time, Marvin ignored it. He didn't want any distractions, not now.

As the small group reached the car and saw the deep scratch down the side, Marvin waited with anticipation. Even in a crowded parking lot, with the car parked beneath the lights, it was easy to make his mark. He'd pulled his cap down low over his face, pulled the collar up on his cheap flannel shirt, and kept his keys in his hand. One slow trip past the car, and Dakota knew he'd followed her.

From the shadows, Marvin watched as she turned this way and that, searching the lot. Looking for *him.* He could picture her expression, and it made him nearly giddy with excitement.

Though it was probably the big man's car, he barely paid attention to the damage. After stowing the packages in the trunk, he unlocked the doors, urged the women inside, and drove away.

No cops. No show of anger. No . . . anything.

His cell phone rang yet again.

Marvin gnashed his teeth and clenched his fists. Snatching the phone out of his pocket, he headed for his car and got inside. "What?"

Barnaby said, "Where have you been? I've

been calling for hours."

"I'm a busy man, you know that. In fact, I'm busy right now, so if you have something to say —"

"I need to know what you've done."

"About what?" Marvin slammed his door and put the key in the ignition. He didn't want to follow too closely, but just in case they didn't go back to the bar, he didn't want to lose them, either.

"Dakota called me. She accused me of pushing her down a flight of stairs."

Marvin laughed. "Like you'd have the guts to do it."

"She could have been *killed*."

"Yeah, we both know for a fact how deadly stairs can be, don't we?" Stupid Barnaby. He got so riled over things, even when they turned out for the best. "But she's fine. I just saw her shopping."

"You're there? You're following her?"

"Yeah." Dakota had left her truck at the bar. She'd go back there. And then he'd follow her again, to her motel.

"Marvin, listen to me. She threatened to call the cops. On *me*. But if they show up here, and realize I had nothing to do with it, they might —"

"What? Come looking for me?" Marvin curled his lip and added a dose of menace to his tone. "Now why would they do that?"

Defeated, almost whiny, Barnaby said, "I don't know."

"Exactly. Unless you shoot off your big mouth, which you know you'd regret, the cops wouldn't even look at me. Besides, I have alibis, Barnaby, so don't sweat it."

"There's no reason to hurt anyone else."

"What makes you think I'd hurt Dakota?" He laughed as he said it. "Tell you what, Barnaby. You worry about getting Simon to cooperate before I run out of patience. Don't make me tell you again." He hung up the cell phone and put it on the seat beside him. Dakota couldn't keep a bodyguard around all the time.

Sooner or later, he'd get to her.

She'd regret making him wait.

Dean wouldn't let her out of his sight. He, Eve, and Jackie all went with her to her motel, waiting while she put her packages away, and then insisting she ride with them to the bar.

They walked her inside, too, and even hung around while Dean talked to Barber. The fact that Marvin had probably followed them to the mall had Dean more grim than the scratch to his car did. In fact, he'd looked annoyed when she offered to pay for the damage.

Barber wasn't happy, either. He wanted her to go on home with Dean and Eve, rather than wait for him to have a late dinner, as they'd planned. But no way would she continue to impose on Dean and his family. And no one liked the idea of her returning to her motel room, as she suggested.

As it turned out, both Michael Manchester and Mitch McGee and a half dozen other fighters were at the bar, so Dakota hung out with them. She had a good time, too. The men were so funny, challenging her in a dozen different ways. Billiards. Darts. Even the mechanical bull. Dakota fared well on the first two and refused to take part in the third. That didn't deter the men.

She laughed as hard as everyone else did to see big muscled hunks clinging to a mechanical bull. It proved a great distraction from her worries, and helped the time to pass so she didn't miss Simon so much.

When Michael got thrown from the bull, the others ribbed him about landing so hard. The way he merely dusted himself off showed why he got the nickname Mallet. He was hard as nails.

A few minutes later, the band announced

the last song and Dakota dismissed herself. "It's been great, but I've got to go." They cheerfully tried to convince her to stay, but she was ready for some quieter time.

Mallet joined her at the door. "You're not leaving alone, right?"

"Nope. Barber and I are at the same motel now. We're having a bite to eat, then we'll head back to our rooms."

Mallet walked with her to the main floor. Because she knew he was one of the men Simon had asked to keep an eye out, she looped her arm with his. It felt strange to have so many new friends. Before coming to Harmony, Barber was it, and with their weird schedules, they didn't get to visit as often as she would have liked.

Now her whole life was different. Everywhere she turned, there was a friendly face. The thought of staying in Kentucky, near Simon and all the guys, with a job she liked, appealed to her a lot.

They stopped at the edge of the main floor so the band wouldn't drown out their conversation. "I heard about Dean's car." Mallet looked at his feet, then at her. "I hate it that someone is bothering you."

It always came back to that. Would Simon be so attentive if he didn't fear for her safety? Dakota just didn't know. "Sooner or

later I'll catch him at it. Then it'll end."

He lightly touched his knuckles to her chin. "Yeah, I'd put my money on you." He dropped his hand. "But be careful, okay? Anyone that nutty can be unpredictable."

Barber reached them, and Mallet said his farewells. As they headed out of the bar, Dakota considered what Mallet had said. Would she stand a chance against Marvin? His strength was in being a dirty street fighter, but she wasn't without her own skills.

Yes, she needed some fine-tuning for sure. But maybe Simon had the right idea: with enough practice, she could confront Marvin and then cut him out of her life, the same way she had cut out Barnaby.

After that, she'd have only the future to look forward to.

"Simon asked me about Barnaby."

Dakota had just taken a bite of the best chicken she'd ever tasted, and Barber's statement made her choke. He got out of his seat to thwack her on the back several times until she regained her breath.

The second she did, she wheezed out, "What? When?"

Sliding her drink toward her, he said, "Earlier tonight. He's chewing on a theory

that maybe Barnaby and Marvin are some-how in cahoots against you."

She shook her head. "No. I wondered about that, too, but I don't think so."

"Why not?"

"Barnaby hardly knows Marvin, but what he does know of him he doesn't like. He was the one who encouraged my mom to take such a hard stand against Marvin."

"I remember you saying so."

Dakota rubbed at her forehead, thinking about how the mere mention of Marvin had affected Barnaby when last they spoke. "What did you tell Simon?"

"Nothing." At his leisure, Barber chomped into another chicken plank. "I wasn't sure how much you'd told him, but it didn't sound like he knew everything."

Relief took the rigidity out of Dakota's spine and she slumped into her seat. At least Simon hadn't heard the awful truth from someone else. "Barnaby is Simon's real fa-ther."

"Because Barnaby said so?" Barber snorted. "Simon told me that theory, but I think you should check the facts on that one."

"Short of asking his mother about it, how am I supposed to check anything?" Dakota did a fair job of helping to locate runaways, but she didn't have access to private, personal records. She wouldn't even know where to start. "And anyway, why would Barnaby lie about something like that?"

As if she were nuts, Barber gave her a "duh" look. "Because he's a grade-A fucking asshole, and assholes don't care about finding long-lost sons, that's why."

"I can't disagree. But that doesn't tell me why he'd want to hook up with Simon."

Barber pushed the food aside and reached for Dakota's hands. "Let's put that on hold for a second, okay? The real question here is why haven't you told Simon that Barnaby is your stepfather?"

Dakota knew she should have by now, but lame as they seemed, she did have her reasons. "At first I didn't tell him because I only wanted to convince him to go see Barnaby. I figured that if he knew of my relationship to Barnaby, he'd read more into it than a simple request from his long-lost biological father."

Barber accepted that, but asked, "Why work for Barnaby anyway? And don't give me that bullshit about owing him."

"I do. Or at least, I did. But not anymore. I'm done with Barnaby." Never again would she let him hold her hostage with guilt.

"That's a start." Barber squeezed her

hands. "So tell me, how did Barnaby convince you to help him?"

Always, when there was no one else to turn to, Dakota could confide in Barber without fear of judgment. He always assumed the best of her — as he did now. She appreciated that special closeness more than ever. "He claims to have some letters that my mother wrote to me before her injury and coma."

For only a moment, Barber went stock-still in surprise. Then, as his anger exploded, he crashed his fist down on the tabletop, rattling the dishes and nearly spilling their drinks. Through tight lips, he said, "That son of a bitch."

Appreciating his reaction on her behalf, Dakota gave a small smile. "He said he found them behind a framed photo. He could be lying, I know. But Barber, that was a special hiding place for us. Mom had used it to tuck away emergency money for me. Maybe she thought —"

"That once you buried her, you'd rifle the place looking for loose cash?" Still fuming, Barber shook his head. "I don't buy it."

Put that way, it did sound harsh, almost mercenary. "Maybe she figured Marvin would need money, and for him, I'd go looking. I don't have too many answers. But if she wrote letters that she didn't want anyone else to see, that'd be the best place to put them."

"I suppose it's never occurred to Barnaby that he should give you the letters whether you do him any favors or not."

"The only way I'd have gotten them is if I convinced Simon to meet with him face-to-face." She looked up at Barber. "I've never told Simon about the letters. He only knows that Barnaby has something I wanted, but not what. And that was before we got . . . closer."

"And since you are closer, he should have gone to see Barnaby."

This time Dakota took Barber's hands. "You can't blame him, Barber, because I don't. He's in training for a big comeback in the SBC. His whole life is different now. And from what he's said, he's real close to his stepfather. The man raised him and to Simon, he's Dad. Simon doesn't want to do anything to damage that relationship."

"If you tell him about the letters —"

"No." Dakota shook her head. "Like you said, Barnaby isn't the fatherly sort. He's barely the human sort."

"Agreed."

"That's why I already told Simon to forget about the whole thing."

"He mentioned that you had."

"From the beginning, I figured Barnaby planned to use Simon somehow. And still I tried to manipulate Simon into agreeing. If I tell him everything now, he'll think I'm awful, worse than Bonnie."

"No way. You're nothing like her and Simon knows it." Barber tapped his fingers on the tabletop. "So what happens to the letters since Simon won't see Barnaby?"

"They'll be destroyed." Before Barber could work himself into another fit, Dakota tried to reassure him. "Hey, don't sweat it. I've decided I don't care anymore."

"Don't bullshit me."

"No, I won't. I'm not sure I could." She rubbed the bridge of her nose as she struggled to find the right words. "Maybe Mom wrote me something nice." She looked up at Barber. "But maybe she didn't. Maybe she was still mad and wanted me to know how she resented my behavior. Whatever the letters say, they won't change anything, so in the long run, it doesn't matter if I see them or not. From here on, I'm moving forward and forgetting the past."

Measuring her resolve, Barber said, "I hope you mean that, considering you and Simon have something going on. A bona fide relationship. Maybe a future together."

She wanted to believe that. "With Simon so busy making his comeback, who knows if things between us will go anywhere?"

Barber looked at her with sober intensity. "I'd say you two were in love, but I don't want you to keel over on me."

Dakota ducked her head. This time, the "L" word didn't rattle her quite as much. "I'd already decided to tell Simon about Barnaby. Not about the letters or any of that, but I'll fess up to the fact that Barnaby was my stepfather until my mother's death."

"Why do I feel a big 'but' coming on?"

"I was just thinking . . . it might not be so bad if I go to see Barnaby first. Like you said, he's a liar. I could feel him out a little, try to figure out why he wants to see Simon so badly."

With every word she spoke, Barber looked more apprehensive. "Okay, hold up. Before you start talking up a visit with Barnaby, can I tell you what I think you should do?"

Dakota snorted. "Like I could stop you?"

He drew a calming breath. "I know it's not your strong suit and with good reason, but you should try a little trust. That's always a good first step, and for a guy like Simon, trust will be top of his list."

"I trust you."

His expression left a twinge in her heart.

"I know, and I love you for it. But Simon's the one, so you gotta extend the trust to him, too. Tell him *everything,* hon, and then if you have to go see Barnaby, see him with Simon, not on your own."

She picked at her French fries while thinking that over. "It's not that I don't want to. I do trust Simon — I think I always have. I can't explain it, but from the day I met him, I felt like I knew him. And for some reason, he's the only man I've been attracted to *that* way, too, if you catch my drift."

"I catch it. And that's another reason to clear the air and get rid of the lies."

Seeing the mess she'd made of a fry, Dakota wiped the salt off her hands and covered the plate with her napkin. "In the short time we've known each other, Simon's had too much of my drama dumped over his head. He made it clear that he doesn't want anything to do with Barnaby. But if I tell him about the letters, he might go see him for me. I don't want that responsibility."

"What if Simon is right about Marvin and Barnaby working together?"

Dakota didn't know what to think. "I talked with Barnaby earlier. I even accused him of sending Marvin here."

"You did *what?*"

"He denied it, and I dunno, Barber. I think I believe him."

"I don't fucking believe this."

Lifting her brows, Dakota said, "What?"

Face furious, he leaned closer. "It's like poking a bear with a stick. Do you want Barnaby to get pissed?"

"Why should I care? Once the letters are gone, pissed or not, there's not much else he can do to me."

In the middle of that debate, her phone rang. Glaring at Barber, she dug it out of her pocket and flipped it open. "Hello?"

"Are you all right?"

"Simon." Her mood lightened, and warmth surged through her. "Hi. I'm fine."

"Are you sure? I heard about Dean's car."

Dakota wanted to groan. "I feel so bad about that."

"I knew you would, but it's not your fault. Dean doesn't blame you. And we're both just glad he was with you, since that bastard obviously followed you."

She, too, was glad Marvin hadn't found her alone. "Same here."

With an added edge of frustration, Simon said, "I don't like you being there alone."

"I'm not. Thanks to you, poor Dean stuck with me for hours. And some of the guys were at the bar, and they helped to pass the time."

"What guys?"

"Fighters. From Dean's gym. Don't worry, Michael was there."

"Yeah, that reassures me." He cleared his throat. "So how are you feeling? Not too sore?"

"For what?"

His sudden laugh sent a rush of heat through her body, and she knew Barber noticed. Half turning away, she said, "I'm fine, really."

"Fibber. But I admire your stoicism."

Changing the subject, Dakota asked, "How was your flight?"

"Boring. And I have some bad news." He let out a breath. "I have to stay in Vegas an extra day. Seems like everyone knew I'd be here, and they all want a piece of my time."

Visions of beautiful women lining up to see Simon added an edge to her tone. "Who's everyone?"

"Sponsors. Fighters. Friends. But I hope to be out of here day after tomorrow."

"Want me to pick you up at the airport?" She glanced across the booth at Barber. "I could get Barber to come with me."

Barber made a face, but didn't refuse.

"That's all right. I left my car there. But I

wouldn't mind if you made some time for me when I get home."

"Guaranteed." Dakota hedged a moment, but she wanted to share. "I have some good news, too."

"Let's hear it."

A little apprehensive, she said, "I talked with Roger, and we came to an agreement."

"You'll be staying in Harmony?"

"For a while at least." Dakota couldn't be sure, but she thought Simon might have sounded pleased. "I'll start after Barber finishes up with his contract."

"Good." Before Dakota could relax, a new tension entered Simon's voice and he said, "I'm starting to sound like a broken record, but I think we need to talk."

"Oh, really? Again?" As Simon laughed, Dakota looked up and saw Bonnie coming into the restaurant on the arm of yet another fighter. "Hang on a second, Simon." She covered the phone.

"Well, look at her, will ya?" Barber slanted Dakota a glance. "Seems you aren't the only one who felt the need for a little shake-up to the image."

Dakota rolled her eyes. Her wardrobe update didn't begin to compare to Bonnie's alterations. The woman had sheared off her long hair into a tousled, and admittedly sexy, shoulder-length shag. Her makeup was brighter, her clothes more revealing. "She looks sexier."

"I'm sure that was the point. And what do you know? She's sent the escort on ahead and she's coming this way. In fact, it appears she was looking for you."

Dakota stiffened, then lifted the phone to her ear. "Um, Simon, I sort of need to go."

"Why? What's wrong?"

"Not a thing, except that Bonnie is fast approaching. I think she wants to . . . talk." Nearly choking on that last word, Dakota said, "Will you let me know what time you're getting in?"

Simon ignored her question. "What the hell does Bonnie want?"

"I have no idea." Bonnie stopped in front of her, so Dakota said, "Should I ask her for you?"

Bonnie looked at Barber and smiled. "Hello, Barber."

"Hey, darlin'. Lookin' good."

"Thank you."

"The new 'do rocks."

Bonnie gently shook her head to ruffle her hair. "I like it, too." Lazily, she turned to Dakota. "I don't suppose that's Simon on the line."

Dakota wanted to tell her to go to hell,

but instead she said, "None other."

Holding out a hand, Bonnie asked, "May I?"

Of all the nerve! Eyes burning, Dakota swallowed her ire and said sweetly, "Why not?" as she handed over the phone.

Bonnie smiled, but didn't thank her. "Simon, how auspicious."

Disregarding manners, Barber stayed seated while Bonnie continued to stand near their table. He even went back to eating.

Dakota didn't budge.

"Now, Simon, don't be surly. I have something important to tell you." She laughed. "Well, if you're certain you don't want to hear, of course I won't bother you. But since it's about Dakota . . . yes, that's what I thought."

Barber stopped eating to stare up at her.

Dakota's heart thumped against her ribs.

"I received the oddest phone call from a man who refused to identify himself. He said if I wanted you back — which I no longer do — that he could arm me with enough information about your little songbird to make you dump her. And those were his exact words for her, not something I made up."

Dakota couldn't move. Her legs felt frozen — like her heart.

"If you raise your voice at me, Simon, I'll not share the rest." Bonnie looked at Dakota while speaking. "Naturally I told him I wasn't interested in gossip. He called me a fool, and told me that if I cared for you, I'd save you from her. It's because I do care that I'm sharing this. Honestly, he had a very odd way of speaking that didn't feel right. After what happened in the parking lot, I thought it'd be best to let you know so that you can protect yourself."

Heartbeat slowing, Dakota went rigid. Her hands curled into fists on the tabletop.

"You're welcome," Bonnie said. "I don't expect to hear from him again, but yes, if I do, I'll let you know." She paused, and then smiled. "Actually, I'm doing quite well. I got a promotion at work, so I gave myself a makeover and I'm taking tonight to celebrate. Thank you."

Dakota began fuming again, especially when Bonnie gave an intimate laugh and made a kissing sound into the phone before handing it back to Dakota.

She started to leave, but Barber took her hand. "Bonnie?"

"Hmm?"

"Thanks. It was real nice of you to share that info."

She glanced at Dakota with pure dislike.

"She's trouble, and she's going to drag the lot of you into that trouble with her. Whoever called me was uncouth and crass, and apparently well acquainted with her." She looked at Barber's hand on hers. "I'll play no part in any of it."

Barber released her and pulled back. "Loud and clear, sweetheart."

"Good." With another fleeting smile, she sashayed away.

Well done, Dakota thought, watching Bonnie make a strategic exit after shoving the knife in her back. The woman was an out-and-out pro at retaliation.

Reluctantly, Dakota put the phone back to her ear. "You still there, Simon?"

"Let me talk to Barber."

She knew that tone too well. "Why? So you two can plan things around me? I don't think so. I'm not stupid. I hear the warning bells the same as you."

"And you'll be extra careful?"

It was how she lived her life. "I repeat — I'm not stupid."

"I'll take that as a yes, but I want to hear you say it. Tell me you won't go anywhere alone. I don't want you to leave your room for ice without letting someone know about it."

This day had not gone well. "Sure, I'll say

it. If you will, too."

"What?"

"Bonnie didn't parade over here for my benefit. She only shared that stuff because she was worried about you. So I want you to promise that you'll be extra careful, too. Being the generous sort I am, I won't forbid you to get ice. Just look up and down the hotel hallways first, to make sure the coast is clear."

Simon chuckled. "Okay, I get it. You're pissed that I'm being overbearing."

"No, I'm annoyed that you think I'm too lame to look out for myself. I don't plan to skulk around in dark alleys or go for midnight drives alone, and I won't even play with sharp objects. So give me a little credit for common sense, okay?"

"I'm sorry."

"You say that sincerely enough, but I can tell you're grinning."

"I really do miss you, honey."

And that easily, he defused her temper. She sighed. "Same here."

"Now that we've got that settled . . ." He paused for emphasis. "Put Barber on the line."

Dakota handed over the phone. "This is getting ridiculous."

Barber grinned evilly. "Hey, Simon."

Rather than listen to them, Dakota put her thoughts to figuring out why Marvin would call Bonnie. What had he hoped to accomplish? Or was it Barnaby? Crass and uncouth sounded more like Marvin, but Barnaby had his moments. She knew what Marvin wanted — to annoy her, to frighten her. He got off on it, for some reason. But what could Barnaby possibly want? Maybe she should ask Bonnie a few questions about the call . . . the hell she would.

Laughing, Barber handed her back the phone. "He wants to talk to you again."

"Right." Dakota put the phone to her ear. "I hope you have a good long-distance phone plan!"

"I'll call again later tonight. And in the morning before my show."

"You don't need to do that."

"I do if I want to hear your voice."

"Then . . . okay. I'll keep my cell nearby."

"Dakota?"

"Yeah?"

"Tonight, after you get rid of Barber, think of me. And only me." Simon hung up, and Dakota put the phone away.

Eyeing her, Barber asked, "Any reason for that ear-splitting grin?"

She shrugged her shoulders. "Yeah. Simon says I should think of him tonight."

"Like there was any doubt?" He uncovered her food. "You understand that if you don't tell Simon everything, and I mean everything, then Barnaby or Marvin probably will, right?"

"It looks that way."

"Perfect. Now that we have that settled, don't you think you should eat?"

She didn't argue the point. Simon did need to know it all. And then he'd understand that being honest with him meant more to her than possible letters from her mother. Surely he'd forgive her for her earlier omissions. "You know, I'm suddenly starving."

"That's the Dakota I know and love."

She'd heard that "L" word more tonight than in all the years since she'd left home. It was growing on her. She liked it.

She'd like it even more coming from Simon. But that could wait. He had a title belt to win back, and she had a past to put to rest. After that, they'd have plenty of time to work out the kinks in their growing relationship.

CHAPTER 16

The spot on the talk show went great, and as Simon left the studio, he continued to grin. Who knew the hosts, camera crew, and everyone else on the set were such rabid fans? Things had veered off course, but in a fun way, and he felt it was a better show for it. The relaxed conversation, the honesty of the questions, and the opportunity to give detailed answers would prove great promo for the SBC.

He couldn't wait to hear what Dakota thought of the show.

Because it was taped, he should be home in time to watch it with her. First he'd kiss her silly, then maybe take her to the hot tub to play a little more, and then . . . Simon didn't want to rush her, but he hoped she'd be ready for lovemaking.

He was more than ready. He couldn't even think of her without his muscles tensing and his dick twitching, yet he thought of her at every quiet moment. Hell, sometimes she crowded his brain when it wasn't quiet. In the middle of his interview today, he'd started wondering if she was at the gym, if she was grappling with Barber, if she was enjoying herself.

He needed her.

Soon.

The dry Vegas heat blasted Simon in a smothering tide as he stepped out of the building. Slipping on reflective sunglasses, he glanced around the lot, looking for the car that'd take him back to his hotel.

His gaze skimmed over a lone man leaning against a black sedan. Then shot back.

Shielded by his sunglasses, he studied the man. He stood two inches taller than Simon and had a bulkier build, especially through the shoulders, neck, and chest. Thanks to the heat, sweat had darkened his shaggy blond hair. He wore his own sunglasses, hiding his eyes, but Simon knew they were dark, piercing blue — something often mentioned by the commentators during a stare-down at the start of a fight.

Harley Handleman.

No doubt about it, he was waiting on Simon. The man had nerve. Or he lacked common sense. Simon wasn't sure which.

Turning his back on Harley, Simon located his ride and started in that direction.

Footsteps sounded behind him. Harley called out, "Sublime."

Simon said nothing. As he'd told Bonnie, what this man had done with her meant nothing to him now. But he wouldn't have it thrown in his face.

"I know you heard me, Evans."

Simon stopped, glanced over his shoulder. "Then you know I'm ignoring you."

"I only need a second."

He snorted. "You need more than that."

Harley stopped a good distance away and put his hands on his hips. Heat waves undulated off the blacktop between them. A bead of sweat slithered down his temple. "I just want to talk, that's all. I'll save the brawl for the cage."

Simon smiled and said, "Go to hell."

"It's important, damn it."

What a laugh. "Are you a fucking idiot? No, don't answer. That was a redundant question. Of course you are, or you wouldn't be here."

Harley went taut. His iron jaw jutted out. "I already know you don't care about me sleeping with Bonnie. I heard that from some of the other fighters."

"They should have also told you that it'd be best to stay out of my way."

"I'm not afraid of you, Sublime, if that's what you're thinking."

Simon shook his head and started walking toward his ride. If he stayed, he'd definitely put his fist through Harley's mouth, and truthfully, he didn't want to do that. As Harley said, he wanted to save it for the cage.

"She came on to me, Sublime," Harley called after him, uncaring of any passersby who might overhear. "I didn't know she'd taken pictures."

Yeah, right. How the hell could a man not know?

As if he'd heard Simon's thoughts, Harley said, "I was a little distracted with other things at the time. She must've set the camera on a timer or something." Disgust filled his tone when he added, "Do you really think I want naked photos of myself floating around?"

Simon's neck stiffened. That explained one thing, but he still couldn't believe Harley had come here to talk about his bedroom activities with Bonnie.

Harley strode after him. "I didn't know she was your woman, Sublime." Then louder, "I met her in a damn bar, for God's sake!"

Simon flagged a one-finger salute and

finally reached the car. The driver, a young man fascinated by the exchange, looked from Simon to beyond him at Harley. His eyes widened.

Harley now stood right behind him. "This isn't about Bonnie, you stubborn ass."

Grinding his teeth together, Simon paused, but he knew he wouldn't get rid of Harley by ignoring him. He slewed his head around to glare. "I'm. Not. Interested."

"Fine. Fuck it." Harley jerked off his sunglasses, showing Simon those eerie blue eyes of his. "Have it your way, then. But it's about Dakota."

It was strange, Simon thought a few seconds later, how one short sentence could change everything.

He went from being annoyed and insulted into a full-blown red-hot rage.

As Simon came after Harley, Harley back-stepped, but he caught himself and stopped to brace for Simon's attack. "God damn it, man, if you hit me I *will* hit you back and then I won't be able to help you or her."

The words didn't register. Barely restraining himself, Simon spoke mere inches from Harley's face. "Understand this, Harley. Bonnie was one thing. Dakota is another. If you touch her, I'll take you apart."

"I don't want to touch her," Harley said,

exasperated. "If you would listen, you'd know that I want to help. That's all."

"I don't need your help."

"Hear me out, and then make that decision."

Simon clenched and unclenched and finally relented. "You've got five seconds."

Harley accepted the opportunity. "A reporter approached me about Bonnie, insinuating that our fight was a grudge match."

Simon eased back an inch. "Shit." It needed only this.

"I told him to get lost, so he asked me how Dakota was involved. I had never heard of her, so I walked away from the guy. He's dogged me ever since, and I think it's going to blow."

Surly and needing to take it out on Harley, Simon said, "Good press for you, huh?"

"You've got it wrong, Sublime. I want the fight, but I want it as fair and straightforward as it can be. Me and you, matching up in the cage. Period. I don't want it to be about anything other than the sport."

"If that's so, then how did the reporter even know about Dakota?"

"I have no idea. Until he said her name to me, I hadn't heard of her. In fact, when he first mentioned her, I thought he meant the state, like maybe he thought one of us was taking a damn trip or something." Harley's mouth twisted. "He was real quick in explaining things to me."

Simon didn't want to admit it, and he definitely didn't like it, but he believed Harley. He had no reason not to. He didn't know that much about the man, but what he did know gave him no reason to think he'd lie, or use underhanded tactics to garner press.

"Fine. You told me. Now I need to go."

Harley grabbed his arm. "Not yet."

Slowly, Simon met his gaze. He wanted Harley to know how he'd erred by touching him.

And the second Harley looked at Simon, he more than understood. Lifting his hands away, he asked, "Did you know that my uncle Satch is my manager?"

"It's common knowledge. I know he's obsessed with you winning a belt, too." Harley hadn't had an easy time in the organization. He often came close to taking a title, but three times now, something had happened to knock him off course.

"When I told Uncle Satch about the reporter, he did some digging. And here's where I can help you if you'll stop trying to find a reason to slug me."

Simon's shirt stuck to his chest and back. The reflection off the blacktop nearly blinded him. "Get on with it."

Harley drew a deep breath. "The reporter told my uncle that he got Dakota's name from an anonymous man who contacted him with what he called the 'whole sordid scandal.' The reporter said he confirmed that you're seeing her."

"How'd he do that?"

Harley gave him a look. "Jesus, man, you can ask just about anyone in the sport and they know. I take it she hangs out at Havoc's gym? And that she's a looker?" He lifted one solid shoulder. "Guys talk. You know that."

Yeah, he did know it. No way could Dakota Dream infiltrate an all-male domain without causing a stir.

"Now this damned reporter wants to paint Dakota as a rebound fill-in for Bonnie, and as a bone of contention between us."

Simon burned. No way in hell would he let the press sabotage Dakota. He'd talk to Drew. He'd —

"But I wouldn't have come to you just over that."

There was more? "I'm roasting out here, Harley. Do you think you can get to the point sometime today?"

Harley chewed his upper lip, looked around the lot, and hedged uncomfortably. "Like I said, my uncle leaves no stone unturned. He used to be military, and after that, he worked as a bodyguard until I took up fighting. He's a mean cuss with contacts everywhere."

"Skip the family history."

After one sharp nod, Harley said, "My uncle is convinced that the man who called the reporter is going to cause more trouble."

Thoughts churning furiously, Simon narrowed his eyes. "And he thinks this because . . . ?"

"He found out that Dakota just took a spill down some stairs at a local club back where you're training. Is that true?"

Simon hid his surprise. Very few people knew of that, and he couldn't see any of them spreading rumors. Old Uncle Satch really did have his sources. "What of it?"

Using his wrist to wipe the sweat from his brow, Harley huffed out a breath and then propped his hands back on his hips. "Maybe my uncle is paranoid, and maybe he sees conspiracies where none exist. I don't know. But he made me promise I'd tell you, so that's what I'm doing."

Simon began to feel ill.

"You might already be aware of this, but

Dakota's mother died a while back."

"I know."

Harley nodded. Eyes squinted from the bright sun, he explained, "Ultimately, it was an infection that killed her. But did you know that it was a fall down some stairs that injured her so bad in the first place?"

A sick foreboding kicked Simon in the gut. He stood there for several moments, taking it in, working it through his brain.

Appreciating his expression, Harley nodded. "Hell of a coincidence, don't you think?"

Simon glanced at his watch, then at Harley. "Got some free time?"

"Nothing until this evening, then I'm running again."

"Hang on." Simon walked back to the driver. He tipped him generously, thanked him, and dismissed him. As the driver left the lot, Simon turned and walked past Harley toward his car. "Come on. You can give me a ride to my motel, then to my next appointment. It'll give us a chance to talk."

Harley jogged to catch up. "So you think it's important? My uncle was right about that?"

"Yeah. He was right." A thousand questions demanded answers. And most of them would start and stop with Dakota. "Let's go. I'm running late."

Simon's trip got extended again and again. It seemed everyone wanted a piece of him while he was in Vegas. After four days away, Dakota was missing him so much that she couldn't stop thinking of him. He called at least once a day, which gave him the opportunity to do a lot of the "talking" that he'd requested.

Starting on the second day of his trip, every sports channel shared quick footage of him. His fame and the attention he got amazed Dakota. Not that long ago, outraged senators who didn't understand the sport had tried to have SBC events banned in their states. Now, most considered it the fastest-growing sport around. It had long since overtaken boxing in popularity.

Simon took the attention in stride, and lamented his delay in returning to town.

Sounding almost bored, he mentioned over the phone that a hit sitcom had invited him to play a bit role. On top of that, he'd turned down offers to commentate select sporting events and even a few other interviews. According to Simon, he'd refused because the timing was wrong and would have interfered with his training.

Dakota hoped that was true, that he

wasn't turning down awesome offers just out of worry for her.

While hitting a heavy bag at Dean's gym, Dakota listened to Mallet and Billy speaking of Simon. They liked and respected him, but more than that, they believed in his ability to win. Though Harley Handleman was considered the top contender and a very dangerous man, most would still put their money on Simon.

She was deep into a series of kicks against the bag when Barber came up behind her. "That's enough for now. Let's practice some moves."

With her muscles on fire, Dakota gladly accepted the switch. How the men practiced full speed for up to six hours a day, she couldn't fathom. She'd only been at it since Simon's departure, and already she felt the strain in every muscle. Of course, compared to the men surrounding her, she looked downright scrawny.

Using the hem of her sweatshirt, Dakota mopped the perspiration from her face. Unlike the guys, who wore only shorts and regulation-weight gloves, she'd bundled up in a jog suit and sports bra. A breath of cool air and a hearty lunch would do her good — but she wasn't about to cry uncle, and Barber knew it.

With the gym packed and the men all working, it took them a few minutes to locate an empty mat. As usual, as soon as Dean came over to oversee their practice, Mallet, Mitch, Billy, and Gregor all stopped to watch, too. The small crowd they made drew the attention of the other fighters.

Dakota didn't like being the center of attention, but at least it spurred her on to do her very best.

Trying to look pumped instead of pooped, Dakota peeled off her gloves. In a real competition, the fighters would wear them. But she didn't practice in order to compete, and the others accepted that. "What's first?"

Standing there in nothing more than black nylon shorts and a big grin, Barber said, "Standing guillotine defense." He moved behind her, put his right arm around her neck, locked it in, and said, "Let's see what you've got, sweetie."

Dakota went through the defensive moves, knowing that Barber allowed her to do them by offering very little resistance. With the right move, he went flat on the mat beneath her. Keeping her grip on his left wrist, she stepped over his head with her right leg and finished by leaning her weight onto her left side and onto Barber's stomach for a reverse bent arm lock.

Barber tapped. And snickered . . . as did most of the guys watching.

Of course, her derrière was inches from Barber's face, with her legs on either side of his head.

Dean narrowed his eyes. "You're making it too easy on her, Barber."

Dakota rolled off him, but Barber just lay there, sprawled out and still smiling. "Like you wouldn't?" A rumble of agreement came from the spectators, and a few even volunteered to coach her next.

"No." Dean strolled onto the mat. "I won't." He took a stance. "Let's go, Dakota."

She stared at him. Somewhere along the way, Dean had not only decided that he liked her, but he'd made it his personal goal to better her skills. "You're not kidding?"

"Afraid not."

Barber said, "She's learning by repetition."

"At first," Dean agreed. "Now she'll learn by actually defending herself."

She didn't know if she liked the sound of that.

Without softening, Dean asked, "Do you want to improve?"

"Yes." She wanted those same fast, automatic reflexes that the fighters had.

"Then you'll have to take your knocks." He signaled for her to come closer. "So let's go."

Did he plan to maim her? With everyone watching, Dakota couldn't back down. Barber moved out of the way, but sprawled on his side to watch. Mallet crossed his arms and grinned. Gregor, standing a head taller than the others, shouted, "Go get 'im, Dakota."

Chin up, Dakota walked to Dean. "All right. What first?"

"We'll do an arm lock series — from the mount." So saying, Dean went to his back. He braced his bare feet on the mat, which emphasized the muscles in his thick thighs and calves. Chest muscles bulging, he lifted his head and motioned her forward.

He wanted her to mount him?

Sure, she knew the mount was a vital part of positioning. She wasn't attracted to Dean *that* way, so she supposed it would be okay. And at least he wasn't planning to mount *her.* That would have been worse, because it might have caused her to panic, given how she reacted when in a submissive position.

Hoping to brazen through what she considered an awkward moment, Dakota shrugged. "All right. Sure." She put her knees on either side of Dean's hips and . . .

sat down. Other than embarrassment, she felt nothing.

Judging by Dean's expression, he didn't, either. She might have been another male. That made it easier.

But the men watching sure liked the show. Typical.

"Forearm choke?" Dakota asked.

"Whatever suits you," Dean agreed. "But be ready to defend it."

Seconds later, when Dakota found herself in a rather uncomfortable position, she realized she wasn't ready at all. Dean sat up with her, patiently explained each move that she'd done incorrectly or that she hadn't finished, and then went to his back again.

By the fourth try, they ended with Dakota on Dean's left, his arm secured in hers with his pinkie aimed at his chest. She dug her heels into the mat, lifted her hips — and got the armlock.

Dean tapped.

"Good job," he said as soon as she let up. "Now let's do it again."

And so it went for over an hour. Each man had something he wanted to contribute to her education, offering up suggestions, encouragement, and a few bawdy jokes. One by one, they took the mat with her to show her something from a different perspective.

They were all good at what they did, some more than others. They were careful with her, but diligent, and overall, Dakota found it so tiring that her embarrassment faded away. She learned a lot, and despite the male teasing from their audience, she had fun.

It was in the middle of an arm-bar counter against a standing front choke that she heard a familiar voice say, "What kind of welcome is this?"

From her position on the floor, Dakota cranked her head around to look up. And there stood Simon, arms crossed, feet planted apart — and looking so gorgeous she couldn't help but grin. "Simon!"

Twisted together with Dean, Dakota had his arm locked against her chest, her legs around his head, with both of them belly down on the mat.

Tone dry, Dean said, "Now might be a good time to let me up, Dakota."

"You think?" Laughing, she scrambled to free herself and get to her feet. Everyone watched them. Feeling conspicuous at the gym was starting to be a habit. But it didn't stop her from rushing over to Simon and saying quickly, "I've been practicing and I *think* getting a lot better."

Simon's gaze moved from her face to

somewhere behind her and a second later, she got locked in a tight embrace from the rear.

Without even thinking about it, Dakota executed several moves, countering each new one until she was able to do a sweep with her right leg, dropping her attacker to the mat. Keeping her own balance, she shifted quickly and caught him in a standing arm bar.

Barber groaned and laughed at the same time. "Yep, she's definitely better, Simon."

"So I see."

Dakota scowled. "That was to give a demonstration to Simon?"

From flat on his back, Barber winked. "You know you were dying to show off for him."

She had been, but . . . "Doofus." Dakota helped him up and, one by one, the crowd dispersed. "You know you could still brush me off like a fly."

"Maybe, if I was really pissed. But most guys without training would have their hands full."

"You mean it?"

Barber smoothed her hair. "Yeah."

Suddenly she felt herself hauled to the side. Simon leaned forward and put a warm kiss to her mouth — right in front of Barber.

"You smell like male sweat."

She wrinkled her nose. "That'd be Dean, Barber, and Mallet."

Expression carefully blank, Simon asked, "No one else?"

Barber chuckled. "Sorry, bud, but I'm afraid the whole gym took part."

Simon gazed around the crowded room. He didn't look happy. "I suppose they had good intentions?"

"Dean made sure they did."

Simon relaxed. "I owe him."

Dakota shook her head at both men, then said to Simon, "I'd be showered and fresh, but you weren't due home for hours."

"I got done ahead of schedule and was able to catch an earlier flight." His attention went to Barber. "Everything go okay?"

"Haven't seen hide nor hair of anyone suspicious." Barber clapped him on the shoulder, picked up a towel, and headed off.

Left somewhat alone, Dakota moved from foot to foot. She wanted to throw herself against him. She wanted to take him to the mat and kiss him senseless.

"What are you thinking, woman?"

"I was thinking that this time I'm the one who's a sweaty mess, otherwise I'd greet you with . . . more enthusiasm."

"Soon." He took her chin in his hand and moved her face from side to side. "Your bruises are fading."

"I'm a fast healer."

"How are you feeling?"

"Wrung out like a limp dishrag. But that's from working here. Dean is ruthless. But he's also real clear about what I should do and when."

His large hand went to the side of her neck. "Other than that, you're okay?"

"Good as new."

"How about we get out of here, then?"

"I need to go to the motel to shower and change."

"You rode here with Barber?"

"Yes."

"My car is outside." He held out a hand. "Let's go."

CHAPTER 17

After barely sponging off the worst of the sweat in the locker room, Dakota joined Simon and they went to his car. Unlike the men, she couldn't use the shower room at the gym. It was a big open space with no privacy.

Of course, the guys always volunteered to wash her back — not that she'd tell Simon that. Somehow she didn't think he'd appreciate their humor.

"What's all this?" His backseat overflowed with shipped boxes.

"Freebies. You might want some of it. There are some energy drinks and bars, shorts and towels. A new type of razor, too." Grinning, Simon ran a hand over his clean-shaven head before fastening his seat belt. "They'll be sponsoring me in exchange for a few ads."

After Dakota latched her belt, too, Simon started the car and left the gym parking lot, saying, "That other box, the one near the door, is filled with SBC T-shirts and sweatshirts. I figured with your fondness for printed tops, you could make use of them."

The way he said it with so much nonchalance gave him away. "You mean instead of the shirts that Barber gives me?"

"Exactly."

His possessiveness thrilled her. He wasn't overbearing with it, and he never tried to bully her. It just . . . showed that he cared. And that never ceased to amaze her. Dakota stared at him, and smiled.

Afternoon sunlight limned his profile, highlighting the straight line of his nose, the sensual curve of his mouth, his strong chin and firm jaw. "You're too handsome, Simon, do you know that?"

His grin flickered. He lowered the visor to block some of the sun. "I'm glad you think so."

"Don't be modest. It's true. You're like . . . better than good-looking." She shook her head. "It's unnerving. And almost scary."

"Scary?"

His concern only baffled her more. She was an okay-looking woman. Not a hag, but not a real beauty, either. She had a strong figure, not a supersexy bod. In almost every way, she rated average. Simon was so above average that she didn't even know what to call it.

And he wanted her.

"Not that kind of scary." She pulled at her sweat-soaked top. "Look at me. At my best, I'm no match for you. And right now, I'm bordering on gross."

Without smiling, without a word, Simon reached out a hand to her. When she took it, he carried it to his lap and pressed her palm to his growing erection. "Whatever you are, Dakota, I like it. A lot. I can't recall ever wanting a woman as much as I want you."

His bold honesty had her heart beating double time. She started to curl her fingers around him, but he returned her hand to her side of the car. "None of that or I won't make it to the motel, and you definitely won't get your shower."

That snapped her out of the fog. "Trust me, Sublime, no matter how irresistible you are, nothing's happening until I'm done bathing."

Stopping at a red light, Simon turned toward her. He studied her in silence for a few seconds. "You do realize that you're touching on a sore spot, right? I mean, all the other fighters have great names. Havoc. Mayhem. Spider. Viper."

Dakota fought back a laugh. "Yeah. Makes them sound real adorable."

"Adorable isn't the point."

"I suppose not."

The light changed so he pulled away. "Almost from jump, I got stuck with Sublime."

"Poor Simon," she teased. "You don't need a badass name to shore you up. You do well enough without it."

In an odd mood, he said, "So far."

That surprised her. "You're worried about winning your comeback?"

"No. But I'm always aware of possibilities." He studied their surroundings as he drove. "Harley came to see me while I was in Vegas."

Dakota didn't know what to make of that. "He lives there?"

"No, but he was in town, too, for promotion."

A wisp of anger unfurled. "He wasn't there trying to challenge you, was he?"

"No." Simon grinned. "Actually, he's a good fighter, and from what I can tell, a good man. I believe Mallet and Gregor are friends with him. They've trained at the same camps, sparred, that sort of thing. Harley's had some rough breaks that've kept him from getting the title belt, but he's due.

It should be a good fight."

"So what did he want with you?"

Simon pulled into the motel lot. "Back when he slept with Bonnie, he didn't know she was living with me."

"And?"

Shrugging, Simon said, "He wanted me to know that he hadn't sought her out on purpose. She was in a bar and, according to him, she gave the come-on, not the other way around."

"Does it matter?"

Turning toward her, Simon smiled. "Not really." He leaned forward and kissed her lightly. "Let's go, woman. My patience is running thin."

Simon took her gym bag and, after escorting her from the car, locked it. No one paid them any attention as they entered the motel and went to her room. Once inside, Dakota said, "I'll make it quick."

But Simon caught her hand. "I'll shower with you."

She looked down at her grungy clothes, thought of her sweaty hair, and said, "Wouldn't you rather —"

"I'd rather be inside you right now. It's all I've been able to think about for three damn days."

Her mouth went dry. She could almost

feel him pushing inside her, and it excited her unbearably. "Well, if you put it that way . . . Sure. Why not?"

In minutes, Dakota had the shower adjusted, her hair out of the ponytail, and her sweatshirt and sneakers off. Steam swirled around her as she wrestled with her socks. She heard a noise and looked through the open bathroom door to the sleeping area in time to see Simon toss his slacks and boxers on the bed. He'd already removed his sweater, shoes, and socks. He straightened, and then just stood there, totally naked, looking at her — mostly at her bared breasts — and she almost melted.

She'd never survive this. Still balanced on one foot, she whispered, "Lord have mercy."

Simon's expression darkened even more. "Finish undressing."

"Yeah." Dropping down to sit on the side of the tub, unable to take her gaze off Simon, Dakota peeled off the socks. She stood again — and felt a twinge of shyness.

Simon stepped into the minuscule bathroom with her, but he didn't reach for her. "Take them off, Dakota."

She nodded. "It's good that the lights are on. I mean, I don't think I could do this in the dark because my mind would start thinking ignorant things. About Marvin, I mean, and what he did. But I wouldn't want to miss seeing you anyway. And the light in here is pretty bright, don't you think?"

Simon frowned. "Don't be nervous, honey."

"No."

"I don't want anyone else occupying your thoughts but me."

Looking at his body, Dakota raised a brow and said, "I think that's doable."

"Get naked."

"It comes back to that, huh?" She firmed her mouth, hooked her thumbs in the elasticized band of the jogging pants, and pushed them down, taking her panties with them. She stepped out of them and glanced at Simon.

Breathing deeply, he looked her over from head to toes, lingering everywhere in between.

"Do I pass?"

"Yeah." He sounded hoarse. "You pass." Then suddenly he was there, pushing back the shower curtain and lifting her into the tub. Seconds later, when her back flattened against the icy tile wall, Dakota gave a small shriek. Simon smothered the sound with a deep kiss, at the same time turning so that it was his back to the wall and she had the dominant position.

One of his big hands held the back of her head, keeping her there for his kiss, for the teasing of his tongue and the nip of his teeth. His other hand went down her back to her bottom. He gave a gentle squeeze — and groaned about it.

Wow, he was impatient. And with his erection pressed solidly against her belly, she knew he was more than ready, too.

He was so tall and hard all over that he overwhelmed her, and little by little, the ruthlessness of his touch and kiss eased into a tender exploration. Dakota ran her hands over his shoulders, loving the bulk of his muscles and the sleekness of his skin. She trailed her fingers through his dark chest hair, over his pecs, and down to his tight abdomen.

Pulling his mouth away, Simon tipped his head back against the shower wall and groaned. A split second later, he caught her wrists. "Sorry. I can't take too much of that right now."

Dakota stared into his dark brown eyes, inspired and excited. "What if I don't want to stop?"

His eyes glittered beneath wet lashes. "I'll come."

"I don't think that sounds so bad." With their gazes locked, she pressed against his restrictive hold until he released her. Watching him, loving the strain in his face, she wrapped both hands around his jutting penis.

His breath caught.

Her breath caught, too.

The shower sprayed against them until her hair was soaked, streaming down her back. Steam rose around them. Dakota couldn't recall ever feeling so connected to a man and what he wanted. It was . . . exhilarating.

"Relax for me, Simon. Let me enjoy you for a little while."

Breathing harder, his nostrils flared and his body taut, Simon dropped his hands to his sides and braced his feet apart. "Have at it, sweetheart."

A challenge? Slowly, Dakota smiled and let her gaze drift from his face down his body. "You are such a treat." She leaned forward and opened her mouth over his chest, tasting his skin, breathing in the hot scent of him. And all the while, she held his flexing erection tight in her hands. She didn't stroke him, not yet. She just held him.

Every so often he twitched, as if he couldn't control himself.

Because she didn't want to relinquish her hold on him, Dakota caressed and explored the rest of him with her mouth. His throat, his shoulders, his jaw. Simon turned his head and caught the kiss, taking over for a brief moment, kissing her long and deep. He didn't raise his hands or in any way touch her, other than with his kiss.

It was so erotic that Dakota felt herself on the edge, too.

To put things back on track, she squeezed Simon. He tightened all over, giving up the kiss so he could lock his teeth against a harsh groan. Expecting to see his eyes closed, Dakota looked up at him.

He stared at her, and there was so much there in his dark gaze that she wanted to both cry and smile, and beg him to love her.

Instead, she slowly lowered herself to her knees, trailing her tongue along his heated flesh until she reached his navel. Her chin bumped the head of his cock and he jerked hard. She liked that reaction, and turned to rub her cheek against him.

Simon made a small sound, and his hands curled into fists. Teasing him, Dakota left a warm, wet trail of love bites along his hip bone. His scent was so much stronger here, drawing her, heightening her awareness.

It quickly became too much. Still holding him in both hands, she drew the head into her mouth and sucked.

Simon went rigid with a curse. His hand caught the back of her head, his fingers tangling hard in her hair. "Dakota. Baby, don't."

His response amplified her own. Awed by the silky texture of his flesh here, the way he swelled even more, grew harder and longer, she worked her tongue around him. A bead of fluid escaped, giving her his taste.

She loosened one hand from him so that she could stroke his thigh, feel the muscles so bunched and rigid. With the other hand, she stroked in counterpoint to the glide of her mouth over him.

Simon sank both hands into her hair and began guiding her. With each stroke his breath grew harsher, deeper. *"Last chance,"* he warned in a low growl, and he tried to draw her away.

Dakota wanted everything from him.

Giving up, he pulled her close, pushed himself into her mouth two more times, a third. And then he was coming, his moan rough and loud in the small shower, his body tensing in rhythm to his release until he was completely spent.

Feeling warm and soft, Dakota drew away and looked up the length of his gorgeous body. Eyes closed, head back, chest still billowing, Simon looked like a female fantasy.

And for right now, he was all hers.

More than satisfied, Dakota licked her lips, then slowly stood and hugged herself to him. Simon managed to loop one arm around her, and again, he tangled his fingers in her wet hair. She indulged that quiet comfort for half a minute before she pushed away and made use of the soap while Simon barely opened his eyes.

"God, you are a sexy woman."

Covered in lather, Dakota laughed. "Yeah, that's me. A regular femme fatale." Teasing him, feeling powerful, she licked her lips again. "You taste very good, Simon."

His eyes narrowed. "And what about you, sweetheart?" He levered away from the shower wall and took the soap from her. "When do I get to taste you?"

Her heart started pumping double time. "Um . . . maybe after I'm clean and sitting down somewhere?"

His smile did crazy things to her. "We'll see."

Turning her so that she faced the shower spray, he took over washing her. Taking his time lathering her breasts and belly in a diabolical way that soon had her squirming in need. "Simon . . ."

"My turn." His soapy hands came back up to her nipples. The lather left her slippery so that his fingers slid over her, around her, pinching lightly, tugging at her.

"I'm not you, Simon." So much sensation swelled inside her, she wanted, needed, to lie down. "I can't do this standing up."

His mouth touched her ear, and he whispered in challenge, "Wanna bet?"

Dakota tried to turn, but he held her secure with one arm. She really didn't think she could take too much more, not with how much she wanted him already. "Simon, no."

He went still. "Are you afraid of me, Dakota?" His arms hugged around her. "Does this position alarm you?"

She shook her head hard. "No, it's not that." Other than that one time after discussing Marvin with him, she'd never been distressed with Simon.

"Good." He went back to teasing her.

"But I —"

His hand cupped over her mound. "Quiet down, Dakota. No talking. Just feel."

Pressing her head back against his shoulder, she tried to do just that. He had one arm around her upper body, supporting her but leaving his hand free to toy with her breast. With his other hand, he fondled between her legs, exploring her. The soap washed away, but the water left their skin slick.

Simon said, "Hold your breasts for me."

"What?" She didn't understand him at all.

He took her hands and lifted them up to her breasts. "Right here, honey."

Arms crisscrossed, she covered her own breasts. It wasn't nearly as exciting as Simon's touch.

"Now I have both hands free to play with you." And that's just what he did, slipping his fingers inside her while also exposing her small clitoris, rubbing lightly, rhythmically. It was wonderful — but it wasn't quite enough and Dakota grew so frustrated that she wanted to scream.

Suddenly Simon said, "My turn now." He eased her back against the shower wall and went to his knees.

Anxious for her release, Dakota groaned and braced herself. She clamped one hand on the towel bar, the other on his shoulder, and she moved her legs apart.

Simon ran his hands down the length of her body, from her breasts to her upper thighs. She felt his sudden hesitation and peered down to see him lightly touching the faded knife scar on her thigh. He looked higher, at the similar scar on her ribs.

Some strange emotion showed on his face,

prompting Dakota to ask softly, "Do they bother you?"

"They infuriate me," he whispered back. In the next instant, he leaned forward and gently kissed each sign of past violence. "You're a remarkable woman, Dakota Dream."

"I'm a horny woman."

Laughing, he put his face against her belly and hugged her. "That's it, honey. Make it easier on me."

He continued to kiss her, down her stomach, lower. His fingers opened her more, and his mouth covered her and Dakota nearly shouted from the joy of it. The flick of his tongue, the heat of his mouth, the sheer awareness of Simon kissing and tasting her there, and she didn't last more than a minute.

Helping to keep her upright, Simon caught her hips until the roiling climax eased and the ripples of release weakened. Easing her down until she sat in his lap, Simon held her.

He kissed her ear and said, "I'll give you one minute to recover, and then we're drying off and trying this in a bed."

Dakota managed a chuckle. "A bed? How boring."

"I want to be inside you, Dakota." He

tipped her head back so he could see her face. "I want to feel you squeezing me when you come."

As he said it, she felt it, and desire sparked again. It amazed Dakota, but she wasn't about to question it. She liked it too much. "Simon?"

"Yeah, honey?"

"Turn the shower off."

He smiled, brought them both to their feet, and turned off the water.

"I like mounting you," Dakota whispered as she lowered herself over him. "It's much more fun than when I'm sparring."

Lying flat on his back in the bed, Simon held her hips, keeping her on her knees. Her nipples were tightly puckered, her skin flushed.

He knew he wanted to grow old seeing Dakota just like this.

She'd towel-dried her hair, but it was still damp, hanging in long, tangled clumps around her proud shoulders. The faded bruises on her forehead and cheek didn't detract from her feminine features, especially when need softened her blue eyes and fast, shallow breaths parted her lush lips.

He loved her. He knew it. And he didn't give a damn if it hadn't been long enough yet. "I hope you wore more clothes when you mounted the guys at the gym."

"Yeah." Her eyes closed and she braced her hands on his chest. "Lots of clothes." Her eyes opened again and she stared down at him. "But it wouldn't have mattered because none of them are you, and they don't even come close to making me feel the way you do."

She'd closed the curtains, but every lamp glowed in the room. Simon could see the scars of her past, the scars that had kept her from feeling anything sexual for far too long. Already, he wore a condom. He didn't want to take chances with her future, a future she had to decide.

"For my peace of mind, whether it matters or not, keep on wearing clothes, okay?"

She started to laugh, but as Simon worked two fingers into her, she gasped instead. He felt the bite of her nails on his pecs and said, "Easy, honey. I just want to make sure you're ready."

She pressed herself against his hand, driving his fingers deeper. "More than ready."

Yeah, she was wet and hot, swollen and soft. *Ready.* Pulse racing, Simon pulled his fingers away and guided her onto him. Her small, anxious sounds of excitement filled his head. He watched as, slowly, his cock pushed past her pink lips, as her thigh muscles flexed and her belly drew tight. Little by little, he sank in — and it was such a turn-on that he had to fight to hold back another release.

Clasping her knees, Simon opened her legs more, then reached down and touched her where she joined with him. She gasped again.

"So tight, Dakota. But nice and wet."

Moaning, she leaned closer to his chest, but that wasn't what Simon wanted. He took her shoulders and held her away. After a deep breath, he said, "Sit up, honey."

She shook her head. "I can't."

"Yeah, you can. Do it."

She sucked in several shaky breaths, and drew herself upright by small degrees. Simon watched her face, relishing each nuance of sensation as he went deeper, filling her more, possessing her completely.

"Lean back on my knees."

Squeezing her eyes shut, she did as he asked, and the position arched her back, offering her breasts to him. She bit her lip on a whimper.

He loved it. Strong, capable Dakota, reduced to burning need. He could spend his every free moment loving her like this. "You are beautiful, Dakota."

441

She said nothing.

Simon kept one hand between her legs, gliding a fingertip over her turgid clitoris, and with the other he took turns working her nipples, tormenting each in turn until Dakota trembled with near desperation.

"Do you like the feel of me filling you?"

She nodded, gave a small sob, and to Simon's shock, she came again. He'd been so involved in enjoying her that he hadn't realized she was so close. He felt her inner muscles milking him, clasping and squeezing in undulating waves, and he lost his tenuous hold on control.

Grabbing her hips, he lifted into her.

She cried out. Then cried out again, and again in time to his thrusts, each sweet sound of release rising as her orgasm took her, pushing him that much closer. He drove into her one last time and came, his mind and body totally spent.

When Dakota slumped down against his chest, Simon clamped her to him. He groaned at the overwhelming sense of it all, and felt Dakota idly stroking his chest.

They stayed like that until Simon knew he had to get up before he lost the condom and ended up taking chances with her after all.

He kissed her shoulder and lifted her to

her back beside him. "Stay put. I'll be right back."

She didn't move, didn't speak. Simon smiled at that, and went into the bathroom.

When he returned, she'd rolled to her side and had the sheet over her lower body. He walked around the bed and got in beside her. Immediately, she crawled back on top of him.

In a whisper, she said, "Do you mind?"

"Having you for a blanket? No."

"Good. I like breathing you in and feeling all of you." She snuggled against him. "I could sleep like this."

No time like the present, Simon thought. "Honey?"

"Yeah?"

"Before you doze off . . . Harley didn't come to see me about Bonnie."

As if she really didn't care one way or the other, she kissed his chest. "No?"

"He didn't want to talk about the fight, either." As Simon spoke, he trailed his hand up and down her spine, luxuriating in the silky texture of her skin. "I'm sorry, Dakota, but I need to —"

"Talk. I know." Around a lusty yawn, she said, "You *love* talking."

He smiled at her, but didn't relent. "I wish there was a better time to bring this up, but

I don't think there is."

Looking wide-awake, Dakota jerked up her head. "You're not giving me a kiss-off, are you?" She tweaked his chest hair playfully. "Listen up, Sublime. If you were only biding your time till you got what you wanted —"

"I'm not sure a decade would be long enough to get everything I want from you."

"Really?" Dakota's smile wobbled, then she lay back down on him. "A decade, huh?"

Refusing to go off course, Simon cupped the back of her head and said, "Honey, how did your mother die?"

She went very still. "What are you talking about?"

Tenderly, Simon sifted his fingers through her drying hair. "You told me your mother passed away, but not how or why."

"She had an accident."

"What kind of accident?"

Long seconds went by in silence before she shrugged. "We had this tiny deck off the back of our house. Wooden stairs led to the yard. Somehow Mom fell."

"Lots of people fall." Dakota had fallen.

"I know. But she . . . I guess the railing had rotted, because halfway down, it broke away and Mom went over the side into a large woodpile." Her voice faded with the memories. "She had multiple rib fractures. A broken leg. So many cuts and bruises. But they told me it was the severe head injuries that put her in a coma."

"She never came out of the coma? She never had a chance to say what happened?"

Dakota shook her head. "I'd already decided to leave Marvin, so I moved back home. It was close to the hospital. I spent each day with her. And I prayed a lot. But the doctors told me not to get my hopes up. She had so many injuries and every day she looked more frail until . . . one day she was gone."

Simon pressed a warm kiss to the top of her head. "I'm sorry to bring it up."

She pushed up to her elbows to look at him. "Why are you?"

"Because you also fell down some stairs."

Confusion had her shaking her head. "It wasn't the same."

"Wasn't it?"

Her brows came together. "I was pushed."

Wishing he didn't have to put the possibility into her head, Simon touched her cheek. "Maybe your mother was, too."

She jerked upright, her expression contorted with anger and suspicion. "You think someone pushed my mother?"

"I don't know." Simon sat up beside her.

"Was Marvin ever around your mother? You think he's the one who pushed you. Could he have pushed her, too?"

In a near panic, Dakota searched his face. "God, no. If he did, then it was my fault."

"No. Shhh. I didn't say that."

She left the bed in a rush and paced across the room — as far from him and the awful possibility as she could get. "You don't have to say it. I brought Marvin into our lives. I know that and I accept the responsibility for it."

Simon didn't go to her. She looked ready to charge from the room naked if he did. "I want us to think about this rationally."

"The night Marvin . . . hurt me" — she ran a hand over her forehead, pushing her hair away from her pale face — "he left and didn't come back. But that was days *after* my mother had already fallen. She was in a coma almost a week before the detective found me. It doesn't make any sense that he would have done that to her before that night."

"Had you argued at all before that?"

"No. If she'd been hurt that night, I'd believe it in a heartbeat. He was capable of that. He *is* capable of that. But before that night . . . we had our spats and God knows our relationship sucked, but I don't think he had anything against my mother."

Simon moved to sit on the edge of the bed. "You told me that you had wanted to see your mom, and Marvin refused."

Dakota went white. She swallowed hard. "Oh, God." Her gaze sought his. "Simon, what if he did that to her?"

"Then we'll let the police know and he'll be punished."

And just like that, right before Simon's eyes, she changed. One moment she had looked ready to sink to the floor with guilt and remorse and pain, and in the next she stood taller, her hands fisted, her eyes bright with determination.

Simon went to her and clasped her upper arms. "Dakota, I don't want you to do anything on your own."

"No. I wouldn't." She looked up at him and drew in a calming breath. "Marvin always has alibis. If he did something like that, it'd be hard to prove."

"He'll slip up, honey. I'm sure of it."

She nodded. "I'm really tired. Do you think we could go to bed now?"

Simon didn't trust her odd mood, but what could he do about it? "All right."

Dakota frowned. "You are spending the night, aren't you?"

She'd have a hell of a time throwing him

out. "If you don't mind." He smiled and held out his hand. "You want to be on top still?"

Rather than answer, she tumbled him into the bed and wrestled her way atop him. He thought she'd have a hard time falling asleep, but within minutes, she was out. And even in slumber, her hold on him remained tight throughout the night.

Simon stroked her hair, kissed her forehead, and made plans. Tomorrow he'd get things started. One way or the other, he'd put an end to Dakota's fears.

CHAPTER 18

They arrived at Simon's rented house early the next morning only to find the mailbox spray-painted with obscenities.

In the bright morning sunlight, with autumn leaves crunching beneath her feet and a brisk wind making her shiver, Dakota stared at that awful reminder. "Damn it." She shook her head. "I'm sorry."

Simon looked at the damage. "You didn't do it, so you have nothing to be sorry for." Absently, his hand cupped the back of Dakota's neck and caressed. "I'm going to enjoy meeting him, honey. I really am."

The idea of Simon tangling with Marvin didn't sit right. Shielding her eyes from the sun, Dakota turned to him. "I have faith in you, but don't forget that he's a thug, not a good sport, okay?"

"Noted." His smile seemed genuine enough as he started them into the house. "I'll call someone to clean it, then we need to get to the gym."

"No, I'll call someone."

"Dakota . . ."

"Hustle up, Sublime." She playfully smacked him on his muscled tush. "Time's wasting. I've been enough of a distraction from your training. I don't want to add to it. So get what you need and I'll make some calls from the gym."

As Simon went into the house and down the hall, he said, "I want to practice with you while we're there."

"I'd love it. Maybe after you're done with everything else, and if Dean says it's okay." Dakota had made up her mind about many things. Tonight she'd tell Simon all about Barnaby, then together they could ask Barnaby more about her mother's death. If Marvin had been around at all, Barnaby would know it.

Last night had given her plenty to consider. The thought of facing Marvin still sent chills down her spine, but she knew she had to if she wanted him out of her life.

Before that happened, she planned to get in as much practice as she could. When she saw Marvin again, she'd be ready.

They arrived at the gym a little later than usual, and although Simon didn't seem to notice, there were plenty of sly glances sent their way. Did everyone know that they'd slept together?

Probably.

Did she care? Nope.

As she stowed her satchel and thermos in the corner, Haggerty came over to her. "Betcha won't guess who dropped in."

He looked anxious to tell her, so Dakota asked, "Who?"

"You gotta guess."

Looking around the gym, she saw Simon in close conversation with Dean. They both appeared engrossed, but not disgruntled, so it couldn't be an unpleasant caller. "The media?"

"Nope." Haggerty rocked back on his heels and announced, "None other than Hard-to-Handle."

So much for guessing. Dakota peered around the crowded floor again. "Harley Handleman is here? Where?"

"In the back, yakking it up with Mallet and Gregor."

He must have left Vegas around the same time Simon had. "What does he want?"

"Don't know. But I reckon Simon will find out." And with that, Haggerty swaggered back to his position out front.

Dakota didn't want to interrupt Simon or Dean, and she didn't feel comfortable grilling any of the other guys. Resigned to waiting before she'd know why Harley had come calling, she sat down in the corner with her stuff and pulled out her phone with a pad of paper and a pen. Hopefully she'd find a repairman who could clean the paint off the mailbox.

A few minutes later, she had just made arrangements with a company when a shadow fell over her. Still speaking into the phone, Dakota looked up, and found herself snared in mesmerizing blue eyes. Her eyebrows lifted.

With his sun-streaked blond hair and dark tan, the man standing over her looked more like a surfer than a contender for the SBC championship belt.

Dakota covered the phone. "Harley Handleman?"

"That's right. And I take it you're Dakota Dream?"

She nodded, but had to return to her call. "Thanks. Yeah, that'll work. Okay, see you then." She closed the phone and stood. "You know me?"

"You're a legend in your own time."

That made her laugh. "Now I wonder how that happened."

He tipped his head to study her. "I imagine it was effortless on your part."

Confused, Dakota frowned at him — and Simon stepped in between them. "Harley. Dean said you were here."

"Hope you don't mind, Sublime, but you did issue the invite."

"It's fine." Simon slipped his arm around Dakota. "I didn't get a chance to tell you, honey, but a few of the sports magazines are trying to make it look like Harley and I have a grudge to settle."

Comprehension dawned. "Ah. Because of Bonnie."

Simon shrugged. "I figured the best way to put that bunk to rest was to have Harley here, where anyone can see that this fight will be like any other."

"Not about a woman," Harley clarified. "But about the sport."

"Just one more competition," Simon added.

"Yeah. Got it." Dakota wasn't sure she liked it, though. And she'd be willing to bet Bonnie would hate having the spotlight reduced. "So you're going to train here?"

"It's always good to mix it up with other fighters, to learn their techniques and defend against them."

"Makes you better rounded."

"Exactly. I'll hang out for a few weeks, then head back to my own camp."

Simon nodded at her phone. "Any luck?"

"I have a contractor coming over tonight to look at it. He says he thinks it can be cleaned."

"Great." Simon brushed his thumb over her cheek. "I'm going to get busy. Go get changed so you can do some work, too. Barber should be here any minute."

And so the day went.

Dakota pushed herself to keep up with the men, but she still needed more breaks than anyone else did. By the time Simon called it quits, she was ready to keel over, but not ready to stop. Especially since Simon wanted to use the last hour of the day to work with her himself.

She'd thought Dean was good, but had to admit that Simon was an even better coach. No wonder he was known throughout the SBC as a trainer of champions. Dean had certainly fared well under his instruction.

After Simon took her through several sets of defensive moves, Dakota took a few deep breaths, wiped the sweat from her face, and said, "Let's do it again."

Simon propped his hands on his hips. "I don't think so."

Something about his tone got through to her. "What's wrong?"

"You're pushing yourself too hard."

"Not nearly as hard as everyone else here."

Dark brows lowered over the bridge of Simon's nose. "Everyone else here is a man used to training." He took a step closer. "Everyone else here outweighs you by at least sixty pounds, most by a hell of a lot more." He stepped again, and loomed over her. "Everyone else is a professional fighter."

Back stiff, Dakota shrugged. "Fine. You want to quit, we'll quit."

He caught her arm before she could walk off. "What's going on, Dakota?"

"Nothing."

"From day one you couldn't lie to me, so why do you think you can now?"

Jerking free, she said again, "Nothing. I'm trying to learn, that's all. You said you wanted me to, remember?"

"I didn't say I wanted you to kill yourself in the process, damn it."

She had no idea what to say to that. They both sounded angry for no good reason. With nothing else to do, Dakota snatched up the water bottle, took a long swig, and then tossed it to Simon. "If you don't get a move on, we'll miss the contractor."

To her relief, he accepted that. "I'll grab my stuff and meet you up here in five minutes."

By the time they got on the road, Dakota

was fading fast. She drank the last of the coffee in her thermos, but there wasn't enough there to give her a much-needed caffeine kick.

"If you really want to get in prime shape," Simon told her, "give up that artificial adrenaline."

"And drink what?"

"Water is best."

She wrinkled her nose. "There are some things a woman can't live without." Knowing it was sure to cause conflict, she broached a new topic. "I need to go by the motel."

"We can run back over there later."

"Just drop me off on the way. I'll shower, change, and drive over to your place. We can do dinner or something if you want."

Simon's hands flexed on the steering wheel. "I don't want you to be alone."

"It's still light out. The motel is busy. The road is busy. Other than when I shower, I won't be alone." She tried ribbing him a little. "But I assume you don't want me to shower in a crowd."

His jaw worked. "Why don't you just grab some things and bring them to my house? We can shower there together." His dark gaze touched on her for a brief moment before returning to the road. "You liked showering with me."

"Ha, are you kidding? I *loved* showering with you. But that's not the point and you know it."

"You're going to be stubborn about this?"

" 'Fraid so."

Making the turns that'd take him to the motel instead of his house, Simon stewed in silence. Dakota couldn't take it.

"Come on, Simon. Stop acting like a dog left out in the rain."

"The stuff you say . . ." He shook his head. "I'm not acting any way at all."

"Yeah, you are. It's not like I want to run through a minefield or something." She reached over for his thigh. "Tell you what. I'll shower with you again tonight if you want."

He parked in the lot and turned off his car. There was no smile to soften his mood. "Does that mean you'll be spending the night with me?"

Because he didn't look too enthusiastic about that notion, Dakota winced. "I'm a little rusty here, Simon. Give me a clue so I know if you want me there or not."

"I want you there, damn it."

The unexpected confrontation took her off guard. "Well, such a sweet invitation." Frustration put an edge in her tone. "Look,

I've been thinking, maybe we're moving kind of fast here."

His eyes narrowed.

"I mean, I'm not dodging out on you or anything. God, no. And I do want to stay over sometimes. I definitely want more sex."

Something shifted in his expression. Dakota feared it might be humor.

"The thing is, I don't want to be dependent on you and that's where you're pushing it. I get it that Marvin could be trouble, believe me. Hell, I've lived with that reality for a while now. But you have to trust me to use good judgment."

Simon reached across the seat and lifted a lock of her hair. "What is it you want?"

"Are we going to be blunt here? Because I'm not good at sugarcoating things, but I don't want to scare you off."

The corners of his mouth tilted. "You won't scare me."

"Well . . . good." Simon could be so hard to read sometimes that he left her floundering. "I want to get closer to you. I want to keep on seeing you."

"That's a start."

"But I don't want anyone to look at me like one of those featherbrained broads who gets in the way of the important stuff."

"Like my training?"

458

"Yeah. Dean seems to like me okay now, and I don't want to give him reason to change his mind."

"Dean likes you fine. Mallet and the others like you more than fine." He half smiled. "Hell, Harley told me he could see what all the fuss was about."

"What fuss?"

With a grin, Simon shook his head. "I'll explain it to you later. So you'll spend the night but you don't want to move in?"

"Right. I don't want to crowd you. I don't want you to think I expect to be there every night." She gestured lamely, hoping he'd understand that she didn't want to be crowded, either. "I'm sure you have other stuff to do sometimes."

"What about you, Dakota? Do you have other stuff to do?"

"Well . . . yeah. I mean, I'll be working for Roger soon, and that means our hours will conflict. I'll be up late so I'll sleep late. But you're always up with the roosters."

"I suppose you have a point." He got out and walked around the car to open her door. He walked her only as far as the lobby. "How long do you think you'll be?"

"An hour or two?"

"To shower and change?" But rather than push her, he looked at her mouth, bent to kiss her, and whispered, "I'll see you in a few hours, then."

Dakota watched him go with mixed feelings. It'd be so easy to let Simon take care of everything. He didn't make unreasonable requests, and he wasn't obsessive in his concern. But if she relied on him, she wouldn't be herself anymore, and she'd worked too hard to gain her independence, to become a person she liked, just to give it up at the first opportunity. She'd slipped a little with Barnaby's last scheme, but she was on the right path again, and by God, she'd stay there.

Even loving Simon wouldn't change things. She wouldn't let it.

It nettled Simon to leave Dakota alone. He trusted in her common sense, in her ability to stay out of potentially dangerous situations. The problem wasn't with her, but with Marvin.

Any man ruthless enough to rape his own wife would be unpredictable. Marvin might not wait for the ideal time to further his harassment of Dakota. He might not be content to sit idle until she showed up alone and vulnerable.

Would he force his way into the motel?

Would he come at Dakota with more than

a knife this time? Maybe a gun? Maybe the same two cronies who had attacked Barber in the parking lot?

Even as Simon considered all those possibilities, he understood Dakota's side of things. He was an independent man and not for a second would he let anyone hover over him with worry. Dakota was just as independent, maybe more so, given her past. She deserved some time and space.

No matter how badly Simon hated being away from her.

When Simon pulled into his driveway, the contractor was already there. He spent a little time discussing his mailbox and possible ways to clean it, then he went inside. He wanted to make good use of his time away from Dakota.

He called Barnaby.

So that he could see Dakota if she pulled in, Simon stayed by the front window. He watched the contractor work as the phone rang once, twice.

In a faint, hesitant voice, Barnaby said, "Hello?"

It infuriated Simon that he had to deal with the man. Not only because he'd skipped out as a father, but because he'd used some underhanded advantage against Dakota. "Where are you?"

Barnaby drew a breath. "Simon? Is that you?"

"Yeah."

"I'd about given up hope! I thought —"

Impatience ripped through Simon's tone. "Where do you live? What state?"

"Why, I'm in Ohio."

"Where in Ohio? How far are you from Harmony, Kentucky?"

There was a pause. "Only a few hours, I guess."

"Perfect. If you want to meet, you can come to me."

"But —"

"Take it or leave it. It's my only offer and it expires quickly."

"I'd be glad to." Barnaby sounded like a gleeful child. "When? What's your address?"

Simon didn't want him that close to Dakota. "There's a diner outside of town, right off I-71 South." Simon gave him the exit number and general directions. "I'll meet you there tomorrow, six o'clock."

Barnaby started to say something more, but Simon hung up. He tossed the phone onto a chair and rubbed the back of his neck. By the minute, it seemed things got more complicated, not just the way he felt about Dakota, but everything surrounding her.

He had an awful suspicion that she planned to confront Marvin, and Simon knew that if she did, it'd be his fault. He'd put the thought in her head that Marvin might be responsible for her mother's accident and death. While Simon applauded her courage, he detested the thought of her getting anywhere near Marvin.

With any luck, Barnaby would be able to provide some answers. If nothing else, maybe he'd tell Simon where he could find Marvin. Picking on a woman was one thing. Facing a man was another.

Simon would help him understand that when he messed with Dakota, he messed with a whole team of SBC professional athletes. If nothing else deterred Marvin, that ought to do it.

Dakota kept watch as she left the motel and walked to her truck. With every step, her muscles complained from the long workout. The shower had revived her so she wasn't quite so tired, but she was cold and hungry and . . . happy.

She had a knit hat pulled low to cover her ears, and a scarf around her neck. Every day it got colder. Before long, the holidays would arrive.

Would she still be with Simon? Would he

expect her to meet his parents?

Thinking it made her nervous, so she blocked it from her mind and instead looked at the road in front of the motel. Traffic raced back and forth in a blur. Off to the side was a shabby convenience store, and behind the motel was a wooded hill. Dakota saw nothing suspicious — but she felt it. Marvin was around, and sooner or later he'd make a play for her.

The last time, she'd panicked.

The next time, she wouldn't.

No matter what happened, she would never again show him fear. He could rot in hell before she'd ever again show him a weakness.

That decision had liberated her in many ways; the future looked brighter, the past less painful. She felt stronger and more determined. Between her new mindset and the specialized fighting techniques she'd learned, she could face the world with confidence.

By rote, Dakota again looked around the area, and just in case Marvin lurked about, waiting for the right time to get her alone, to try to intimidate her, she put her shoulders back.

She smiled, too.

After pulling off her hat and loosening her

scarf, she held out her arms and turned in a circle, presenting herself to Marvin — if he was around.

It felt so good to snub her nose at him that Dakota laughed. A few people looked at her strangely, but she didn't care. She waved at them and went on to her truck. Just as she reached it, the motel's outdoor security lights flickered on. This time of year, it got dark earlier.

Because she didn't trust Marvin, Dakota walked a circle around her truck to make sure she didn't have any slashed tires or key scratches. It all looked good, so she got inside, kicked on the heater, and drove away.

Marvin waited for her; she knew it deep in her bones.

But Simon waited, too.

All in all, a fair trade.

An overgrown empty lot separated the convenience store from the motel. Harley leaned against the brick wall outside the store and stared after Dakota Dream's truck. After meeting her earlier in the day, he felt he had a handle on her personality and her appeal. Seeing her antics just now reaffirmed his assessment: Kooky broad. Lousy dresser. Very sexy.

At Havoc's gym, he'd watched her work

with a few men and though he admired her gumption, when it came down to it, she was still just a woman and therefore no match for a man. At least, not a skilled man.

But she worked at it plenty hard.

Her low-key appearance cloaked beneath baggy sweatsuits and bulky layers couldn't keep him from seeing the obvious.

Tipping a beer to his mouth, Harley recalled the noticeable swells of hips and breasts, and the long length of her legs. Sublime wanted her, and that alone meant she had to look really fine beneath the ugly duds. Not quite in the same way as Bonnie, but in some ways, better. Earthier. More real.

As he tipped his beer up again, Harley noticed a man standing across the street from the motel by an idling car. He had his back to Harley so he, too, could stare after Dakota.

Lowering the beer, Harley studied him. Medium height, decent build. So was this Dakota's ex, the guy stirring up all the trouble and bringing up bad press?

Possibly.

While Harley tried to decide if he should investigate further, the man got in his car and drove away. Harley committed his license plate number to memory and headed back to the motel. He wanted to stretch out on the bed, watch a movie, drink another beer, and ponder ways to beat Sublime when they finally faced off in the spotlight.

When Dakota reached Simon's door, she lifted her hand to knock and it opened. Simon stood there in well-worn jeans and nothing else. His gaze went over her, from her hair pulled into a ponytail to her thick coat to her new jeans and boots.

"Come on in." He held the door open, and once she was inside he reached for the buttons on her coat. Without a word he opened her coat, looked at her new figure-hugging thermal top and snug-fitting jeans, and bent to kiss her.

Dakota started to put her arms around him, but he stepped back. "I like the new look."

"Dean helped me pick out stuff. I don't think he likes shopping any more than I do."

"Next time, I'll shop with you." He took her coat, tossed it on a chair, then turned and headed toward his kitchen. "I was just finishing up some dinner. You hungry?"

"I could eat." Appreciating how very sexy Simon looked, Dakota watched his bum in the low-riding jeans as she followed him through the house. "What are you cooking?"

"Grilled chicken fillets, baked potatoes with salsa, and salad." He opened a small grill and removed the chicken. "I made coffee for you if you're interested. Help yourself while I get the potatoes."

Seeing him bent at the oven, how his back and shoulder muscles flexed, Dakota couldn't take it. She strolled up behind him, ran both hands down the long line of his back and then onto his behind. "If you really wanted dinner," she whispered, "you should have worn a shirt."

He didn't jump, as she'd expected. He just forked the potatoes to lift them out onto a plate and stepped back from the oven. "Patience, Dakota. A man needs sustenance, you know." He walked away to the table.

Dakota folded her arms. "I think you're a tease."

"And you're a delight." He winked. "But you had a hard workout, too, and you need to eat."

"So this is about my needs, not yours? Because if it is, I'd say some needs take precedence over others."

Acting very put out, Simon sighed, looked her over, and said, "You really don't want to eat first?"

Put that way . . . what the hell. She didn't care if she sounded irrational. "No. I'd rather have sex."

Simon laughed. He gave a look at the food, shook his head, and started toward her. "I guess dinner can wait. It won't be as good cold, though."

Dakota opened her arms. "Maybe you should make it quick, and then we can manage both."

"Whatever you say, honey."

CHAPTER 19

Simon told himself to go easy, that Dakota didn't know how her bold come-on affected him, or the tenuous way he'd held on to his control. Before she'd ever gotten to his house, he'd wanted her. With every minute that he waited for her, the need had grown.

When she showed up dressed so differently, looking hot and happy to see him, he'd had a hell of a time stepping back to focus on dinner. She did need to eat, just as she needed him to remember that this was all new for her.

But the second he reached her, she went on tiptoe for his kiss, her mouth open, her breath already coming fast — and Simon lost it.

He had her backed to the wall in a nanosecond, his kiss voracious, touching her everywhere, needing to feel her naked skin. He pushed up the thermal and fumbled at her front-closure bra. It opened and he

470

cupped both breasts in his hands.

Dakota made a sound, but he had his tongue in her mouth and her nipples were tight and his impatience grew by the second. He released her mouth to suck at her throat as he struggled with the closure of her jeans. Her hands pressed on his shoulders, her nails biting into his flesh.

"Simon."

The jeans opened and he shoved them down her hips. In the next instant, he had one hand pressed into the front of her panties, feeling the heat of her, prodding, opening her.

In a faint voice, she said again, *"Simon . . ."*

He bent, closed his mouth around a taut nipple — and Dakota went rigid.

Opening his jeans in a rush, Simon lifted his head to look at her, and he froze. Her eyes were squeezed tight, her face turned away. Breathing hard, he touched her cheek, smoothed her hair. "Dakota?"

She didn't answer.

Damn. He looked down at their bodies, at how her jeans hobbled her legs and her shirt bunched up under her chin. He'd left a hickey on her neck. Her hands clenched his shoulders until her nails left half-moons in his skin.

Carefully, feeling like an ass, Simon kissed

the corner of her mouth. Small, barely there kisses. He touched his mouth to her jaw, her cheekbone, her ear. This time when he cupped her breast, he did so lightly, barely caressing her, brushing tenderly at her nipple with his thumb.

He felt her stir, and closed his eyes in relief.

"Have you ever had sex against the wall, Dakota? No, don't answer that. I know you haven't. Not the way you will now."

He ran his hand along her waist to her hip and back up again. "You wanted a quickie. That means I leave my jeans on, but yours are going to have to come off so I can get your legs opened really wide, wide enough for you to wrap them around me. What do you think of that?"

She whispered, "I don't know."

"When we're done, you'll know that you like it. A lot."

Her fingers unclenched, and she slid one hand up to his neck. "Will you kiss me again, Simon?"

"Yeah." He put his mouth on hers, but let her set the pace this time. Against her lips, he murmured, "After dinner, when we've got all night, I'll kiss you everywhere. But for now, I'm going to finger you instead."

She went still — but not in worry or fear.

Her breath hitched and, in a rush, she kissed him deeper, her tongue twining with his, her body trembling.

Pleased with her, Simon lightly teased his fingertips down her stomach, then trailed them along the waistband of her panties, over the crotch, back and forth, until Dakota moaned.

"Open up for me," he said, "as far as your jeans will let you."

She did, planting her feet apart until she'd drawn the denim material taut. Simon dipped his hand into her panties, moved lower, and pushed two fingers into her.

Dakota put her head back on a gasp.

"Nice, Dakota, but not quite wet enough. Not for standing up."

Without opening her eyes, she asked in a low rush, "Standing up?"

"Yeah. I'm going to take you right here, against the wall. What do you think?"

Her teeth sank into her bottom lip; his fingers got dampened by her response.

Simon smiled.

"You like that idea, huh? Will it bother you to be against the wall, honey? Because that's how it works." Jesus, he was turning himself on with all the sex talk. He visualized everything he said, and knew he'd have to be in her soon, or he'd embarrass himself.

"You'll have your back braced on the wall with me driving into you."

"Yeah. Okay."

Simon released her and went to one knee. He found the zipper on each boot and tugged them off her feet. Dragging her jeans and panties down her legs, he said, "Step out."

She still wore thick white socks, and Simon half smiled as he stood again and fished a condom from his wallet. He tossed the wallet on the table and opened the condom with his teeth.

Resting back against the wall, her shirt above her breasts, her eyes dazed and her cheeks flushed, Dakota watched him.

"You're okay?"

She nodded, and her gaze went to his dick as he rolled on the rubber. Simon pushed his jeans lower on his hips and stepped back up to her.

He cupped her face. "To do this, I'm going to be hard against you." He moved his thumb over the corner of her mouth. "But I don't want you to feel a single twinge of uneasiness. If you'd rather go to the bedroom —"

In answer, she looped her arms around his neck. "Just keep looking at me, please."

Not a problem, since he loved watching

lust twist her beautiful features. "Hold on."

Once she'd tightened her arms around his neck, Simon hooked his arms behind her knees and lifted her. Surprise made her gasp. Her legs were wide open and she had no way to control him or herself; all she could do was hold on to him.

He positioned himself, looked into her eyes, and in one long firm push, drove himself into her as far as he could go.

She cried out, and squeezed him tighter.

He growled at the sensation of sinking into her, possessing her.

God, she felt good, so snug and wet and open. It took iron control for Simon to restrain himself. "Okay?"

Breathing hard, her eyes locked with his, Dakota whispered, "You're so deep."

And Simon lost it.

He kissed her again as he began the rhythm that'd put them both over the edge. He could feel her puckered nipples on his bare chest, heard the slap of flesh to flesh, felt her getting wetter, hotter, and he knew he wouldn't last.

"Come for me, Dakota," he rasped. *"Now."*

She broke eye contact, arching her back and closing her eyes on a shattered moan. Her internal muscles gripped around him, squeezing in small spasms. Dakota heaved in his arms, forcing him to hold her tighter, nail her closer to the wall, and then he lost thought of everything but the awesome relief.

His legs quivered, barely keeping them both upright. With his face on her shoulder, he asked, "You okay?"

She swallowed twice before saying, "Yeah."

He released one of her legs and flattened a hand to the wall. "Ready to stand?"

"No, but go ahead anyway."

Levering himself away so he could see her face, Simon carefully let her other leg drop. From ribs to knees, they remained pressed tightly together, and Dakota whispered, "You're still inside me."

"Don't." He closed his eyes and struggled with himself. "Just be quiet."

He sensed her smile when she said, "Okay, Simon."

It took him another thirty seconds to gather himself enough to separate from her.

"That was . . . incredible."

Emotion, sensation, and something else, all conspired to overwhelm him. "I said to be quiet."

"Simon says, huh?" She ran her hands over his sweaty chest. "Well, I don't think you're in any position to give orders. You're even shaking." She kissed his shoulder, and when he glared at her, she kissed his mouth.

"I did all the work, woman."

"Yeah. Thank you."

Her eyes were vivid blue, her ponytail ruined, and her mouth looked swollen from his kisses. Simon couldn't keep himself from cupping her face, kissing her again. But he did manage to swallow back melodramatic words that would be totally out of place, and said instead, "Do you think we could eat dinner now?"

"God, yeah. I'm starved."

It wasn't until hours later, after he'd made love to her again and they were lying face-to-face in his bed, that Dakota apologized.

"I'm sorry that I lost it earlier."

When she was near, he couldn't keep himself from touching her. He smoothed her thick blond hair, traced her eyebrows with a fingertip. "I pushed you too fast."

Her lashes lowered, hiding her gaze. "I don't know why it happens sometimes, but I know that it'll probably happen again. I'm not afraid of you. I never have been. And I know you're not the type to ever hurt a woman."

"Memories can be a son of a bitch. They come at you out of nowhere, sometimes when you least expect them. It's not a problem for me, Dakota. I just want you to tell me if I ever do anything that makes you uncomfortable. If you try to tell me, and I'm not listening, give me a good smack."

She smiled. "No. I like you too much to hit you."

Wanting more of an admission than that, Simon said, "Like, huh?"

Her gaze locked with his. "If you want me to be truthful —"

"I do."

"Then I more than like you."

That answer didn't really appease him either, but he didn't plan on making declarations, so it wouldn't be fair to expect them either. "I more than like you, too, Dakota Dream. You fascinate me."

"When I'm pinned to a wall and you're inside me, or do you mean now, when I'm having a hard time expressing myself?"

Simon grinned. "All the time." He caught her to him so that when he moved to his back, she ended up atop him. "When you walked into the gym that first day, acting like you owned the place and uncaring that a lot of men were eyeballing you, I admired your courage. When you were hurt from going down those stairs, your strength amazed me. When you make love with me, your naturalness is so refreshing."

"Even when I freak out?"

He put both hands on her bottom. "Even then." She was so honest that even in fear, she didn't hide herself.

"Simon?"

"You've worn me out, woman. I need some sleep. It's almost midnight and the alarm is set for six."

Groaning, she dropped her face back to his chest. "I'm interfering again."

He patted her backside. "The way you interfere would make every other fighter envious, trust me." Leaving the light on, as he knew she preferred, Simon said, "Good night, honey."

He felt the gentle press of a kiss to his sternum. "Good night, Simon."

"You should follow your own advice, little lady."

Dakota kicked out, and Gregor blocked it easily. Tsking in a way that Simon could see annoyed Dakota, Gregor said, "Remember when you chewed my ear about telegraphin' kicks? Well, doll-face, you keep using that right and I'll keep blocking it. If you can't switch up —"

Just that quick, Dakota switched and kicked with her left, catching Gregor in his shoulder. Given that Gregor was a freak of nature with shoulders like boulders, it didn't hurt him, but it did make him stagger.

He grinned, saying, "There ya go. Let's mix it up a little."

Simon grinned, too. They'd been sparring for a while, and Gregor was being very careful with her. He kept teasing her, and Dakota kept taking the bait. She needed to learn to fight with less emotion.

Not being an idiot, Simon knew exactly why she wanted to put so much into training: she hoped to meet up with Marvin. If she ever did, she'd need to put the emotion on hold. More than strength or speed, fighters needed to use their minds. They had to anticipate each move, plan each attack. That was best done cold, without the disruption of emotion to throw off the balance.

Simon would talk to her about that later, though. For now, he had a meeting.

He walked up to Dean, who was busy watching Harley and Mallet grapple. "I'm taking off for a few hours. If I don't make it back before she heads out, will you see that Dakota gets to her truck okay?"

Still watching the fighters, Dean asked, "Without her knowing?"

"Preferably."

"Got it." He turned to face Simon. "Where are you going?"

"I'm meeting with Barnaby."

"You think that's smart?"

Simon looked at Dakota. Sweat darkened the back of her shirt. Her face was red with exertion. "Yeah. I have to figure out what the hell is going on, the sooner the better."

"Should you be going alone?"

Simon snorted. "If you're asking me if I want backup, the answer is no. I would love for Barnaby or Dakota's ex or anyone else to try something. I'm in a killing mood today and I'm not even sure why."

Dean lifted an eyebrow. "Don't do anything stupid that'll keep you out of the competition. It's only a few weeks away now."

Simon gave his attention to Harley. Anyone could see he was good. Damn good. "I'll be there. Don't worry about that." Simon clapped Dean on the shoulder and walked out. He didn't want to draw Dakota's attention, or answer a lot of questions from her. Tonight he'd tell her that he'd visited Barnaby. But he didn't want her to try to talk him out of it now.

On the drive to the diner, Simon considered all the possible reasons why Barnaby might have wanted to meet him. But more than that, he wanted to know what hold Barnaby had over Dakota.

It took him over an hour to reach the diner. The dinner hour had come and gone, so it wasn't very crowded. Only ten or twelve people sat at tables and booths. The moment Simon laid eyes on him, he knew he'd found Barnaby. Before walking in, he looked around to see if Barnaby had brought anyone with him. It appeared not. The man sat alone at a small table in the back of the diner, his hands folded together on the tabletop.

Suddenly he swiveled around and stared at Simon. He rose from his seat, and then just waited.

Dread churned in Simon's gut, but he kept all emotion from his face as he moved forward. "Barnaby Jailer?"

"Yes." The smaller man reached for Simon's hand. For some reason, Simon didn't want to touch him, but to refuse a handshake would put things on an awkward stage from jump.

"Simon Evans."

"Yes, yes, of course I know that. Thank you for meeting me."

Eyeing him, Simon took his seat. Barnaby looked . . . haggard. Neatly dressed, well groomed, but overly tired and stressed.

A waitress approached, and Simon ordered a juice over ice.

"Don't you want something to eat?" Hopeful, Barnaby said, "My treat, naturally."

Simon shook his head. "I won't be staying that long." He didn't tell Barnaby to order himself food. He refused to be any more polite than necessary.

Undeterred, Barnaby smiled at the waitress and asked for coffee and pie. It took her only moments to serve them, and then they were alone.

"So let's get to it." Simon folded his arms on the tabletop. "What is it you want from me?"

Stirring sugar into his coffee, Barnaby tried to hedge for time. "I thought we could talk for a while, get to know each other better. After all, as I told you, I'm your father and —"

"And as I told you, I'm not interested in knowing you better. I came here because you have something Dakota wants."

Taking his time, Barnaby sipped his coffee and ate a bite of his pie. "So you're here for Dakota?"

Simon stared at him. "That's right. To get whatever it is you have that she wants."

After a brief laugh, Barnaby shook his head. "Please excuse my confusion." He took another drink of coffee. "But it's very odd. Dakota specifically told me she doesn't want them anymore."

When had Dakota talked to Barnaby? And why hadn't she told him? Simon just waited.

Barnaby smiled. "You didn't know, did you? She called me in a foul mood, issued some threats, and told me to destroy the letters. She's a bold one, you know. Always has been."

Letters? Despite his better efforts, Simon's eyes narrowed. "How well do you know Dakota?"

"Better than I know you, that's for sure. You're a fighter, aren't you? In the SBC?"

When Simon said nothing, Barnaby lost some of his congenial good humor. "A very successful fighter?"

His success would only be mentioned if Barnaby hoped to gain from it. Relaxing a little, Simon leaned back in his chair. "Yeah, I'm successful."

"I thought so. You've been all over the news lately." With an oily smile, Barnaby added, "I've been overcome with pride." Then he scooped up another bite of pie.

Simon grew impatient. He took the plate and moved it out of Barnaby's reach. "What do you want?"

"I can see small talk is a waste of time."

Again, Simon said nothing.

"Fine." Barnaby, too, sat back in his seat. "I need your help. There's no one else for me to turn to or I wouldn't be bothering you."

Simon laughed at his audacity. "If you're counting on me, then you're really sunk. I have no intention of helping you in any way."

"Perhaps you should let me tell you what I need?"

"I have about two drinks of juice left. That'll give you three minutes, tops."

Barnaby narrowed his eyes. "I need cash."

"No. Anything else?"

"It's important." Hands flat on the table-top, he leaned toward Simon. "I've been ill. I can't work. I'm going to lose everything if —"

Simon wanted to walk out, just not yet. He still had to figure out what hold this man had over Dakota. "There are government programs to offer assistance to the needy. I'm not a program." He swallowed the last of his juice and set the glass aside.

"I'll lose my home." Barnaby's eyes shone with malice. "Dakota's home."

In the process of pulling a few bucks from his wallet, Simon froze. Slowly, he brought his gaze to meet Barnaby's.

Sensing he had an advantage, Barnaby

rushed into the rest of his speech. "Do you want her to lose the only real home she's ever had?"

"I have no idea what you're talking about."

"Really?" Barnaby laughed. "You mean she never told you?" Another laugh.

Simon wanted to kill him. "Told me what?"

"I'm her stepfather."

It felt like his heart stopped beating. Simon couldn't move.

"Poor girl lost her daddy long ago. I married her mother and filled in the best I could. But Dakota was a difficult child. Too determined to have her own way. Too stubborn." Barnaby propped his head on his hand. "She and her mother did not part on good terms. Dakota knows that her disrespect nearly destroyed Joan. If it wasn't for me, I'm not sure Joan could have borne the pain of it."

Simon stared beyond Barnaby. Had Dakota been as innocent as he assumed?

"Joan always had the hope that they'd one day reconcile. Of course, with Joan dying so unexpectedly, that didn't happen."

Anger made Simon's movements awkward and stiff. He threw a ten on the table and closed his wallet. "How do I know you're not lying?"

"About what?"

"Being her stepfather."

"Well, isn't that just like Dakota?" He shook his head as if amused. "I'm sure she has her reasons for not telling you. But I'm curious. Did she do anything at all to convince you?"

Simon kept silent.

"She told me she'd try everything." Leaning forward, Barnaby closed the space between them to speak in a low, conspiratorial hush. "Did she work to gain your sympathy? Ah, I see that she did." He smiled. "I thought she'd try a different tack, given what she said."

A strange hollowness expanded inside Simon. "Meaning?"

"I assumed she planned to crawl into your bed. That's the impression she gave me, anyway."

It was all Simon could do not to strike Barnaby. "This meeting is over." He stood and walked toward the door of the diner.

"Wait." Laughing, Barnaby followed. "Maybe in that, she succeeded. Did she? You won't say? That's very gentlemanly of you." Once outside, Barnaby stepped in front of Simon, blocking some of the light from a street lamp. "What about her letters? Did Dakota tell you how important they are to her?"

Once before, with Bonnie, he'd been played for a fool. This time was worse. Far worse. He hadn't known about any fucking letters, so what could he say?

"They were from her mother."

Car lights flashed by in a steady flow of traffic, keeping Simon from crossing the street to reach his car. He stared straight ahead. "I thought her mother died after a bad accident."

"She did. But she wrote to Dakota before then. I have the letters."

"Then it's a matter between the two of you."

"That poor girl. So anxious to save her home and her mother's last thoughts to her. And you won't even give her a chance by lending me a little —"

Pushed past the breaking point, Simon grabbed Barnaby by the front of his shirt and carried him backward until he slammed him into the clapboard wall of the diner. "Stay away from me, Barnaby. Do you understand?"

As if thrilled by the emotional display, Barnaby looked elated. "Just throw the fight."

Simon released him. *"What?"*

"Throw the fight." Barnaby straightened

his shirt. "If you won't loan me cash, then you can help me make the money in a bet. I'll win enough to cover the debts and Dakota will get her letters."

The idea of deliberately losing a fight was so absurd that Simon laughed. He stepped away from Barnaby. "You're pathetic."

"If you don't, Dakota won't be the only one sorry."

"Threatening me?" The laughter stopped and Simon took advantage of his height and bulk to loom over Barnaby. "I'm not a woman who might be intimidated by you."

"It's not me you have to worry about."

"No?" He clasped Barnaby's arm and hauled him toward the curb. Traffic or no, Simon surged into the street. Brakes squealed, horns blared. Barnaby cursed in fear, but Simon kept walking, giving only a quick wave of apology to the drivers.

When he reached his car, he opened the passenger door and shoved Barnaby inside. "Don't move."

Slack-jawed with alarm, Barnaby stayed put.

Simon quickly circled the hood and got in on the driver's side. He turned toward Barnaby. "Let me see the letters."

Barnaby licked his lips. "Not until —"

"Now."

Scurrying, Barnaby reached inside his jacket pocket and withdrew three folded, worn envelopes. Simon took them from him, lifted one flap, and saw that handwritten paper filled them. "I'll see that Dakota gets these." He stuffed them into his coat pocket. "Now, about these asinine threats of yours. Are you referring to Dakota's ex, Marvin?"

As if seeking escape, Barnaby looked around in a panic.

Simon wrapped his long fingers around Barnaby's wrist in an unbreakable hold. He drew him nearer. "Do you know what happens in an arm lock, Barnaby? When done correctly, if the opponent doesn't tap out in time, elbows dislocate. Wrist bones break. Tendons snap. It's not a pretty thing." He tightened his hold. "I know how to do them correctly."

White-faced, Barnaby shook his head. "You wouldn't dare."

Simon stared at him.

"I don't know what to tell you, damn it! Yes, Marvin is a lunatic. I told Dakota that. I told her that when she was a kid and wanted to run away with him."

"Did he kill Dakota's mother?"

Genuine shock left Barnaby's expression blank. "What? *No.*"

490

"You're sure about that?"

Barnaby sucked in a deep breath — but he deflated just as quickly. Putting a hand to his head, he said, "God, I don't know. Marvin has hinted . . . He's capable of such a thing, I'm sure of that. And he was there at the time. But Joan fell down the outside stairs."

"Dakota was pushed down stairs."

His mouth opened and closed until he scowled angrily. "If Marvin had anything to do with it, I didn't know. I *don't* know."

"But it's possible?"

"Anything's possible." Barnaby rubbed the bridge of his nose and gave an odd, disgust-filled laugh. "The oddest things inspire Marvin. He told me many times that Joan's death was a stroke of luck."

Thank God Dakota wasn't here to hear that sentiment. Simon could only imagine how she'd react. "How so?"

"I owed him money, he was threatening me, threatening everyone. After Joan's death, I got her life insurance and paid him off."

"And you owe him money again now."

"No." Barnaby glared at him. "I'm not a fool. I want nothing to do with him. Unfortunately, he knows things about me, about my past."

491

"Barnaby, Barnaby." Simon clenched his wrist a little tighter. "How bad have you been?"

"It's not like that! I'm not Marvin. I hustled a little, I admit it. I gambled and lost. I ran some scams. But I'm not in Marvin's league." He tugged on his wrist, but gave up on that when Simon just increased the pressure, making him wince. "Now Marvin is squeezing me for money. I only want to live my life and be left alone."

"The way you've left Dakota alone?"

"Why shouldn't I have involved her? This is all her fault anyway! If she hadn't brought that goddamned Marvin Dream around, he'd never have recognized me, and we wouldn't be going through this now."

Feeling ten times the fool, Simon considered all the options, but it wasn't easy. His calm demeanor was a ruse; he was in such a killing rage, he wouldn't trust himself to get in the ring with anyone.

He wanted to see Dakota.

And he would. Right now. The sooner, the better.

"This is what's going to happen, Barnaby, and I suggest you pay close attention." Simon let him go, but warned, "Fuck it up and I can promise you won't be happy."

With his face twisted in impotent anger,

Barnaby rubbed his wrist.

"I want you to get hold of Marvin. Tell that cowardly prick that you want to meet with him here tomorrow at noon." Simon would be there, waiting for him. And he'd make sure that Marvin understood a few things.

"With what excuse?"

"I don't care. Tell him whatever you have to, but get him here, Barnaby."

"You're insane."

"No, but I am going to end this farce." He had to. Even now, knowing Dakota had lied to him, deceived him, he wanted to make sure she was safe. That meant he had to talk to Marvin before the police got hold of him. If Marvin managed to sidle out of this one, if he had alibis as Dakota feared, she might never have a chance to erase Marvin and his stamp of fear from her life. As added insurance, Simon explained, "After I have a little chat with him, I'm going to see the police and when they ask you questions, you will answer them."

Horrified by that prospect, Barnaby pressed back in his seat. "I can't."

"Wanna bet?"

"I could lose everything!"

This man could be his father, Simon thought, but he knew he didn't care, not even a little. In a flash of time, so many things went through his mind, moments with his dad, holidays and vacations as a family. He thought of long talks and the occasional scolding, looks of pride and fatherly advice.

His dad was a man of strong convictions, a man who loved his family and cared for them. His father would never cower this way, never abuse others for his own gain.

Blood didn't make a father; Simon had no confusion about that.

But the same as he would for any sniveling coward, Simon felt a twinge of pity for Barnaby. He wouldn't forgive him or make excuses for him because he had robbed Dakota of what she should have had. He'd robbed her of all the things that Simon had gotten from his stepfather. But at the same time, he despised seeing fear in anyone.

"Look at it this way, Barnaby. Talking to the police and starting with a clean slate is better than waiting until Marvin gets fed up and shoves you down some stairs."

An arrested expression came over Barnaby, and he half laughed in utter defeat. "Yes, I suppose you could be right about that."

"I am." Simon watched him — and saw the moment he began calculating again.

"If you gave me a little time to sell the house, a little money as a cushion, I could disappear after telling the police everything."

Simon shook his head. "I won't give you a single thing. Ever. Now get the hell out of my car. And Barnaby, call Marvin. Do it right away. Don't make me come looking for you."

CHAPTER 20

Dakota was really starting to get worried, when the knock sounded on her motel door. She peered through the peephole, saw Simon, and jerked the door open. Thrilled to see him, she reached up for a tight hug. "I've been waiting on you for hours."

"Have you?" Sounding strange, he moved her aside so he could step in and shut the door.

In one quick glance, Dakota noted the odd tension in the set of his shoulders and the stiffness of his spine. "Where'd you go? All Dean said was that you took off. But you didn't say anything to me —"

"Was I supposed to clear it with you before leaving?" Eyes dark and cold, he stared down at her.

Dakota frowned. "No, I didn't mean that, but —"

His gaze went to her chest, and though she knew he noticed the SBC shirt she wore, he didn't comment on it. "Did you check before opening that door?"

His mood put her off, but twice now she'd lost her chance to explain about Barnaby as she'd planned. "I always do, not that I get many visitors here at the motel." As Barber had said, Simon had to know about Barnaby, so despite the way he acted, she took a fortifying breath and bit the bullet. "I'm glad you're here. For a change of pace, I'm the one who wants to talk to you about something."

"Really?" The sardonic smile made him appear almost cruel. He moved away from her to take off his coat. "Go right ahead. I'm listening."

He tossed his coat on a bed and Dakota's heart began pounding in dread. She could feel some strange, angry pressure surrounding him. "Are you okay?"

His hand slashed through the air and, because of his hostile mood, she ducked without meaning to. When his expression turned more volatile, she rushed to explain.

"Sorry about that. I just . . ." She didn't know what to say, so she tried to be honest. "It's not that I'm afraid of you, Simon. But you have to admit that you're acting strange."

Beneath a dark, long-sleeved pullover, his

solid chest rose twice. Out of nowhere, his eyes narrowed and he reached for her, easing her closer. "I want you."

As always, it took very little for Dakota to feel seduced with Simon. But damn it, she had to tell him everything. "Hold up, big boy," she teased. "I want to talk to you, remember?"

"It'll keep." He nuzzled her neck. "If I wait, I might change my mind, but I need you."

"Damn it, Simon. What does that mean?" She tried to straight-arm him, to put some distance between them, but he kissed her and, where Simon was concerned, she had no willpower.

"Say yes, Dakota."

He was so close that she felt his breath as he spoke. She could still taste his kiss. And he wanted her, he'd said so.

What the hell, she could tell him everything after they'd made love. Right now, he seemed so distressed that if she could make him feel better, she wanted to. "Okay, Simon."

Something new and a little scary burned in his eyes. He took her hand and led her over to the side of the bed. Dropping down, he sat on the side of the bed and pulled her down on his lap. In the same movement, he kissed her hard and fast, deep and hot.

Dakota wore only a T-shirt, panties, and flannel pants. After working at the gym, she'd showered and changed into the comfortable clothes. Simon seemed voracious, licking and sucking at her skin along a damp path down her chest until he could latch on to a tightened nipple through her shirt.

She moaned at the shock of pleasure. It seemed every time they were together, the sexual tension was worse, sharper, and more frenzied.

To get rid of her clothes, Dakota tried to stand, but Simon kept a tight hold on her.

"No," he said, and dropped back on the bed so that she sprawled over him. With both hands now in her bottoms, he palmed her backside, squeezed and caressed, then shoved the flannel pants down. Dakota struggled to kick them the rest of the way off while still touching and kissing Simon. Grabbing her shirt, Simon jerked it up and off over her head, then tossed it across the room. Completely naked, Dakota went to her side to help him undress.

He brushed her hands away from his shirt and urgently opened his jeans. Pushing them down only far enough to free his erection, he pulled her back atop him.

"Ride me, Dakota." As he said it, he

guided her thigh over his hips, helping her to straddle him. "Now. Right now."

His hands were on her thighs, stroking, inciting her. Heat rose between them, scented by Simon's unique smell. He dipped one hand between her legs, sought through her pubic hair, and then, with a groan, pushed a finger into her.

Dakota felt the bold intrusion with shock and excitement.

"You're ready," he murmured low as he pressed his finger deep, retreated, thrust in again. "More than ready." Taking his hand away, he ordered again, "Ride me."

With one hand he held himself at the ready and with the other he guided her hips down. Breathing hard and fast, Dakota stared at him as he entered her.

His eyes half closed, his jaw locked, and a feral sound came from him. His hand on her hip clenched as he encouraged her to sink lower, down, down, until her knees completely bent and she sat flush on him. The position drove him deep, so deep that it took away her breath.

For long moments they stayed like that, joined but unmoving, each anticipating the flood of sensations to come. Watching her, his expression both intent and somehow distant, Simon held her firm and lifted up

the smallest bit. Dakota sucked in air —
and released it on a moan.

"If we could stay like this . . . ," Simon
whispered. His gaze went from her face to
her breasts, then down to her belly. "But we
can't."

Lost in need, Dakota didn't understand.
"Simon?"

Gently, he caressed her hips, up to her
waist, her ribs, and over her breasts. Again,
more softly this time, he ordered, "Ride
me."

Saying nothing, Dakota gathered her wits
and looked at him. The dark, soft cotton
shirt had ridden up above his abdomen, and
Dakota ran one hand over the solid ridge of
muscles there, through the trail of dark silky
hair that descended from his chest, bisected
his body down to his navel, then lower still.
The muscles tightened even more, and
inside herself, she felt his erection flex.

He was the most gorgeous man she'd ever
seen, but she didn't think it'd matter what
he looked like. It was just something about
Simon, some unnameable nuance that affected her in a mind-numbing way.

For the first time since breaking her
mother's heart, she needed to please someone else. Having sex with Simon was inde-
scribable, but she wanted more. She wanted

his respect and affection, and admiration.

She wanted his love.

Bracing her hands on his chest, she used her knees to slowly lever up — then dropped hard.

They both groaned.

She did it again, and again, each time metering the pace, making it last, going as slow as she could until Simon began playing with her nipples, working her, stealing her control.

"Faster," he whispered.

Dakota worked over him until her thighs began to burn, and still he didn't move, didn't help her in any way except to roll her nipples, tug at them. She wanted to scream in frustration. She needed to come.

"Simon."

The second she cried his name he took over, driving up into her while holding her hips tight so that she felt the full impact of each deep thrust. It was enough. It was almost too much.

As an orgasm sizzled through her, Dakota cried out and at the same time, she heard Simon groan hard in his own release. When the sparks of pleasure gradually faded to oblivion, leaving them both spent and limp, Simon pulled her down to him, holding her tight, his face in her throat.

A few minutes later, two things occurred to Dakota at once. Simon hadn't worn a rubber. And she didn't care.

She pressed a hand to his chest, feeling his slowing heartbeat. Emotional words of commitment burned in her throat, but Dakota held them back. She wouldn't pressure him with her feelings. She wouldn't burden him this close to his comeback fight.

"You are one phenomenal man, Simon Evans. Thank you."

Not only did he not reply, but his hands fell away to his sides, leaving Dakota with a sinking feeling in the pit of her stomach.

Something was wrong, damn it. She had to know what.

"Simon?"

Their heartbeats mingled. Like the brush of velvet, he felt her warm inner thighs still around his hips.

His sperm was inside her.

Simon felt sick. At himself and his weakness and what he'd just done. He never took chances, damn it, yet he'd just made love to Dakota without protection. "What?"

"I need to tell you something."

She wasn't going to blast him for forgetting the condom? "What is it?"

She pushed to sit up on his lap. "But first,

I want you to tell me what's happened, why you're acting so distant."

He was still inside her, and damned if her shifting around didn't stir him. Again. Would it always be that way? Would she keep him on the edge with that unfamiliar, emotional, overblown lust?

Her beautiful breasts were right there, her nipples now soft, her skin dewy from exertion. But more than that, he was aware of her face, of her uncertainty mixed with sated pleasure.

God, it was too much.

To close her out, Simon shut his eyes. But that didn't help much, not with the taste of her still on his tongue, the scent of her in his head, her warmth wrapped all around him. What was it about her? Why did she have this god-awful effect on him?

He'd walked out on Bonnie without a qualm.

With Dakota, he felt so connected, walking away would leave him permanently hollowed.

But he would not, could not, tolerate deception. "I didn't use a rubber." Damn, but he was a fraud.

Time stood still. Dakota said nothing until he opened his eyes and looked at her.

Her small, cool hand cupped his face. Appearing introspective and solemn, she said, "Don't worry about that now. It'll probably be okay. The timing is wrong."

"But you'll let me know?"

"I wouldn't keep something like that from you."

She'd kept other things from him. Important things. Determined to get it together, Simon braced himself. "Did Barnaby call you?"

Caution kept her still. "When?"

That made him laugh, but not with humor. He could see it in her eyes; she planned to hedge, to continue with her manipulations. "Let's start with recently. Like today."

"No."

It was odd having this conversation with her straddling him, totally naked while he wore his clothes. He wasn't inside her as deeply now, but they were still joined.

Very odd.

But then everything with Dakota had been that way. "Are you sure, Dakota? And before you answer, let me tell you that there's no reason to lie. Not anymore."

The acceleration of her heartbeat left her trembling. She licked her lips. "Someone said something to you. Barber? Did he tell you everything?"

"No." Barber knew everything? He should

have assumed as much.

Dakota didn't seem to hear him. "I wanted to tell you, Simon, I really did. I planned to. But we kept getting off track. Like now. I was going to tell you as soon as you walked in, but then you looked at me and you wanted me, and I can't seem to resist you at all."

"Convenient."

Her shoulders stiffened. "Are you calling me a liar?"

Ignoring that, Simon asked, "What did you want to tell me? Tell me now, Dakota." He crossed his arms behind his head and gave her nude body a mocking glance. "I've got nothing better to do than listen."

Challenged, as Simon had planned, Dakota lifted her chin and said, "Fine."

Would she give him the complete truth? Or, not knowing for sure what he knew, would she continue to spin tales?

"There are things about Barnaby that I need you to know. First, he's not a nice guy — but I already told you that. And because of that . . . well, and because you and I are kind of involved —"

"Kind of?"

She scowled. "With you acting so strange, I don't want to make assumptions!"

Smart girl. "Go on."

She drew in a breath. "While you were in Vegas, I called Barnaby and told him I was done. I told him that I wanted nothing more to do with him. I told him that I wouldn't be bringing you to him and that if he bothered us again I'd call the police."

Simon refused to believe her. The timing was too perfect, too pat. But . . . had Barnaby said something about her calling it off? "I thought Barnaby had something you wanted."

As if it no longer mattered, she shrugged. "Letters. But I'm not sure they exist, and even if they do . . ." She looked him in the eyes. "I decided they aren't worth losing you."

She sounded so believable, Simon put his head back on the bed and laughed.

"Simon?" Dakota leaned forward, worried, insistent.

Her position pressed him deeper into her. His breath caught. "God, don't move."

"Simon, listen to me. I know I tried my best to get you to go see Barnaby. I had a lot of reasons, and I'll explain them all. But now . . . I don't want you to. Will you promise me?"

It couldn't get more ironic. "Too late. I already saw him."

Her eyes went blank with incomprehension. "When?"

"Earlier tonight." He brought his hands down from behind his head and laid them on her thighs. Smiling, watching her expression, he said, "That's why I left the gym."

"But . . ." He could see the way she tried to sort it out in her mind. "You didn't tell me you were going to see him."

"Just like you didn't tell me he's your stepfather."

Her reaction was immediate. She gasped for air and tried to shove herself away from him.

Simon held her still. He felt mean. He felt used. "No, Dakota, don't rush off. We're both comfortable, right?" He smirked. "I want to know what else you haven't told me. What else have you lied about?"

"I didn't lie."

"No? Barnaby swore you'd do anything to get my cooperation, even sleep with me. But you knew that wouldn't do it, didn't you? I blew you off when you first showed up, so you knew you needed a new plan. Is that why you played the victim?"

"You're wrong, Simon."

"Like a fool, I was noble and worried about you. I've been creative in the sack, hoping to get you past your fears." He looked at her heaving breasts. "But the thing you feared most wasn't sex, was it, Dakota? Hell, you love sex. You're insatiable."

"Simon, shut up now before you say too much."

He didn't listen. "You feared not getting those damn letters from your mother."

Her fist almost caught him. Sharpened reflexes kept Simon from getting decked. He caught her wrist, then also caught the next punch she threw. "Settle down."

She did the opposite, surging away from him, jerking and twisting. He'd never wrestled with a naked woman, especially while still inside her. He hooked her legs with his own and flipped them both, landing atop her on the bed.

He was no longer a part of her, but he was aroused. From the beginning, he'd loved Dakota's strength, her courage. Even now, with her lies exposed, she heaved and struggled, cursing him.

And he wanted her. Again.

Simon raised her arms above her head. "I'll let you up if you can contain your violence."

"Go screw yourself."

So vehement. "I just screwed you. I'm sated. But thanks."

Her beautiful eyes narrowed. "You're going to regret that."

"You think so?"

"Yeah." She jerked one hand free and with the speed of a professional, used her forearm to clip him hard in the side of the jaw.

Seeing stars, Simon lowered all his weight on her. "Damn it, woman, that hurt." He flexed his jaw.

"Poor baby." She damn near head-butted him next.

Yanking back just in time, Simon stared at her in awe and disbelief. "That's an illegal move." He cautiously contained her. "You fight dirty."

"Turn me loose and I'll show you how dirty I can fight."

He shouldn't have been surprised, not with Dakota. "You actually think you can take me?"

"No, but I can hurt you." Her eyes glittered. "Right now that's good enough for me."

Simon could tell she meant that, and for some reason, it bothered him. "I just realized something."

"That you're an obnoxious ass? I could have told you that two weeks ago."

"You're not afraid."

Dakota stilled. She was breathing hard and fast — and looking stunned with his disclosure. Her mouth tightened. "No, I'm not."

"Was that a lie, too, then?" God, he didn't know what to believe anymore.

"Everything was a lie, Simon. You have it all figured out." She jerked again, trying to get free. "Now let me up and I'll be out of here before you can count to ten."

"Why would you leave? We're in your motel room."

"I'll leave the motel. I'll leave Harmony."

Simon began to wonder just how little he had right — and how much he had wrong.

"I'm not afraid of you right now because I'm too mad to be afraid."

"That wouldn't have helped you before."

"Before I didn't . . . I wasn't . . ." Her mouth pinched.

"What?" If she said she was in love with him, he'd laugh in her face.

Instead she whispered, "I stupidly trusted you. I guess I'm an idiot after all."

She had every reason to trust him. He wasn't the one making up stories. "Why did you come for me in the first place?" She started to give another smart answer, and Simon said, "The truth, please, and I swear I'll let you up."

Even flat on her back, she looked independent and capable. "In the beginning, it was because I felt I owed Barnaby. He'd ignored my mother's wishes and let me come home when she got hurt. Later, when you refused to see him and I wanted to give up, he said he had letters written to me by my mother. I thought he might be telling the truth about that. I've lived with the idea that my mother died disliking me. But if she wrote to me, maybe it was to forgive me. Maybe it was because she still loved me." She turned her face away from him. "It doesn't matter anymore."

"Why?"

"Because if there were letters, Barnaby would have destroyed them by now. I *told* him to destroy them." Her gaze came back to him. Her mouth twisted. "I decided you were more important than anything from the past."

Simon studied her, but he just didn't know. "Isn't it ironic that you'd tell me about these grand sacrifices after I've already seen Barnaby and learned the truth?"

"Think what you want, Sublime, but get off me. Now."

Simon rolled away from her. In a flash, Dakota was off the bed. She disappeared into the bathroom, no doubt to clean up from their lovemaking, and returned a few seconds later.

Simon watched her jerk on the oversized SBC shirt. It hung to the middle of her thighs. Not bothering with underwear or pants, she wrapped her arms around herself and turned her back on him.

After adjusting and refastening his jeans, Simon stood and went to his coat. He retrieved the letters. "Here."

Over her shoulder, Dakota looked at him. She saw the folded envelopes, but said only, "What is it?"

He shrugged. "Barnaby says they're the letters from your mother."

And right before his eyes, Dakota crumbled. Going pale, she unfolded her arms and stumbled toward him. She reached out a shaking hand, and in a breathless whisper, she asked, "You got my letters for me?"

Definitely not an act. She looked ready to fall apart. Afraid and hopeful and amazed. "I hope they're what you want them to be."

Once they were in her hand, Dakota didn't read them. Crushing them to her heart, she closed her eyes and a single tear went down her cheek.

Simon stood there, ripped apart, undecided. He had no idea what to say or do — but he was glad he'd gotten the letters for her.

Finally, Dakota sniffed. After swiping the back of her hand over her cheek, she looked at him with a trembling smile. "Thank you, Simon. Thank you so much."

Shit. He shrugged on his coat. "I need to go."

"But . . ." She looked down at the letters, clutched them tight in her hand, and followed him to the door. "I . . ."

Simon shook his head. "You should have told me about Barnaby."

"I know."

"One lie always leads to another. Now I don't know what to believe."

The soft gratitude faded from her features. "You can believe me."

"Can I?" He nodded at her fist, clutched around the letters. "It looks to me like those were pretty important to you."

"Yes."

"So why shouldn't I believe you'd do anything, say anything, to get them?"

She looked at the letters, too, then walked over to lay them on the dresser. She hesitated, smoothing them out carefully, and in a rush she came back to him. "I'm not an expert on relationships, but I know that walking out mad isn't the answer."

"It is if I'm too pissed to stay."

"But you weren't too pissed to have sex?"

Good question, not that he knew how to explain it. And that only infuriated him more. "Temporary insanity." He chucked her chin. "You have that effect on me, I guess." And with that, he opened the door and stepped out into the hall.

Dakota followed hot on his heels. "So that's it?" she yelled. "You actually think it's over?"

In the long hallway, her voice carried. Annoyed, Simon turned — and the sight of her standing there with her hands on her hips, her hair wild, and her legs bare reminded him that she wore only a T-shirt and nothing more. She didn't even have on panties. Sure, she was covered, but just barely.

Simon stormed back to her. "Are you out of your mind? You're damn near naked."

"You're through with me, so what do you care?"

A door opened down the hall and Barber stepped out, followed by Harley and Mallet. What the hell! Were they having a frigging party?

Simon couldn't believe his luck. The men took in the scene with curiosity, amusement, and pure male appreciation.

Shit. In a low growl, Simon said to Dakota, "Get back into your room."

Instead, she shoved at his chest. "Back off, Sublime. Even when you liked me, you weren't my boss. Now that you're done with me, you sure as hell aren't going to give me orders."

Barber straightened. "You two are through?"

Seeing Dakota's friend as a new target, Simon snarled, "You'd like that, wouldn't you?"

Barber shrugged. "Well, yeah."

Dakota shoved him again. "Don't start on Barber just because you're done with me."

Why the hell did she have to keep saying it like that?

He looked again, and saw all the men grinning. They'd stationed themselves comfortably against the wall, settled in for the duration of the show.

It was more than Simon could take.

He glared at Dakota. "Fine. You want to flaunt yourself, go ahead." Again he turned to leave, and he had to force his feet to take every damn step.

Dakota raised her voice even more. "You should know, Simon. I'm not Bonnie."

What the hell was that supposed to mean? Simon turned back to her. "Your point?"

"I won't come chasing after you the way she did. If you want to be a big baby and stalk off without giving me a chance to explain, that's fine. But I won't beg you to listen to me, damn it. If you think I will, you can forget it."

They already had an audience, so what would be the point of discretion? His voice rose, too. "I'm not stalking off, I'm just leaving."

"Ha. You're flaring your nostrils like a bull's. You look ferocious enough to step into the ring."

"But you're not afraid of me, are you, honey? That was all an act, too, wasn't it?"

"Think what you want, but I already told you I trusted you and that made all the difference."

Simon's brain couldn't go there. Not right then. "You lied to me! How the hell would you explain that?"

Scornful, she said, "You'll never know, since you won't give me a chance!"

He threw up his arms.

From behind them, Barber said, "I take it he knows about Barnaby?"

Dakota whirled, saw the other men with Barber, and rather than be embarrassed over her state of undress, she sought an alliance. "I didn't have to tell him. Barnaby did."

Barber winced. "Tough break, doll. I take

it you hadn't gotten around to it yet, as planned?"

So she *had* planned to tell him — just not soon enough.

"I tried! But *he*" — she pointed a finger at Simon — "never gave me a chance."

Lazily, Harley unglued himself from the wall. With a brow raised, he said, "If you were dressed like that, I can see why."

Mallet slugged him. "Don't look."

Harley laughed. "Yeah, right."

And they *both* did some more looking.

Simon rubbed his brow. He couldn't believe this. In a calmer voice, he asked, "Why are you guys here?"

"Just visiting," Mallet said, and then he explained, "Barber's going to be leaving soon."

"No reason to stay," Barber said, and he looked at Dakota with meaning. "At least, I didn't think there was. Now . . ." He shrugged.

That set off Simon's temper more. He knew if he walked off on Dakota, Barber would step in.

Would she let him? Would she replace him that easily?

Fed up and frustrated beyond belief, he yelled, *"Son of a bitch,"* but verbal venting didn't help that much.

Because he wasn't a man to lose his temper, everyone stared at him, and into the chaotic mix, his phone rang. All but snarling, Simon turned his back on all of them and snatched up the phone. "What is it?"

"You want to see me, champ?"

Marvin. Though he'd never spoken to him before, Simon knew it had to be him. Obviously Barnaby hadn't followed his instructions, not that it mattered now. He'd take any chance to meet up with Marvin.

Simon glanced back at Dakota. She stood watching him with her arms crossed and her bare foot tapping.

Furious, but safe. He'd made sure of that.

Taking two more steps away from her, Simon said, "Damn right I do."

"I'm outside your buddy's gym."

"The gym?" That didn't make any sense. Not only was it a busy section of town, but a few fighters might still be there.

Surely Marvin knew that.

To get what he wanted, Simon played along as if he believed him. "You're dumber than I thought."

Marvin didn't take the bait. "You think you want some, then come on. I'm here, and I'm ready."

Anticipation sizzled through Simon's

veins. "Fine. I'll be there in ten minutes."

"Dakota know you're doing this?"

"No." Simon looked at her again. "And if you have any smarts at all, you'll keep it to yourself." He disconnected the call, gave himself two seconds to think, then strode back to her.

At his approach, she straightened. "What's going on? What's at the gym?"

Damn, she had good ears. Slipping an arm around her back, he got her moving. "Come here."

Trotting alongside him as he led her to her room, Dakota said, "What is it?"

Simon propelled her inside. "You're almost naked."

Glancing down at herself, she shrugged. "I'm covered."

"Just barely. It doesn't take much imagination to rid you of that shirt, and trust me, those three in the hall have plenty of imagination."

She curled her lip. "Gee, and here I thought you didn't care anymore."

"Stop pushing me, Dakota." She could be the most infuriating and sexiest woman he knew. "We have a lot to sort through, but right now, I need to go."

"Why?" More alert, she studied him. "Who are you meeting at the gym?"

Simon hid his evasion behind annoyance. "Stop grilling me. And please, if you're going to play in the hall, put on some jeans." He rethought that, and added, "A bra would be nice, too."

He turned to go, and she grabbed at him. "Simon, what are you up to?"

Because he couldn't help himself, Simon cupped the back of her neck and drew her up. "I used to be such a calm, reasonable man, but I swear you're making me crazy." He kissed her hard and fast. "We'll talk later."

More than a little confused, she said, "Yeah, right. Where have I heard that before?"

Simon left before he could do anything else stupid. Like apologize. Or declare himself.

One thing at a time, he decided. His explosive relationship with Dakota would wait. Right now, he needed to focus on Marvin Dream and his plans to get him permanently removed from Dakota's life.

CHAPTER 21

Within seconds, Dakota pulled on her flannel pants, grabbed her car keys and room card, and shot out the door. Halfway down the hall, someone caught her by the arm. She swung around in surprise.

Barber released her and quickly backed out of range. "Whoa. Take it easy, slugger. I just wanted to know where you're rushing off to."

"Damn it, Barber, you startled me." Rather than go barefoot through the lobby, she went down the hall to the side door. "I have to get to the gym." She was aware of not only Barber following, but Michael and Harley, too.

"Why?"

"Because Simon's up to something."

"Like?"

Crushed gravel bruised her feet and hobbled her headlong dash to her truck. A cold evening wind made her hands shake as she tried to get her key in the door lock. If Michael and Harley listened in, it didn't matter. She didn't have time to worry about that.

"Simon went to see Barnaby, today. Then he gets a call and shoots out of here." She bit her lip. "I heard him mention the gym."

"So?"

"I think he's going to meet Marvin there."

Floodlights showed Barber's surprise. "Hell."

"I have to go." Though shivers racked her body, the key finally went in and Dakota unlocked the door.

Barber again pulled her back. "Don't be a doofus, Dakota. You're not dressed and you don't even have shoes or a coat."

"I don't care."

He halted her climb into the truck. "I'll go. I'll take Mallet with me." He turned to Harley. "You in?"

Harley's piercing gaze went to Dakota, and he shrugged. "Why not?"

Dakota felt the panic setting in. "I'm not going to wait here, Barber, so forget it."

"I figured as much. Remember, Dakota, I know you." He took her keys and handed them to Harley. "Get dressed, and then you can ride over with Harley."

Michael scowled at that plan. "I'll wait

with Dakota."

"No, you're coming with me. Simon and Harley have a fight coming up. If we do find Marvin up to no good, they can't chance bruised knuckles."

Michael's brows shot up. "Meaning if Marvin is there, I get to kill him?"

"You can help me kill him."

"Well, why didn't you say so?" He rubbed his hands together. "Let's go."

Dakota fretted, and damn it, she was not a fretting type of woman. She snapped at the men, saying, "Neither of you gets to kill Marvin. That would just get you in trouble, too." On impulse, she hugged Michael. "He's a dirty fighter. He carries a knife. Please don't let him pull a fast one on Simon."

Michael patted her back. "Sublime will be fine, I promise."

Barber pulled Dakota from Michael and into his arms. "We'll be careful, so don't worry." He turned to Harley. "Don't take any chances."

"Wouldn't dream of it."

A few seconds later, Dakota watched their taillights disappear down the road. As she stepped past Harley, she said, "I appreciate your help."

"Not a problem." He kept pace with her

toward the motel. Though he, too, only wore a T-shirt, he didn't look the least bit cold.

He reached the door before her and pulled it open. Just as Dakota started in, running footsteps sounded behind them and someone kicked the door. It shut hard and fast, yanking Harley forward and causing Dakota to stumble back. Harley let out a curse, but he turned so fast he was a blur.

Three men had their faces hidden behind ski masks. Dakota knew one of them was Marvin, and her heart dropped to her knees. As Harley attacked, she backed up a step, so scared that her vision blurred. Pandemonium exploded.

One man stood to the side while the other two fought. Harley threw kicks and took some punches. Dakota noticed that his right arm hung funny and that he wasn't using it for much. Dear God, had he gotten hurt when the door slammed?

She couldn't tell by Harley's manner because he smiled as he kicked out, catching one of the men in the chin and sending him flat to his back. With a fast left jab, he staggered the other man.

And suddenly, Gregor stepped out of the shadows. "Howdy, folks."

The two men tried to scatter, but they didn't get far. One fell beneath Gregor's enormous fist, and the other took Harley's knee to his solar plexus. Slumped on the ground, neither of them looked capable of much movement.

The third man looked back and forth between them before staring at Dakota with palpable rage. Gregor pointed a finger at him. "Don't even think about movin'. I'll be pissed if I have to chase you down." He bent to the first man and yanked off his mask. "That him, Dakota?"

Shocked, Dakota stared at the man. She'd never seen him before.

"Dakota," Gregor said again. "Is that him?"

Marvin? She shook her head.

"Huh." Gregor reached for the other man's mask and dragged it off, too. "This one?"

"No." Both men were scruffy, already bruised up, and unrecognizable to her. "I don't know them."

Gregor straightened to his full impressive height and crossed his arms over his chest.

"You know what that means, darlin'?" Gregor nodded his head toward the last man. "This one here has to be the burr in your backside. Now, if it was up to me, I'd let Harley hold him while I broke all his joints. But Simon has other ideas."

"Simon?" She had no idea what Gregor meant. In fact, she had no idea why Gregor was here. "What —"

Knowing he didn't stand a chance against Harley and Gregor, the last man let out a roar and surged toward Dakota. Taken off guard, she tried to stumble back, but fell.

He wrapped an arm around her neck and yanked her back to her feet. Fear immobilized her. It was Marvin. She felt it.

Harley moved to the side. Gregor did the same. What were they doing? She clutched at the arm restraining her, gasping for breath, until she heard someone say, "Easy now."

That voice sank through her fear and she whispered, "Simon?"

"Right here, honey." Simon stepped forward. "Marvin's not going to hurt you. You won't let him."

With his free arm, Marvin jerked off his mask. "The hell I'm not. Back off, all of you."

"Ain't happenin'," Gregor said.

"Not on your life," Harley agreed.

And then Barber and Michael were there, too, all of them surrounding Marvin and ensuring her safety.

Marvin brought up his arm, and Dakota saw the flash of his knife. "You think I'm afraid to cut her?" He laughed. "Keep pushing me and you'll be sorry."

He began dragging Dakota backward, and though the men all kept pace, she knew she had to do something.

They all expected her to.

Besides, with Simon close, the fear wasn't as bad as she had imagined it might be. Seeing Marvin again, comparing him to the men all standing in front of her, made him seem small and weak, not quite a man, much less a monster.

"Dakota," Simon said, "listen to me. He's nothing. You can kick his ass, baby. I know it. I've seen you in action."

That really got Marvin chuckling — and just that easy, the moves she'd learned came to her. For courage, Dakota looked at Simon, then acted.

Instead of struggling, she dropped her weight, throwing Marvin off balance. That was all the advantage she needed. With every ounce of strength she had, she brought her elbow back for a liver shot and at the same time, ducked away from the knife. She didn't have the power that the fighters had, but she had enough for Marvin.

Now that she was free of his hold, she faced him. "Did you hear him, Marvin? Simon says I can take you."

Marvin caught his breath and straightened, the knife clutched in his hand. "You're fucking with me, aren't you?"

"No. You took me by surprise, but not again."

She heard Simon say, "That's my girl."

Marvin laughed. "This has to be a joke."

Dakota circled him, and when he started to laugh again, she kicked away his knife. Marvin grabbed his wrist in pain. The knife flew to the side and Barber picked it up.

"I'm actually dead serious, Marvin." She kicked again, landing her foot on his temple.

He fell on his ass with a grunt. Glaring at her with hatred, he said, "You're going to regret that."

"Stand up, Marvin."

"Bitch." He shot to his feet, lunging for her. Using his momentum against him, Dakota drove her knee into his groin. When he doubled over in pain, she caught the back of his head and brought her knee up again, this time into his chin, once, twice, a third time. When she released him, he fell to the side.

She could hear the smile in Simon's tone when he asked, "Dakota, you done, honey?"

"No."

"Take your time."

Since Marvin wasn't moving much, she

spared a glance at Simon and saw his small, proud smile. For some reason, tears suddenly burned her eyes. "Thank you, Simon."

"Anytime, sweetheart."

Dakota walked a circle around Marvin. "You think you're so big and bad. Get up and prove it."

He curled into a ball and groaned.

"Get up, or I'll kick in your ribs with you lying there."

Slowly, Marvin struggled to his feet. Blood trickled from his grotesquely swollen nose and the side of his mouth. He bent forward like an old man, one hand still cupped over his jewels. "You're insane."

"No, I'm mad. There's a difference." For the first time in years, she felt truly free. As independent as she'd always tried to be. "Can you defend yourself at all, Marvin?"

"If I had my knife —"

"I'd take it from you and break it off in your kneecap."

Simon winced.

Mallet laughed. "Jesus, I love it."

Barber said, "I've got your knife, Marv. Want me to give it to her?"

Dropping back to his knees, Marvin said, *"No,"* and everyone laughed.

It struck her; to them, Marvin was a joke.

A coward and a wimp and now, to her, he was the same. More tears burned her eyes as she stared at him, slumped on the ground in the dirt, sniveling and afraid. He was so much less than a man that he was nothing at all.

Not to her. Not anymore.

She didn't realize she was truly crying until Simon tucked her hair behind her ear and used gentle fingertips to wipe her cheeks. "You are remarkable."

Sniffing, Dakota turned to him. "I thought you were at the gym."

"Marvin thought so, too. But remember, I asked if you'd be okay with someone watching your back?"

"While you were in Vegas."

He shrugged, still tenderly wiping her cheeks. "I figured a few more days couldn't hurt. Especially after meeting Barnaby."

"So when you left —"

"I knew Gregor was here, keeping an eye on things. He called me as soon as the three stooges showed up."

Dakota tipped back her head and stared up at him. "I thought you were too mad to care."

"Never that." He pressed a kiss to her forehead. "I was pissed, but I think it's because I was hurt — though I won't admit that to anyone else."

Laughing, Dakota hugged him. "I'm sorry I hurt you."

Gregor cast a big shadow over them when he approached, and they both fell silent.

"For a badass Amazon lady, you sure are a wuss 'bout the cold." Gregor laid an enormous jacket around her shoulders, and it was only then that Dakota realized how badly she trembled.

"Thank you."

Gregor thwacked her on the shoulder, almost knocking her over. "I owe ya for the great show."

Harley was the next to approach. "For a woman, you do good work."

His arm still hung at his side, filling Dakota with dread. "Harley, I'm so sorry."

"For what?"

Simon nodded at his arm. "Is it broke?"

Brows drawn, Harley looked down at his arm. As if just noticing the injury, disgust twisted his mouth. "Well, hell."

Simon released Dakota to check on him. After gingerly testing his elbow, he sighed. "I hate to tell you, but your elbow is dislocated."

"Damn. Must've happened when I was holding on to the door and that bastard kicked it shut." He glared at Marvin. "Guess

I should have let go sooner."

Covering her mouth, Dakota said, "How could you not have known it was dislocated?"

He winced. "I don't know. It's suddenly hurting like a son of a bitch."

Barber and Mallet watched over the men, making sure they didn't try to get away, until the police arrived with ear-splitting sirens full blast. Simon called Gregor over, and he took Harley to the side. As soon as the police finished talking to him, Gregor would drive Harley to the emergency room.

Simon put his arm around Dakota. "Come on. You need to put on warmer clothes and some shoes before the cops start grilling you, too."

On the way inside, they passed Marvin and the other two men. Dakota stopped to look at them.

"What do you want?" Marvin snarled.

"I was just thinking how long you'll be in jail. Everyone here heard you say that you planned to cut me. You wore the same masks that you wore when you jumped Barber and Bonnie in the parking lot. The same night that I was shoved down the stairs." She tipped her head. "You really aren't very bright, are you?"

He started to stand and Mallet planted a

boot in his chest, shoving him back to his butt.

Shaking her head, Dakota said, "You are a very pathetic . . . thing."

With a hand to the small of her back, Simon started her walking again. "Let's go. You've wasted enough time on him."

They'd almost reached the door when Dakota said, "Simon?"

"Yeah, honey?"

"You lied about going to the gym."

"I was going."

"But to meet Marvin, right?"

"If he showed up, which I doubted."

"So it was sort of a lie of omission." She slipped her hand in his. "Same as my lie of omission about Barnaby being my step-father."

His hand tightened on hers. "No, Dakota. This was different."

"Maybe. But the fact is, we're both human and both bound to make mistakes. Right?"

He pulled the door open for her. "We can talk about all that later."

"I was going to tell you about Barnaby. Today in fact. It's been pretty crazy, that's all. Everything has happened fast."

"Shhh." Simon led her down the hall to her room. "Do you have your room key?"

It was still in the pocket of her flannel lounge pants. She handed it to him. "I know I made mistakes. I know I'll make more. But the important thing is that I love you."

Simon paused with the key card stuck in the door. "What did you say?"

Dakota stared up into his eyes. "I love you." The admission had her shrugging with helplessness. "I know it hasn't been that long. And with you making your comeback and the fight we just had and everything, the timing is off. You're still ticked at me, and I've sort of got this rush of adrenaline going that makes me want to molest you, but —"

"You love me?"

She nodded. "Yeah. Sucks, huh?"

Simon grabbed her close and kissed her hard. He kept trying to stop, but couldn't seem to manage it. They stood in the hall outside her room and he had her backed up to the wall, his mouth devouring hers.

Dakota pushed him back. Seeing the heat in his eyes, she took a breath. "Maybe it doesn't suck?"

He cupped her face and smiled. "No, it doesn't."

"So . . ." She suddenly felt shy, when she didn't have a shy bone in her body. "Does that mean you care a little, too?"

Slowly, Simon's smile turned into a laugh. "Yeah. I guess it does."

Dakota slugged him. "How little?"

He laughed harder, put his forehead to hers and said, "I love you, too." Then, teasing, he added, "If your sexual energy didn't do it, the way you fight would have tipped the scales. You really are one impressive lady."

With that resolved, Dakota wrapped her arms around him. New worry settled on her and she wanted Simon's support. "I haven't read the letters yet."

"Afraid to?"

She nodded. "Dumb, huh?"

"Not dumb at all." He turned her face up to his. "Would you like me to look at them for you?"

Dakota bit her lip, but in the end, she gave up some of that hard-won independence. "I'd appreciate it if you did. Just in case it's bad."

"Come on." He led her inside the room and shut the door. "Get dressed, okay?"

While she did that, he picked up the envelopes and pulled out the letters. Dakota could barely change her clothes with the way her heart thundered and her hands shook — until she saw Simon smile.

He laid down one letter and went on to

the next. Then the next. Finally he sat in a chair and said, "Come here, Dakota."

She went to him, and he pulled her onto his lap. "Your mother loved you a lot, honey. You have no reason to fear reading these."

"If you say so."

"I say so. Trust me."

"Of course." So with Dakota held in Simon's arms, she read her mother's last words to her, words of forgiveness and remorse and understanding.

Words of love.

Dakota twisted out of a move, but not fast enough. Barber ended atop her in the mounted position. "Tap," he said.

"No."

Leaning closer, he pinned down her arms. He could feel her straining, and said again, "You're beat, woman. Admit it."

Trying not to laugh, Dakota shook her head. "Never."

She looked adorable sweaty. Why had he never realized that before? Barber stared at her, she stared back.

And out of the blue, without really thinking it through, he kissed her right on the mouth.

The kiss was a revelation for him; short and light, but definitely not of the friendly sort. As he lifted his head, he knew he'd made a terrible mistake. Good God, he loved her. He wanted her happy, and she was.

With Simon.

If he'd just caused a rift in their friendship, he'd kick his own ass.

"Dakota . . ." He loosened his hold, saw the spark in her eyes, and suddenly she punched him.

"Damn." Barber flinched in pain before laughing. Leave it to Dakota to react so strongly. "Well, that's answer enough."

Shoving him away, she sat up. Seeing his bloody mouth only made her angrier. "What the hell is wrong with you?"

He fingered his lip, licked at it, and shrugged. "I just wanted to be sure, that's all."

"Sure of what?"

"That I don't have a chance."

Her face fell. "Oh, Barber. Simon said . . . that is . . ."

Sitting up beside her, Barber patted her knee. "Simon told you I was interested."

"I didn't believe him."

Playfully, hoping to lighten her mood, Barber mussed her hair. "Hey, don't look so glum. I'm a big boy. I can handle rejection."

"I would never reject you, Barber. I love you."

"Like a brother." He grinned to ease the sarcastic bite. "I know."

"Barber . . ."

"It's okay, doll. I swear. I love you, too, and nothing's going to change that. Not even a fat lip."

"Or a wedding?"

Barber eyed her. "So he finally proposed?"

"There's no *finally* to it. Shoot, I'm the one who wants to wait until after the fight. Harley's out of it. Simon says he'll be rehabbing that elbow for six weeks. I feel so wretched for him. If it wasn't for me —"

"Hey, Harley and I have become friends, and I can promise he doesn't blame you. He just has bad luck when it comes to title fights. Although this time, I think luck was on his side, because I have a feeling Simon would have creamed him."

"Yeah," Dakota agreed, having complete faith in Simon. "This other guy, the one Simon will fight now . . . I don't know much about him."

"My money's on Sublime."

"Mine, too, but I don't want a wedding to distract him." She shouldered Barber. "I know you're leaving tonight for your next gig, but you will be at the wedding, right?"

He slanted her a jesting look. "I don't know. That depends. As your best friend, do I have to be your maid of honor?"

They both laughed. "No. Dean's wife will take the honors for that. She's pretty nice. I like her." Dakota leaned on him. "But I still want you there."

"I wouldn't miss it."

Suddenly Simon spoke. "Someone want to tell me what's going on?"

Though he hadn't heard him approach, Barber had no doubt Simon had seen everything. He kept such an eagle eye on Dakota that it almost seemed he had a sixth sense where she was concerned.

Not all that concerned, Barber just shook his head.

But in guilty haste, Dakota jumped to her feet. "Nothing's going on."

"Uh-huh." Simon didn't look angry, just curious. And maybe possessive, too. "Then why does Barber have a bloody lip?"

"Because I hit him when I shouldn't have." Dakota quickly crossed the mat and hugged herself up to Simon's side. Barber noticed that when she was with him, she glowed, no matter the situation.

It really was damn nice seeing her so happy.

Simon looped his arm around her, but

stared at Barber. "I dunno. I think he deserved a punch in the mouth."

He thought right, Barber silently agreed.

Going on tiptoe, Dakota said to Simon, "Next to you, he's my best friend in the whole world." She turned to look at Barber. "Don't do anything to piss me off."

Grinning, Barber climbed to his feet. "Yeah, Sublime. Don't piss off the lady."

"Wouldn't think of it." He kissed Dakota's forehead. "Why don't you go get your things and we'll get out of here."

She lowered her brows. "Simon."

Her warning tone amused both men. "Go. I'll behave."

"You promise?"

"Yeah."

She looked at Barber again. "You're okay?"

"Count on it."

Simon watched her walk away. Casually, as if discussing something mundane, he said, "You had to try, didn't you?"

"You'd have done the same."

"No, because I wouldn't have waited around until it was too late, like you did. I'm smarter than that. But the point is, you don't get a second chance." All grave seriousness, Simon gave him a direct look. "It's only because Dakota cares for you that I'm not smashing you right now. She's mine. She's going to stay mine. You might as well accept it."

Barber slung a towel around his neck and stepped off the mat. "I have."

"You should find a woman of your own, Barber."

"Ha." He dried the sweat from his face, glad that Simon didn't feel compelled to use him as a punching bag. "I'll tell you, if I ever do settle down with a woman, she'll have to be every bit as gutsy, strong, and earthy as Dakota. I don't think I could take the other kind now."

"The other kind?"

"Yeah. You know. Whiny. Weak. The type who cries over a broken nail or spends three hours on her hair. If I ever settle down, and all things considered, that's a big if, she'll have to be tough."

"Famous last words." Simon shook his head. "I'm pretty sure love doesn't give you a choice in the matter. When it hits, it hits. I know, because I hadn't been looking. Just the opposite."

"You'd sworn off women for the comeback, right?"

"Yeah. And it didn't feel like much of a sacrifice until fate brought Dakota Dream into my life. I haven't been the same since."

He put himself in Barber's path. "Maybe because I left Bonnie without a qualm, you're a little confused on something. But as Dakota said to me, she's not Bonnie. I wouldn't fight over most women, but for Dakota, I'd take a man apart. Even a friend of hers."

Running a hand over his hair, Barber nodded. "Yeah, I hear ya. I overstepped myself and I know it. I apologize."

"Just don't let it happen again."

Grinning, Barber held out his hand. "I don't think you need it, but good luck with the fight next week."

After a slight hesitation, Simon accepted the gesture of peace. "Thanks."

Keeping Simon's hand, Barber said, "I really am sorry about . . ." He waved a hand. "You have my word, it won't ever happen again."

Simon's smile said many things. "It better not."

"I saw you and Barber talking." Dakota tried to read Simon's expression. "Everything okay now?"

"Yeah, it is." He started the car and pulled away from the gym. "I don't want you to worry about that."

They hadn't ridden far when she said, "Simon? I'm not pregnant."

After a quick glance at her, he nodded but stayed silent. Dakota didn't know what to think, until he said, "How do you feel about that?"

She shrugged. "I wouldn't fall apart if I was pregnant, but I'd rather wait until after we're married."

"Same here."

"So you want kids?" It wasn't something they'd ever discussed.

"With you? Yeah, sure."

"It won't interfere with your career?"

"Dakota." He reached for her hand. "There's nothing about you and me that could ever be interference. I love you and I want a life with you. That includes a house and kids, your own career, and anything else you want. I'll still have to travel when I fight, but I hope you'll be able to travel with me sometimes, too. When we have kids, then they can come along as well."

That sounded nice to Dakota.

Simon stopped at a red light. "I've been thinking. The SBC is into using new bands for the musical openings at events. It's always something hard and edgy — like Barber's music. Do you think he'd be interested?"

Dakota's mouth dropped open. "You'd do

that for him?"

"I'd do it for you." Simon half smiled. "And he's not so bad." Under his breath, he added, "He's got good taste."

Dakota laughed. "That'd be wonderful!"

"I can't make any promises, but I can take Drew Black to hear him play sometime. It's up to Barber from there. But I'd say he's good enough."

"If you say it, Simon, then it must be true."

"Is that so? Well, I say you're the most wonderful woman in the world, and I love you."

She leaned across the seat to kiss him. "I love you, too, Simon." Grinning, she added, "Whoever would have thought I'd be marrying Sublime? I mean, you're famous with the female fans."

"It's a joke, nothing more." He glanced at her. "Did I tell you that the guys gave you a nickname now, too?"

Her eyes rounded. "They did?"

"Yup. You're now officially Divine."

"No way."

"According to the fighters you are. Dakota 'Divine' soon-to-be Evans." He lifted her hand and brought it to his mouth. "I'll be calling you something else, though."

"Really? And that is . . . ?"

He grinned. "All mine."